DUAL EARTH

The Experiment

Mary Louise Hurford

Printed in Australia

First Printing: July 2021
Shawline Publishing Group Pty Ltd
www.Shawlinepublishing.com.au

Paperback ISBN- 9781922444837

Ebook ISBN- 9781922444844

CHAPTER 1

Louis Blackwell awoke to the sound of smashing bottles and ugly muffled voices. Loud voices were screaming obscenities at each other.

It was Thursday night, which meant payday for those on welfare. Louis got out of bed and sat on a rickety old timber chair near his window. He loved to look at the stars and the moon. An old torn lace curtain flapped in the spring breeze, brushing against his face. Sighing, Louis thought about his life and wondered if it would ever change. The days ran into each other. Nothing pleasant ever happened. Louis was unsure how old he was. He never celebrated birthdays, but ten or eleven sounded about right. Small for his age, he had dark curly hair, sea blue eyes and freckles scattered across his cheeks and nose, highlighted by his creamy coloured skin. Lucy is always saying he is a funny looking thing. He's now used to his feelings being shattered.

Lucy Blackwell lay snoring on the lounge. Sprawled out on the floor was some other body, another hopeless life his mother had dragged home from a day's drinking in one of the local pubs.

Lucy and Louis live in a country town called Lambert Central, NSW, Population, nine thousand. Lucy hasn't worked for years. They live in a commission house, row upon row of fibro houses in various stages of disrepair. Yards bare of vegetation because of underfed dogs continuously pacing looking for a way out. Toys and dolls lay ruined and forgotten, a reflection of the lives within. Other yards were overgrown with Kikuyu growing up drainpipes and broken windows boarded up, some containing old lounges disappearing in thistles, torn to pieces full of happy rodents breeding uninterrupted.

Playing on the roads were children of all ages, fighting over bikes that still have some life in them, trying to get the best out of what they had. Some adults had jobs at the local meatworks, they were the lucky ones that could afford a second, third, or fourth-hand car. The cycle of alcohol and drug abuse is continuous, escaping reality being the main goal for most adults. Children learnt early what to expect from life. Getting to school and living class distinctions confirmed their life's path.

The only real part of community housing that Louis actually enjoyed was the night and its darkness. The nights somehow softened the harsh landscape of daylight. Imperfections faded with the light.

Lucy Blackwell had been visited on many occasions by D.O.C.S in regard to Louis's behaviour at school, resulting in many suspensions. Many times, Lucy was told to ensure Louis had proper food and clothing and his hygiene maintained. It would last a few weeks, but then Lucy would fall back into her neglectful ways. Louis hated going to school. It wasn't so much the schoolwork, he actually liked to learn about many things, the mysteries of the world.

Louis had a passion and a special gift with animals, not that he had any. He was never allowed. Lucy felt animals were a waste of money and time. Louis loved to feed and watch birds. He had begun nurturing a family of Blue Tongue lizards living under the old garden shed in the backyard by finding any scraps suitable.

Every day going to school was humiliating. He didn't have a proper uniform and his old black shoes had holes in the soles. His clothes were faded and dirty. The washing machine had been broken for 2 years. Lucy filled the bathtub up when they ran out of clothes, threw in handfuls of washing powder and stirred every couple of days with the broom handle. It was then Louis's job to rinse over and over, wringing out by hand and hanging on the rusted Hills hoist. There was never enough pegs so slinging over the line had to do. Louis always stood back, looking at his work and thought they looked like dead souls, captured by an alien clothesline.

Lucy's days all started the same, waking with a cheap wine headache, and feeling nauseated, vomiting and wishing she had never woken up.

Life was not always this way for Lucy. She had a functional family life and married the man of her dreams, Jason Blackwell. He was tall with dark curly hair, a classic handsome face with a smile that fascinated women, making men feel inferior. Lucy and Jason had a modest home on the North shore of Sydney. Lucy's mother Maeve Llewelyn Beaumont had given them the deposit. They were the envy of young couples around the area, always photographed and in the society pages, looking so good together.

Jason worked as a town planner at the local council whilst Lucy worked part-time as a hairdresser and beautician. Lucy always looked perfect. Her beautiful long blonde hair, her shapely movie star body, and her stunning photogenic face. Jason Blackwell was her leading man - the perfect centrefold.

At any opportunity, the Blackwell's loved to get to the Gold Coast. Lucy loved the atmosphere, the shops, the cars, the wealth, and most of all the beach. Lucy loved to strut around the beach, having her perfect tanned and shapely body, admired by men of all ages. Women looked at her with envy. Lucy loved that even more.

It was one of these organised holidays to the Gold Coast that was to change the entire direction of both Lucy and Jason's lives forever.

CHAPTER 2

Lucy looked down on the beach from their holiday apartment. European cars lined the beachfront. This was where she belonged. She noticed activity on the beach. It looked like a film crew. She grabbed her bag and keys, checked herself in the mirror and headed toward the excitement.

Lucy stood in awe watching the frenzied crew set up for the shoot. It was a shampoo commercial. She could see all the producers and her hungry eyes missed nothing. The model appeared and Lucy was amazed at her beauty, long shapely legs and perfect features. Lucy felt she could improve on perfection.

Lucy began daydreaming, drifting into her own world of glamour, lights, beautiful clothes, loads of makeup and someone to apply it. A perfect picture of herself lingered in her mind. This is what she loved about this place.

'Hey cutie! You alright?'

Lucy jumped and looked into the eyes of Rick Jensen, photographer for a top shelf magazine. Lucy mumbled something in response. Rick began scanning Lucy's face, then moving down her body absorbing everything he saw.

'You like the look of this?' said Lucy, moving into a sexual pose.

'Yes! As a matter of fact, I do. It looks very exciting.' Rick Jensen handed Lucy a card, 'Give me a call, maybe I could take a few pics.'

Lucy looked shocked, 'You think I'm good enough?'

'I can see you on a cover already!' With that Rick Jensen turned and walked away, shouting over his shoulder 'What's your name?'

'Lucy.'

And he was gone.

An unbelievable swell of excitement began rising throughout her body. Staring at the card, her mind racing, uncontrollable laughter came forth, then that voice in Lucy's head, warned her to think and be smart. She had to get around Jason, she had to stay on the Gold Coast. Lucy was excellent at plotting, her mind worked things out methodically, especially when money, glamour and a chance to be famous was on offer.

Lucy was well aware Jason would be jealous and she loved to act.

'Hello Jason, I'm home.'

'On the deck.'

Lucy launched into her scene pouring Jason a fresh drink. Sitting together Lucy remained aloof and handed Jason the business card.

'What's this?'

'This was given to me from a photographer who works for a top shelf magazine.'

'So?'

'He feels I have the potential to be a top model.'

'Oh, come on Lucy, are you that stupid? The guy was making a pass at you!'

Lucy, feeling her anger rising, held it in. 'No, he was very serious and professional. He actually approached me while he was doing a shoot.'

Jason, looking thoughtful replied, 'So how does this work, and what sort of money are we talking about?'

'We?' thought Lucy but smiled. 'Thousands I believe. Remember it's one of the best, so I could be famous. Well possibly!' said Lucy very casually. Knowing they were due to go home tomorrow, Lucy said in haste, 'How about I phone tomorrow and see what happens?'

'Okay babe!'

And there it was. Jason calculating dollars. She smiled to herself and gently led him to the bedroom. Lucy woke early to start her beauty regime, paying careful attention to her makeup and her hair. It had to be perfect.

Two hours later, Lucy's efforts paid off. She was magnificent. Standing in front of the floor length mirror, she scrutinized every part of her reflection, willing this day to be the best day of her life. Looking at her watch, it was time to make the call. The appointment was made. Within an hour she could be beginning her new life.

CHAPTER 3

The camera loved her and it did her justice. Rick Jensen loved what he saw. Lucy modelled in various outfits, bikinis, seductive evening wear and skimpy underwear. Her energy was ferocious. The camera crew were stunned, she was a natural and they just loved watching her.

Rick and Lucy sipped champagne, relaxing in luxurious lounge chairs waiting for the shots to be processed. Lucy looked relaxed on the outside, but internally every nerve was tingling in anticipation.

At last, the knock came, Rick spread the photos on the table. 'Oh my God,' Lucy looked terrified, Rick burst out laughing, 'they are magnificent!'

Captivated with herself, she touched them gently, and tears welled in her eyes. 'Well Mrs Blackwell, I am happy to inform you, your modelling portfolio will be sent to the best agencies in town, and you my love will be booked solid for the next six months - and that's just to begin with.'

Lucy hugged Rick; she was nearly bursting. 'I have to tell Jason,' And ran out of the lounge squealing.

That night Jason and Lucy sat dining at the most expensive restaurant money could buy. Other patrons couldn't help but admire the attractive couple. Jason was in an incredible mood. Lucy was going to earn two hundred thousand dollars for three months work. He too saw a different future. A new house and money to move forward with a political career. Jason left the following day, leaving his wife on the Gold Coast to chase her career and earn lots of money. Real estate was his new priority.

Lucy's life was like an incredible dream. The attention she was getting was like life giving blood, feeding her ego, inflating her personality and becoming very ugly on the inside. In contrast Lucy's beauty was radiant and every day in front of the cameras she was an enchantress.

In international fashion houses Lucy was becoming known. She was receiving invitations to high society parties. Hollywood had received her photos and serious conversations about acting roles had been entered into. Agencies were sending out invitations to Lucy, cameras followed her everywhere, she was now a woman of the world. Magazine editors hounded her for some life stories and glamour shots.

The private jet landed at Sydney; she hadn't seen Jason for eight months. To be honest she hadn't really missed him, he had become an inconvenience, 'like a burr in your pants', Lucy laughed at her comparison.

Jason checked his watch. He had to meet Lucy and after eight months he was feeling a little nervous. Jason's life was also moving ahead. He was now Mayor of a large coastal city with quaint little suburbs, and all had huge tourism potential. Rayford had a beautiful mountain range and over the mountains the Pacific Ocean could be heard rolling endlessly. Hugging Bay jutted out of the coastline. Two long curving land formations, like arms wrapping around to protect its precious creation.

Jason had big plans to make a fortune in a resort, exploiting a natural landscape, especially a lake and a magnificent mountain. The phone rang interrupting Jason's dreaming.

'What, for God's sake?!' he yelled, picking up the phone.

'Your wife's plane has landed Mr Blackwell.'

Jason slammed the phone down. He was not particularly interested in seeing Lucy, it was her money that interested Jason. That was going to get him what he wanted. He had her contracts scrutinised to ensure he was getting the most he could extract. Their bank account was bulging.

CHAPTER 4

Lucy sat in luxurious surrounds, waiters and patrons trying to get a good look at her without being obvious. Bodyguards stood like sentinels discreet in their presence.

Jason arrived at the restaurant. He stood watching his wife and watching others intrigued by her. They embraced, like business partners. They talked about themselves to each other, both aware they were the centre of everyone's interest.

The couple drank too much that night knowing they had to spend the night together, nervous in each other's company.

The sun spread its rays across the bed, Jason studied Lucy's face, she was so beautiful, so famous and he actually felt intimidated. They spent the day together relaxing, tormenting the paparazzi, exercising and having beauty treatments and massages. It was a superficial time spent together. All was surface conversation about themselves. It was an agreed situation that they would pursue their careers and make as much money as possible, to live the life of the rich and famous. That was who they were now, and it suited both perfectly.

As her private jet left Sydney airport, Lucy barked out demands ensuring her pampering needs are met. Paris Fashion Week was her next show, and she was the most famous model booked for the event. The rich and the best fashion houses would be coming just to see her.

Lucy had been pushing herself solid for nearly three months, so she was enjoying the beautiful day sitting beside Rick Jensen in his new BMW. Her beautiful hair danced around her head, the wind controlling its destiny. Lucy looked good. Her body was tanned and tone with perfect makeup on a beautiful face.

Rick looked over at Lucy admiring her from head to toe, Lucy returned the look with a smile, Rick had a quizzical expression.

'What's the matter?' asked Lucy.

'Have you put on a little weight? Your abdomen looks swollen.'

Lucy's hand went to her abdominal area, face flushing, deep in thought.

'That time of month is it?' said Rick smiling.

It was like a heavy weight fell on her, her heart started to race, it was pounding in her ears. She hadn't had a period, she felt a bit sick in the morning, she was pregnant!

'The camera does not like fat models, you know that, right?'

Lucy's mind was in a state of seizure, something was rising inside her and then it spewed forth, screaming, hands smashing the dashboard, her face twisted in uncontrollable rage.

The sound of screeching tyres, the smell of rubber burning, glass shattering, metal crunching, wheels spinning nowhere to go, flames flickering to life. The smell of blood mingled with the toxic smoke and fluid. The beautiful shiny symbol of wealth groaned to its end, unrecognizable.

CHAPTER 5

It was headline news in Paris, 'Famous photographer killed in car crash, well known model seriously injured.' The description of the crash was horrendous across all the media.

Lucy's condition was upgraded to critical. Jason sat by her bedside wondering what lay beneath the bandages covering her face and entire head. A broken left leg, fractured ribs, massive bruising, internal organs intact.

Jason was informed that his wife was pregnant, but unfortunately the foetus aborted during surgery to her face and fractured leg. He knew that there was going to be a difficult road ahead. No amount of counselling or psychiatric medications was going to give anyone a peaceful life.

Maeve Beaumont held her daughter's hand, waiting for her to respond.

Maeve was an educated woman. She was a retired veterinarian and had a degree in Environmental science, spending her time teaching at various universities. On many occasions she travelled the world writing papers on the effects of global warming, overpopulation, the impacts on environments and the decline of natural flora and fauna.

Maeve was the opposite of Lucy, she was spiritual, mysterious, and very gentle, hence why Lucy did not get along with her mother. Maeve liked to give back to the world, considering how fortunate she had been. Emitting an elegant presence, she was tall and graceful, with lively blue eyes that highlighted an interesting, sculptured face.

The love of her life Harley Beaumont had passed away twelve months ago. They had met at university, married, and were like one person. Harley taught science after gaining his master's degree.

Their academic minds intertwined, pushing their intellect into the unknown realms of modern man. Together they travelled the world to secret destinies, compiling writings that were secreted away in a bank security box.

When Maeve discovered she was pregnant, they decided to buy a house in the Blue Mountains. It was secluded. A perfect Shangrila.

The day their daughter was born was an amazing gift to Maeve and Harley Beaumont. They loved being parents, just nurturing and teaching her when she was a toddler. It was incredible to be parents. As Lucy grew, it became very clear that she was very much the princess. Clothes, jewellery and all things sparkling, and pink intrigued the little girl.

Harley and Maeve often joked there must have been a switching of babies at the hospital.

It was unfortunate that Maeve and her daughter had nothing in common. It was even more obvious as she got older.

CHAPTER 6

The day had come for the bandages to be removed. It was six weeks since the accident. Lucy's thoughts kept going around in her head, the life she was having, and then nothing, she couldn't remember how this happened, over and over it played, but no outcome.

Maeve left the room, deciding it was Jason's place to be with his wife to give her the love and emotional support she was going to need.

The room was darkened. The surgeon and nurse talked Lucy through what was going to happen. She didn't respond but grabbed in the air for Jason's hand.

Very gently the nurse cut away at the heavy bandages, using a gentle tone of voice to soothe the Lucy's nerves. The last of the dressing was removed using saline, loosening its grip to reveal the traumatic facial damage.

The silence in the room spoke volumes to Lucy, slowly she opened her eyes, shards of light, dark figures and strange shapes moved around until the visions gathered clarity. The first thing she saw clearly was Jason's expression.

Maeve heard the scream from the waiting room. A low guttural sound, it permeated the vicinity, making people freeze from whatever they were doing. They then quickly continued on their way, interpreting what just happened in their own minds.

Jason emerged from the room. His face was white, and his hands were shaking. Maeve gathered Jason up and sat him down. Jason searched her face. 'My God Maeve. Her face is butchered!'

Back inside the room, pain could be felt in the silence. All three people looking from one to the other, she raised the mirror slowly until her entire face filled up the mirror.

Lucy studied what used to be her beautiful face. The right side of her face looked like it had melted. A train track ran from her hairline above her ear to the middle of her bottom lip where the side of her mouth hung open, which resulted in a trough of saliva trickling slowly down her chin. Lucy's right eyelid hung down like an old, faded blind. The bottom lid was slack exposing the soft pink tissue. In contrast the left side of her face was almost perfect. Her fingers delicately probed the melted meaty mess that now replaced her beauty like some invading parasite.

As the mirror smashed into tiny pieces, an injection was administered into the saline drip. Slowly darkness fell, providing relief from the horrible reality that was now hers.

CHAPTER 7

It was going to be a long journey for Lucy to try and rehabilitate. Maeve thought her house in the mountains would be a private peaceful environment.

Maeve did her best to help her daughter. Physically she could walk again with a slight limp. Mentally, Lucy was damaged. She retreated into a place in her mind that she could stand being in. She was emotionless and life was cold and dark.

The police had tried to question Lucy on many occasions and each time Lucy just shook her head, stating she couldn't remember, hiding her face and scurrying away like a wounded animal. Lucy decided to wear a patch over her right eye, inside a liner was used to soak up her weeping fluid.

All her days were the same. She stayed in her room watching TV and videos, followed by reading magazines about celebrities. Lucy didn't respond to psychological intervention. She found contentment in her medications to keep her calm and stable.

Maeve and Jason had many conversations about the future. Jason felt he had no place in Lucy's future or her life and perhaps he should move out. Maeve couldn't really argue or find a positive angle. It was decided with Maeve's blessing, Jason would move on with his future.

A discussion was held with Lucy. Jason and Maeve approached the subject delicately. Jason explained his feelings and his needs. Lucy responded with a grunt, saying ''Days of Our Lives' is starting,' she got up and left the room.

That night Maeve sat at her desk looking out the large glass door into her native garden, surrounded by tall trees and native shrubs. It was a full moon. It shone so brightly; it was like early morning. Two figures sat high in a tree, silhouettes in the moonlight. Maeve left her desk and walked outside to greet her visitors. At that moment, a golden light enveloped all three beings.

As the brilliant light disappeared all three remained in silence - a huge Wedge tail eagle, a Tawny frog mouth and Maeve - watching the night. It was quiet, nothing moved. Stars became restless in the sky racing in all directions, an exciting event was unfolding.

Stars formed a roof over the house in the shape of a dome. At that moment in time in the galaxy above, the planets were in alignment.

Lucy too was restless tonight. Her powerful medication had not sent her to that place she craved every night. She was feeling a powerful emotion, her thoughts of Jason were overwhelming, and she wanted to be with him, to feel the warmth of her husband. She couldn't stop the feelings of desire.

Jason woke in fear. He felt something getting in his bed, when he realised it was Lucy he couldn't speak. He felt revulsion. Her voice was frightening and desperate, and he could see her hideous face. She demanded Jason make love to her. He felt sorry for her and then he thought it didn't matter, he was leaving the next day and taking her money with him. That thought in itself made it bearable, he never had to see this ugly creature again.

Lucy woke around 4am, the light outside was bright and she felt strange.   She yawned, feeling tired and snuggled back down slipping into a relaxed sleep.

She could feel the wind lifting her silky blonde hair, exposing her beautiful face. She felt wonderful and she looked magnificent. Rick Jensen looked at her with pure adoration. Lucy was smiling in her sleep, then her face changed to a frown, then horror, her twisted mouth opened as Rick began to scowl at her.

'You're fat, you're fat. You're ugly'.

Lucy sat bolt upright, sweat springing out all over her body. Lucy grabbed her abdominal area, then she remembered the conversation about her weight with Rick. She was pregnant. She screamed, losing her mind. The car crashed and she had been pregnant with Jason's baby. It was his fault. Lucy's voice shrieked like an animal being killed. Jason woke in time to avoid the base of a large lamp coming down on his head.

Leaving the house that morning, Jason vowed to never see the 'ugly bitch' again. He was relieved. Happy. His life was now his own. He didn't have to feel guilty, after all she did try to kill him. Jason began laughing, turning the music up as he drove away.

CHAPTER 8

Lucy became slightly more motivated, deciding to go off her meds, which Maeve convinced her to since she had found out she was pregnant again. Maeve gave her healthy juices and fresh food, all for the baby growing inside her, a very important baby to Maeve.

Lucy enjoyed the pampering, magazines galore and movies. They even exercised together. Maeve purchased deep moisturising creams and tempted Lucy with hairdressing and nail polish, Lucy enjoyed everything, but there was little conversation.

Louis Harley Blackwell was born on the 7.7.2007 at 7am, he was a beautiful baby and Maeve Beaumont fell in love all over again. There was no interest from his mother. She went through the motions of motherhood and found the only positive aspect was the single mother's pension. She finally had money to spend on herself.

Maeve and Louis became very close, Louis considered Maeve his mother. She taught him about the world, the life of animals, and she taught him how precious the planet was. They studied together, they laughed, and they were soul mates. Lucy chose not to join in. She had feelings of jealousy and life was boring with a kid. As life continued, Maeve became more Louis's mother than grandmother. Lucy lived in her own world oblivious to the real world and that's the way she liked it. The years rolled by, the older woman and the young boy loved their life together, they were made just for each other. The contentment and adventures never became boring, the wonders of the world enthralled them both. Maeve told Louis of the incredible places of the world. They read many books together and watched many documentaries.

It was Louis's sixth birthday. Maeve had organised a party with friends, interesting games, and Louis was so excited. Lucy had taken the car to the nearest town and purchased soft drinks for Louis and his friends. Arriving home, the party was in full swing as she staggered in the front door. She was drunk. No one noticed until she began her tirade of abuse, targeting Louis and Maeve. Her words were vicious, accusing Maeve of ignoring her and spoiling Jason's bastard. How Louis was a reminder of what Jason did. It was his fault her life was over. Lucy's saliva flew out of her mouth, her nerveless lip wobbling around like a fish out of water, Maeve directed Lucy to her room, gave her medications, talked to her like a child, and she went to sleep like an emotional infant.

Maeve spent many hours over her years together with Louis teaching him multiple skills and knowledge he would need in the future. How to cook, how to shop and all the tasks to survive in the world, including the intricacies of technology. Louis loved doing anything with his grandmother. He didn't spend any time with his mother nor invited to, except when Lucy wanted him to do something for her.

Louis woke early on this particular morning to the sound of birds protesting and squabbling, waiting for their morning feed that Maeve did every morning. He looked out the window with a thoughtful expression. His grandmother was always up early and then he remembered she was out in the yard late last night looking at some night birds high up in the trees.

The boy headed for Maeve's room. She was still in bed, so he did the usual and crawled in to cuddle the warm secure body and receive his daily kisses. Something didn't feel right thought Louis. There was no warmth. Maeve wouldn't wake up. She was pale, her blue eyes still and milky. Fear began to rise in Louis. He felt stunned, a loud scream filled the room, and it didn't feel like his voice. Birds called out desperately and took flight, then calm darkness took over Louis's world.

It was a mournful sight. A small, frightened boy, a woman holding his hand their heads turned downwards. Slow drizzling rain. Tears blurred Louis's vision whilst his body shook. He just wanted to get in the coffin with his beloved Maeve and go wherever she was going. Louis was worried his Nan would be cold and lonely. Prior to laughing, Lucy rather bluntly informed Louis that his grandmother was dead and gone, and he would never see her again.

All the grownups looked at him with saddened eyes. Louis believed his Nan would be waiting at home for him, this was all wrong, everyone has got it all wrong. He ran through the house searching for his Nan. She was gone. The sorrow was overwhelming. He went and got into her bed and sobbed himself to sleep.

The days that followed the death of Maeve Beaumont were empty and cold for Louis. Gone was the human contact, the laughter, and the good smells coming from the kitchen. The excitement for knowledge and adventure lost forever. Louis sat with his mother, forced to watch romantic movies and eat take-away.

Many visitors came to the house. Lucy informed him that they would be moving, she said horrible things about Maeve.

'Your precious grandmother made the will out in your favour. The house has to be sold and all proceeds to go into a trust account for YOU when you turn eighteen. I get the household items and that's all.'

Lucy ranted and raved for days. She drank lots of wine and threw up, when she could no longer stand up.

Louis withdrew into himself, he spent hours alone thinking about the things Nan had taught him, how to not let things hurt him.

A furniture truck came and moved them to a town called Lambert. Lucy decided that if she moved to a country region the public housing would be cheaper, there would be less chance of being hassled to find a job, and she wouldn't have Maeve's nosey friends watching her. She sold a lot of household items, her mother's jewellery and all her potted plants. She made over eight thousand dollars. Louis watched as all the precious belongings of his Nan's disappeared, until it was like she never existed. He found all Maeve's photos in the recycling bin torn into tiny pieces. Louis couldn't understand why Lucy hated his grandmother so much.

It was a long journey to Lambert, Louis watched out the back window of the car, until the house, the trees, the birds, his whole life and the Blue Mountains disappeared forever. Huge tears of emotions cascaded down his cheeks landing in his lap.

Lucy looked at her son in the rear vision mirror.

'Oh, really Louis! It's time you got over that old bag. I'm your mother and we will be doing things my way from now on.'

Finally, after about eight hours of driving they arrived at their destination. Louis enjoyed watching the farmlands and the farm animals, losing himself in the beauty of nature. Many times he made the mistake of calling Lucy 'Maeve', drawing her attention to something interesting he sighted. Lucy reacted badly, yelling at the top of her voice, her melted face twisting into a demonic being from one of Maeve's ancient books.

Number twelve Curlew St, Lambert was to be their home, the furniture truck was being unloaded, and Lucy parked Maeve's immaculate Saab in the carport.

'Well Louis, here we are! Let's check it out!'

Louis looked at the house and looked up and down the street.

'They all look the same Mum.'

'That doesn't matter, it's cheap and I'll have more money to spend.'

'Can we have a dog?'

'No! Definitely not.'

'Can I have a kitten or a guinea pig?'

'I'm not wasting my money on stinking animals.'

Louis's heart sank into his boots, he just wanted something to love and look after.

'Your grandmother had a bad influence on you, now just get over it.'

Louis thought the house was ugly. It looked like it was built out of blue cardboard. A half dead bottle brush leaned over the back fence looking like it was trying to commit suicide. The floors in the house were covered in a brown orange patterned lino, highlighted by many cracks and burns. He suddenly remembered the thick cream carpet in Maeve's house and how good it looked and felt on bare feet.

Stained torn lace curtains hung on every window, with dark blinds to block out the daylight. The kitchen had brown cupboards, chipped and scratched from years of frustrated abuse. The walls still had globules of old yellow fat stuck firmly on them an around the top of the stove, mouse poo lay throughout the cupboards. Where the fridge was once positioned the lino was torn bare to reveal the floorboards. Louis checked out the bathroom. It too was in a state of disrepair. The old enamel tub had that many chips in it, it looked like a Dalmatian. The grey lino was lifting in the corners, from years of water seeping into the floor. The hand basin had rusted taps with matching rust stains in the basin, calcium had built up around the spouts nearly blocking the flow of water. Louis poked at the walls assuming they were cardboard, and his fingers went straight through.

Lucy was in a frenzy of excitement placing her mother's furniture and belongings around the house. Louis hated the house it was ugly and smelt of urine and vomit, Maeve's furniture looked sad and pathetic trying to inhabit a hideous cardboard box. He loved to sit on his Nan's lounge. It smelt like her rose perfume, the same as the ones that grew in the garden. Sometimes Louis would sit in his Nan's huge bedroom cupboard, just sitting in the dark smelling the Tea Rose perfume. The darkness felt good, and he could remember her without his mother's abuse.

The next day Lucy pulled up at the front of the school, waiting for Louis to get out.

'Can you come with me Mummy?'

'No Louis! I've got more important things to do.'

At 9 years of age Louis felt frightened. He didn't know what to do or where to go, tears started to blur his vision, he felt like running away. As those thoughts gathered, a gentle hand touched his shoulder. Louis looked up to see an older woman, dressed a bit like Nan used to. A soft voice and a gentle direction soon bundled him off to his classroom under the guidance of Ms Noels, the headmistress. Louis informed them of his name and said his mother was too busy to come into the school. He noticed the exchange of looks between Miss Mills, his teacher, and Mrs Noels. Maeve's lessons on being observant of the world around him and people's expressions had certainly proved worthwhile today. He felt like a total loser.

Primary school life was lonely and humiliating, none of the kids wanted to be friends with him, he was just called a weirdo and left in isolation, just a fringe dweller.

The teachers thought it unusual that a child of obvious neglect performed well in all subjects, but his social skills were not developing. Many times, Louis had to be supplied with decent clothing and fed nearly every day.

CHAPTER 9

Lucy's lifestyle was starting to affect Louis's life and his mental health. He was even more withdrawn, spending lots of time in the dark cupboard or under the bed locked in his room. The only time Lucy spoke to him was to blame him for her life and make him clean up her mess of vomit, food and ashtrays. She started to drink heavily. Watching soap operas on television was her favourite pastime and she became deeply involved in the characters' lives.

Louis felt dead inside, nothing pleasant ever happened. He spent hours in the local library. Each time he returned home with books Lucy would make fun of him, 'You're just like your stupid old grandmother.'

Lucy started to hang out in the pub all day when her pension was deposited into the bank. Louis learnt very early to disappear into his room to avoid being ridiculed and abused by his mother and her friends. He just hoped they forgot he existed.

One particular day he got off the school bus, it was a Thursday - pension day - and he knew what to expect. One of the kids threw an apple core at him.

'Hey weirdo, your ugly mother hitting the grog tonight? Big party with all the dropkicks?'

Louis ran towards home as tears started to bulge out of his eyes. He so wished he had somewhere to go besides home. He often wished he had died with his Nan, and he missed her so much. Even now her death seemed like it was only yesterday, and he was having many thoughts about dying himself. As he got closer, he heard the music from six houses away. He had a bad feeling. Nervously, he slowed down and sat in the gutter, tears streaming down his face. A strange noise broke his misery. Looking upwards to the sky trying to locate the source of the sound, he spotted a huge Wedge tail eagle, drifting and floating. Spiralling, the eagle soared higher. It was mesmerising and calming to watch.

Continuing home, he was faced with a lot of people in the lounge room. The music was loud, so no one noticed him. He went to his room and made a safe haven under his bed, locked the door and tried to sleep whilst envisaging the eagle, free and happy. He concentrated on that over and over. He was peaceful at last.

Around 11pm Louis awoke to the sound of music in the backyard and the smell of smoke. Looking out his window, drunken men were pulling palings off the fence to burn. Everyone was staggering and swearing amidst drunken maniacal laughter. Lucy was dancing around the fire like a visiting demon.

Counting, Louis could make out there were at least twenty people filling up the yard with ugliness. Out of the corner of his eye he noticed one of them went behind the old garden shed. His lizards lived in a hollow log that was half embedded into the ground. His heart started beating fast, as he felt it shaking in his chest. Fear and anger began taking over his mind.

With a drunken sway and maniacal laugh the partygoer came from behind the shed holding the female Blue Tongue by the tail and began walking towards the fire. Ferocious anger drove Louis out of his room. Years of frustration and anger spewed forth like a volcano erupting as the end of Nan's big garden broom connected with the man holding the Blue Tongue.

Louis felt a hard blow to his lower back, then a sharp pain penetrated the right side of his face. He was on the ground. The last thing he saw and heard were ugly faces scowling, laughing, swearing and calling him disgusting names.

The sound of buzzers and bells rang in Louis's head. It was bright and the bed felt strange. He could smell strange odours. A soft voice spoke.

'Good morning.'

Looking up Louis saw a pretty face leaning over him.

'Hi, my name is Virginia, your nurse for today. How are you feeling?'

Louis was informed that someone in the street had called the ambulance and police because they heard him screaming. He was told his mother was at the police station and he would be staying in hospital until things were sorted out. Louis kept worrying about the lizards and wondering if he was going to go to jail for belting that bloke. He slept for the remainder of the morning. For the first time in years, he felt safe.

At 3pm Louis was visited by a lady dressed in a black suit and a really white blouse.

'Hello Louis, my name is Karen Landy, I'm a social worker and if it's okay, I would like to talk to you.'

'What about?' Louis replied, unsure what a social worker was, he guessed she was a detective. 'Am I going to jail?' he continued, sinking into his bed.

Karen Landy smiled and touched Louis gently on the arm.

'No Louis, I'm sorry, let me explain what I do. My job is to make sure that children in your situation have a safe home. After I investigate and feel a child is in danger, then I find them a safe home.'

Louis felt frightened, he asked in a tiny voice 'Am I going to a Juvenile Centre place?'

Continuing to smile at Louis, Karen replied, 'No Louis, you are not in trouble. Hopefully, I'm going to make your life much better, not worse.'

It had been decided that Louis be taken away from Lucy. All events had been taken into consideration, including the past visits and school issues. An eyewitness saw Lucy assaulting her son with a fence paling and kicking him in the stomach when he was on the ground. She had been screaming that she hoped he was dead and to join 'that rotten bitch in hell'. Louis sustained severe bruising and multiple skin lesions and was left feeling very lost and alone.

CHAPTER 10

Bridget Sherwood heard someone calling her name, she looked up from kneeling in her vegetable garden dressed in old blue overalls, long brown curly hair pushing its way out from under her old straw hat. Bridget was a small woman, pale skin, her eyes the colour of the sea on a stormy day, kind and generous. Bridget's pretty face exploded into joy when she saw who it was, she quickly threw off her hat and gloves, and hurried to the verandah door.

Karen Landy stood there, folder in hand looking a bit frazzled.

'Hello Karen. Come in, it's been ages.'

Bridget quickly put together a cup of tea and heated some homemade scones served with fresh cream and jam. Karen was grateful for the morning tea; it had been a busy morning.

'It's been ages since I've seen you, Karen!'

'I know Bridget and I apologise for being so slack! But, I have some news that I hope will please you. Oh Bridget, this jam is amazing!'

'Native plums Karen, they make the best.'

'You're amazing you know, how you grow all this beautiful food. This place it's just magical.'

Karen looked around Bridget's beautiful little home, so abundant with plants, preservatives and interesting art. 'This tea is amazing Bridget! What brand is it?'

'I just mix different leaves to get an interesting flavour.'

The two women enjoyed their morning tea, savouring that moment in the day that everyone looks forward to. Karen sat back in her chair looking at Bridget.

'I suppose you're wondering why I am here?'

Bridget smiled, 'That had crossed my mind.'

Karen pulled a file out of her large handbag. 'How about I give this to you. You read and I'll eat. I will not interrupt until you finish.'

Bridget read with intrigue. Through her facial expressions Karen could almost tell what part of the story she was up to. Large heavy tears made their way down her face. She studied the photo of Louis and she looked up at Karen simply stating, 'I'll take him.'

'Do you need time to think about this? He has been through some awful events.'

'This child needs me, and I've waited long enough.'

Bridget lived in a small suburb called Tirrana, located north of Sydney. The area was thriving with tourism. Considered quaint and alternative, it was heavily forested with many boutique industries of food and wine. To the east of Tirrana was the Pacific Ocean, but before the ocean was a range of unusual mountains - one in particular. It was a huge ancient giant and nestled at the foot of these mountains was hidden a beautiful, pristine natural lake. From the lake you could hear the ocean rolling in and out. Two land formations similar in size jutted out resembling arms, cradled that particular part of the coastline. It was aptly called Hugging Bay.

Bridget's small but unique cottage was situated at the end of a road close to a natural forest not far from the hidden lake. Her cottage was split level incorporating a combination of stone and timber. Inside was like a fairy tale house. A staircase, timber floors and a beautiful oak kitchen. There was a rich purple feature wall, with unusual ornaments and colourful rugs. Brilliant, coloured cushions adorned lounges, the floor, they were scattered everywhere. Glorious potted ferns and other plants, accentuated by batik prints highlighted every corner of the house. Chimes and coloured lanterns hung from the back verandah, as soft sinking furniture invited bums to sit, and everywhere colourful objects caught the eye. The yard was lush and inviting, despite being somewhat tangled. The bedrooms overlooked the gardens, each one having their own balcony. Night noises and aromas drifted into one's sleep. Stained glass doors reflected soft pastel colours into the house each morning. The bathroom was burgundy, black and silver. A deep, old restored tub had soothed many bodies throughout history and yellow glass windows reflected a beautiful amber light on the ferns hanging from the heavy timber beams overhead. Shelves of multi-coloured glass bottles housed herbal creams, tonics and remedies, compliments of her beloved friend Isobel. An old fireplace in the bathroom was the centrepiece. Cherubs carved out of mahogany timber framed a beautiful ornate mirror. Candles and a fire in the wintertime enhance a deep soak in the beautiful burgundy tub.

Bridget had created a sanctuary of peace and she desperately needed someone to share it with. She had lost a baby boy at birth years ago and her partner left her not long after. It was after this she decided to leave the city and move to Tirrana, finally to live the life she needed to live. She wanted to live amongst nature, grow her food and just create. It was six months ago she decided to be a foster carer, finally the right one had arrived. Louis Blackwell had been a long time coming.

Bridget's dearest friend, Isobel Crane, has a son named Charlie around the same age as Louis and a daughter Simone who is six years old. The Crane family are of Aboriginal origin. Isobel is very spiritual and a clairvoyant. She practices naturopathy and runs a business from home. Both she and Bridget study the ancient practice of witchcraft and tarot. One of her favourite things to do is purchasing old books relating to her interests. Bridget and Isobel's family have an unbreakable bond, doing many things together, sharing their homes and their lives. They have no secrets.

Strangely, Bridget's characteristics were similar to Louis. Long curly hair, freckles, dark blue eyes that smile with ease and an aura of serenity.

When Bridget closed the door after saying goodbye to Karen Landy, excitement nearly sent her crazy.

Isobel Crane answered her mobile, she had trouble deciphering the babbling on the other end.

'Bridget is that you? You need to slow down.'

'I've got a child!'

'What?'

'I've got a child!'

With laughter gurgling down the phone from both ends, plans were made for Louis Blackwell's arrival.

Walking out of the Lambert hospital, Karen Landy at his side, Louis was told in depth of the proceedings, and he had agreed to be fostered. He decided he liked the sound of Bridget Sherwood and her home. It reminded him of his Nan.

There was one stipulation that Louis insisted on. That was to see if his Blue Tongue lizards had survived and if so, he wanted to take them with him. Karen asked Louis how he felt about seeing his mother again. He looked out the window, and there was a long pause before he answered.

'I know it was my mother who belted me with the fence paling, I remember what she said before everything went black.'

Karen looked at Louis in shock surprise. 'I didn't realise you knew all that.'

'It doesn't matter anymore. I just want the lizards.'

The car pulled up in front of Number 12 Curlew St. The woman and the nervous boy entered the front door after their knocking went unnoticed. Simultaneously, the stench of the house hit their nostrils. It was repulsive. The smell of vomit, cigarettes and putrid food mingled together.

Lucy lay sprawled out on the lounge with a bucket beside her which she had been using as a toilet. The smell of faeces and urine added to the other unbearable smells. Stirring, she slowly sat up.

'Hello' said Karen in a sympathetic voice.

Lucy's eye patch sat on the coffee table amongst the debris, she had not attended to her eye for some time. Dried tears and pus stains encrusted her face. The scar bulged red and angry. Oily and lifeless, her hair hung over her shoulders like a mass of rat's tails. Her old flannelette pyjamas stained with all manner of things. Louis looked at her with pity.

'Hello Mum, I've come to get a few things.'

He left the room unable to stand the look of his mother. He walked through to the back door. Amongst the rubbish strewn over the kitchen bench he noticed an official looking envelope and picking it up, read the contents. It was from a firm of solicitors in the Blue Mountains. It stated that Nan's house had sold for $525,000 and the proceeds were in a trust for Louis to have access at the age of eighteen. Applications needed to be made for funds to be released to support Louis for all his needs. It stated that the firm would be managing the funds as instructed by Maeve in her will. There was a feeling of guilt for his mother, but common sense told him that the money would destroy her. He resolved he would talk to Karen and put the letter in his pocket.

Walking into the yard he was relieved to see the Blue Tongues had survived and their bodies healed. They both had received scars for life that night. Deciding a vet check was in order, he put his friends in an old shoe box, stuffed some clothes in his school bag, some old treasures in a drawstring bag and left his room, not wanting to look back.

The goodbyes were said between mother and son, he said he would write, although he knew that was a pointless statement. A tiny pathetic voice whimpered.

'What about me? What will I do? I won't get the single mother's pension, my rotten mother left me nothing!'

Her voice now grew louder.

Karen Landy intervened. An anxious Louis waited in the car. Fifteen minutes later Karen got in the car and drove off silently. Two hours later the travellers sat in McDonalds having lunch. Louis was hungry. Burgers and chips disappeared at a hasty speed. Once full and his hunger satisfied, he handed Karen the letter out of his pocket.

'No wonder she's pissed off, she needs some sort of help.'

'I know,' said Karen, looking at Louis with admiration.

'I've spoken to your mother and I'm going to arrange for a heap of things to happen to improve her life and help her get back on track.'

'Can some of that money be used to help her? I think Nan would have wanted that.'

'I'll see what I can do.'

Once back on the road Karen entered into the heavy explanation stating what Louis's future would be. Karen discussed in depth the process of fostering and described Bridget's home, her jobs and her friends. Karen explained how his inheritance would work to support his needs. Louis didn't say much. He just listened imaging the woman and a life much like his Nan's.

The nerves were starting to stir in Louis's stomach. The thought of trying to fit in with strangers felt overwhelming. Karen's voice interrupted the dilemma in his mind.

'I was wondering, when you start school, if you would feel more comfortable taking Bridget's surname to avoid long, drawn out explanations.'

Sad confused eyes stared out from the car window.

'Just think about it Louis, there's no rush.'

The familiar smell of Nan's tea rose perfume awakened his senses.

'What perfume are you wearing Karen?'

'None.'

'Do you have air freshener?'

She shook her head. 'What's wrong Louis?'

'I can smell the perfume my Nan used to wear. It smells like roses.'

'Perhaps it's because you have been thinking about her.'

'Yeah.'

Turning his head to the window, heavy full tears rolling down his cheeks, memories hurtling through his mind, his gaze turned to something far away in the sky. It looked like a speck. Focussing hard, the speck started to take on a form. A wedge tail eagle was floating and surfing the thermals. Watching it felt soothing and calming. He was magnificent.

CHAPTER 11

Pulling up at Number 20 Lavender Lane, Louis couldn't help but notice that the name suited the cottage perfectly. His eyes feasted on the vision before him, reminding him of his Nan's place. The colours, the organised chaos and the comfortable verandah housing old furniture. Plants and cushions, chairs that swallowed you up, multi-coloured mats scattered randomly, and ceramic pots scarred with unwanted seconds positioned to show off their imperfections.

The ground covers and weeping shrubs created a tunnel around the cottage. A crazy path enticed any visitors to explore. Hidden garden seats, wind chimes and bird feeders supported the vision. Tiny grottos, perfect to hide away in, housed wooden stumps to sit and watch the birdlife. It was a busy place. Birds of all breeds fed off seed bells as the wind chimes tinkled in the breeze.

Karen and Louis waited nervously at Bridget's front door. When the door opened, all Louis's senses were on alert, as he began studying the woman that he was to spend a big part of his life with. She looked kind. Her eyes smiled and her voice was gentle. Feeling his heartbeat in his ears, the smell of roses happened again. Louis's heart slowed.

'Are you alright Louis?'

His mind gathered, she looked concerned.

'Yeah, um yes, I'm okay.'

Together Bridget and Louis waved Karen off, both nervously looked at each.

'Why don't I show you the yard and the rest of the house, then I'll help you unpack. That sound okay?'

He followed Bridget down the crazy path.

'We're lucky to have a national park beginning at the end of the yard. I have all sorts of visitors drop in.'

'Visitors' said Louis.

'Yes. Birds. Echidnas. Lizards.'

Louis then remembered his Blue Tongues.

Bridget heard the story of his lizard rescue. 'I have the perfect place for your family, an old pile of wood, plenty of hollow ones a perfect habitat.'

It made Louis feel so good inside to see the family of lizards finally find a place to call home.

Introductions were made, the chooks, a rather clownish raven called Rodney, and a multitude of wild birds. It was a beautiful, serene place.

'There's a secret path that leads to a beautiful lake at the end of the yard', Bridget pointed in the direction.

'Can I go there sometime?' said Louis looking at Bridget with an air of intrigue.

'You certainly can, now let's go and get some dinner.'

The two new friends sat together eating homemade hamburgers, mud cake and ice cream. They relaxed in each other's company watching a comedy Bridget picked specifically for this evening.

Later that night Bridget ran Louis a warm bath, then added some of her friend's aromatic oils to help relax and sleep. Bridget folded back his bed, leaving him a book 'Wind In The Willows', a couple of old comics, a diary, as well as pens and pencils.

The sounds of birds and the rooster, Mr Big, greeted the day. Louis stirred and waking, laid in his bed looking out the window. He thought of Lucy and that horrible house. He felt guilty and sad for his mother, silently hoping Karen Landy could help her get better.

After they finished a homemade breakfast, they went shopping for school clothes and casual wear. Louis couldn't remember shopping with his mother for anything new. They tried caps, sunglasses and lots of shoes. Bridget made it a fun trip dressing in boy's clothes and making silly jokes. Louis giggled and made funny comebacks to her comments.

They ate lunch at the Coffee Club, Louis ordering his own food, excited and feeling very grown up.

Bridget decided to give Louis a guided tour of the town and Hugging Bay. Looking out over the ocean, Bridget asked how he would feel about meeting her very dearest friend Isobel Crane and her son Charlie.

'Charlie, he's your age just turned thirteen and her daughter Simone, I think she's six. I really want you to be happy here Louis.'

Louis looked at Bridget and smiled, 'It's nice and green, it reminds me of my Nan's place in the Blue Mountains. I loved living there, the mountains are beautiful'.

'You must miss your Nan?'

Louis didn't respond he looked confused. 'What is that?'

Bridget looked startled 'What's wrong Louis?'

'I keep smelling Nan's perfume she used to wear.'

'What was it like?'

'Roses, it smelt like roses.'

'Was it Tea Rose?'

'That's it.'

Bridget's face softened and smiled at Louis, she reached for his hand, realising she was being pushy, but he didn't pull away.

'Would it be okay if I told you something Louis? But please don't be scared or upset.'

'I think I can handle it, you know, considering my past.'

'Do you understand when I say that your Nan is with you?'

'I do' said Louis unperturbed. 'Nan and me used to talk about the spirit world. I didn't really understand. So, Nan is kind of still here?'

'Yes, she is Louis.'

From that moment on Louis Blackwell, now Sherwood started his transformation to his new world with confidence and hope.

Before Louis started school, Bridget asked the Crane family over for one of her homemade breakfasts. On the back verandah six comfortable deep cane chairs with soft cushions were all placed around an old oak table covered in baskets full of baked goods all laden with Bridget's fruit, homemade quiche and French toast. Bowls full of fruit were scattered across the table cut up and ready to dip into fresh cream. The smell of freshly brewed coffee and hot chocolate drifted on the air.

The Crane family arrived, lots of chatter and laughter came rolling through the door. Bridget stood with her arm around Louis. Introductions were quickly dispensed with, then Simone stood in front of Louis and wrapped her arms around his waist. Louis wasn't quite sure what to do. Laughter broke the awkward moment.

Charlie Crane was the same age as Louis, aboriginal, full of life and fun. Curly black hair, large brown eyes, and a smile that could melt ice. The boys began to talk and from that moment forward their friendship was sealed for life. They went off together to check out the lizards and other life forms that had set up house in Bridget's yard. Giggling could be heard above the garden. It was a perfect family setting, relaxing and at ease in each other's company.

Louis Sherwood slowly evolved into a well-adjusted thirteen-year-old. Bridget's gentle communication, her attentive care, kindness and routine was absorbed like a sponge. The memories would wake him at night, and at times when he woke in the mornings, it took some time to understand where he was. A day never went by that he didn't reflect how his life changed and he was proud to take Bridget's name. Many time's Bridget reminded Louis of his Nan. He finally had trust again.

The friendship between Louis and Charlie became stronger, they were great mates. Every weekend the families got together and did lots of activities. Isobel Crane was a very interesting woman, her beautiful thick hair dancing in the wind and her all-knowing mysterious dark eyes suited her spiritual nature. Louis loved her alternative practices, and on many occasions, she told stories of the dreamtime. She studied and practiced the ancient art of tarot. Isobel was a qualified naturopath and made a comfortable living treating many people in the area.

A strong bond was developing with the Crane family, Simone had adopted Louis as another brother. The affection and closeness with the two families amazed Louis. He was astounded how much they accepted him. It was like he had known them over many lifetimes.

When Isobel Crane first met Louis, she felt a powerful force surrounding this young boy. She kept it to herself until she understood more clearly what it meant.

The sun had been up for an hour, Louis stared out his window, he then locked eyes on a spider. His little friend was busy repairing his web, damaged from insects struggling for freedom. The sun glistened on the dew clinging to the web. All things in nature enthralled Louis.

'Well little fella you can mend your house from a string in your bum, just look at what we have to do in comparison.'

Smiling and in a contented mood, jumping out of his bed, he dressed quickly to feed the animals and birds before they went to the local markets.

CHAPTER 12

Isobel and Bridget have a stall together. They sell homemade food items, eggs, moisturiser creams, soaps, books and magazines. Isobel does tarot readings and numerology. The locals loved Bridget's jams and pickles, the two women were legendary up and down the coast for the quality of their produce.

Louis fed the chooks put out seed and cut up meat, all the while, Rodney the orphaned juvenile Raven pecked at his feet and pulled on the bottom of his trousers. Rodney was a rescue from the side of the road. It was presumed he took flight in a storm, far too young to fly. He was found floundering around unable to fly, and terrified.

'Rodney, you ratbag! Get off my foot.'

Louis loved this crazy bird. It followed him around the yard, sat on his windowsill just watching him. On many occasions Rodney follows Louis to school and meets him on the way back, the thinking is that Louis has become his mother and he's fine with that.

The morning was hot, a cool breeze kept it pleasant, fluffy cumulous clouds floated across the sky. Locals and visitors strolled around the beachfront stalls. The locals gossiped, kids played, the smell of sausages and onions drifting in the air, mouths salivating. People tasting local foods, everyone rummaging for a bargain or relaxing under trees. Humanity working together. Louis loves the markets, all the stuff people don't want anymore, and the homemade products. The sights, the smells and the connections all these people have.

'Hello Bridget.'

'Hey Louis.'

'Sold anything?'

Bridget smiled, 'Two bottles of pickles, 2 dozen eggs and a few magazines.'

Bridget handed Louis twenty dollars.

'Thanks Mum.'

Bridget's head jerked upward and looked into Louis's eyes. That was the first time he had called her Mum.

'Um, you better take a bag.'

A small tear trickled down her cheeks, Isobel wrapped her arms around her friend and the mood at that moment was absolute bliss.

Louis was busy rummaging through a second-hand book stall stacked high on a handmade shelf. The seller had gone to a lot of trouble to present his wares. Louis found a book on 'Strange Events and Creatures of the World.' Charlie Crane came up behind Louis in his usual tormenting style, flicking Louis behind the ear.

'Found anything?'

Louis turned around laughing ready to greet his friend, but stopped midway, eyes growing like saucers, looking straight back at him were the saddest most forlorn eyes you could ever see.

Eyes the colour of egg yolks, dirty matted black hair covered his body.

Skinny and panting for a drink, he was wearing around his neck a piece of cardboard attached by wire the words in black texta 'TO GIVE AWAY'.

'Charlie look!'

'Look at what?'

Louis pointed, his voice near to hysteria.

'God it's ugly.'

Louis made his way towards the dog, their eyes locking on each other. Fate was busy today.

Louis knelt down in front of the dog and allowed him to sniff. Slow movement began to beat from his tail. A great big lolling tongue fell out of the side of his mouth, which formed what looked like a smile on the dog's face. Louis gave the dog a good pat down and talked to him in a low, soothing voice.

'Hello old fella, so you're not wanted anymore.'

'That's right.'

Louis stood up quickly and turned to greet the gruff voice. A deep involuntary breath of shock came from Louis.

Before him was a man who was anywhere from fifty to a hundred years old. He looked like a big burnt sausage and deep crevices went in all directions over his face. Long dirty grey hair fell over mean calculating eyes the colour of raw coal. Louis broke his gaze, observing his old flannelette shirt, shorts, but his eyes remained on the man's feet. Long black toenails curled over the front of his toes lengthy black hair curled on the top of his feet.

'You want this mongrel?'

'Yes, I do' said Louis, mustering all the strength of voice that he could.

'Got any money?'

'It says 'TO GIVE AWAY'.'

Louis looked deep into the cavity of the man's smelly mouth, mesmerised with all the dags of food clinging to his multi-coloured beard.

'I'll give you this.'

Louis handed a $10 dollar note towards the man. A black gnarled claw snatched the money. He gave Louis one last look, and turning, spat, hobbling away into the crowd. The smell of urine, tobacco and sweat followed him.

'Holy shit! What was that?' Charlie stepped out from behind Louis, mouth gaping watching the strange figure disappear.

'He looked like something out of 'Lord of the Rings'.'

Both boys turned to look at the big dog.

'Mate, this dog is going to need some serious bathing. Not to mention a good feed,' said Charlie reluctant to touch him.

Louis bent down to take the wire and cardboard off him, a big wet tongue swept up the side of his face. The bond between boy and dog was formed.

'Oh dude, you let him lick your face, you might need that wire collar to lead him.'

Louis looked at the big dog, 'Nah I don't think so.'

'Now,' said Louis 'comes the hard part. Some heavy grovelling to my mother.'

The weather during the last hour had changed dramatically. The light wind was now menacing and gathering force. Dark clouds brimming with rain moved overhead. Stall owners' goods began to come alive, flapping and dancing in the wind. Items started to fall over. Bags took off. Anything loose was escaping into the turbulent sky. People were puzzled, nothing was predicted. It was meant to be clear skies.

The big dog was looking up into the sky, Louis followed his interest. High above a huge Wedge tail eagle soared on the high wind.

'That's unusual,' said Louis 'he's flying around in the middle of a storm.'

He looked down at the dog, then back to the sky. The eagle was gone.

Isobel and Bridget madly packed away their goods.

'Mum.'

'What is it, Louis?' All flustered, Bridget turned around, arms full of books, ready to stuff into bags.

The big dog sat smiling doing his best to look attractive and needy.

'He didn't cost anything, he's a giveaway!'

'Umm, technically' announced Charlie.

'Okay, I donated ten dollars to the owner. He was derelict and homeless Mum! Please Mum can I keep him. PLEASE?!' Louis was on his knees. 'I'll look after him, he'll be a great guard dog.'

Bridget looked at the large forlorn dog, and started to laugh, hair whipping around her face.

Okay he's yours, load him into the car.'

The rain started; the wind blew like an angry argument.

'Come on boys quick shove everything into the car.'

Isobel and Bridget were in panic mode, to avoid their possessions getting wet, Isobel's hair, now looking like wildfire dancing in all directions. Wind chimes screamed to be rescued, no longer a tinkling sound of serenity.

Once in the car, Bridget screwed up her nose.

'Oh my god, a bath big fella as soon as you get home.'

It took three soapy baths to remove built up dirt and kill all residing fleas. Once dried off and brushed he looked very handsome. He was very regal.

'I think perhaps he is mostly Labrador, what are you going to call him? He's got a big head and big feet.'

Bridget and Louis laughed together while the big dog sat looking all haughty as if he knew they were making fun of him.

'I'm thinking 'Boofy'.'

The dog banged his tail on the floor in response to his name. A big bowl of leftover beef and vegetable casserole for dinner, a pile of old blankets beside Louis's bed and Boofy was content and snoring in his new home.

Louis settled into bed, arm behind his head, thoughts of the day ran through his mind. Three things kept becoming prominent in his thoughts, the strange little man, the dog now beside him and the eagle floating in the storm. The smell of roses was again in the air.

Louis smiled 'Hello Nan'. The curtains above his bed billowed out, however the window was closed. Louis didn't feel fear only safety.

Louis rolled over to get comfortable and settle into sleep, just as he was about to turn off his bedside light, he noticed a green enviro bag leaning up against his clothes cupboard. For some reason he felt compelled to get up and look in the bag. Putting his hand in the bag, he realised he had picked up the wrong one. He pulled out packets of soap, a bag of potpourri.

'It's Isobel's stuff.'

In the bottom of the bag, a heavy old book, bound in thick leather with frayed laces and faint writing.

Louis sat on his bed and read the cover ''Chants and Spells, The Secrets of Medieval Times'.

'Wow' said Louis out loud, 'This is ancient.'

Boofy banged his tail on the floor and sat up very attentive.

He patted the big dog on the head.

'Let's read some of this 'A spell to protect you from evil spirits', 'A spell to protect you from the Forest Lord'. Oh, look Boof, 'A spell to receive wisdom', one to protect from Ancient Souls. 'A chant to increase fertility'. 'A spell to make your enemy weak'. Hey Boof, look at this one, 'A reduction spell to enter the magical world of nature' Let's read this one!'

The dog seemed excited.

'Hey, you like being read to big fella.'

Louis read...

'Firstly, to invoke your Guardian, you must send out messages of love deep within you. Invite your Guardian to appear before your being. You must communicate as with anyone else. The forces of light and truth shall enter your life. The power of the Universe will be yours. Invoke the vision of your Guardian and they shall appear. Expand your lungs, expand your mind, and take it beyond what you know. Fill your lungs with fresh clean air. Feel the calm and peace permeate your soul, call to your guardian to come forth.'

Louis read on to understand how to set out an altar, marking out elemental symbols for every direction. He read about magical tools and all the items required to conduct the spell of his desire. The room was electric, you could touch the excitement.

He looked at Boofy.

'We're going to have to get back to this tomorrow my friend. I have a lot of work to do in the morning.'

Louis couldn't understand why he felt so intent on doing something so incredibly stupid.

Slowly drifting off to sleep, a shadow stood beside the bed, the dog watched unperturbed. Moonlight fell upon the ancient book, the shadow of a huge bird flickered across the beam, then the night fell silent.

CHAPTER 13

Lucy Blackwell was a desperate picture dressed in stained black track pants with cigarette holes on the front from falling asleep after a big night on cheap wine. Her jumper was stretched and three sizes too big, dirty joggers with no laces. It was pension day. Since Louis had been removed, she was transferred to a one-bedroom flat closer to the CBD. She had to attend counselling sessions fortnightly. Louis had insisted she have a small allowance and some new furniture. Her life, however, was pretty much the same, living in a fantasy world of glamour magazines, movies and daytime soaps.

Sandra Thompson sat opposite Lucy, waiting for a response on how her life was going. Lucy had no interest in talking, she used up time talking about characters and events in her favourite dramas.

'Have you heard any news about your son Lucy?'

There was silence, Lucy's face went flushed, then spitting her words at Sandra.

'I don't want to talk about that thing, and don't mention my bitch of a mother. Look how they left me. I hate them all to hell and I never want to set eyes on that bastard I married, he ruined my life.'

Lucy's scars became red with rage, her face twisted, her scars becoming alive on her face like some parasite wriggling under her skin. Sandra was again feeling inadequate, unable to reach this pathetic creature that sat before her.

She started again with the uncontrolled raving about her famous modelling career. Lucy would pull out the much-handled photo of her modelling a skimpy bikini. The beautiful girl in the photo was no longer. A broken and mangled substitute took her place - like an evil body snatcher.

Her notes always sounded the same, no progress was ever recorded. Lucy left the office, made another appointment spitting her dribble on the floor as she left.

Lucy headed for the supermarket, doing a minimal shop of food, mainly processed food, snacks and a cask of wine.

She was used to people staring at her, the eye patch, the scarring, now looking at her ugliness and not her beauty. The allowance allowed Lucy to buy all the top shelf glamour magazines, she read them front to back. Lucy was fascinated by all the latest beauty therapies, the surgeries and where the rich and famous go to be reconstructed, she knew everything beautiful people go through to remain beautiful. The latest models' procedures, the clothing and makeup, Lucy lived in the magazines. Her daily soap operas became reality to her she saw herself in the leading roles.

Lucy put all her magazines on the counter, waiting to be served, she checked the credit on her phone, and she had plenty, not as though she had anyone to ring. Her good eye looked above the counter, all sorts of gambling games available. At that moment someone shoved Lucy aside wanting to be served, she was about to hurl abuse, but she was busy picking up money she dropped so she let it go. While she was gathering her coins off the floor, she noticed a $50 note under the counter. She quickly grabbed it without saying a word. The thought of extra booze and maybe some drugs made her feel good inside. For once something nice happened in her life. Handing over the money from her allowance to pay for her magazines, the Twenty Million Lotto Draw caught her eye. The girl behind the counter smiled feeling sorry for Lucy.

'You can get a few games for not very much.'

Lucy handed over the $50 dollars.

'How much can I get with that?'

The girl smiled.

'Plenty.'

With that she processed an automatic pick.

'Shall I register you?' asked the girl.

Lucy nodded. She didn't know what that meant, and her identification was recorded.

Arriving home thinking today had not turned out too bad for her, she had what she needed plus a little extra came along. The pain in Lucy's face began to get intense, it was time for her strong painkillers they always worked better, washed down with some wine. She giggled at herself as she settled into the lounge and drifted into another world.

'Hey Lucy goose', 'Lucy goose!'

Who was touching her, that stupid voice, again someone was touching her, shaking her?

'Come on.'

'Oh for Christ's sake Donk, how did you get in here?'

'The usual way.'

Lucy sat up, feeling very groggy and stiff.

'What time is it?'

'Nine o'clock in the morning.'

'What! I've slept all night?'

'I dunno, I just got here.'

Donk is the local drug dealer. He visits people on welfare in his area, on the day pensions come in, hoping they will buy drugs before anything else.

'No! No, No.'

Lucy was frantic, looking through her handbag.

'What's up Goosie?'

'I've run out of painkillers! I must have taken more.'

Lucy found her script at the bottom of her bag, and then she found her lotto ticket.

'Can I get a lift downtown Donk? I really need to fill this script!'

'You better clean yourself up. You stink like piss and vomit. You're not gettin' in my car smellin' like that.'

Lucy felt the pain of those words, she looked in the mirror, and she looked dreadful, like something designed for a horror show.

Once showered and clean clothed, Lucy had her script filled and got a short lecture from the pharmacist about medication abuse. The newsagent was two doors down. She noticed the nice girl was at the counter. Reaching into her handbag she found the ticket thinking 'I don't suppose it would hurt.' Handing over the ticket, it ran through the computer. The nice girl just stared at Lucy. The manager was alerted, and Lucy was taken to the back of the shop. She felt sick and nervous. What the hell had she done?

Why were they acting so weird? Her heart started to race. Lucy was guided to sit in a chair.

'Miss Blackwell, I'm happy to inform you, that you have just won eighteen million dollars.'

Lucy sat quietly. She did not speak. She did not move She did not react. Her mind was racing, swirling, a thousand thoughts fighting to be selected. A voice demanded to be heard, Mr Matheson was holding Lucy's hand. Then it happened, the thought she needed came with clarity, she was tuned in. Mr Matheson explained the process, helped her with the form, he was so excited. A switch went on in Lucy's brain, it was like travelling at incredible speed through a tunnel heading for a breathtaking light, and at the end, precise focus.

When he finished, Lucy asked if it could be kept a secret, she didn't want any publicity. Mr Matheson was confused at her reaction, but then he figured by looking at her, she had lots of problems. Shame really, a waste. Someone like her winning so much.

Donk was watching at the front door of the newsagent, Lucy thought quickly, he must not find out.

'Hey Goosey what's goin' on?'

'Oh, they thought I shoplifted.'

'How come you're not pissed off?'

'I couldn't be bothered.'

'So Goosey, you want some drugs, you got money?'

'Yeah why not,' said Lucy. Anything to get rid of him.

At last, she was alone, a long list was written, her mind was tuned in, no drugs, no alcohol, it was like a transfusion of life, she knew exactly what she wanted and how to get it. She began a list for her future, writing everything in sequence as it would be needed. Flight schedules, a list of the chosen surgeries and the outcome she expected. Surgeons to be contacted, book in dates. Luggage, Lucy would need clothes, makeup, hairstylist to be booked, airline tickets. The cheque would be deposited in ten working days. Credit cards would need to be organised. Lucy was calm, she was coming back. She thought about that day. If she had not dropped her money, the man that pushed her out of the way he would have won, the $50 note, it was meant to be and she hugged herself with glorious excitement. From this day on, the cigarettes went in the bin. No more daydreaming, she started to clean the flat. She needed healthy food. All the rags she was wearing as clothes went in the bins. She washed three sets of decent clothes. Ten days until freedom. She must be patient, calm and ready. She phoned the bank to organize a credit card. She demanded $50,000 credit.

Lucy paced the flat. The waiting was excruciating. She exercised, took walks, scrubbed herself, did her nails and applied makeup. Trying to concentrate on her TV shows was impossible, they no longer interested her. The magazines bored her. She was going to be one of them. Lucy decided she was leaving every part of her behind. She checked all her arrangements that were needed over and over. Lucy kept dreaming about the intriguing chalet where she would be booked in for her surgery, the privacy and the secretive location due to the exclusive clientele. Nothing could be confirmed until the money is deposited.

It was six in the morning. Today was the day and Lucy dressed ready to walk to the bank to check her account. The morning was fresh and clean. Not many people around at this hour. Lucy inserted her card, then nervously pressed account balance and there it was. She withdrew two thousand dollars, then walked to Macca's for breakfast. Now she had to wait until 9am for businesses to open. She could scream with the expectation, never had she felt so good in such a long time.

At 9am Lucy entered the bank for her credit card, followed by the exclusive boutique she selected. She chose seven complete outfits underwear, jewellery and shoes. The shop assistant treated her with a touch of contempt, she used her credit card and asked for the items to be delivered. Lucy attended her hairdresser appointment and makeup. Next was the Telstra shop for the latest and best iPad and phone. The travel agent had her tickets ready. Lucy then went to a department store, purchasing trendy casual wear, changing into a tailored pants suit, with high heeled shoes, matching bag and loads of expensive make up and toiletries.

Lucy then headed towards the taxi rank.

'Hey Goosey is that you? Wow you win the lottery or somthin', can only recognise you by the patch.'

Donk was like a parasite, sensing and sniffing money in the air. Lucy had to think quickly.

'Yeah, I got money for my birthday.'

Donk jumped in the cab.

'If you're cashed up Goosey, then you'll be wantin' you know what.'

Lucy had to think.

'I was thinking I might find a job, you know clean up my life.'

He followed Lucy into the flat and seeing how clean it was, Donk became suspicious. Just then a taxi pulled up outside her flat.

'Shit' thought Lucy. Quickly she gathered up the parcels she purchased, her other purchases waiting in the taxi. Donk followed her.

'You've got money ain't you? 'Where you goin?'

Donk tried to get in beside her.

'You lyin' bitch, you got a shit load of money, look at all this stuff.'

Her anger was rising. This scum was not going to ruin this day. With all the force she could harness she pushed him hard and he fell into the gutter. Slamming the taxi door, she yelled at the driver to take off, she threw Donk a couple of fifty-dollar notes and watched him scramble after them laughing out loud at the pathetic sight. She watched his angry face disappearing and laughed more.

'Take me to the airport and please do not talk to me, I have work to do.' This was it! Lucy turned around to take one last look at her old life, for the first time in a long time, she smiled.

CHAPTER 14

It was the beginning of a new day, mist hovered in the valley. An enormous orange sun peeped and shimmered over the mountains. Tentacles of light reached the highest trees in the ancient forest. The Bunya Mountains stood majestic, overlooking their kingdom. Freshwater springs trickled everlasting into the river and nourishing the fertile valley below.

Lush forest growth set their roots firmly in the rich soil, a tapestry of colours displayed native flora, beautiful, untouched for millions of years. The early chatter of birdlife starts to echo around the valley. Colours and sounds complement the glorious creation.

Forest animals stirred, to begin their day searching and hunting for food. All who lived in the forest drank from the pure water supplied from deep within the earth.

In a secret place in the valley, an old cliff face of an enormous mountain stood erect, deep crevices sculptured by time. Displays of rich colours red, black and shades of grey. If you looked and concentrated, a face of an ancient soul reached out to catch the human sensory by surprise.

At the base of the mountain, a lake rests in absolute serenity, feeding nature, and in return the rich earth feeds the glorious flora, joined by timid fauna that drink and feed daily. In the background gentle grasses, frothy ferns lush dense shrubs protected the ancient lake.

Tall old trees since the beginning of time, stand guard over the mysterious scene. A magical sensation seeps into the essence of anyone who takes the time to absorb such a vision engineered by Mother Nature.

On the far side of the mountains the Pacific Ocean can be heard rushing and rolling endlessly. Hugging Bay juts out of the coastline, two long curving land formations, like arms wrapping around to protect its precious creation.

High on the mountain at the very top of a huge Bunya tree sits a lone figure, wise alert eyes scan his domain.

It was Mooki, a wedge tail eagle, distinguished by a white streak running from the top of his beak over his head all the way down his majestic body. Mooki was feeling uneasy today something unwelcome drifted on the morning wind. Today the bushland and forest creatures are gathering at the sacred lake. Disturbing feelings were tormenting all who lived in the mountains.

Bookatee landed on the same branch as Mooki.

'Well, my trusted old friend what news do you have today from your night journeys?'

Bookatee, an old Tawny Frogmouth, looked at Mooki then back to the valley.

'As usual many arguments with those parrots over domains, and who is supposed to be feeding where. I have disturbing news from the magpies and no doubt you will hear all at the lake.'

'Very well my old friend, we best make a start and join the others.'

It was a majestic sight. Mooki soaring down the mountainside, floating on the thermals, directing his wings to his destiny.

Birds of all colours, shapes and sizes rested on the soft grasses around the lake. Those more nervous, perched in the trees, loud chatters, screeching and squawking rang in the valley.

The bushland marsupials sent representatives. Other forest animals arrived but remained secreted in the protection of the forest floor.

Reptiles sniggered and chuckled amongst themselves, unable to stop the thoughts of what a bountiful smorgasbord of tasty morsels surrounded them.

Magpies positioned themselves in front row, full of information and busting at the beaks to tell Mooki.

'Here he comes!' screamed a cockatoo gathered with his mates in a tall eucalyptus.

All eyes followed the direction of his wings. A regal sight, perfect aviation skills prepared for a landing on a ledge protruding out of a cliff face. Bookatee preferred to travel via the trees and remain undercover, touching down beside Mooki.

Mooki surveyed the crowd.

'Welcome to you all, and I hope all is well in your territories.'

A big buff magpie jumping up and down, excitement urging him on.

'Hurry up open the meeting, I've got something to tell you. It's very important.'

'Alright Mr Magatelli please begin' said Mooki, giving Bookatee a sideways glance.

'Well, as you know we magpies mix very closely in the human world. I have families living and working in towns and cities and anywhere where humans live. Some patrol footpaths and school grounds. Some of us hide in parks watching and listening. We hang around house yards.'

The magpies' wings were doing overtime, jumping from one foot to another. Chests puffed out, many onlookers stifling outbursts of laughter.

'You can laugh, my brave families are infiltrating shopping centres.'

'More like scavenging because you're too lazy to hunt.'

This outburst coming from a cockatoo named Boss. Pent up laughter exploded in the crowd.

'You ought to talk big bag of screeching feathers!'

'That's enough.'

Mooki pointed his powerful wing over the crowd.

'Continue Magpie.'

'I have information from my town family living on the other side of the valley, and it could disrupt our lives, and put us in danger.'

'Go on' said Mook.

'My family hang out in the lovely gardens at what they call 'Council Chambers'. They heard a gathering of humans through a window, discussing this very place.'

The big magpie watched the crowd, enjoying the anticipation he was creating.

'They talked about plans and bulldozing, and how it will build 'tourism'.'

'What's tourism?' screeched a galah from the top of a treetop.

Mooki waited for the crowd to settle.

'It means many humans will be coming here and taking over and we will be forced to move out.'

Individuals looked at each other. Fear could be felt, and nervous chatter accelerated. A large grey kangaroo's voice boomed over concerned voices.

'What's going to happen?! What do we do Mooki? This is our place. It feeds and waters us all. Even when the seasons are dry, this place keeps us alive.'

Mooki and Bookatee finished a brief discussion. Mooki stretched his wings indicating calm and quiet. The crowd turned their focus on Mooki, silence fell they waited for his words.

'I have been informed by Bookatee that a young human is coming. He is being directed to us.'

'A human!' roared the great grey kangaroo. 'They will kill us all, that's what they do.'

The crowd hushed and all eyes turned towards the cliff face, especially the cave entrance. A great sadness overcame the inhabitants of this perfect place. Many times their homes, water and food sources have been taken and destroyed. How could a young human possibly prevent this?

CHAPTER 15

'Is there something I can help you with?' said Bridget, watching Louis's bum disappearing into the cupboard under the kitchen sink.

'Just lookin' thanks Mum.'

Bridget loved being called 'Mum'.

'I'll see you and your bum later.'

'Yep okay.'

Louis reversed out of the cupboard holding a small bottle of lavender oil.

'Well, that's item number one.'

Louis had a list of everything he needed to cast his spell.

He searched the linen cupboard, the garden shed, and the garden. In Bridget's room he found tarot cards. He found the candle he needed, that was easy the house was full of them. A small stone, soil from the forest, black cloth, a white feather, and a vial of rainwater. Louis found the tools for his altar – a wine goblet, old coins, an old knife, and then he made a wand.

He didn't know what anoint meant, but all was revealed on the internet. He sat back on his bed looking at his gatherings.

'What the hell am I doing this for?'

He could not understand why he felt compelled to do such a stupid thing.

'Hey Bro! What's up?'

Charlie stood at the glass verandah door, skateboard in hand.

'Ready to hit the beach? Let's make the most of school parole.'

'Sounds good to me.'

'Hey Louis, I don't suppose you found a stray bag of Mum's rubbish? It's got some old book in it. Old girl is having a rat attack about losing it and she's all devo about it. It's old and worth money!'

'Follow me,' said Louis 'I've got what you want.'

'Oh, thank god for that' sighed Charlie.

'So, what do you think of spells and stuff?'

'I dunno, it would be totally sick if it worked.' Charlie laughed out loud, he was a constant source of his own amusement.

'I've been reading some of the spells, I've decided I'm gonna do one.' Louis watched Charlie's face wondering what he really thought.

'Cool' said Charlie unperturbed.

'Can I write one out before you take it back?'

'Yeah, I guess so. I'll ring Mum and tell her I've found it. So, dude, when are you turning into Harry Potter?' giving Louis a playful flick on his head.

'Tonight, you wanna sleep over and see the magic unfold?' Louis doing his magician's actions.

'Okay,' said Charlie. 'I'll go and pack my Nimbus 2000 broom.'

'So where is the big dumb mutt?'

'Good question, I haven't seen him for a while.'

Just then Boofy appeared.

'Jeez doesn't he look different, very good looking.'

The big dog nuzzled Charlie's hand demanding a head pat.

Louis, Charlie and Boofy caught the bus to Hugging Bay. The bus driver was related to Charlie, one of his many cousins. Boofy was passed off as a companion dog. It was only a short trip.

The day was magnificent, the best that nature could offer. Warm sunshine with cool breeze.

'You know Louis, you can get to this really mad inland lake from your backyard.'

'Really?'

'Yeah, I found it some time ago. I just followed this track.

'Oh yeah Mum mentioned that. You can hear the ocean at times, it's kinda tucked away at the bottom of the mountain range. One big mother in particular.'

'Magic' I would call it' Charlie shoving Louis in the back giggling.

Louis wrapped Charlie's head in a towel.

The boys skated towards the beach and spent hours frolicking in the Pacific Ocean. Boofy was having the time of his life, loving the water and waves.

All three laid side by side on the warm sand.

'Hey Charlie.'

'Yep'

'What do you think about spirits and stuff?'

'Louis in case you hadn't noticed I'm aboriginal.'

'Oh yeah! The dreamtime.'

'Well,' said Charlie, 'I kinda believe, but I've never seen anything spiritual, I reckon it would be mad.'

'I reckon too.'

'I'm starving,' said Louis. 'I'm thinking fish and chips.'

The boys woofed down their feed, Boofy had his biscuits and water.

Three very tired bodies returned home, all jobs done and dinner in front of the TV with Bridget. Louis then confirmed it was okay Charlie could stay the night.

'Is it okay if we go to my room and play games?'

'Of course it is. Make sure you get to bed at a reasonable hour.'

Bridget smiled at both boys, said goodnight, followed by the big dog.

'So?' said Charlie. 'You gonna do this spell thing?'

'Yep, ready to go. I've gathered it all up.'

Louis turned on his lamp. Boofy sat on his bed as if he knew what was happening. Charlie sat in the lounge chair.

A round table sat in the middle of the room. Louis set out his altar and read aloud all the instructions to harness all the power of the elements for magic.

The smell of the anointed tarot cards swirled around the room, creating a sweet aroma. The candles were anointed and lit, and the cards placed accordingly. The room was silent and warm. Louis put on a long black coat that came to his ankles.

He then followed the words to invoke the Guardian and achieve a close connection with the forces of the universe. The atmosphere in the room was intense, Charlie began feeling restless and unsure, the big dog sat silent and alert.

Louis kept repeating the words. On the sixth repeat, the candles went out, the curtains moved, and a small beam of moonlight fell across the room.

For a brief moment a very tall silhouette shrouded in a cape appeared and then vanished. Louis spoke out loud his wishes of magic, and a desire to become small and experience the enchantment of nature. He followed the inviting words step by step.

All items were placed in order, the feather, the soil, the stone and the water. The lavender oil burner was lit, the tarot cards placed as directed. A picture of a body of water sat in the middle of the altar. Louis repeated the chant one more time.

When the spell was completed, everything was to be left undisturbed and repeated for two more nights. At the completion, a walk was to be taken deep into a forest and the water, the soil, feather and stone to be buried in moist soil. This to be done at the stroke of midnight.

'That was kinda weird', Charlie's eyes like saucers.

'I think there was something in the room with us.'

'I know, I felt it too.'

Louis felt very tense, slowly getting into bed excited, but tired.

Charlie jumped into his bed, both silent for a time.

'You know we have to complete this!'

'Yeah, I know. Just not looking forward to that midnight thing.' Charlie pulled the blankets up to his neck, 'It's a bit freaky dude.'

'I was thinking, why don't you take me to that place you found?'

'That's an excellent idea bro', we'll make a day of it, food, drink and swimming.'
'Sounds good.'

Settling down for the night, Louis reached over and turned off the light. An hour later nothing but snores could be heard. The big dog went to the window and sat watching the night sky.

The tawny frog mouth arrived quietly and perched in a Bunya pine beyond the backyard. A wedge tail joined him, settling his feathers. The birds watched the curious event unfolding in the night sky. Stars moved across the sky forming patterns in the shape of multiple rainbows. It looked like a celebration of the universe, that only the spectators knew about.

CHAPTER 16

Bridget rushed through the door of Louis's bedroom. She was greeted with excitement by Boofy. 'Louis! Charlie! Wake up and come outside quick. Come on!'

The boys yawning and staggering behind Bridget, stood dead still following Bridget's gaze.

'I can't believe my eyes Louis, am I dreaming, quick come outside.'

The entire yard looked like it hadn't been tended to for a long while, untouched by human intrusion.

'It's magnificent.' Bridget started to laugh.

Louis and Charlie looked at each other and burst out laughing. Everything had grown madly, vines and flowers, huge leaves, healthy and robust, and the colours are magnificent.

Boofy jumped up and licked Bridget's face. A great big sloppy one from the bottom of her face to the top. The boys laughed even harder.

Sitting on the verandah having baked beans on toast, followed by ginger marmalade on crumpets, the family watched Bridget's garden in wonder.

'And what are you boys going to do today?' Bridget felt like she was the luckiest person alive on this day.

'Well, we thought we might take a bushwalk and follow the path down the back.'

'That sounds like a great day out.'

'Food. What about food? We must have food!'

Louis pushed Charlie, laughing together. Bridget began piling all the food in front of Charlie.

Peanut butter sandwiches for human and dog consumption, homemade raisin cookies, bananas, mandarins and frozen bottles of water.

With backpacks filled, single file the trio made their way to the secret lake.

The day was warm, lenticular clouds like spaceships hovered in the sky, a mysterious cloud formation for such a calm day.

'How far is it?'

Louis noticed the bushland getting thicker. A loud splash could be heard ahead.

'There's your answer', Charlie laughed and raced ahead.

They broke through the clearing. Louis stopped in his tracks, his face reflecting amazement. Charlie joined Boofy splashing and frolicking in the clear, clean water. It was the most beautiful natural sight he had ever seen.

Louis observed every aspect of the lake and mountain. It felt strange, the oddly shaped cloud seemed to have followed him. The sun was blocked out casting eerie shadows across the lake.

'This is amazing' said Louis to no-one in particular. His trance was broken by Boofy barking and snapping at the water.

Louis put the backpack in the cool under growth, then joined the others in the water. He floated on his back, the water seemed to massage his body, he was almost drifting off to sleep. The silence and slumber came to a noisy end, Charlie and Boofy splashed and dunked Louis under the water. The trio skylarked and swam for an hour.

'I'm starving', announced Charlie.

The food disappeared quick, the big dog enjoyed sandwiches and dog biscuits.

The moment of complete tiredness came when bellies are full. They all moved to the dappled shade.

'I'm stuffed,' said Louis making himself comfortable.

Tall trees stood guard over the peaceful place. Boofy started snoring, both boys laughed and mimicked the big fella.

'Louis.'

'Yep?'

'Can I ask you something?'

'About what?'

'Where you came from and what happened to you?'

Louis said nothing and watched the leaves above flickering on the breeze.

'Sorry Bro. It doesn't matter.'

'No, it's okay, but it's a very long story. I'm just thinking where to begin.'

Louis talked for about half an hour, and it felt good to get it out.

'So, where's your mother now?'

'Well, that's the weird part. According to Karen Landy the social worker, my mother has just left all the items in her flat and vanished. Karen said her pension had been cancelled, she's ow on the Missing Persons List. Strange thing is, apparently, she had her hair done, then purchased clothes and was sighted leaving in a taxi. Karen Landy said they have checked for weeks and found nothing.'

'Aliens that's it.'

Louis looked at Charlie and burst into laughter.

'Can I ask you something?'

'Yeah, let's have it.'

'Does it piss you off at school when some of the kids say stuff about being black?'

'Yeah. It makes me feel like shit sometimes, but the old girl has drummed it into my head that I'm not to react.'

'I can tell you I feel like smashing them at times.'

'You realise Louis, you're gonna cop a lot of shit for hangin' with me.'

'Already have, but listen you skinny little black fella, we're mates and that's that. No matter what!'

Both boys went silent for a while, deep in their own thoughts, listening to the world around them.

'How do you feel about your real mum?'

'I'm not sure. She was cruel to me most of the time. I used to try so hard hoping she would at least like me a little.'

Louis kept going, memories started to surface, falling out of his mind onto his tongue with ease.

'She hated my Gran because I loved Gran so much and we were so much alike.'

Charlie rolled over and leaned on his elbow, looking at his friend's face, the pain in his eyes was so visible.

'She was a famous model, had a fantastic career – her words. She was pregnant with a baby. Apparently, she and her photographer were driving to location and he noticed she had put on weight. At that moment she realised the pregnancy, she went off her head, he freaked out and lost control of the convertible and it burst into flames. He died and she suffered heavy facial scarring. Well, that's the story I have heard over and over again.'

'So,' said Charlie 'when did you come along?'

'According to Gran my mother and father lived with my Gran after the accident, suppose they got together, but then she kicked him out. Then my Gran died, so Mum took me and moved away. Mum was a drunk and derelict, everything just got worse. Mum bashed me, I ended up in hospital. The Department of Community Services sent me to Bridget for foster care. That's kinda brief,' said Louis.

Silence fell again.

'Do you think I'm psycho? You know, doing that spell thing.'

'Yep, you're as mad as my mother.'

Both boys started to giggle.

Louis rolled up the towel and made a pillow his eyes moved around the cliff face, studying the colours and layers. High up on the cliff there was a ledge leading out from what looked like an entrance. With eyes half closed and the feeling of sleep taking over his body, blissful calm. Then it appeared. Louis kept watching through squinting eyes, he rubbed them for clarity. It was a tall human like being, long black hair trailed down to his waist. It was dressed in a long green gown, standing perfectly still like a statue. It was holding what looked like a crystal ball. Louis couldn't quite make it out.

'Charlie' whispering for his attention.

'Charlie!'

'What?! What Louis?'

'Don't move anything but your eyes, look towards the cliff face right up the top.'

Charlie blinked several times.

'I see it. What the hell is that?'

'Don't move Charlie.'

'I can't bloody move!'

The vision was mesmerising.

'It's gone!'

And it was. Vanished from their gaze.

'It just disappeared' said Charlie, sitting bolt upright, panic rising. 'Man, my heart's thumping like mad.'

Louis was about to say something, he sniffed the air, the smell of tea rose, it was comforting and a signal that all was okay.

'Nan.'

'What the hell was that?'

'I don't know Charlie but it's okay.'

'I'm outta here brother. You comin?'

Boofy was at the water's edge, looking towards the cliff, a huge wedge tail circled above.

'That's the third time I've seen that eagle' said Louis, getting ready to head home.

'So? You really think there's only one wedge tail eagle remaining in Australia?'

'Very funny' said Louis, flicking Charlie around the legs with a towel.

Walking home, Louis was deep in thought, and then it came to him, he stopped dead still, Charlie ran into the back of him.

'What are you doin?'

'That figure on the cliff.'

'Yeah, what about it?'

'I saw it last night doing that spell.'

'Holy shit. You mean that stuff could work?'

'I dunno, but that's what I saw, this is creepy.'

Louis looked at Charlie raised his shoulders and walked on.

That night, Louis fed the animals in silence. Rodney the raven jumped around kicking a tennis ball and generally tormenting Louis. The whole yard remained in unusual bloom and the speedy growth continued. Louis felt strange. It felt like he was being watched and he kept seeing a shadow in his peripheral vision. Something in his very being was driving Louis on and he didn't know why.

Bridget cooked a very tasty spaghetti bolognaise using all fresh herbs to enhance the flavours. Plump juicy tomatoes with home grown - flavours to wake the tastebuds.

Charlie chatted openly to Bridget.

'You alright Louis?' asked Bridget looking at her child with concern.

'Yep, I'm good.'

Boofy let out a big pig grunt laying on his blanket, full of tucker and sound asleep and dreaming. Laughter and mimicking of the big dog changed the atmosphere immediately.

The boys washed up to the sounds of their favourite music. The house was alive with fun and laughter. At nine o'clock they said goodnight to Bridget, went into the bedroom and spent a noisy hour playing the PlayStation.

At ten o'clock Louis became very focussed. He carried out his spell to perfection. This time he saw clearly the Guardian, tall, elegant in a shimmering green gown, long black hair, and the most incredible purple eyes. Intense, wide and ancient.

At the hour of eleven the two boys left through the doors leading onto the verandah, even Boofy somehow tiptoed quietly. Backpack in place and torches ready, the boys disappeared into the dark, following the track they had walked during the day.

'God this is scary. It's almost as black as me.'

Louis giggled at this and kept moving on.

'Oh no.'

'What's wrong now Charlie?'

'My torch has died I can't see a bloody thing.'

They both suddenly stopped and looked up at the movement in the sky. Stars were gathering in the night sky, they were gathering in a line and then dropped at an incredible speed hanging like lanterns to light the way. Louis looked at Charlie.

'Just walk don't ask questions.'

The big dog was excited and ran ahead, he stood waiting.

'What's up big fella?'

'I think this is where we are meant to bury the stuff,' pointed Charlie.

Louis dug a small hole under a bush fern, the soil was soft and moist.

The stars remained in place until the boys were safely home. Sitting in their room drinking cold juice, trying to comprehend what happened on this night. Excitement and nerves brought on fits of laughter until they were exhausted.

A noise was heard on the verandah. Sitting on the rails looking through the glass sat a very odd pair of fluffed up birds. A frogmouth and towering beside him a huge wedge tail eagle.

All eyes locked on each other.

'You know Charlie,' spoke Louis in a very calm voice, 'I swear they're talking to each other.'

'Maybe,' said Charlie 'these peeping toms want a game on the PlayStation, maybe we could challenge them.'

The situation remained like this for another thirty seconds. The birds looked at each other and then vanished.

'Louis! They didn't fly, they just disappeared. This shit is getting weird.'

Charlie got into his bed and covered his head with his blankets.

Louis sat staring out the window.

'Charlie.'

'What?'

'You're aboriginal. What about the Dreamtime?'

'Exactly the word 'Dream', this stuff is real. You have your own personal wedge tail.'

Louis giggled in bed.

'Not funny' came a muffled voice from under the blankets.

Louis laid back processing the day and night events.

'I wonder what tomorrow will bring?'

'Oh, we're probably going to end up experiments.'

Yawning deeply, both overcome by sleep, the room fell silent. The big dog sat looking through the window, watching the night sky, his big tail thumping on the floor.

A celebration was taking place in the sky, stars shooting and falling in all directions. A silhouette of the two birds crossed the beam of a fluorescent white moon. Bridget's garden was growing again.

CHAPTER 17

Isobel arrived with Saturday morning papers, hot quiche and pancakes for the ritual of breakfast together.

The big table on the back patio was laid out in waiting. A mixture of homemade jams, a pot of fresh thick cream, freshly brewed coffee and as always Bridget's assorted teas.

'My God Bridget. What's happened to your yard? It's magnificent, the perfume is delicious.'

'I have no idea, it happened over the last week.'

'Well,' said Isobel, 'there's something mysterious going on here. Almost magical.'

The women smiled at each other.

'I'm going to have to look into this' said Isobel.

'You just do that', laughed Bridget winking at her friend.

Everyone at the table was engrossed in their particular interest from the papers.

'No this can't be right!'

All heads snapped up looking at Bridget.

'Look! Look at this.'

Everyone gathered. The heading on the third page read 'Tourist development a win for locals.' Isobel read on. There was a photograph of Lavender Lane and the wilderness beyond Bridget's house. Bridget was enraged and bewildered, her face a mixture of emotions.

'I haven't been approached about this.' Bridget sat in shock.

The two boys read on, Isobel and Simone trying to comfort Bridget.

As the boys read on, it went on to say that a naturally forming lake would be the centrepiece of the development. The article described how up to thirty private villas would be built plus restaurants with bars, boutiques, health spas and tennis courts. Entertainment galore. This would provide that extra touch for people wanting a private hideaway. The lake itself was said to have healing and rejuvenating powers. It went on to describe Louis and Charlie's secret and special place.

'What's the name of the bloody MP behind this?'

'It says Jason Blackwell.'

Louis dropped his cup of tea. It clattered loudly and attracted the attention of all.

'You alright Louis?' asked Charlie. 'You went kinda funny lookin'.'

'Oh um, yeah, just upset for Mum, you know it's a strange coincidence about the lake and all the weird stuff happening.

'Tell you what, let's go to the lake tomorrow, we might see that mysterious figure again!'

'Excellent idea Charlie. Now let's go skating.'

Louis was deep in thought. The Blackwell name, the lake, his spell, everything was connected. He was meant to be here, but why? Was he supposed to do something?

About six boys were at the skate park, all friends with each other. The sounds of rolling and crashing skateboards echoed in the atmosphere. Those who tumbled on the concrete, could be seen pretending they weren't hurt. Challenging each other to perform greater skills.

Jokes and laughter went back and forth. Good friends having fun, until the arrival of four older boys.

'Why don't you little jerks clear out this is our park.'

Louis, Charlie and their mates all stood together in defiance.

'Who says it's yours?' blurted out a brave Charlie.

'This park is for everyone!' announced Louis, bolstered by the safety in numbers theory.

'Don't you little piss ants know who I am?'

'Yeah we know' said Tim, a rather hefty kid standing behind Charlie.

'So, who is he?' asked Louis in a confident voice.

'I'm Tristan Blackwell and my old man has got a lot of pull.'

'Oh, what a wanker,' said Charlie, unaware of the danger he was in.

'You smartarse little black prick, and I suppose that's your little white boy and you're hangin' out with black fellas and losers! You all belong in a zoo. Now piss off, I've got business to attend to before we smash your faces into your skateboards.'

Charlie was about to lurch forward and take his revenge, Louis grabbed the back of his t-shirt.

'Come on let's go and have a feed.'

Laughter could be heard as the boys walked away.

'That bloody Tristan Blackwell, he's gonna cop it one day.'

Charlie was angry and mumbling his protests and throwing stones at the ground.

It was just one of those days that turns in on you and going to bed and sleep was the best option for all at number 8 Lavender Avenue. That night as all slept, a tall spiritual being, with radiant green eyes cast his vision over the house. Louis's spell was beginning to make itself known. Not only was the magic starting to take effect, but other powerful forces had also joined in, because Mother Nature was in trouble.

The next morning Louis woke slowly, feeling a weight leaning up against him and hot breath on his face, Louis put his arms around the big dog. Together they laid quietly, Louis's mind racing from one event to another.

Charlie slowly woke rolling over to face Louis.

'Oh, that's so romantic, shall I leave?'

'Very funny.'

Louis landed a pillow square in Charlie's face.

Bridget was sitting in her big cane chair on the verandah, just looking at her garden, dried tear tracks staining her face. Louis's heart ached for her. She's such a good person, he put his arms around her.

'Everything will be okay Mum.'

Bridget responded by hugging Louis. Together they gave each other strength, the smell of tea rose drifted in the air.

'I feel like I have let you down. Everything was going so well and on track.'

'It's not your fault Mum. No one is going to take your home.'

'Our home Louis.'

Bridget didn't want Louis to witness her internal turmoil.

'So, what are you boys going to do today?'

'We're going back to the lake.'

'Oh, I'd love to come with you, but I've had a call from the Aged Care Centre to start at 11am. God Louis, I don't want to grow old. No one wants you, and it's harder to find people with a compassionate attitude that manage these places.'

'I'll look after you,' said Louis. 'I remember my Nan, she always said she would put herself down when her turn came.'

'You miss your Nan don't you?'

'Yeah. You two would have got along real good.'

'Why is that?'

'Well, you both love the same things. Nan was good to be around, she always made things interesting.'

'Mum hated her you know. They were like strangers, nothing in common.'

'Do you think about your Mum Louis?'

'Not much to think about, anyway no one knows where she is. You know it's really weird.'

'What's weird?'

'That man running for parliament Jason Blackwell and his son Tristan.'

'What's the weird bit?'

'Don't you remember that was my surname before I took yours?'

'Good Lord Louis, I had forgotten. You have become so much my child. I for one am glad Karen Landy found you. I suppose you and Charlie had better get going.'

Bridget was on the verge of tears. Everyone went their way for the day, connections between all becoming stronger.

The backpacks full of food again, and loaded with towels, water and sunscreen, they set off for the lake.

'What do you think is gonna happen with your house?'

'I don't know, I just wish this wasn't happening. It's just so weird that snothead Tristan is related to that other Blackwell wanting our lake.'

'What do you mean dude? I'm not following.'

'My name used to be Blackwell.'

'Holy shit! You're right, this is weird. Could you be related?'

'I bloody well hope not.'

Charlie put his arm around his mate's shoulder.

'Come on let's go and enjoy our day. Boofy certainly is.'

Worn out from swimming and eating, the boys rested and Boofy snored, stretched out in the shade.

'You know Charlie, the water in the lake makes you feel relaxed and calm inside.'

Louis watched the cliff face fascinated by its structure, on either side of the façade, a significant ledge with two trees stood like sentinels guarding something special. Sleep was starting to overcome him like a warm blanket. He took one last look with a deep sigh. He sat up rubbing his eyes and looked again. Every leaf on each tree was an eye and all looking his way.

Dead silence came over the lake, nothing stirred.

'Charlie, are you awake?'

'I am now.'

'Look at the cliff.'

Charlie was speechless, they sat mouths open, not moving.

The lake water began to swirl in the centre, now all eyes on the lake. The big dog looked on, his tail banging in the sand. The swirling intensified creating waves, something was coming out of the water. It was huge.

'Holy shit! It's a whale.'

It was mauve. The entire body began to emerge. It was a magnificent sight.

'He's got purple eyes and looking directly at us.'

A great noise was in the air getting closer with every second. Charlie touched Louis on the arm without taking his eyes off the whale.

'What's that noise? Should we run?'

'No, it's okay Charlie, trust me.'

'Oh right, I feel so much better! I'm going to die.'

Something was coming. There was a noise in the distance. A whooshing noise came from the lake. The two boys and the dog were showered with purple water as the whale released its blowhole.

The noise in the distance was now with them, birds of all variety lead by a majestic wedge tail eagle circled the lake. When the eagle settled on the edge of the ledge of the huge mountain, all others found a resting place. Slowly the eagle transformed to an amazing being. It was the same Louis had previously had a glimpse of. A tall pale body, long black hair, they couldn't see him properly. It was clouded in mist. A beautiful tranquil voice spoke.

'Welcome Louis. Welcome Esouli.'

'Who's Esouli?'

Then a shadow fell across them. The boys turned and looking upwards, at what used to be Boofy. There stood an impressive, frightening figure. Standing seven feet tall, the face the same with long black ears, twitching and moving. The creature bore a massive, muscled chest, strong huge forearms and legs. His feet long, with seven toes and webbed. Resting wings laid on his back. Strong claw like hands, small wings on his heels.

'Oh my God Boofy. What the hell?!'

'It's okay. Don't be frightened.'

'Dude this is totally sick.'

'For once Charlie I agree.'

Both sat looking up at the creature in awe.

'Louis.'

The voice called from the mountain.

'I am Arume, I am the Guardian for planet Earth and all her creatures, along with others of my kind and Esouli's. It's been a long journey for you to finally arrive at your destination. Your pure spirit and your strength will be your key to freedom, enabling you to be who you are meant to be. We welcome you and in a matter of time you will join us and the very reason for your being will be imparted to you. You may now go safely on your way, and remember, whatever happens there is a reason.'

In a matter of seconds in an illuminating light, all went back to normal. Louis turned to his friend and the dog, which had only moments ago been introduced as Esouli.

'Let's go home.'

'One question, what's 'imparted' mean?'

'I think it means tell me stuff.'

'Oh cool! It's the spell, isn't it? You were meant to find that book. What's going to happen Louis? Where are you going?'

Charlie's voice was desperate. He sounded frightened.

'What will I do? What will I tell people?'

Louis turned around and looked at Charlie, he put his hands on his shoulders.

'Charlie, this is something that needs to happen. You're my best friend and I'm never going to lose that. Everything will work out.'

After arriving home, Louis set about to do his routine jobs, many thoughts going in and out. Charlie helped collect the eggs, his mind also alive and confused.

'Come on you chooks. Hand over those bum nuts. I don't want any trouble or heads will roll.'

'God, you crack me up Charlie.'

Louis's voice rang out with a strange strangling sound. Charlie dropped the eggs and ran. He stopped in his tracks.

'Holy shit! It's happened!'

Louis stood amongst his clothes.

'What are we gonna do?'

Charlie was becoming hysterical. Louis grabbed his shirt sleeve and wrapped it around himself signalling for Charlie to come closer.

'Run home and get me Ken's clothes.'

'Ken who?'

'You know, Ken and Barbie.'

'Oh dude that's so weird. Ken's clothes? Do you want me to bring Barbie back so she can look at her new dude?'

Both boys cracked up laughing excitement, fear and confusion fuelling their emotions. Charlie bolted out the back gate adrenalin feeding his heightened senses.

Louis dragged his clothes under a flowering May Bush and sat quietly trying to take in what had just happened. Mixed feelings flooded his brain, ecstatic happiness, panic and laughter.

A soft voice calmed Louis' sense. Boofy laid down beside the bush, he looked enormous.

'Did you speak Boofy?'

'Yes Louis. Stay calm, you are safe.'

Louis moved and snuggled up to the big dog's chest. Louis could hear the loud thumping of Boofy's heartbeat, strangely the rhythm served to slow Louis's own. They waited in silence. Louis found his voice, tiny but audible.

'What's going to happen now?'

'Be patient Louis, as soon as Charlie returns you will be taken to the secret cave, from then on your purpose will be explained. You are about to experience the ancient world and secrets of different dimensions that are unknown by the planet Earth.

'Oh God Boofy, this is hard to take in.'

'Be calm Louis, I'll be with you.'

'Louis. Where are you?!'

Charlie's feet looked like boats. Boofy emerged from the May bush. Louis followed wrapped in his massive t-shirt. Charlie handed the clothes over.

'I didn't bring 'Ken on Safari' clothes that would be just weird.'

Louis emerged wearing Ken's shorts, t-shirt and thongs.

'So, what happens now?'

Boofy barked to the sky. Within seconds Rodney the big black raven landed like a jet fighter.

'Listen carefully Louis,' said a calm, majestic voice.

'You talk as well?'

'I do and now we must hurry. Climb on.'

'Wait,' said Charlie in a panic.

'Where are you guys going? What am I gonna tell his mum? What about school and stuff? This is crazy.'

'Listen carefully,' said Boofy to a very distraught Charlie, 'Louis has been chosen and it all began the day he was born, his journey to this place was not a coincidence.'

'Can I come too? I want to be with Louis.'

'You want to be with Louis?' said Boofy in a confused manner.

'Well, I know I'm not chosen, but can't I be the Chosen One's sidekick?'

'Mmm this is not what I expected, we have to go now Charlie, but if it is deemed possible with Arume, you will join us in time. Now we must go.'

The wings of the shiny blue-black bird began their flight mode, Louis tightened his legs into the raven's sides, gathered a handful of feathers and closed his eyes. He had never felt anything so soft. He lifted his head, and the air was cool on his face. Looking down, eyes fully open, familiar sites began zooming past. Louis smiled; he had never felt so free. Ahead, he could see the lake, but he couldn't see the entrance to the cave.

'I don't see an entrance, Rodney.'

'Keep watching.'

Louis studied the cliff face. It began with a black circle in the centre then swirled around and around becoming bigger with the swirls. Beams of all colours in the world lit up the sky, so bright, Louis had to squint to watch the spectacle before him.

Rodney flew into the centre of the beams. Then they were gone. The cliff face stood as a sandstone rock face undisturbed in its natural state.

CHAPTER 18

Charlie sat on the garden seat in Isobel's garden, head hung and feeling totally lost.

'Do you really want to join Louis?'

Boofy sat facing the boy.

'He's my best friend. Shit, I sound like such a loser.'

'Well then Charlie you need to be prepared, strange events are upon us.'

'Do you mean I better carry around some Ken clothes?'

'Firstly Charlie', spoke the big dog, 'you must explain to Bridget and Isobel what has happened and what's going to happen.'

'But I don't know what's going to happen.'

'Listen to me Charlie.'

Boofy's gentle tone and caressing voice told Charlie that the world was in trouble. Something important had gone missing and shocking events were going to happen unless this object was found.

'Louis has come to us to try and find this, it has to be a human, but a special human.'

'How do I say this,' Charlie's voice unsettled 'where will you be?'

'I'll be with you. My help is yours. Remember Charlie, Bridget and Isobel are spiritual beings of the Earth.'

'Yeah, suppose you're right.'

'So, what is it about Louis that's so special?'

That night, as organised, the small family sat together. Charlie's job was to try and explain everything that had happened.

'Charlie, what on earth is wrong with you? Are you not feeling well?'

Isobel checked his forehead.

'Where's Louis?' said Bridget looking at the backyard trying to sight him.

'Um, just sit down please. Louis is um, a bit busy at the moment.'

Charlie knew he was sounding crazy his voice was excitable and his thoughts being all over the place. The family just sat looking at Charlie.

'Perhaps I could explain what Charlie is trying to say with more clarity.'

'Oh, and the dog talks, I forgot to say that in the beginning.'

The two women looked at each other, unable to make a sound come out of their mouths.

The big dog began slowly, starting with Louis's birth to present day, explaining all the events experienced up until Louis leaving on the back of Rodney.

Charlie looked at both women. He noticed an exchanged glance between the two of them. He was starting to feel uncomfortable and scared. Isobel's voice was quiet, however her face expressed awe.

'I knew that book was powerful, I could feel it whenever I picked it up. I could feel a surge of energy and it was intense. This is a miracle in the making.'

'Does that mean you believe me? I mean us?'

'Of course!'

'What's going to happen to Louis? How am I going to explain his disappearance? Will I see him again? I love that boy with all my heart.' Bridget's eyes looked pleadingly at the big dog.

'Please don't be upset Bridget,' spoke the big dog calmly. 'Louis is safe, and he will return safe. Let me show you something that will reassure you and finally explain what is going to happen.'

Isobel put her arm around Bridget.

'Just trust this Bridget it's going to work out, all will be well.'

'It's lucky Simone is staying at her friend's house,' said Charlie. 'This would send her batty.'

'Does she have to know?' said Bridget.

'I'll tell her when I feel it's right, she will understand, she is a wise old soul.'

Charlie closed the blinds.

'What are you going to witness, is totally mad.'

Boofy sat before his audience in quietness.

'Hang on,' said Bridget, eyes popping, an expression of realisation, 'the lake, the land behind us, this is all connected.'

'What do you mean Bridget?'

'Read this.'

Bridget handed Isobel a yellow envelope. Isobel read the communication out loud in bits and pieces. Isobel then threw the letter on the coffee table.

'So, they reckon this house is illegal and it has to be demolished and you get $185,000 to relocate.'

'Do you see the connection?' said Bridget. 'How convenient, they need all this land for the tourist development, and incorporate the lake.'

'That arrogant local member,' said Isobel, pacing behind the lounge.

'What's his name?'

'Jason Blackwell.'

'Blackwell' said Bridget. 'That's Louis's former surname.'

'Jesus,' said Isobel, 'this is getting weird. Blackwell is behind this you don't suppose he knows about Louis?'

'He couldn't,' said Bridget. 'He abandoned him when he was a baby.'

'We have to go to the lake tomorrow,' said Isobel looking at Charlie.

The big dog interrupted, 'You can see it now if you wish.'

'We are in the dark side of the moon,' said Isobel. 'We will need torches.'

'Hey Boofy, now might be the time to show these gals your stuff big fella.'

'What an excellent idea' Boofy stated in a very posh voice.

'How about you do the whole show, you know, change from this to that.'

Everyone sat quietly waiting. Black mist began to swirl from nowhere, strange little objects with wings, at a closer look they looked like tiny little people with insect legs. It was like watching a fairy-tale. All eyes became drawn to Boofy. The change was slow but magnificent. A huge warrior was emerging.

A seven-foot figure stood before them. Huge muscular forearms with menacing claws catching the lamplight. Long webbed feet, wings on the back of his legs. Shiny black wings in his shoulder blades. Long black pointy ears moved to catch every sound.

'Holy shit,' said Charlie. 'I think you're bigger this time.'

Bridget and Isobel sat very still absorbing the sight before them.

'This is just magical,' said Isobel.

Her small voice trying to find its way to the surface, 'Mmm', was all Bridget could manage, eyes fixed on the warrior.

Boofy stood erect with his wings wrapped around him, a black veil fell across the figure, as it cleared a large smartly plumed rooster stood before the people with a very indignant look. Before anyone had a chance to comment, a beautiful red deer appeared. Then, a regal tiger yawned in tiredness. The black veil manifested again, only to reappear again as a red sports car right in the middle of the lounge room. Charlie was so excited. He burst into nervous laughter. Then in moments Boofy once again sat casually panting his big pink tongue lolling out the side of his mouth, and his tail thumping the floor.

'That was incredible. You can change into everything?' asked Bridget.

'I can,' said Boofy 'although I have never tried a skyscraper.'

Charlie laughed loudly with a tinge of nervousness.

'Are you alright?' asked his mother.

'Well, um, you know how we have school holidays now and Louis is by himself, and I'm here? Well, Louis has this thing he has to do, why don't I go with him?!'

You could hear a pin drop!

Bridget cleared her throat. 'Can you tell us Boofy, exactly what it is Louis is doing? I must admit, I am starting to feel nervous and frightened.'

Isobel put her arm around Bridget and pulled her close.

Before an answer came, the big dog transitioned to his warrior self, his voice was low and comforting.

'Louis's journey to you and this place, Bridget was no coincidence. Louis possesses many qualities he was born at a special time when the universe was in complete balance to form precise planetary alignments. This phenomenon was only maintained for a short time. Events in his life were purposeful, he has been guided and protected, and that will remain until he returns safely to you. You were all chosen to be part of his journey.'

'But what does he have to do?' asked Bridget in a strained voice.

The big warrior looked deeply in Bridget's eyes.

'He has to find an object that is paramount to the continuance of Earth and return it to the mountain. This means he will be travelling through many galaxies in safety, to find this object.'

'But that's impossible,' said Charlie. 'We've only been to the moon. It's the mountain and the lake, isn't it? blurted out Charlie.

'Exactly.'

'But how can we get to other galaxies?'

'Technology Charlie. Advancement from other planets.'

'What is this object?' asked Isobel, leaning forward fascinated.

'It's a sphere made of powerful elements from other planets.'

'What is the importance of the mountain and the lake?'

'Well to put it in simple terms, these sites are imperative to the planet's survival. There is so much that mankind does not understand.'

Each person in the room looked at each other, an understanding silence confirmed their thoughts.

The big warrior stood tall. 'I hate to rush you, but the time has come for us to leave. I would like to show Bridget and Isobel the site. Now Charlie, would be a good time to ask again what you need to ask.'

Charlie sat down beside Isobel and held her hand. 'Mum, it's school holidays, and well, Louis has this thing he has to do, and he can't be by himself. I know I'm nagging, but please can I go?'

Isobel looked at the stunning alien figure.

'What do you think?'

'He will be safe, and he is part of this, as both you and Bridget are.'

There was silence then Isobel's voice broke through in a quiet whisper.

'Alright, okay you can go.'

'Yes!' said Charlie, punching the air, falling into Isobel's arms giving her a huge loving hug and kisses all over her face.

'If you could all gather out the front, we need to leave.'

The big warrior left the room. Charlie was busy shoving clothes into his backpack. He had a last glance at the room and joined his mother and Bridget out the back.

The night outside was clear. A cool breeze stirred in the overgrown garden. Aromas from multiple plants floated on the air. The two women and the boy stood on the steps.

The glorious being stood before them. The trio looked puzzled wondering and waiting. The black veil drifted in and like a huge glove being taken off, Boofy's warrior body slowly changed and a majestic being replaced him. A horse's nose, a full horse's head, shiny and black as onyx. Before their astonished eyes, a massive black horse appeared. Something else was happening. From the sides of the horse, like a moth squeezing out of a cocoon, magnificent strong wings emerged. Smaller wings from his fetlocks, all wings moving up and down in unison.

'Holy shit.' Charlie's squeaky voice broke the silence.

Bridget and Isobel couldn't find their voices to respond, just looking in awe!

'Please come onto my back, use my wings as steps.' The voice was still Boofy's. 'Come, time is wasting.'

Charlie, grabbing both Bridget and Isobel's hands, slowly and silently mounted the big Pegasus.

Strong wings began to move up and down. The massive horse and his passengers lifted into the air. High above the treetops, the passengers looked into the darkness the higher they went. Isobel sat in front holding the horse's mane for dear life. Bridget's arms wrapped around her, Charlie's arms around Bridget.

'I wish it wasn't so dark,' yelled Charlie. 'This is awesome.'

No sooner said, a line of stars from the heavens dangling like fairy lights appeared, lighting their path. The beauty rendered all speechless. All eyes feasted on the scenery below. Twinkling township lights, the wild ocean, the cavernous valleys and the dark mountains.

'Look!' said Charlie, 'I see the lake ahead.'

It wasn't hard to miss. The lake glowed purple lighting up the mountains and the cliff face. A huge white whale lolled in the lake and thousands of birds edged the lakeside. Animals of all species sat quietly in the surrounding bushland.

As they descended to ground below, the face of the mountain slowly opened. Shards of brilliant light splashed across the scene below.

Gently the huge magical beast landed safely beside the lake. All three dismounted and watching in awe, looked up at the cliff face.

'My God,' said Bridget 'this is just pure magic.'

Both women had tears rolling down their cheeks. Isobel nodded holding Bridget's hand.

All eyes were fixed on the cliff face. Two forms appeared. One very tall and regal, the other, the figure of a child.

'Louis!' called Bridget frantic to see him properly.

Immediately their animal chariot lifted off the ground heading towards the cliff face. As it arrived Louis mounted the big warm animal and within seconds was in Bridget's arms. They all embraced. There was much chatter and excitement amongst the family. When all conversation had been exhausted, Boofy's voice interrupted them.

'The moment is here.' His voice familiar and calm.

Louis looked at Bridget. 'Please listen Mum, you know we will be safe. You have only witnessed a very tiny glimpse of this force and you have to know we will return.'

'Yes, I see that Louis.'

'If you should need me, there will be custodians around you and Isobel, just call to them and help is on the way.'

'But how will we know who they are?'

'Trust me, you won't miss them. Time to go.' With that all exchanged farewell hugs, words of love, tears, confused laughter, and then the boys climbed aboard.

As the strange big horse circled once above the lake, the boys huddled together, glad to be back in each other's company.

'Hey Louis, I wonder if we could enter this dude in the Melbourne Cup. I certainly wouldn't name him after fish eggs!'

Louis burst out laughing.

'Now that's what I have missed, you weirdo.'

After circling the lake and dismounting, the boys walked either side of the tall being standing at the entrance to the mountain and then simply vanished.

The two women were forlorn figures, so many thoughts again. Mounting the huge horse for the glorious trip home, their big friend decided to extend their journey to lift their spirits.

The women's senses stirred, giggling like teenagers with excitement. Higher and higher into the night, the air becoming colder. Below all the lights twinkled along the coastline. The new moon was high, deep gold against the blackest of nights.

Up and down through soft clouds, in the distance Isobel sighted an aircraft descending to land. Flying closer, people's heads and faces could be defined by the internal lights, staring into the darkness, consumed in their own thoughts.

Bridget shouted into the night.

'What if they see us? They might think we are a UFO or they've drank too much.'

Both women laughing into the wind.

Secretly one small pair of eyes, that of a seven-year-old girl, fascinated by the moon, clinging to the window of the aircraft spotted the strange vision in the distance, her eyes not game to blink in case it disappeared. The little girl alerted no one, keeping the incredible vision to herself. She smiled. It confirmed in her mind that magical things do exist, and grownups don't know everything – and then it was gone

Gliding down through the cloud's moisture caressing their faces, the air became warmer, and they were met by the smells of earth. Touching the tree tops familiar sights came into view and they rested gently in Bridget's yard.

The women watched the big horse ascend again into the clouds. It had been an incredible night.

'Time for a cuppa?' smiled Bridget taking Isobel's arm.

'Time for a conversation,' said Isobel.

CHAPTER 19

Jason Blackwell sat in his oversized leather office chair; his long legs stretch out before him. Jason's looks had matured over the years. He now bore a rugged handsome face and a strong lean body. He ran his fingers through his thick brown hair, which now had just a touch of grey at his temples. All combined to create an impressive image that could turn heads of women all ages.

He sat with his hands now resting relaxed on his thighs. Before him stood a short rotund figure, holding papers in his hands, that shook as he spoke. His pale pudgy fingers and palms, sweating under Jason's scrutiny.

'Well Paul? I assume the property at Lavender Lane has been sorted.'

'I have given her documents explaining the illegal development.'

'And?' Jason's voice raised.

'She didn't really respond much.'

'What about the offer?'

Jason was looking like a lion ready to take his prey out.

'Well, like I said she really hasn't responded.'

Jason leaned over the miserable Paul Handy, the council's General Manager.

'Get the legal department to do up some threatening legal papers. Now get the hell out of my office and get that woman out of Lavender Lane. Do I have to remind you of your financial gains in this venture? If you fuck this up, you overstuffed pig, it will be the Centrelink line for you. Now get out!' Jason yelled, his face flushing dark red with anger.

Paul Handy scurried like a disgraced dog from the office, red faced and sweating.

Jason Blackwell's life was moving perfectly, he was the Local Member of Parliament, and his popularity was sure to see him elevated to State Parliament at the next election. The lake development was set to make him millions, his lifestyle was nothing but the best. Beautiful women found him irresistible. Men felt inferior around him, no one dared argue with him.

When the miserable Mr. Handy left, Jason turned on his television and replayed the many DVDs of himself. He was transfixed with the images.

After the gazing was over, he moved to the table beside his matching leather lounges. He flicked a switch that lit up the model of the lake resort. It looked like a Vegas casino. Luxurious high-rise apartments, swimming pools, sports grounds, restaurants, and endless shops. Jason caressed the model, then fell back into the lounge chair, just gazing at his future.

A distraction came slowly to disturb his fantastic dream, movement outside his office window. Five magpies sat perfectly still all warbling, watching the human within.

'What the hell are they looking at?' Jason dropped the blind mumbling to himself. 'I'll get someone to poison those bloody things.'

A knock at the door distracted Jason. His secretary entered holding the newspaper and Jason's special coffee.

'Anything interesting today Jill?'

'Um, oh there's a picture of this socialite model Genevieve St Day, it says she's arriving some time in Australia for Fashion Week as their international guest. She's very beautiful, she has apparently been the world's top model for some time, and part time Hollywood actress. Then it goes on to say she is looking for real estate in Australia.'

Jason grabbed the newspaper. His eyes fell on Genevieve St Day's face, he was speechless.

'My God she is stunning.'

Jill cleared her throat.

'It also says she is looking for a husband.'

She was smiling mischievously at Jason.

'Well then Miss Secretary, find a contact and her schedule. I have the perfect opportunity for Miss St Day.' Jason grinned, glancing toward the lakeside model.

'Oh, by the way Mr. Blackwell, your son Tristan rang. He said to tell you he has settled well into boarding school, and he has been invited to a friend's place for the school holidays and he needs money.'

'Oh good, just transfer a couple of thousand into his account.'

'A couple?'

'Yeah. Keeps him out of my hair.'

Tristan Blackwell was a real thorn in Jason's side.

Jason prayed he would die at birth. That grubby woman who trapped him remained a dark secret he continues to pay to keep quiet. It was a night of too much alcohol, beautiful women, and a great public relations opportunity to be seen with the rich and famous.

One encounter with Stevie Wills, who refused to terminate her pregnancy, to use for a life on easy street. Many times, Jason had contemplated an accident for the two problems in his otherwise perfect life.

He sat back smiling, his mind racing with all sorts of possibilities.

'Anything else Mr. Blackwell?' asked Jill, halfway out the door.

'Yes. Find out how much Miss St Day is worth and get someone to poison those bloody magpies. They're always hanging around my windows.'

'Poison? Those birds are native.'

'I don't give a bugger what they are. Just get rid of them!' Jason continued, raising his voice, his face flushed with blood.

Jill left the room in a hurry, close to tears. This was becoming a typical day for her. Internal thoughts bursting forth from her mouth as she closed the door.

'Contemptable Bastard!'

Jill was the third secretary in two years to suffer the temper of Jason Blackwell, but she was determined to go the distance. Besides, she didn't have a choice, it was getting tougher to find work. She sat at her desk pondering what to do about the magpies. There was no way she was going to organise a poisoning; she was not that kind of person.

It was time for a break, so making a coffee she headed outside walking up the side of the building to the outside of his office.

She stood watching the family of magpies in the tree, warbling without a care, arguing amongst themselves. She approached the tree, looking up, feeling very stupid. All eyes looked down at the strange human.

'Listen you lot, you have to leave. Don't come near this place, he's going to have you poisoned. Please just go.'

She began contemplating to herself. I don't believe what I'm doing, on the verge of hysterical laughter.

'Go on, leave.'

All the magpies studied Jill in silence, then looked at each other. A minute went by and then as if someone said 'After three', the family of birds flew off, not just to another tree, they flew towards the distant mountain.

Jill stood watching, wondering if they understood, then burst out laughing. Jason Blackwell's voice broke out through the open window, disturbing the moment of absolute pleasure.

'What the hell are you doing? I'm not paying you to stand out there laughing like a demented hyena.'

'Oh, I was just sorting out the magpie thing.'

Jason slammed the window shut. For the next week, Jill was nervous watching and hoping the magpies did not return. To her great relief they never did.

CHAPTER 20

When the mountain closed slowly around the three figures, silence and absolute darkness surrounded the trio.

'Don't be afraid, everything is about to change.' Arume's strong caressing voice eased the fear.

Slowly, light was forming, then faster and faster, colours and long tubes could be seen.

'Close your eyes. Do not open them until I say.'

It seemed like a lifetime to both boys with their eyes closed. The excitement and fear, nearly unbearable.

'Open slowly.'

The boys did as they were instructed. Before them was a spectacle beyond imagination. The floor was no longer a dirt cave, it was like pure white ice. Veins of colour pulsated underneath. Long tubes like stalactites the shape of crystals, liquid swirled inside, the veins of colour continuously moving, energised as if living beings. The boys' vision was then diverted upwards. Little creatures like dragonflies flittered above their heads.

One of the creatures hovering in front of Charlie squirted him in the face with something wet, a tiny human like face smiled into his. Charlie wiped his face with the back of his hand, his hand sparkled, fluid danced around his fingers. To Charlie astonishment the sparkles turned into even smaller little human dragonflies and flew away.

'Did you see that, Louis?' Charlie laughed with excitement.

'They can be very mischievous little creatures' said Arume.

Louis and Charlie looked at each other and laughed.

'This is incredible' said Charlie, his mouth open taking in this strange new world.

Arume spoke. 'Firstly, Louis and Charles, I need to explain to you both what all this is, what it means, and why you are here.' Arume spoke softly and asked the two boys to follow.

Charlie sat mesmerized by Arume's voice, his looks and the feeling of absolute calm.

'You are very observant Charlie,' Arume said, looking into Charlie's eyes.

'Oh, um, I was just thinking how tall you are, and you have very long hands and stuff.'

Arume laughed, 'Yes you are right Charlie, and I do have different looking 'stuff', as you put it. Let me show you.'

Arume rose and unbuttoned his gown. It fell off his shoulders.

They stared without a word or movement, barely able to take a breath. Arume's body was long and thin, his body was white with tiny coloured scales with a human shaped body, but more advanced. The fingers and toes twice as long as a human, down Arume's back vents that opened and closed.

'Wow,' Charlie finally broke the silence 'that is so cool!'

Louis nodded in appreciation.

Arume's face was beautiful, slightly triangular, the colour of milk. Long slender green eyes the colour of grass, and purple at intervals, black triangle shaped pupils appeared to look into their souls. Arume's mouth was much wider than a human's, with tiny teeth all the same size. Each ear was long and folded to seal off. Long black hair fell gracefully to the floor, a startling contrast to his near opaque body. His feet were long with retracting webbing with four long toes, a nose much like a human's, however it had the ability to close when under water. Arume's hands were long with five long elegant fingers, that had retracting webbing and long nails that shone like pearls.

Arume put his gown back on and looked at the boys who remained looking stunned.

'Let us sit and be comfortable. Food and drinks for our guests.' Arume said.

From the very floor the boys were standing on, movement started, something was pushing up through the floor.

'Holy crap Louis. What's happening?'

'I don't know Charlie! It's not like I've been here before.'

Three large comfortable chairs appeared.

'How did you do that?' Charlie's voice rather squeaky and excitable.

'Sit boys and I will explain' said their majestic host calmly.

The boys sat taking in everything before them. A pool of what looked like melted crystal lay before them surrounded with large tube-like structures.

'It's like a palace of white ice. It's unreal,' said Louis.

The next minute something was tugging at Charlie's coat. A strange little creature like a miniature elephant appeared, except his trunk had a small hand at the end with four tiny fingers. It had a squat little body covered in fur with a pair of loose wings down its back.

'May I introduce Dorfund. He is from the planet Nollid Dune, a long way from your solar system,' Arume spoke softly. 'He is helping to try and save your planet, as are others.'

Before Charlie or Louis could speak the little creature handed up a tray. Louis took the tray and looked at Arume totally confused.

'Look at the tray, both of you. Concentrate on what you would like to eat and drink.'

Louis and Charlie did as they were instructed. Before their eyes, cubes and two glasses of sparkling crystal formed.

'Oh, that's very pretty. Doesn't exactly look like a burger,' said Charlie.

'Taste it' said Arume, looking intrigued by the boys' actions.

Louis picked up the cube and bit into it reluctantly.

'It's a chicken sandwich.'

He grabbed the glass and drank it warily.

'Wow! It's chocolate milk!'

Charlie picked up his cubes and ate them.

'It's a burger.'

Another bite.

'With the works!'

Quickly he took a gulp of his drink.

'Oh man, it's a caramel milkshake.'

After eating the boys began to relax, perhaps a little too much. It was obvious to Arume' that the boys needed to sleep.

'It is time for you both to rest. I want you both to visualize a bed to lie on.'

Slowly the chairs changed to soft welcoming beds. They laughed at the amazing world they found themselves in.

'This is totally mad,' said Charlie.

Louis agreed. The boys stretched out sighing and slipped into a well needed sleep. As they relaxed into a deeper sleep, a crystal dome formed around their beds, forming a cocoon for silence and rest.

Arume' watched them sleep, stating to himself, 'I hope you will be strong enough to accept what you are about to learn.'

The boys were unaware their food had been laced with an additive that would give them deep sleep, to rest the entire brain in preparation for what they were about to witness and absorb.

CHAPTER 21

Genevieve St Day sat opposite her manager in his luxurious office, which possessed the best sweeping views of Paris. The woman opposite him tantalised every fibre of his manhood. She was an absolute picture of exquisite beauty. Luxurious platinum blonde hair waved delicately over her breasts and cascaded down to her waist. Her sculptured body was perfectly proportioned.

The mysterious woman's face glowed a honey colour, unblemished skin, highlighted by her vivid blue eyes. Maxwell Dupree actually thought she was almost the image of a Barbie doll.

'Well? What is it that you had to see me so urgently Max?'

'I have an invitation for you to attend and be their international guest at the Australian Fashion Week.'

'Australia?'

Genevieve's voice was high and for an unnoticeable moment she lost her educated English accent. She quickly recovered, sitting forward so Max could get a glimpse of her breasts. Genevieve knew her beauty would distract any questionable irregularities.

'I have taken it upon myself to accept your invitation.'

Maxwell put his hand up to stop her protests.

'Please listen Genevieve. You have accumulated a lot of money and we need to invest some of your money to avoid a large tax bill. I have an email from a gentleman in Australia. He has heard of your imminent arrival via my press release which stated your interest in investing in Australia - you know public relations - and people are scrambling for your attention.'

'Have you quite finished organising my life?'

'Well, that's what you pay me for Genevieve!'

'Well perhaps that arrangement can be changed.'

'Please Genevieve, I'm sorry, let me explain. We need to keep you prominent in the public eye. It's been a while since a contract in Europe or America has come across my desk and this will give you great exposure in the Southern Hemisphere. You are looking more beautiful than ever. You never seem to age. You know it's been a pleasure to be your manager. In my opinion, the world should not be denied your beauty.'

'Oh Maxwell, I'm sorry, of course you're right. You have always looked after me. Please tell me about this investment.'

Max smiled internally, congratulating himself. His ability to soothe and play these pretentious people never ceased to amaze him.

'Now in relation to this investment. My people have investigated the proposal. It's about two hours from Sydney and it's to be a five-star luxury resort, surrounding a natural lake. The clientele of course will be wealthy internationals.'

'Sounds fantastic Maxwell. Send the details to my secretary, the dates and what not. I have a fitting in half an hour.'

'Of course. You do and do what you do best – look beautiful. Before you go, would you like to know how much Australian Fashion Week have offered for your presence?'

'Yes of course Max. What is it?'

'Two million.'

'Excellent, how long for?'

'One week.'

'Good. Ta-ta Max.'

She left the room like and exotic bird taking flight.

Max sat back and laughed. The actual figure was three and a half million.

'Go my beauty. Go get your injections and adjustments, more money for me.'

Max pressed the button on his intercom.

'Yes Mr. Dupree?'

'Send all Miss St Day's Australian trip details to her secretary. Please ensure Mr. Blackwell's introduction is included.'

'Yes Mr. Dupree.'

Genevieve St Day boarded the private jet Max had organized. Each of her staff loaded down with clothes, shoes, expensive jewellery, special foods, drinks, vitamins, top shelf cosmetics, creams and oils.

The internals of the jet showcased a beautiful bedroom. Luxurious in its furnishings, it was like a flying penthouse, designed especially for Genevieve's needs.

Rosa Lebosi, a small Italian woman with attractive features, always had a stressful expression. She had been with Genevieve for six months. Every day she kept wishing she could tell her boss to shove her job.

'Do come on Rosa, I'm ready for my massage, then I want my deep tissue massage. Then I'll need my hair washed and nails touched up. My lunch needs to be prepared. The menu is in Vivian's briefcase. Then I must sleep and whilst I sleep, I expect all my clothes to be ready and laid out.' Every day was the same. Excessive demands, never a thought for another human being.

Vivian James, Genevieve's secretary, ran from one end of the jet to the other.

Vivian and Rosa took side glances at each other in expressions of sympathy. Once everything was sorted, the women settled into the chairs for takeoff. The two employees finally relaxed for a moment with a hot tea.

'This is going to be a long hard trip.'

'Yes Vivian, and if she does not get enough paparazzi attention, we are going to pay big time.'

Vivian picked up the briefcase, heavy with paperwork. It went everywhere when Genevieve travelled. It contained her life and all her important contacts.

Both ladies closed their eyes while the aircraft climbed higher into the heavens.

The door slammed open waking Vivian and Rosa.

'What the hell are you two lazy sluts doing?! I'm not paying you to sleep and sip tea.'

'Just having a break until it's safe', said Vivian in a shaky voice.

Rosa jumped in quick, 'Are you ready Madam for your massage? You look tired.'

'Yes, yes, I am. Come and massage me until I fall asleep, then have everything ready for my stopover.'

'Yes Miss St Day.'

Vivian stood up from her seat in a frenzy when Rosa took their boss to her bedroom. In her haste and fear of Genevieve, the briefcase dropped hard on the floor.

Something had fallen off the bottom of the briefcase, it was a secret compartment. An envelope bulging with items was jammed inside. Just at that moment Genevieve appeared in a tirade. Vivian quickly shelved the briefcase and kicked the piece of metal under the chair. The minute she turned to face Genevieve a sharp sting from her boss's hand landed on Vivian's face.

'I told you to pack my oils, you useless lump of ugliness. That stupid peasant can't find them. Get them now!'

Her heart was beating that fast with anxiety, it actually hurt. The blasted oils were found, and the beast was temporarily calm.

Inside the bedroom Rosa's abuse continued, her wrists ached from massaging, she was finally asleep. Rosa quietly left, backing out watching her sleep and snore.

The two women sat together eating and enjoying their quiet time. Rosa put her cup down and sighed. Vivian grinned.

'I nearly forgot to show you, look what fell out of the bottom of her briefcase.'

She gently removed the large envelope.

'Let's go up the back of the plane, in case she comes back.'

They sat on the beds and laid out the contents.

Photos of Genevieve when she started modelling when she first started. In another envelope articles of her potential success. Next was clippings of an accident describing the unfortunate death of a successful photographer and injuries to a beautiful model. Hidden and folded many times, a photo fell out of a piece of folded paper, it was a picture of her face post-accident.

'Oh my God! That was her, she was hideous.'

In another envelope, written words stating her hate for a child, her mother and an ex-husband. The words were constructed by someone very bitter and resentful, blaming them for her accident and injuries.

'Where are you, Rosa?'

She was awake.

'Quickly Rosa, go to her before she sees this, or I swear she will throw us off the plane.'

'Here we are again, get up and do something. I can't wait to see the last of you two. What is that you are looking at?'

'Just pictures of my small children.'

Both women froze with fear.

'Oh lovely, more little peasants. I hate children, so don't think I'm going to admire them. Get them out of my sight. You Vivian, better have everything organized. How far are we from Sydney?'

'Four hours Miss St Day.'

'Rosa. Come! I need your attention.'

Vivian busied herself organizing meetings, times and introductions, first class accommodation and hire cars. Specific diet and drinks were organized, as too were beauticians and hairdressers.

Rosa's hands moved like a magician's over her body, perfect in its structure. Rosa slipped on her glasses looking closely for scar suture sites. There was something odd about her scalp.

'What the hell are you doing? I can feel your breath on me. Go away now, I've had enough of you.'

The women took a break, both having thoughts regarding their employer.

Vivian finally spoke, 'You know Rosa, that information about her could be sold to a journalist. I wonder how much it would be worth?'

'Vivian don't even go there we could end up in court. I wonder if she remembers it's still hidden?' Rosa laughed.

'That would mean thinking about someone else. Well, I have photocopied all the paperwork and put it all back. You know what is really weird?'

'It's all weird Vivian.'

'There was a mention of a boy.'

'She had a baby?'

'His surname is the same as some hotshot politician she has an appointment with. Anyway, we have a backup, perhaps down the track.'

Genevieve St Day exited her private jet like a true movie star. Cameras flashed and the paparazzi called her name to get different angled pictures. She adored these moments. This is what her life was all about. To be admired and envied. She was what common women could only dream of.

Alone in her luxury apartment overlooking the harbor, French champagne in hand, Genevieve twirled around, her delicate feet sinking into the pure wool carpet. She relaxed back into the overstuffed, oversized lounge.

'Where are those two ugly peasants?'

She then laughed to herself.

'Oh, that's right, they're entitled to time off. I'll give them permanent time off when we get back to Paris.'

Sitting back, she sighted the briefcase.

'Oh hell, I forgot.'

Scrambling to her feet she grabbed the case. She carefully opened the compartment, sighing with relief.

'I should burn this.'

Momentarily, she thought about Louis.

'I would like him to see me. How beautiful I am and how wealthy, no doubt he'll want his Mummy then. I'll take great pleasure in turning my back on him.'

CHAPTER 22

It was a long flight, but that didn't bother Lucy Blackwell, because this was the beginning of a totally new life. It was night, the plane was due to land in Zurich in twenty minutes. Lucy had arranged through the travel service to have a car waiting to take her to the Swiss Alps. Hidden south of Bern and Luzern and east of Lake Geneva was a world-famous chalet. Within the walls of this chalet, the world's leading plastic surgeons, general surgeons and the world's best health professionals were employed to turn ugly ducklings into beautiful swans.

Lucy was given a sedative to relax and sleep for the trip. This was standard protocol for all patients. The identity and location of the chalet was to remain secret. She had stumbled across a contact for this place in one of her expensive magazines that catered to the wealthy and the beautiful. Models and movie stars, absolutely anyone who made a living with their appearances.

When she woke from her drug induced sleep, slowly her surrounds became clear. A luxurious room took her breath away. Warm colors, beautiful prints, exotic timbers and a balcony with a view resembling a postcard. Snowcapped mountains, lush green valleys and dense forests. There was a gentle knock on the door and breakfast was delivered. Freshly baked croissants, fresh fruit, thick yellow cream, and the tantalizing smell of coffee. Lucy was starving. The maid disappeared without a word.

Lucy showered after breakfast and dressed in the special robe left for her. She was enlivened and nervous. She was to wait for a knock on her door and then she was to be directed to her surgeon.

She sat opposite a very beautiful man feeling so vulnerable and hideous in front of him, she put her hand up to cover her face.

'Please Lucy that is not necessary, I want you to take deep breaths and relax. We have a lot to discuss. I will turn your face into a masterpiece.'

Lucy's entire body was put through rigorous testing. An MRI that examined her bones, her nervous system, muscle tissue and her skin. Her face was examined for hours. Pathology was collected and tested. Every part of her pathology was matched in preparation for her surgery. She was visited by nurses, physiotherapists, dieticians, beauticians, dermatologists and a personal trainer. Each of these people explained Lucy's regime that she must commit to after her surgery. She was shown DVDs of what she was to expect. She was instructed to watch these numerous times until she understood every expectation she had to commit to. She did as she was instructed watching intently what to expect. As she sat watching, a knock came at her door. A very well dressed, perfectly groomed woman stood before her holding a briefcase.

'Good morning Ms. Blackwell, my name is Casandra Appledorf. May I come in?'

Lucy sat, unsure of what was going to happen.

'Today I want to ask you, who you desire to be, when you are 'changed'. I need to know your deepest desires in life. Lucy began slowly, again embarrassed about her face, trying to hide it with her hand. Casandra was beautiful. Lucy talked about her modelling, how successful she was, and how much she was in demand before the accident. Lucy became excited within herself.

'I want to be on top again. I want to be worshipped I want to be admired.'

Lucy shook, then seemingly returned to reality.

'You are very determined. Tell me Lucy, how old do you think I am?'

'Um, oh, about 23 or 24.'

'I am 57 years old Lucy.'

'Wow! That is fantastic.'

'Yes, I am. Now Lucy, let me explain to you what we can offer you. We need to know how far you want to take your transformation. Let me inform you how much we have to offer.'

Lucy sat back to listen.

'It is obvious you want to resume your modelling and movie career we can help you achieve this. However, to be on top you will undergo many rigorous changes. We need to know if you have enough ambition to do this. Let me take you through what is required. Firstly, you need to have elocution and deportment lessons. You need to know how to manage the world stage. We can get you onto the world's most famous catwalks and open up doors to the world of movies. Is this what you desire?'

'Yes! Yes, oh yes please.'

Casandra smiled at her reaction.

'In my briefcase I have four photos your surgeon Dr Semese has designed specifically to your pathology and results of your tests.'

Lucy's mouth was open, pure elation caused her to dribble out of her crooked mouth.

'We have a list of new names, new addresses, a total new identity.'

Casandra handed Lucy all the information.

'Please, take your time. I shall return in an hour to seek your instructions and you will notice the price list matching your selection.'

Lucy studied each photograph closely, they were all beautiful, but the one she was attracted to most was a photo of a beautiful platinum blonde, in fact she was the image of a glamourous Barbie doll. Lucy was transfixed with the image looking back at her, this was going to be her. She laughed, she cried, she dribbled and danced with the photo. Then it was time to choose a name and a place to live. The name choice was easy Genevieve St Day. Lucy said it over and over hugging the photo. She chose Paris to be her home.

The knock came, Lucy was daydreaming, and she could see her new self on the catwalk.

Casandra studied Lucy's choice, it was predictable for Casandra, Lucy oozed Barbie doll. She accepted Lucy's choices.

'What happens now?' Lucy's voice nearly squealing.

'Are you happy with the price of five million?'

'Oh yes, it's worth every cent.'

'Good! As of now you commence 'the change'. I note you have chosen Paris as your home.'

'Oh yes,' said Lucy 'it's so romantic.'

'Good! You shall begin with French lessons after your surgery. Tonight, you will be given a sedative. Tomorrow you will be collected by your nurse at 8:15am sharp. Your face will be operated on first. Your doctor will then sculpt your body to the photo you chose. This will require many procedures to achieve perfection. Your teeth will be attended to as prescribed by our orthodontist. When you wake you will be heavily bandaged, they will remain for ten days. Underneath these bandages is a special solution developed by our scientist to remove scars and increase collagen production. Any blemishes, discolouration will disappear, your skin tone and skin integrity will be perfect. After ten days you will commence your rehab, including exercises, diet, vitamins. You will commence elocution lessons, deportment and French lessons. This Genevieve, is going to be a long hard road, I hope you are committed to achieving your dreams.'

'Oh yes Casandra, I am ready.'

Lucy, soon to be Genevieve St Day, had her sedative arrive. The nurse settled her into bed and injected her, the darkness was welcomed.

Under anaesthetic, photos were taken of her face and body before they commenced. All the team members were ready. A large photo of Lucy's chosen image was visible for all to see.

Ten hours later, it was done. Lucy was bandaged from head to toe and placed in a chamber breathing air mixed with atomised vitamins and minerals. Later she awoke in her luxury room. For the next 9 days she was nursed, fed, assisted to the toilet, given passive exercise. She didn't complain. She did as she was told. Her emotions were controlled, her determination was intense.

It was day ten and Lucy was impatient, she wanted this new life so badly. Everyone was ready, the entire team that worked with her. Precise delicate cuts were made into the special bandaging, slowly unravelling, for a moment Lucy remembered another time with bandages being removed, there was silence, she held her breath, and finally all bandages were taken down. Smiles on everyone's face told her it was a success.

'Can I please see?'

Casandra stepped forward.

'To begin we are going to bathe you, do your hair and makeup, apply some prescribed skin food designed by our dermatologist and then, and only then, will you see Genevieve St Day.'

Lucy didn't argue. Another four hours to create the most beautiful woman in the world, she didn't mind. She was quite prepared to enjoy every moment of pampering, she deserved it.

Photos were taken of the finished product. She was then guided to a full wall mirror. The refection was mesmerising, she couldn't move, she was even more beautiful than before. Lucy burst into tears. Casandra stood beside her.

'Are you happy Miss St Day?'

'Extremely.'

'We shall leave you for now and return in one hour.'

Genevieve walked up to the mirror and began looking at herself closely. She touched her long, soft and luxurious hair. It came to her waist and a soft wave highlighted the platinum colour. The figure-hugging dress displayed superb lines, her breasts were plump and perky, the low-cut dress showed them perfectly. Studying her face intensely, there were no signs of scarring, instead they were replaced with perfect skin, eyes turquoise blue and pouting lips. Ripping the dress off over her head, she took off her underwear examining her body bit by bit, turning slowly as she did so. She was perfect. Her legs, shapely, with no hair were smooth golden brown. Her teeth were a brilliant white colour, all even and small. Her feet and hands were petite, French tips on all her nails. She looked nothing like her previous self.

Knocking at the door, Casandra entered observing the new creation studying herself.

'Tonight, Miss St Day we have a ball where we would like to present you. Amongst the guests, you will recognise many famous faces. I have to remind you that we have a confidentiality clause. You are never to repeat to anyone who you speak to or see. If you do, your true identity will be revealed, plus your 'before photos.' And any future you would have had will be destroyed. This evening you will be the centre of attention, you will meet people that will open doors for you. You are not to drink, your manners will be impeccable, and you will be demure. Try not to enter into too much conversation, your speaking voice is yet to be perfected. You have 15 minutes to prepare yourself and your escort will present you.'

Finishing, Casandra left as abruptly as she had arrived.

Genevieve looked at herself.

'Well young lady you are going to show that has been! How dare she speak to me that way. Let's give them a surprise Miss Day.'

She laughed and twirled. She couldn't improve on perfection, so fifteen minutes devouring the image of herself was the best pleasure ever. Her escort arrived charming and handsome. She was announced and her entrance was like that of a professional movie star. Slowly descending the staircase into a sea of the world's most famous and wealthy. Long platinum hair bounced around her waist, trailing from the most perfect face money could buy. A figure hugging white sequined dress showed off luscious breasts and a perfectly sculptured body. A strategically placed slit revealed long elegant legs, exposed to the thigh. Every head in the building turned towards the staircase. When she reached the bottom, she was handed a flute of champagne, she was then surrounded by the world's beautiful people.

Genevieve's composure, her sophistication, and mystery fascinated those who sought her company. That night she collected many business cards from Hollywood, Fashion Houses from around the world, and men looking for a beautiful companion.

Lucy Blackwell definitely got her 5 million dollars' worth. She was a star pupil. Her language was perfect, English and French. And after her lessons she exercised to the regime designed for her, she was massaged and spent an hour each day in a deep mineral bath of secret ingredients never to be exposed. A special diet was designed for her and it was for life. She was given special vitamins and oils for her skin. One single contact number was given to replenish her therapies. A list of what activities she could and could not do was read out to her, her surgeons explained that she had extensive work and it remained delicate, due to the detrimental scarring and aggressive surgery to repair her wounds. She was given a briefing in a leather- bound document of all her surgeries and treatments.   The newly created Genevieve St Day moved like liquid, she floated like an exotic bird on the wind.

'Be careful with my bags. You people are impossible idiots. Where the hell is my personal assistant?'

'I'm here Miss St Day.'

'Well open up the bloody door.'

Genevieve was empowered and people were going to notice her and obey her. The apartment was magnificent. Situated in the Avenue Montaigne, a very wealthy part of Paris, she had now created the perfect fantasy and she intended to live it to the fullest. People would admire her, be jealous of her beauty, and want to be her. She hired a manager, a secretary and a maid with therapeutic skills to manage all the aspects of her life. All she had to do was enjoy it and look gorgeous.

CHAPTER 23

Charlie's eyes opened slowly, blinking to focus and at the very same time a pair of bright blue eyes surrounded with fuzzy white hair looked back, fascinated by Charlie. Tiny little hands rested upon the crystal dome.

'And I wonder which planet this comes from?'

'You say something Charlie?'

'You can hear me?

'Yep! Have you met our friend? His name is Fudgunkel, he looks like something left over from Christmas.'

Little Fudgunkel jumped to his feet all of one metre tall. His red suit trimmed with gold brocade, a long pointy hat, his red curled toe slippers, both topped with bells. His slippers trimmed with red gold stitching, all matching his red jacket. He certainly was a sight to behold. Fudgunkel clapped his little hands together and both domes disappeared.

They got to their feet slowly looking confused.

'What the hell is that?' Charlie's squeaky voice looking at Louis for answers.

'Never mind that!' came Fudgunkel's voice, full of authority. 'Follow me and be quick about it!'

They followed in silence, totally in awe of their surroundings. The huge dome of stalactites was pulsating with coloured liquid. It was like watching a gigantic kaleidoscope.

'Stand here.'

Fudgunkel interrupted the boys looking in stunned delight at the environment. Before they had time to ponder anything, they were inside a crystal cylinder travelling downwards.

'Louis, we must be in the centre of the Earth by now. This is crazy!'

Charlie was nervous, and mumbling things about trying to escape. Before Louis had time to settle Charlie they came to a stop and the cylinder disappeared from around them.

Arume was welcoming. Louis and Charlie smiled nervously.

'Please don't be afraid, you are safe.'

The strange but beautiful creature gestured for them to enter. The dome of stalactites with their swirling liquid wove their magic above the boys' heads.

'This is amazing...but I can see an empty space.'

'Interesting that you have noticed Louis, and it's extremely important. That is the reason we need your help.'

Charlie and Louis moved forward, towards what looked like an area with tiered seating, reaching high to the dome. In the centre, a large pool of liquid crystal swirled around. Everything was pure white. Arume stood before the pool and spoke some beautiful words, foreign, but not of earth.

'Duark Tabe, Luar Lator Emde Diazm.'

From the centre of the pool on a clear crystal pedestal, arose a small vial of fluid. It was a brilliant shimmering silver in colour. From out of nowhere the strange dragonfly with its little primate face appeared. It gently gathered the vial and placed it in Arume's delicate hand.

'Thank you.'

Arume bowed to the tiny creature.

'Come, sit. I am going to show you some history of your world, and why we need your help to preserve the future of planet Earth. You are going to see what no other human will ever see. Far beyond your solar system. Incredible visions, lifeforms, planets, dangerous beings, sights that you could not imagine, you will feel fear, joy and shock. But most of all, your journey here has been preordained.'

'Umm...' Charlie put his hand up. 'Am I, what's the word? Pre...'

'Preordained?' said Arume. 'It means something that is going to happen in the future or influence it to happen.'

'Am I really part of this?' asked Charlie, feeling very unsure.

Louis put his arm around Charlie's shoulder.

'I need you Charlie, and that's all that matters. Right Arume?'

The gentle being nodded in approval. Charlie looked at Louis smiling.

'Sounds like Star Wars. Hey Louis?'

'Your jokes are even worse when you're nervous.'

The dome area darkened. Magnificent, iridescent colours from the entire spectrum bounced around the whole area. The pool in the centre swirled, vapour rose to nowhere in particular, and then dispersed. The pool then cleared.

The first vision appeared. It was Earth, covered in lush, thick forests, rivers and oceans, everything in nature was perfect in a pristine state.

'In the beginning the Earth was a perfect planet. Beings from another solar system tended the Earth ensuring a complete balance.'

Arume's voice was passionate and precise.

'Did they look like you?' asked Charlie.

'My people arrived here as the caretakers.'

The two boys stared open-mouthed, watching strange people living in small colonies inside crystal domes. Shapeshifting into different creatures enabled them to move among the animals without fear.

'Unfortunately, Earth was restless, she had not finished evolving. The solar system was still very active. We had to leave and observe its evolution from afar. It was a dangerous place to be.'

The boys watched the pool intently. They witnessed the Earth heave, roll and crash, lava running wherever it wanted. Great mountains were pushed over. Volcanoes spewed forth its contents. Massive canyons began appearing all over the planet. Coastlines moved and crashed into the sea. Forests were swallowed up. Great oceans began surging into every opening finding their way further and further. Watching from above it was like seeing a giant jigsaw puzzle forming in slow motion on its own.

'Then stillness and quiet.'

Arume's voice broke the moment.

'Over the millions of years different beings came to earth looking to colonise.'

The boys began to witness an alien visit, not taking their eyes off the pool. Domes spinning with what looked like giant flying spiders. Powerful and pulsating, nearly silent in their landing, the strong landing gear settling gently. Louis and Charlie were bewitched by the spectacle. The boys waited to see who was going to emerge from such an advanced beautiful spaceship.

A leg appeared first, covered in a creamy soft shell, four long tapered toes. The figure exited quickly. It was beautiful. It was dressed in a film of gold with a tiny body, much the shape of a child. The creature's head was definitely the point of beauty. The head was shaped like a diamond. Its long eyes slanted upwards. Each time they blinked they were a different colour. The long pointy nose continuously moved, sniffing the air for every intriguing scent. Its tiny little mouth made a chattering noise. Long tentacles on its head moved like radars with suction caps opening and closing. It was truly magnificent, sleek and highly evolved. Just as fast as they arrived and did sensory tests of the atmosphere, they boarded the ship and left. With a spinning glow of bright light, the giant flying spider simply disappeared.

'Holy crap.'

Charlie's mouth was hanging open.

'That was incredible!'

Louis's voice soft and fading.

'Why didn't they stay?' asked Louis, gathering his composure.

'The air,' said Arume, 'too much oxygen. It would have disintegrated the outer shell. Are you ready to continue? Shall we begin from there?'

'Yep. Can I ask a thousand questions?'

'Certainly,' said Arume, 'no one visited earth until after the ice age.'

'Umm...' said Charlie, hesitating. 'When did we arrive, you know 'Us', Aboriginals?'

Arume looked at Charlie.

'Roughly 80,000 years ago, your race inhabited Australia. We watched their arrival, we watched how they adapted. The deep understanding of the land, for fauna and flora, they were as one with the environment. You are from a very special race of people. Now you need to know about who I am, where we come from, what we are doing here, and what is our purpose.'

Arume pointed to the pool. Slowly forms started to take shape.

'Our planet is three galaxies away.'

A beautiful, mystical vision appeared. A landscape of mixed colours, mauves, pale greens, blue, yellow, orange and purple, all in differing shades reflected in the environment. Trees with crystal leaves shimmered, scattering more vivid colour to be admired. Strange objects hung off them in abundance. Squares, triangles and rectangular shapes all joined together constructed from massive crystal walls. Crystal columns held it all in place, pulsating with liquid energy. Beings like Arume and Esouli were moving around in clear egg shape domes. Shields were being constructed over the civilised areas of living and industry. A small sun feeds the planet mixed with its powerful energy source. Enormous domes grew all forms of vegetation, many similar to Earth. Then, a vision of what looked like Earth appeared. Beautiful green valleys, tropical jungles, snow-capped mountains, grass savannahs, open plains and rivers. All untouched. Clean oceans gently rolled onto large islands. It was like Earth untouched.

'This is just some of our planet, soon you will see our very advanced buildings and technology so far into the future, it will be hard to process. Our home planet is called Helomedes. We found this planet in need of great care. We infused it with our energy force of crystal liquid and Vodoxium. Our people created everything you see before you, much of it borrowed from Earth. This was done to suit some members of the human race from your planet, whom we trust and admire, and from who we seek their guidance. We have tried for many years to infiltrate our people into high positions, in a total shape shift to show the way of sustainable living future. We wanted to protect your planet to continue the survival of your kind. Unfortunately, we are not making any progress. We don't seem to be influencing enough people. Your planet will die, as it is now, slowly. We have great difficulty understanding the thought process. The majority of your societies congregate in vast overcrowded cities, detached from each other and the world around them. The natural environment gives life, air, food and water, and yet, it is not seen as important. We fear your evolution and intelligence is failing and going backwards. Earth is the most perfect in its solar system, the natural beauty is breath taking. The wildlife is the most fascinating of all that we have ever witnessed. There are many on Earth who have a high awareness of what is evolving. There are many people, who we know the contents of their souls. They have been identified because they resonate a special vibration which we have watched since birth.'

Louis and Charlie were engrossed with Arume's words, almost forgetting to swallow, hanging onto every word.

Louis looked at Arume, the words falling out of his mouth.

'My Grandmother.'

'Yes,' said Arume.

'Our families, our mothers, I mean Bridget and Isobel?'

'Yes,' said Arume.

'All of you.'

'As you know already, the lake and the mountain are very special. It is our southern energy point on the Earth and the far point is Greenland. So too is the island of Madagascar and Chickayoo off the coast of Peru. Four points on the planet, North, South, East and West.'

As Arume spoke, visions of countries appeared.

'Hidden within the Earth, at every point, each contains a space carrier similar to the one we are in at present, and within each is another craft capable of vast travel. We have spent years gathering species, plants, soils, animals, blood, hair and so on. Literally every conceivable reproduction sample that lives.'

'It's unbelievable to think we are not only in one spaceship but two! Can we see it?'

'When the mother ship leaves Louis, you will be able to observe, as they will all leave together.'

'This is just so totally awesome. What will happen to the planet Arume, will it survive?' asked Charlie somewhat distraught.

'Yes Charlie, nature will survive. It will regenerate. The future population will be guided to ensure harmony and a world free of war, hate and excessive needs. A new dawn. A higher intelligence will ensure the survival of the human race.'

'Why then,' said Louis with a thoughtful frown 'is it so hard for people to see the entire picture of earth and its survival?'

'Many people do. Louis, the human race has a strange system of governing and I'm afraid the health of the earth is not a concern. The wars for natural resources will decimate the planet and many of its people.'

Louis spoke up.

'What will happen when the development goes ahead and the mountain is destroyed, when all of this is destroyed?'

Louis gestured with his hands.

'What about the lake? Surely you are able to stop this. You must have some power?'

'I can feel the sorrow in your voice Louis,' said Arume. 'Everything is on track. What happens, is meant to happen. The intervention will come. Your mothers have the spirit and the magic to keep the mountain safe. I would like to now show you how we are preserving for the future. The mother ship expands and contracts as needed, the other craft within is for vast travel, it's the shape of a Tetrahedron, it is also a shape shifting craft, and it will be your ship for future travels.'

As they walked the internals just appeared and it was magnificent. Thousands of stored cubes, all with life preserved within. Fruit and vegetable, including many other foods. Some were dried and others living in their own juices, all grown in Vodoxium. Charlie was in awe of the food, the strange shapes and multitude of colours.

'Looks like we will never run out of food and thank god for that I say!'

Arume smiled at Charlie.

Continuing on they saw pods that were used for sleeping and bathing. All the little creatures on board helped the processes run smoothly, each under the watchful eye of Mr Fudgunkel.

'At the moment we have another problem that will devastate many planets in many solar systems including Earth, and that Louis and Charlie is the reason you are here.'

The boy's traded looks, a cross between fear and intrigue.

'On our planet,' continued Arume 'we have a substance, remember it was shown to you?'

'You called it Vodoxium?'

'That's right Louis, let me explain what it is. It comes from the centre of our planet. There is only one external outlet, and it has to be handled carefully, as it has emotions. It has extreme powers, and energy. The energy I speak of generates our entire planet, it allows our crafts to travel through galaxies and black holes. It has the power to grow food, create water, heal, as well as sustain and enhance life, as you have seen.'

'How exactly does it have emotions and energy, and why don't we have it on earth?'

'For your first question Louis, we are not exactly sure how it fits together, all we do know that combined together with liquid crystal it is most powerful.'

'How do you get liquid crystal?'

'It's plentiful on Helomedes.'

Louis was fascinated.

'For your question about Earth and our energy we thought it over and over. The long history of the human race would not allow us to even contemplate introducing it. The wars already waged over resources has devastated the planet, our priority is to preserve the planet Earth. The Vodoxium has been examined thoroughly by our scientists for all its elements. However there still remains a mystery. We have been supporting other races for millions of years to keep them safe and sustainable.'

'So how old is your race? Sounds like you guys are ancient.'

'From all accounts and our ability to explore the universe it is possible we are extremely ancient. Because of the Vodoxium we are able to travel through black holes that sit at the centre of most galaxies. Dark matter are threads holding the universe together. Your own Milky way has a supermassive black hole in the middle, and time is not an issue for us anymore. Black holes are the gateway to new galaxies, and we can travel back in time and into the future.'

'That is incredible!' Louis was totally gobsmacked. 'So many life forms exist?'

'There is life everywhere Louis, suns and moons and viable planets. The atmospheres are different therefore lifeforms are very different, microbial organisms and indigenous lifeforms exist on most planets.'

Charlie listened intently.

'So, what you are saying is that we are in a spacecraft at the moment that can go anywhere out there, and we can do it in normal time and speed?'

'That is right Charlie, you are going to travel and see images that will leave your mind enthralled and exhausted.'

Louis was very quiet and thoughtful, his mind racing, trying to understand the journey he had travelled to get to this point in time.

'What is it that Charlie and me are meant to be doing? I kinda figure it's a little bit dangerous.'

Arume touched Louis's head gently with his exquisite hand. It was cool and surprisingly soft.

Does this have something to do with that missing sphere?'

'Yes Louis, let me explain.'

The boys settled back.

'I shall begin to explain what your mission is. Please stop me if you are confused or don't understand anything. For many years, as I mentioned before, we have been helping races on many planets. Our Vodoxium spheres have assisted their energy needs. We return the spheres to the stalactite dome for replenishment. You may not realise, but not all races are advanced. However, some are aggressive, without any emotions or empathy for each other or anything else. They can be extremely dangerous.'

Louis frowned.

'What do you mean about the emotions in the Vodoxium?'

'It's not fully understood, it's a form of communication. In the outer reaches of the third galaxy, there is a planet which is desolate, dark and cold. This planet is known as Dradask. The inhabitants match the climate. Please look to the pool. These beings are difficult to describe. We have not been on this planet, and the inhabitants live within the planet. They constantly tunnel and make chambers, that's as much as we know.'

The boys leant forward. Slowly a figure shrouded in mist became slightly visible. The first noticeable attribute was the creature's mouth. Large and round, rotating long sharp teeth, row upon row, something coming out of its mouth. The fog got thicker it was hard to see. They were a tall cylinder shaped, tentacles or something similar for feet then the vision was gone.

'Oh God, that was hideous, very unattractive.'

Louis nodded in agreement with a stunned Charlie.

'So, if they're so dumb, why are they of a concern?' asked Louis.

'Let me begin. Another race of beings from planet Aramist who we gave a small vial of Vodoxium to for their craft and one sphere for energy for their planet are intelligent, but fragile. The craft went close to planet Dradask, before the Vodoxium was fully applied. At this time, the Dradask moon was in a very bright phase and because it was close to the planet the craft lost control. The gravitational pull disabled the craft and it landed heavily as they couldn't reverse the ship in time. The Dradask appeared out of their tunnels and took over the ship. Distress signals reached our planet, due to the emotional element in the Vodoxium. It is our belief the Aramist will now be forced to fly the craft to wherever the Dradask want.'

'What is the likely outcome of this?' asked Louis.

'The Dradask are driven by food, therefore they will destroy all planets in their path. This race has eaten everything on their own planet. According to sources, they breed their own offspring to eat.'

'Shit, that's just sick,' said Louis.

'Yes, I agree,' said Arume 'however, we are not sure how they breed.'

'I guess we are going to find out,' mumbled Louis. 'What happened to the Aramist?'

'We're not sure.'

'And I guess we are going to meet them as well?' said Charlie.

'We hope to rescue them safely. The Dradask will force landings on each planet, killing and feeding until it's barren. One of those planets in their path is Earth. The forest, the food and the population could sustain them for years.'

'You mean the trees and stuff?'

'Yes Charlie, everything that lives in any form. They will multiply by the millions until the earth resembles Dradask. They don't have future visions for the future, only the present.'

'How do we know that they haven't already started on the way?'

'The Vodoxium on the spacecraft will react with that on our planet should they travel too near.'

Louis looked at Arume, his eyes searching Arume's face,

'We have to get that Vodoxium sphere, we have to stop the Dradask.'

There was a moment of silence, thoughts swirling and racing in each boy's brain.

Louis broke the silence.

'How the hell are two scrawny kids going to stop marauding aliens, getting on a spaceship, or another planet?'

'Training' said Arume.

'We gonna become athletes?' said Charlie with a silly laugh. 'We can challenge the Dradask.'

Charlie had a hearty laugh at himself, nerves running high, not really knowing how to react.

'Listen to me carefully. You boys will be fully prepared. Do you remember how you watched Esouli shape shift?'

'Are you saying we are going to learn that?'

Almost immediately their big friend appeared, accompanied by Fudgunkel standing tall, well as tall as he could. The boys jumped up and wrapped their arms around the big warrior.

'Well, it looks like someone is popular.'

Fudgunkel kicked the floor, feeling left out.

'Oh come here little dude.'

Charlie bent down and hugged him.

'Look out you're touching my suit!'

Louis laughed at the funny couple.

Arume spoke.

'Your friend – my warrior – is going to teach you how to shape shift and how to harness the power of Vodoxium. Your physical fitness will be assessed and improved. Tomorrow my friends your journey begins.'

'It's okay boys, don't look so worried.'

Esouli put his big hands on their shoulders.

'I'm here as always, you are safe, and I will make sure nothing happens to either of you.'

CHAPTER 24

'My God, you get more beautiful every day.'

Genevieve St Day laughed openly at her reflection in the full- length mirror, looking closely for any imperfections.

'Nothing. I am epitome of perfection. The perfect living Barbie doll.'

She hugged herself.

Looking again closely into the mirror she continued talking to herself.

'So, Mr Blackwell, I'm going to have fun playing with you. You will fall madly in love with me again, then I will destroy you.'

'Excuse me Miss St Day.'

'What is it?!'

'Your car is waiting downstairs.'

'Good! Clean up this mess and I want a massage when I get home. Make sure it is with my special oil.'

Rosa watched as her boss swept down the stairs and into the waiting limousine. Turning, she looked at the lavish bathroom and bedroom.

'Such a pig.'

Jason Blackwell sat back mesmerised by the beautiful woman across from him.

'It's kind of you to invite me to dinner Mr Blackwell. My accountant informed me of your business offer. I must say it is very generous.'

'Yes, Miss St Day...'

'Please...My name is Genevieve.'

Leaning forward she gently touched Jason's hand.

'I would really love to show you the model of the site.'

Jason Blackwell felt like a schoolboy in the presence of such a sophisticated beauty.

Rosa and Vivian sat together drinking tea, waiting for the ogre to return.

'I wish we could just go home and have a different life.'

'We could you know with all that secret paperwork.'

'No Viv, I think that could possibly backfire, they have too much money. Why do you think she is bothering with the past husband?'

'Who knows? She's so full of revenge. I wonder where the child is, you think it would be a priority. I found his address, but I'm waiting for her to ask.'

'It's amazing,' said Rosa.

'What?'

'To be who she is now, compared to how she looked and where she came from. That's what money can buy.'

Rosa started laughing.

'Maybe we could get transformed.'

Vivian got up flicking her hair and mimicking Genevieve's actions. Rosa then did the demanding and strutting, both then broke into hysterical of laughter.

CHAPTER 25

Bridget Sherwood sat across from the local solicitor, Stephen Colade, watching as he shuffled through papers pertaining to her house.

He was holding the demolition order and after what seemed like an eternity of beard rubbing, adjusted his glasses.

His conscious was now getting to him, and he was becoming increasingly uncomfortable. His bank account had increased considerably due to this development and investors wanting his advice on how to proceed. The solicitor shook his head, took off his glasses, sighed, and pulled together his best attempt at a sad, hopeless face.

'I'm afraid Bridget you would be better off taking the offer of $185,000.'

Bridget leant forward in her seat.

'Surely this can't be legal? I purchased this house legally and renovated it. What about my beautiful garden?'

'I know Miss Sherwood but unfortunately, in previous years there seems to have been some impropriety between developers and previous council employees.'

'That's not my concern.'

'Look you are dealing with people who have a lot of money and influence. You wouldn't stand a chance in court. Lastly, how would you pay me? I would need $60,000 upfront, just take the case.'

Bridget felt everything sink inside of her. She wanted to cry, she wanted to scream. Her throat ached with held back tears. She would not give this weasel the pleasure of seeing her destroyed. She got up gracefully, thanked the predator for his time and walked out.

Approaching the reception desk, she asked to settle the account.

'How much do I owe for this visit?'

'Oh, we can send an account out.'

'No. I'll pay now.'

The young receptionist flicked her hair, angry that someone would dare question her authority.

'Excuse me while I confirm your fee for today.'

Whilst waiting Bridget's eyes wandered around the office and she was immediately drawn to an image of a familiar sight. Sitting on the receptionist's desk was a photo of the area behind her house with a cover letter to Stephen Colade. Bridget moved sideways to try and read the print.

'Thank you for your interest in the proposal, you are invited to attend...' Miss Efficiency had covered the rest of the communication.

'That will be $190 thank you.'

'Oh, on second thoughts,' said Bridget in her best authoritative voice, 'you can send me an account.'

Getting into the car, she closed the door and burst into tears.

'You devious bastards! Karma can't come soon enough.'

Verbal explosions released her frustration between her heart wrenching sobs.

That evening, Bridget sat on the verandah in silence looking at her flourishing garden. The beautiful smells, the abundant wildflowers, it was near perfection. What the hell was she going to do? Tears gushed down her cheeks with overwhelming sadness. A noise broke the moment. A beautiful big Tawney frog mouth landed quietly on a branch. It settled, then made direct eye contact with Bridget. After a long pause, just looking at each other, Bridget decided she may as well talk it out with the visitor.

She told the owl how much she missed Louis and Charlie and hoped they were okay.

'I remember,' said Bridget to her guest, 'I was told that someone would be looking out for me, I hope that's true my friend, because the bulldozers are going to destroy this beautiful Shangrila.'

The night bird responded with a soft noise of acknowledgement.

Bridget couldn't help but laugh.

'Thank-you my friend for listening.'

That night strange events happened at the lake that would reveal themselves at a moment in time when needed.

CHAPTER 26

Jason Blackwell felt intoxicated, but not by alcohol, instead the beautiful woman that lay sleeping in his bed. She was famous and he was about to become famous. A perfect couple. Jason stood in front of the mirror, studying himself.

'I still look really good.'

He flexed his biceps.

'The muscles in my legs are still hard, the six pack had reduced slightly, I can get that back with a little extra effort.'

That tiny bit of grey hair gave him that distinguished look. Standing back, he admired himself once more.

Unashamedly he said aloud, 'Mr Blackwell you are extraordinary.'

'Yes, you are Mr Blackwell.'

A tiny voice came from behind and soft arms wrapped around his firm abs. Genevieve moved into the light semi-naked. Together they stood looking at their reflections.

'We are, shall we say, 'The Beautiful People', don't you think Miss St Day?'

'I couldn't agree more Mr Blackwell.'

The doorbell chimed interrupting 'The Beautiful People' gazing at themselves.

'That will be my car,' said Genevieve, gathering her shoes.

Jason reminded Genevieve, 'I will pick you up at 3pm and we can go and look at your future investment.'

'Sounds lovely, I shall be ready.'

Genevieve laid back in her milk bath laughing and talking to herself.

'He's falling in love with me already, it was so easy.'

'Did you say something Miss St Day?' Rosa's voice came from the bedroom.

'Oh my God, you wouldn't understand. I doubt anyone could love you, an ugly old housemaid.'

Genevieve continued, laughing hysterically.

'I'm such a bitch and I love it.'

Rosa, listening on the other side of the door, shook her head.

'I'm ready to get out. Bring me my towels.'

Genevieve stood out of the tub, her glossy hair pulled high, a beautiful sheen on her perfect body.

Rosa looked at her thinking, 'Yes! You may be beautiful in the outside, but you are dark and ugly on the inside.'

'I'm being picked up at 3pm, I want to look seductive, but not overdone. I think I will have my hair up and wear those soft slacks with a seductive blouse. Now hurry up! My makeup needs to be alluring. I want my skin massaged in sweet oils. I want to smell good enough to taste, oh, and I think pearls.'

'I want, I want, I want, never a 'thank you', never a nice voice, never treated like a human.' Rosa whispered under her breath.

Jason looked across at his passenger. She was gorgeous. Genevieve returned his gaze, smiling as the BMW convertible chewed up the road, gliding around corners with ease. At that moment on the bend Genevieve began having a flashback. She was suddenly filled with panic.

'Could you slow down slightly, I suffer a tad from motion sickness. Besides, I want to take in the view.'

'Oh, of course. I'm sorry, what was I thinking? My first wife was injured badly in a car accident.'

Genevieve nearly choked.

'Oh, you were married?'

'Yes, she was a model.'

'Really, what was she like?'

'She was attractive, but I'm afraid that was about it!'

'What do you mean?'

'Her beauty didn't hide the fact that she was selfish, self-centred and oh, so boring.'

Genevieve felt her anger rise. Fortunately, her acting training saved the moment.

'Where is she now?'

'Last I heard she was living in public housing, drinking herself to death.'

'Why would she do that?'

'She sustained a lot of scars and burns. She wallows in nothing but self-pity. She felt there was nothing more in life than looking beautiful. I knew she was never going to be famous, but she couldn't see that.'

'Do you see her anymore?'

Genevieve's anger was bubbling and boiling internally.

'Bloody hell no! She wanted me gone, so I moved on and up.'

'Did you have children?'

'Yeah, we got one. Got together once after the accident. It was just pity sex really. After I'd left her mother phoned me telling me she had become pregnant. I've never seen it, nor do I want to.'

The BMW slowed down.

'Here we are. This will be the entrance. The shack with the overgrown crap will be bulldozed shortly and this my beautiful woman, is our future.'

Genevieve got out of the car looking around, watching Jason, the contempt for him rising with each breath. Pretending she was totally absorbed, she turned to Jason smiling.

'Yes, I see what you mean Jason. My imagination is running wild.'

Bridget watched from her bedroom window as the two people pointed, gestured, and laughed. Continuing to watch them, she then recognised the man from his picture in the papers and on TV.

'Blackwell. Could that be Louis's Father?'

She began, talking to no one.

She studied his looks. Bridget got the binoculars for a better look. They certainly were a stunning couple. Studying his face, Bridget saw something of Louis. She turned the binoculars to Genevieve.

'God! She is the perfect Barbie doll.'

Jason put away the plans and escorted Barbie to the car. Genevieve pointed at Bridget's house.

'It looks like something out of a fairy tale.'

They both laughed and drove off.

'How about lunch at my townhouse? It's all been arranged, all your favourites!'

'So, you've been investigating me?'

'Just so I can impress you.'

'Well, I would love to have lunch with you Mr Blackwell.'

Genevieve's plans were unfolding perfectly. Her training kept her emotions in check.

CHAPTER 27

Bridget had finished packing. Everything she owned was now in storage, with her animals housed at Isobel's safely. Simone was enjoying her extended family and couldn't wait for Bridget to move in.

Bridget took a last walk around her garden, saying goodbye to all she had loved, nurtured and created with her own imagination and hands. The tears would not stop. The pain could be felt in every cell of her body. Bridget's internal voice told her to be strong, as more tears and hopelessness flowed.

A voice behind broke into the sadness. Isobel placed an arm around her shoulder.

'Let's go for a walk to the lake.'

Bridget smiled, wiping away the last of her tears. Together they walked to the lake and the mountain.

'My God Isobel, I miss Louis.'

'I was just about to say the same thing.'

'I hope they're safe. I hope we've done the right thing.'

Isobel's words were lost to the wind. She stopped listening.

'What's wrong Izzy?'

'The wind. There's something, a message. All is not as it seems. Come on, let's keep walking.'

'Is it bad?' said Bridget.

'It's not bad, but it's incredibly mysterious.'

'It's your ancient aboriginal instincts again. Have I told you how amazing you are?'

'I know Bridge, I'm the Black Witch with a lot of hair. I would have burnt well!'

Both women giggled at their silly words. The closer they came to the lake, the more the tension and anxiety began to wane. Pushing their way through shrubs and grasses, they finally exposed the hidden beauty of the lake.

Animals of all species gathered around the lake. Hundreds of birds perched silent in the tall trees. A Tawney Frog Mouth and an eagle rested on the ancient Bunya pine. The two women merely stood there, devouring the scene before them. Isobel began a slow chant, her arms open wide, then silence fell all around. Bridget watched without comment, it was a glorious magical moment. The environment turned a strange amber colour, everything seemed transfixed, as if watching in awe. It was exotic and haunting at the same time. Isobel, in a trance like state spoke softly.

'There is a hidden gallery on the face of the mountain secreted away in a cavern.'

As she spoke a path cleared to follow. Together the women made their way up the mountain, the path still clearing as they moved on. All eyes watched as they moved higher and higher in silence. They kept going.

'We're nearly there Bridge. You alright?'

'Yep, right behind you.'

'This is it!'

Exhausted but excited, Isobel's face was a picture of pure delight.

Behind what could only be described as a screen of rock face, hid a cave. High on the ceiling of the mountain itself, ancient drawings, some with ghostly faces, seemed to follow as you moved. Hands of different proportions, beautiful circular dot art, so many recognisable animals.

Isobel spoke softly.

'These are religious and ceremonial aspects of life. This is so important to my people. It's an integral part of our traditional life. I can guarantee these have never been recorded. They could possibly date back 2,500BC.'

'My God Isobel, this is incredible.'

Bridget's eyes took in this beautiful ancient vision.

'You know what this means Bridgy?!'

'Yeah, my thoughts are forming, and the words 'Sacred Site' is what I am hearing.'

'Spot on girlfriend! Let's just sit a while and absorb all this.'

Isobel found a place to sit and look out over the lake and feel the awesome power. She found her mobile in her shoulder bag and began a lengthy text.

'You texting someone important?'

'Oh yeah. I'm going to make sure this becomes international news.'

Bridget laughed turning her face to the sun, trying not to think of her own problems.

'You know it's weird Izzy, to think our boys went into this mountain and all that has happened. No one would believe us.'

'You're right there girl.' said Isobel, turning to look at her friend.

'We would be labelled something popular and put on prescribed chemicals.'

The women giggled at their compatible sense of humour. They sat in quiet reflection. Movement in the lake caught Bridget's eye, something swirled in the water creating unusual patterns.

Bridget's voice reached squealing pitch, hitting Isobel in the arm.

'Look!'

She pointed to the lake.

'Holy shit. What was I saying about prescribed chemicals?'

Over the lake a fog was forming. The waters started to swirl more vigorously.

'Something is forming,' said Bridget.

'It's a hologram.'

Isobel stood to get a better look.

The vision was coming together with more visual clarity.

'It's my house...and my garden.'

It was perfect, only lasting less than a minute, then it disappeared.

'What does this mean Isobel?'

'I think we will find out soon.'

She was not feeling a hundred percent confident, but also did not want to worry her friend.

The animals that stood quietly around the lake had silently disappeared into the surrounding bushland. Birds had taken synchronised flight like blankets flying into space. All was quiet as the two women made their way back.

Halfway back from the lake, Isobel suddenly stopped. Standing in front of her, she held Bridget's forearms, looking into her eyes. Both could hear the noise in the distance. Heavy machinery was pushing and shoving. Mass destruction. Bridget's life was being reduced to a pile of rubble.

Shaking in her arms, Bridget looked into Isobel's beautiful brown eyes.

'It's done, isn't it?'

'Come on, hold my hand. Just be very strong, your life will continue. Your child will come home. The power is on our side.'

They came to the opening together.

'Don't look.'

Isobel's voice was firm and controlled.

'We are going straight to my car, get in and don't look back.'

Bridget did as she was told. Once in the car, Bridget held her face in her hands as a torrent of agonising tears began to fall. Isobel's tears however were those of anger.

CHAPTER 28

Jason Blackwell lay back in his black silk sheets, long strands of blonde hair spread across his chest.

'You are a beautiful woman, Miss St Day.'

'Thank you, Mr Blackwell.'

They both laughed, in a state of euphoria after spending an exhaustive afternoon together.

Jason's phone chimed indicating a message. Jason opened the message he was sent, together they watched Bridget's home and life being destroyed.

'Who owned the shack anyway?'

'Just some bloody alternative tree hugging idiot.'

'Did the idiot have a name?'

Genevieve giggled as she watched the trees, shrubs tumbling to their deaths.

'*Bridget something*. Who cares about that, we're about to become very wealthy.'

Genevieve rolled onto her back, smiling to herself. She knew exactly who owned it. Money can buy you anything. The department had forbidden her to have contact with Louis or know who his foster parent is. No one tells Genevieve St Day 'She can't.' She laughed out loud.

Jason rolled over.

'And what is so funny my beautiful lady?'

Genevieve playing her part to perfection held Jason and demanded to be pleasured once again. Jason Blackwell could not be happier everything was falling into place.

CHAPTER 29

The pods opened slowly. In unison both boys awakened, tiny fingers poked Louis in his cheek.

'Get up, come on. Get up!'

Charlie sat up watching and laughing.

'Oh look, it's the funny little Christmas weirdo.'

'Okay, okay. I'm up! I feel different' said Louis, scratching his head and smiling.

'Yeah, me too.'

'Come on.'

Fudgunkel stood with his hands on his hips, moving from foot to foot rubbing his tiny hands.

'Arume awaits.'

'Well then, lead the way.'

Louis fell into line.

Arume and the big warrior waited together, they looked incredible and fascinating in their form. The boys joined them and made themselves comfortable.

Louis spoke.

'We both feel different after being in the pods. Has something changed?'

The boys were directed to look into the crystal pool. Arume spoke in his eloquent voice.

'We are preparing you for the journey ahead and what you need to know. After your time in the pods, your bodies have changed temporarily. Your bodies are stronger and ready to be trained. You are both aware Esouli can shape shift. He has enormous power. You too will have these powers; this will help to end the Dradask's journey of destruction.'

The boys remained quiet, unable to make a noise.

'I need you to both breathe deeply. This is a lot to take in. I want you to look at each other's eyes.'

The boys followed instructions.

'Holy shit Louis, your eyes are all different colours, just like the pool.'

'I know Charlie. Yours are the same.'

'Through the pod process your blood has been infused with an element of Vodoxium.'

'Does this mean we are no longer human?'

Louis was searching Arume's face.

'Just temporarily adjusted. In the next few weeks, you will be training to learn how to use your powers and strengthen your bodies.'

The boys were fascinated with the colours under their skins. Charlie had a light bulb moment.

'Can we still eat food, and you know, the other things?'

'Yes Charlie, you can eat and poop.'

'That's good 'cos I'm starving.'

The training soon commenced. Firstly, weights. They were amazed at their strength. Yoga and stretching followed. They learnt the extraordinary benefits of meditation.

Esouli demonstrated ancient martial arts originating since the beginning of time. This included deadly self-defence that was extremely intricate and lethal. The next few weeks were spent under strict instruction.

'What I need you to do now is concentrate on changing into some other form.'

Together they concentrated, Louis was thinking hard of what he could turn into. He remembered the eagle from the car trip with his mother. He remembered how the sight of it calmed him. A tingling sensation travelled all through his body, like intense goosebumps. His organs started to move. Feathers sprouted from his convulsing body. He was falling into a dark tunnel. Momentarily, Louis felt himself change. His eyesight was brilliant, his mouth was gone, his feet and hands were gone. And there he was, a beautiful wedge tail eagle.

'Oh man, this is crazy shit!'

'Charlie it's now your turn.'

Charlie missed his sister, so his concentration began. The sensation was warm, his internals moved, his skin tingled and instantly Simone Crane was looking at the eagle. They could do nothing but study each other intently.

Louis flapped his wings. He could feel the power and he wanted to feel what it was like to fly.

'Imagine you're outside.' Esouli instructed.

The freedom was astounding. It was euphoric. He had never felt so free. Charlie had already changed back to himself and stood there watching Louis. He too then changed into an eagle. Together the boys in their new forms went higher into the sky, it was magnificent. After a not so delicate landing, their next skill to learn was conjuring.

Lost in deep in concentration, Charlie thought of the ocean on a clear summer day and surfing the perfect wave. Slowly his favourite place became a reality before his eyes. It was like standing on a beach watching himself surf. It was so clear and real. He was smiling.

'Damn I'm good!'

Louis laughed.

'Yeah, you are.'

Louis decided he wanted to see his grandmother's home. He could see it so clearly when he closed his eyes. Upon opening his eyes, not only was it the house and garden, but his grandmother was gardening as well. She looked up in a quizzical manner.

'She knows I'm here.'

Tears welled in Louis's eyes, they made eye contact.

Arume and Esouli looked at each other. Nothing was said, just silence.

As Louis wiped away the tears, the vision faded. Charlie put his arm around Louis's shoulder.

Arume spoke softly.

'For your next ability, and this may frighten you as you both have Vodoxium in your veins. It can be used as a weapon. If you pierce your skin, and let it run down your hand imagine what weapon you need, and it will materialise.'

For the next 6 weeks Louis and Charlie practiced their abilities and exercised and tuned their bodies. Esouli and the boys went through hundreds of shapes, from elephants and insects to birds and cars. They visualised incredible scenes. High rise buildings, herds of cattle, forests, even moles tunnelling under the ground. The boys laughed in hysterics. Esouli couldn't help himself as he joined in. Naturally they revelled in the weapons and soon became very proficient in all their skills. Arume watched silently. He then called everyone together.

'Today we will look into the pool. You will see the galaxies you will venture to. You will see the Dradask armies, and their spacecraft taken from another life form. You will see their planet and the history of devastation the Dradask have caused.'

'Has there been contact?'

'Yes Louis, they are moving, and now you can view them clearly. The first vision is a planet, a dead black planet. What you are seeing is the Dradask planet. The vegetation is gone, all native species are gone, no water, no microbial species, everything is dead, it has disintegrated.'

'Could it be restored?' Louis studied it intently.

'With a lot of hard work, however it is too far gone, and it will subject to dust storms and floods. They cultivate a certain amount of their offspring to eat, they are absolute killing machines.'

Before their eyes from the pool, a vision of horror formed. The boys faces said it all. The image was hideous and they had a close-up view of pure evil. Standing seven foot tall, they looked like grey cylinders with a long neck and a big dome head cutting in sharply to the neck. Long slanting eyes, starting from where a nose should be, going to the top of their head. Long thin arms, connected to three long tapering claw-like fingers, the middle one much longer, with each claw rotating. They didn't have legs. They moved on a circle of tentacles which rotated to give them the appearance of hovering. Worst of all, was the Dradask mouth. A large round opening, that expanded to eat large prey. Sharp pointed teeth, also rotated, row upon row, a strange crunching sound each time their mouths opened. The nose was a hole with flaps that opened and closed.

'What's that on the side of their heads?' asked Louis.

'Gills,' said Arume. 'They have adapted to water using the rotation of unusual legs to gain movement.'

'They are so ugly. They couldn't think this shit up in Hollywood.' Charlie gasped.

'I agree,' said Louis.

The Dradask vision slowly faded. The boys could feel each other's tension, each unsure about what was in front of them.

Arume spoke quietly.

'Remember these skills and abilities that are now yours, you have powers beyond your human heritage. Be confident in that. Please.'

Arume gestured towards the crystal pool that swirled in brilliant liquid form.

Another planet appeared, desolate in appearance.

'This is the planet Lanorigal. They colonised this once fertile planet. They ate all the vegetation. Skeletons formed that looked similar to that of burnt out high- rise buildings.'

'It doesn't look like vegetation,' said Louis.

'It's a form of cultivated protein stacked and preserved for their future. The Dradask left a few untouched because they were preoccupied with catching the Lanorigal beings.'

'Did they eat all of them?' asked Louis.

'They captured many of the little Lanorigal beings. They have them enslaved to look after the spawning Dradask. The Lanorigal are forced to produce their larvae to also feed the Dradask.'

'You said the Dradask spawn. Can you show us how?' asked Louis.

'Oh dude, this will be ugly,' Charlie screwed up his face.

In the crystal pool the boys witnessed a mass of white foam with black blobs. Slowly the slimy blobs burst open. First to emerge were the claws, cutting away at the embryo. Then the familiar sound of the Dradask, crunching, rotating, demanding little mouths. Hovering above the hungry mouths a wasp like creature with tiny hands, five fingers, and no thumbs. With a beautiful face similar to a lemur, elegant blue wings kept them in flight. The little hands dropped white objects into the ugly, crunching, demanding mouths. The eyes of the little Lanorigal reflected fear and horror.

'Oh God, no' said Louis, close to tears.

'Those poor little creatures.'

'Can we rescue them?' pleaded Charlie.

'This is our hope.' Arume continued.

'Now you know how important it is to rescue these harmless beings, or they face extinction.'

'Is that the same craft?' asked Louis.

'No and it's a mystery to us Louis. It's not a craft that we are familiar with.'

A vision of a craft appeared in the crystal liquid. Three circular discs joined together by some convoluted tunnels. This allowed the superbly advanced engineering disc to change direction with ease.

Arume spoke.

'Each disc is powered by an unusual energy field. It could be that they are using the captive beings to navigate the ship. The beings that designed and built the spaceship are advanced, but may be passive, or they may not exist at all now. The silver discs that make up the ship are radiant and mysterious at the same time.'

'It could be their new diet?'

'That's very intuitive of you Louis, and most likely true.'

Arume was studying the information screen, something was coming in, and he looked troubled.

'This is worse than I expected.'

Esouli stepped forward to observe.

'What is it?'

'They have the Vodoxium and adapted it as a power source.'

Arume pointed out the position of the crystal, it was pulsating into the ship's system panel.

'This confirms they have captured another race and another space craft.'

'How long will it last?' Esouli answered.

'More than enough to get to Helomedes and other planets.'

Esouli and Arume glanced at each other.

Charlie spoke up in a small voice.

'And kill everything on the way. They could get to Earth.'

The silence told Louis what he needed to know.

'It's certainly troubling times.'

Arume's voice was quiet with concern.

'At this stage it remains unclear who and what is on board the strange spaceship.'

Louis and Charlie were troubled. They took time out to talk out their feelings.

'Sometimes Charlie, I can't believe how I got here. One minute I'm a welfare case, then I'm preparing to go into space to try and stop the destruction of Earth, planets and aliens. How the hell did this happen?'

'Yeah, I know what you mean. There I was, a skinny black kid on a skateboard just chillin', then this dude turns up, he's a bit weird, then as time passes weird shit starts to happen. So! Do you think that this was kinda sorted before we even met?'

'You know Charlie, I think it was organised before I was born!'

Charlie sat upright.

'I'm terrified Louis. Why do you suppose it's us that they picked out?'

'Planets.'

'What do you mean 'Planets'?'

'The alignments, the time, so we're kinda special!'

'Do you think we can do this?'

'Well, if you remember the abilities we have, I think we can!'

'Pity we didn't have a thousand Esouli dudes!' Charlie laughed, amused by his own funnies.

Louis put his arm around Charlie's shoulders.

'You know Charlie, I would never let anything happen to you.'

'Yeah, I know Bro. That's 'cos you ain't got any other friends.'

The boys laughed together, having a mock fight.

Arume remained looking into the crystal pool, furrowing his brow. He didn't understand or recognise the spaceship the Dradask stole, nor did he know who the species were onboard or their planet.

That night everyone ate together. The boys' favourite food was served, and the diners were relaxed. Arume waited for a lull in the conversation.

'I have an announcement.'

All eyes turned to him.

'In three days we will be leaving planet Earth, all preparations have been made.'

He looked at the boys.

'Upon commencement of the journey, Esouli will be instructing you both on how to fly the craft. This mission has just become urgent, as you have witnessed. At this moment in time, considering everything that has happened in your lives, I need to explain why we need human beings on this mission.'

'Well,' said Louis, 'I've been wondering why we have been selected.'

'Yep.' said Charlie. 'We're not exactly hero stuff.'

Arume began.

'In the history of planet Earth and the evolving of its inhabitants, it has become clear that it's time for the human being to transition to a higher enlightened intelligence.'

'That would be because of our continuing history of wars and destruction of the planet.'

'Yes Louis, unfortunately money and power continue to dominate. The human being is changing, the loss of compassion for each other and the planet that sustains every living thing. It has become critical. Having said that, there are many among the human race that are enlightened and have the vision. They are struggling to make any advancement. There is a spiralling desperation to exist and survive amongst your people. This will be devastating, as the greedy will be complacent and watch the lesser people struggle and die. Your oceans are dying, your forests are disappearing, and your lands are being destroyed for what lies beneath. Powerful greed controls your planet. What you two are going to see on your journey, will be extraordinary to witness. You will travel into the Milky Way and enter into a massive black hole. This is the gateway to ten thousand galaxies of many shapes and colours. You will see other beings existing in perfect harmony with their planet. This I want you to study because Earth has to change.'

'But how can just the two of us change anything?' asked Louis.

'After your journey, and what you experience, you will have knowledge to take you into your futures.'

'Will we still have our abilities?' asked Louis.

'You will have them, and you will have guidance.'

'So I know why Louis was chosen, but why me?' Charlie queried.

'You have a pure soul, Charlie. You flow with compassion and you're Louis's friend, as you will be for your lifetime. You two need each other and you vibrate at the same level, your paths were predestined.'

Esouli spoke softly, his big soft eyes looking intently at the boys.

'I know we seem mysterious and your understanding of us is very limited. Our race is very ancient, we have been in existence for many millenniums. This is not our first mission to Earth, nor the first time we have gone to war with an invading species. You are not the first humans to join us.'

Louis and Charlie's face dropped with shock.

'Really, are they still around? Do they remember?'

Esouli laughed.

'One question at a time.'

There was silence, the big warrior glancing from one to the other.

'Your mothers and your grandmother Louis.'

'Holy crap, our mothers.'

'I knew there was something special about my grandmother, I just knew. Wow!'

Charlie and Louis, laughing, then serious, then laughing.

'Do they remember everything?'

Charlie had now broken into full conversation.

'So.... when they acted all surprised and stuff, they knew?'

Esouli put his hands on their shoulders.

'Not everything, they remember what we want them to and when.'

'I can smell her perfume. That's telling me she is around somewhere and if they can do weird space stuff so can we.'

'Dude, everything we do is weird.'

The two absorbed all the information.

Charlie sighed.

'I'm just glad the big fella is with us.'

'Amen to that Buddy!'

The boys now felt more relaxed and confident, the knowledge just imparted giving them the strength to face the unknown.

Bridget, Isobel and Simone enjoyed being on the verandah of Isobel's beach house, the leftovers of dinner still on the table, everyone knowing tonight was special.

Simone relaxed quietly looking up at the sky. It was clear and the stars glittered by the millions.

'Will they be okay?' asked Simone.

Isobel pulled her closed, kissing her gently on the forehead.

'They will be safe my baby girl.'

They waited in silence, the oceans waters breathing in and out caressing the soft sands. It was calming and safe. Anticipation could be felt like a living touch.

The big tawny fluttered gently to his landing in the pine tree, swaying and whispering into the night. His constant companion touched down beside him. No one on the verandah was surprised. Together they settled to wait.

It was getting late. Lights were going out as people went to bed. Silence fell all around as night birds went quiet and the ocean ceased to pulsate. Clouds descended with haste, dark and turbulent. Everyone sat upright, all eyes turned to the east and Simone wrapped her arms around both women.

'They will be alright, this I know,' said Bridget.

'Yes,' said Isobel.

A white light spread across the eastern sky, lighting up the mountain. Time stood still. It had begun. The tip of a golden triangle appeared; it was a powerful image. Golden, spinning, quiet and unobtrusive. As it emerged in full, the spinning increased, so powerful the human eye could not hold the vision. Then it was gone. A slipstream of brilliant colours soon vapourised into nothing.

They all let out their breath, the night sounds resumed.

'I wonder how many people saw that?'

'Only us my beautiful girl, it's kinda weird, and one day soon I will explain it.'

The ocean roared back into life. Isobel, Bridget and Simone held hands. A pagan prayer of safety and return was being said together. The two birds took flight together, heading towards the mountain, their silhouette disappearing into night. Isobel and Bridget traded smiles.

CHAPTER 30

Genevieve St Day watched the world from her apartment window. Everything was perfect. Jason had fallen in love with her, the investment was going to make her a massive fortune. She was to make her appearance at Sydney's Fashion Week. Every magazine of notoriety hounded her for a statement, a photo, anything to get her on the front page. Genevieve loved to play with them. She decided to model one outfit, only from Paris.

Genevieve's thoughts fell away as Vivian's voice interrupted her daydream.

'Excuse me Miss St Day, the editor from Marie Claire would like to speak to you about your visit to Sydney.'

Genevieve swung around.

'Oh, for God's sake Vivian, just tell her I will call her back. How many times do I have to tell you? You idiot!'

Vivian stood staring at her boss. She couldn't move.

'What the hell is wrong with you?!'

'Your face.' Vivian pointed. 'It's your face!'

Genevieve pushed her aside to get to the mirror. Vivian stumbled, overbalanced and fell down five stairs, hitting her head against the wall. The scream she heard was ugly, like something facing slaughter.

'No, no, no! This can't be happening! Vivian, get in here now!'

Smashing could be heard, more screaming, hysterical demands.

'Get my plastic surgeon on the phone. Get an appointment. Get my jet ready. Get everything ready. NOW!!'

Tears streamed down Genevieve's twisted face, she talked incessantly to herself, telling herself to calm down. Vivian came to the bedroom door, terror on her face.

'Don't just stand there, get me a scarf to cover my face! I have to get out of here without being seen.'

The private jet left within the hour. Genevieve was sedated. Vivian arranged her appointment with a leading surgeon in America, recommended by the surgeons from the Chalet.

Vivian and Rosa stood by her bed looking at Genevieve sleeping.

'What the hell is wrong with her? Why is her face sliding off her bones?'

'I guess something came undone.'

Genevieve's right eye was on her cheek folded in skin. Her mouth hung open, flaccid skin forming a gully for saliva to dribble into. A fold of skin lay on the pillow, it quivered when she moved. Genevieve snorted, her breathing laboured due to loose skin falling around her nose.

They tiptoed out and closed the door, Vivian poured them both a stiff bourbon and dry.

'My God Vivian, she called us ugly!'

'I know Rosa.'

'Do you think the surgeon can fix that ugly mess in there?'

The two women sat, nervous tension dragging on their emotions, waiting for her to wake.

'Imagine if the world of fashion and Hollywood could see her now.'

'Oh my God. That would destroy her. Let's get some rest Rosa, before the frenzy begins.'

Genevieve prepared to exit her private jet. Her face covered with a scarf and wearing large sunglasses, a private car waited her arrival. She demanded the car be as close to the jet as possible, including the darkest tint on the windows. Her recommended surgeon was ready and awaiting her arrival.

'Look Miss St Day, I'll be honest with you, the damage is extensive. I can't guarantee you will look precisely as before. There has been tearing in the soft tissue, we will need a specialist eye surgeon. I have organised a microsurgeon and a significant team of experts. You may not have full sensation to the right side of your face.'

Genevieve sat up slowly, her hands shaking, a tremor in her voice.

'Well perhaps Dr Lester I should return to Switzerland to surgeons who can fix this.'

'I'm sorry Miss St Day, this surgery is going to be difficult for any experienced surgeon, we will seek guidance from your Swiss surgeons.'

'I see,' said Genevieve. 'Well Dr Lester, how soon can you get started?'

'I will need to contact surgeons and schedule your surgery. We will need to take photos and have in-depth conversations on how to proceed and plan your surgery.'

'Before you leave Dr Lester, you are aware I am a wealthy woman, I can pay for the best and I expect the best.'

Dr Lester had a slight look of disdain on his own face.

'Of course, Miss St Day. We shall inform your secretary when we are ready to proceed.'

'Yes, good. Send that fool in will you on your way out. Oh, and another thing I would appreciate your haste with this. I am important in the world of fashion and celebrities. I demand total confidentially; my lawyer will see to that.'

Dr Lester closed the door without comment.

Genevieve had a private apartment at the hospital. Vivian and Rosa's days were filled with abuse and demands. Genevieve thought about her days before her face fell. Jason Blackwell played a prominent role. It was his fault, all his ideas. The beach, wanting to show her off to the public and the paparazzi. The late nights, the lovemaking. The more she thought about it, the more her anger increased.

'Excuse me, Miss St Day.'

'What?!'

'Mr Blackwell's on the phone again.'

'Give it here!'

Vivian hid out of sight to listen into the conversation.

'Hello Jason.' Genevieve's voice as sweet as honey.

'I'm so sorry, I had to leave in haste. I blame my stupid secretary for this. I promised my favourite charities that I would be involved at a hands on level to help raise money.'

Vivian leaned against the wall, disgusted at her horrible lies.

Jason got off the phone to Genevieve, sitting back in his large leather chair, a pleasing smile on his face. What a perfect wife she will make. A beautiful woman, well known celebrity across the planet AND she does charity work.

'Well, after all, that's what wealthy people do to look as though they care.'

Jason laughed out loud.

'The perfect politician's wife.'

A knock at the door made Jason sit up.

'Yes?'

Jill opened the door with some trepidation.

'It's Miss Wills, your son's mother on the phone again.'

'Put it through,' Jason waved Jill away.

'What the hell do you want now?'

Jason roared down the phone his face flushing red.

The response on the other end was equally as loud.

'Your son has been caught with cocaine in his room at that fancy school you pay for and I need money.'

'I just need you two out of my life.'

'Well just give me what I want. If you don't, we might surface in your important life and your fancy woman may not be so keen on you. Just donate to the school as usual and fill up my bank account.'

The phone went dead.

Something went crashing against the wall in Jason's office. Jill sat unperturbed at her desk. This was the usual reaction when Miss Will's called.

Jason rang the private school and spoke to the principal.

'Mr Atwell, this is Jason Blackwell, Tristan's father. I believe Tristan has not been complying with your rules once again.'

'Mr Blackwell I'm afraid this is most serious. Tristan has been selling cocaine to our younger students.'

Jason was flushing red with anger but remained silent.

'We have many parents unhappy and demanding that we take action. To date we have kept your son's name out of this debacle. It's become apparent none of the boys are willing to give up his name. Mr Blackwell your son is driving a brand-new Lexus. He does not attend class. He is just boarding here without commitment. The board has met a unanimous decision has been made that your son has to be expelled, never to return.'

A red flush travelled like an elevator up Jason's neck to his face. Explosive anger swirling in his brain, then that voice of reason jumped on his brain.

'Remember who you want to be.'

Jason exhaled slowly.

'Yes, I understand, and I am so sorry my son has caused this shame. I accept your decision and I thank you for your discretion. I'll see to it that Tristan is removed.'

Jason put the phone down gently then picked up his paperweight and pegged it at the wall, smashing Tristan's smiling face to the floor.

'Jill, could you come in here.'

Jill sighed once again, gathered her notebook and entered the vibrating office.

'Yes, Mr Blackwell?'

'I want you to take my car with my driver and inform my son he is expelled.'

'Shouldn't you do that Mr Blackwell? He's your son.'

'I don't have a son and I do not wish to see him. He's dealing drugs and I have to distance myself. He could ruin my future and I will never let that happen. Now go!'

Jill and the driver Eric arrived at the palatial entrance to Tristan's school. Jill felt nervous, this should not be part of her job.

She and Eric waited and waited. Mr Atwell finally opened the heavy oak door and beckoned them into his office. George Atwell indicated for Jill and Eric to sit. After a long sigh, George settled into his chair.

'It appears Tristan Blackwell has left of his own accord. His belongings and car have gone.'

'I see,' said Jill in her best authoritative voice.

George Atwell pushed a large envelope towards Jill.

'This is all the information on Tristan's progress report in all his studies. Now if you could please relay to Mr Blackwell my sincere regrets in this most unfortunate event. Please assure him that this incident will remain confidential.'

George Atwell was anxious to have these people out of his office. He had to deal with some overprotective wealthy parents.

Jill made the phone call when back in the car. Jason's response was calm.

'Well, he must have enough money to make his own way.'

Jason's thoughts swirled around his son Tristan and how he could ruin his future in politics. He examined his feelings, he felt nothing for Tristan. He was a product of a drunken mistake. His death would be a relief.

George Atwell closed his heavy door and turned the lock, finally he had talked around the disgruntled parents. Unlocking his top drawer, George pulled out a sachet of white powder, relief would soon be his, he was going to that good place in his brain. He was going to miss Tristan Blackwell. Thank God for mobile phones!

CHAPTER 31

Esouli, Louis and Charlie relaxed in the oversized chairs, before them simply an array of stars and space. A huge clear panel was in front of them with lines and number moving, redirecting coordinates all dictating the journey ahead. Planet Earth could be seen below, everything could be seen whilst the craft was opaque.

'This is totally mad,' said Charlie 'it does not feel like we're inside anything.'

Esouli smiled and flicked his finger over the dancing lines on the panel. The craft fell to darkness.

'The ship can blend into any environment undetected.'

'Yep. Reckon that will come in handy,' said Charlie.

'Very soon we will be leaving Earth's solar system.'

Louis was busy working and studying the flight panel.

'We are going to enter the Milky Way and enter a massive black hole. This will take us to the next galaxy. It's going to get very dangerous because of the extreme energy. The black holes your scientists talk about are real and they are dangerous, especially to Earth's limited technology and fuel systems. However, with Vodoxium and the energy it creates, including the design of our craft, dangers are greatly limited. Galaxies are elliptical in shape.'

Esouli leaned forward, touching the panel to show the diagram.

'They are like a spiral. The energy in further galaxies is very powerful, as are the black holes. That is what connects the galaxies. They are gateways to the universe.'

'So, this means,' said Louis, 'that we can just keep going?'

'We can, but we are not certain who or what is that far away.'

'What are we going to see?' asked Louis.

'You are going to see millions of planets, all different in size. You will see suns, moons, with darkness and light changing in an instant. We must remember we are on a mission. Many planets are dust and minerals. Others are fertile and thriving with life. You will see advanced civilisations not relating to any human form.'

Louis sat back and sighed.

'Sup dude?'

Charlie's smiling face looking quizzically at Louis.

'So many questions, so much I need to know and understand.'

'Yeah, I know what you mean. Like, what are we gonna eat and drink?'

Without warning Arume's face appeared.

'Are you troubled Louis?'

He spun around followed by Charlie.

'You can see us?'

'Of course.'

'You are so clear, and yet so far away.'

'Is something bothering you Louis?'

'I have always wondered about our mothers and my Nan, and any connection with this?'

'Yep, what he said!' Charlie throwing in his support.

The hologram stirred to life. Two girls aged around ten years old both happily playing in their own worlds.

'That would have been my Mum, I can tell by the hair.'

'Well, if that's Isobel, the other one must be Bridget. This is a bit confusing.'

Arume appeared again.

'We had been watching Isobel for many years, she showed signs of having special gifts and amazing intuition. Her gentle nature resonates at a high level that is considered superior. When she was nearly eleven, she was left alone in the family house. It was winter and Isobel fell asleep on the lounge in front of the open fire. A log rolled out and the floorboards began to smoulder then ignited. Isobel was unconscious and suffered smoke inhalation and second-degree burns. Esouli rescued her and delivered her into the mountain to be treated with Vodoxium. Isobel was delivered back to the parklands near what used to be her home where she was soon found by family. Isobel retains some images but has no fear. She is aware of our presence but not in its entirety.

Bridget at the same age, also resonated at our level. Intuitive, insightful, empathetic and an artistic mind. She was walking home from school and had to cross a road. This day a motorbike was being chased by police. The bike hit her on a crossing, and she sustained some significant injuries. We had to do some instant intervention that looked natural. Creating a wild storm, heavy rain and hail, people around had no visibility. Esouli shapeshifted into a man, picked her up, and making both invisible he took her to the mountain. Bridget's internal injuries were treated, healed, and she was returned home. She too was aware she had an unearthly experience. She has no fear, but again is vaguely aware.'

'And that's why I'm meant to be here? His sidekick, right?'

'Exactly!'

As both boys spoke, a slight tilt appeared on Arume's mouth.

'How about my Nan?' said Louis.

'That is an entirely different and much longer story. I will however tell you something about your Nan. Do you boys recall when man first walked on the moon?'

'Yep. Learnt about that at school.'

Louis nodded in agreement.

'Your grandmother loved to learn languages and explore she could never get enough adventures. An extraordinary person. She taught us many things. Contrary to the belief of Earth's scientists, there is a lifeform on the moon.'

The boys looked at each other.

'This race did have something unusual that could have been detrimental to planet Earth. We had a plan and your grandmother insisted on communicating with the Kadil. When man landed on the moon, we also landed on the dark side undetected.'

Charlie couldn't wait any longer.

'How did they live and what did they eat? There's just no food!'

'We sent a probe into one of the tubes that indicated a habitat to have a look. Inside the moon are some interesting minerals and deep springs, and their little home came into view. Honeycomb rock structures serve as housing, tiny spring pools are scattered within the cavities. Incandescent veins of mineral serve as light. They need very little to survive and live well inside the moon. The Kadil filter minerals out of the water using their mouths, then the excess drips from their shiny skin. This is the interesting part. The excess drips on the rocks, starts to dry and becomes a fungus. The fungus forms a highly toxic and poisonous element, but not to the Kadil, it sustains their bodies. It has many applications. It can be a sticky substance or powder. They communicate by clicks and low whistles. They were terrified by man, his spaceships and their spacesuits. The vibrations disturbed their homes. The Kadil felt they had to destroy the alien invasion.'

'How could such a primitive race retaliate?' Louis was intrigued.

'Remember I spoke about the fungus?'

'Yes,' replied Louis, trying to calculate the relevance.

'It was a simple plan, attach the fungus to the Apollo 14 Lunar Module. Once it returned to Earth's atmosphere the fungus would multiply and disperse in the high oxygen levels. The toxicity would wipe out warm blooded animals and poison the waters on the entire planet.'

'What did they look like?'

Louis couldn't believe what he was hearing.

'I guess the closest description is a larger wasp like creature, with very active hands and a large mouth. A large head and eyes like black light bulbs.

The Tetrahedron arrived very quietly on the dark side. Your grandmother had studied their clicking and whistling tones and was certain she could communicate with them. Maeve needed them to know that the aliens could not live on the moon and they were not colonising. She sat on the edge of a crater, softly clicking and low whistling using every format she created. Maeve had a vial of Vodoxium that she took in small sips to keep her lungs inflated. She had oxygen panels hidden in her clothes that she inhaled intermittently. The Kadil needed to see the suits were not like those of the aliens. Eventually, they surfaced a few at a time, moving slowly to Maeve, touching and smelling, the clicking and whistling intensified. The eye contact was intense. It was incredible to watch, an ancient race never before having contact with any other being and your grandmother, alone, unafraid, breathing and communicating in a toxic environment. If man only knew, it would have been a far more historical moment then the actual landing. An understanding of information was finally exchanged. They returned peacefully to their inner moon home and your grandmother returned safely to Earth.'

There was silence.

Louis spoke.

'That is totally awesome, just triple awesome dude!'

CHAPTER 32

Tristan Blackwell was in his lavish surrounds, music pulsating around his luxury inner city rooftop apartment. Tristan was tall, dark haired and his looks were very similar to his father. He was working on his body in his own gymnasium. Cocaine deals spread over a large designer coffee table. Money was pouring in, business was good, his life was now platinum and he didn't need his germ of a father.

Tristan's hurt ran deep regarding his father, he was ignored from the day he was born. Jason Blackwell never gave his son any attention or affection, it was all foreign to Tristan. He was often reminded by his mother and father he was a mistake, and he remained invisible to both of them. Shoved away in boarding school since he was four years of age, before that a fulltime babysitter from the moment he was born. He never had a family Christmas or a birthday party.

All contact he ever had was visits to boarding school. Tristan had never experienced family life. Now eighteen years of age, he had money, power and respect. He was going to insert himself into Jason Blackwell's life and just play. His mother didn't matter. Every living cell in Tristan's body generated revenge. But he knew he had to be smart. Years of manipulating teachers and students for his own needs had served him well. Careful thinking, timing and planning. It consumed his life.

Jill sat at her desk feeling confident that the day ahead would be calm and uneventful. That was not meant to be. A very attractive well-dressed man stepped into the office. That man was Tristan Blackwell.

'Oh My God!' was all Jill could manage.

'Hello Jill, is he in? It's okay Jill, I'm not here to cause trouble, in fact it's the opposite. How is your family? Your daughter Jessica must be in High School.'

Jill had to admit Tristan certainly had presence.

'Just let me go in and talk to him first,' said Jill, feeling very uneasy, but also having a degree of sympathy for Tristan.

Jill tapped lightly and saying a quick prayer opened the door.

Tristan heard his pompous voice summoning his servant.

Anger started to overtake his calm demeanour. Then it happened, that little voice in his head, to soothe the anger, reminding him of his mission.

'Mr Blackwell, umm, you have a visitor.'

'Well...who is it?!'

Jill paused, afraid of the tirade.

'It's...it's your son Tristan.'

'What the bloody hell does he want?'

Before Jill had time to do or say anything, Tristan walked through the door, straight up to Jason and held out his hand.

'Hello Dad.'

Jason stood speechless, staring at Tristan. He had to admit he looked good. Handsome and tall (Just like me – his voice jolted Jason back to the presence.).

'It's good to see you Dad. Now, before you start, I would like to apologise.'

Moving forward and grabbing his father's hand, shaking firmly and making solid eye contact.

'I caused immense embarrassment and trouble.'

Jason was still gobsmacked, Tristan jumped in and took the lead, headed towards the lounge chairs. Jason followed, Tristan's voice in his head jumping for joy, 'You're in! You did it! You did it!'

Jill suggested coffee.

'Yes, that would be appropriate.'

'*That would be appropriate*, who the hell does he think he is?'

'Firstly Dad, I would like to say something else.'

Jason nodded.

'My days of drug dealing are over, I realise it's only going to get me in prison, I've gone completely legitimate.'

Jason finally spoke.

'Glad to hear it son. To be honest I was concerned it would damage my career and investments.'

That little voice inside Tristan's head whispered softly, 'Oh God forbid that, you arrogant bastard!'

Tristan smiled at his father.

'I've purchased a travel agency, I know you're thinking 'drug money', I admit that, but mistakes I have made, and my lessons are learnt. I want you to be proud of me Dad, not ashamed.'

Tristan's brain had begun throwing up, his lies were so sickening. He managed to squeeze out a tear, as a closing act. 'Whoops, there it goes, my brain threw up!' Tristan had to control his need to laugh, he looked at his father like a starving dog.

Jason cleared his throat.

'It's alright son, I understand.'

'You got him. My God you're good.'

They enjoyed the coffee. The conversation started to flow.

Jason talked about himself, all his financial ventures, his political aspirations, his love life, his success. Tristan listened with interest, smiling, nodding appropriately. Praising Jason for his achievements, stroking his ego, and it was working. When Jason finished, he suggested he and Tristan have dinner that night. Tristan accepted with humble appreciation.

Tristan laid back on his lounge smiling, aggressive music playing in the background. His plan had gone better than expected, all he has to do is plant the seeds and that fool fertilises them. Tristan jumped up and down on the lounge, laughing like a maniac on steroids.

'Not once did he even attempt to talk about how he abandoned me.'

The voice in his head was screaming. He picked up a heavy ashtray and smashed it up the wall. He laughed even harder, kicked the small bags of white powder into the air, falling to the floor like dying white butterflies. Tristan Blackwell's heart was empty, but hate was feeding his soul.

At the very same time Jason Blackwell sat by his pool pleased with himself. Sipping his brandy, deep in thought about the benefits of reconnecting with his son. Tristan standing at his side while he campaigned, he would attract the younger voters. Jason chuckled, after all he was good looking just like his old man. The vision he conjured in his mind was perfect.

Talking to no one in particular he said, 'All I need now is a human Barbie doll to come home and the picture is complete.'

Jason laughed out loud, tossing his cigar into the pool.

CHAPTER 33

The two boys observed in total astonishment. The spaceship was changing shape.

'What's happening?'

'It's okay Louis.'

Esouli sat between them.

'It's easier to get through a black hole if our craft is elongated. We will experience less turmoil.'

The spaceship accelerated.

'Holy Shit!' were the only words that Charlie could manage.

Louis grabbed Charlie's arm.

'It's okay Charlie, we can do this.'

Both their hearts skipping a beat, the vision was unbelievable. It was like being inside a tunnel of raging rainbows with colours swirling. A massive kaleidoscope spiralling into the unknown. Large chunks of meteor bounced off the spaceship, giving minimal shudder, being drawn in further and further, the tumultuous tornado of random colour and objects. Then suddenly stillness. Quiet, floating, tense bodies releasing one nerve and muscle at a time. Strange webbing wrapped itself around the ship. Luminous creatures stuck on the outside of the ship. Large eyes blinked at the occupants inside, black and penetrating. Webbing continually poured out of their mouths.

'What the hell are they?'

Charlie was almost hysterical Louis however was fascinated with the creatures.

'Don't worry,' said Esouli, 'they just think we are some form of food.'

'They just look like blobs with faces,' said Charlie.

'Killing Blobs,' said Esouli.

The spaceship accelerated.

'Here we go again.'

Charlie grabbing the side of his chair. The hitchhikers turned into long strings of jelly like substance and disappeared. Then, darkness, pitch black.

'What's happening now?' asked Louis.

'The ship is going to change shape, much like that of a bullet, we are now entering the extreme fast zone.'

'How fast?'

'The speed of light perhaps faster. What we are going to do now is enter our pods, filled with protective gel, if we don't take these measures your bones...'

'I get it,' interrupted Louis 'it will be like being put in a blender.'

'What about you Esouli? There's only two pods.'

Just as Charlie finished his question, Esouli began to change, bit by bit he started to disappear, slowly melting until he became a pool of liquid.

Then it started. The spaceship began spinning into darkness looking like a colossal intestine. There were flashes of luminous red, then the tunnel became small, then smaller again. The boys couldn't see what was happening, couldn't move or react, it seemed like hours of travel, when in fact it was only an hour. Millions of kilometres had been covered. Many thoughts ran through their minds, trying to imagine what was happening and hoping they would survive.

When the pods lifted the brightness was incredible, another galaxy. What the boys saw before them was a feast for the eyes.

'We are now in a galaxy beyond your own.'

'This is incredible, I can't believe my eyes.'

'Oh dude, I can't find any words.'

It was beautiful. A place of fantasy. Nearly impossible for the human brain to process. A different world with different beings. There were six fertile planets small, rotating around what looked more like a moon.

Esouli began to grow out of his pool. Charlie couldn't help giggling.

'Dude, were you that scared you turned to water?'

Charlie's sense of humour easing the moment.

'Oh, very funny you two.'

Esouli pointed to the world outside.

Spaceships of all forms floated around the galaxy. Strange discs glittering like Christmas decorations, just hanging in space. The atmosphere had a yellow shine all around. It was awesome.

'What are those light globe things?' asked Charlie.

'The globes contain pure Vodoxium. It energises everything you can see before you, including this craft.'

'Can we land here?' asked Louis. 'This is just astounding. Can we breathe the air?'

'We can breathe the air for an hour. The oxygen content is very high as opposed to earth.'

'Is that because of no pollution?'

'That's one reason. Choose a planet.'

'The first two are the same, lets land on one' said Louis, his excitement evident.

'Oh, don't worry about me,' said Charlie 'I'll just do as I'm told.'

Louis and Esouli laughed.

The craft landed on planet one.

'Do these fellas have a name?'

'Yes Charlie, the inhabitants are Abarist. They use each planet for something different.'

'Well come on fellas, let's go meet some aliens. Oh! Just one thing. Are they friendly?'

'Firstly, what you need to know about these beings, they are cautious, very inquisitive and very capable in defending themselves. Do not make any sudden movements. Allow them to investigate you. I will communicate with them and inform them of our mission. You must walk behind me and do not speak unless I tell you.'

Louis and Charlie were nervous, they had never seen Esouli so stern. On the large opaque panel Esouli programmed the life of the Abarist race. Their physicality, their life cycles and the precise organisation of their civilisation. The panel vision depicted a functioning race of beings similar to ant colonies.

'They are not particularly advanced but have a very strong sense of protection for each other. THAT is what you must be very mindful of.'

Esouli went on.

'Their purpose for existence is to maintain their life. They have a short lifespan equivalent to Earth's five years.'

The screen then showed each individual planet, beginning with the largest.

'The first two planets are their homes. Masses of treelike structures with square shape tunnels branching off the central tower. Inside is like an elevator to taking them to their designated tunnel.'

'It looks very geometrical and sleek,' said Louis.

'This is awesome.' Charlie grinned.

'The next two planets are for production. Large fields cover the entire planets. Thousands of different plants, a multitude of colours and shapes. These are harvested every cycle of the planets. Each inhabitant feeds daily and the young are looked after. It's their priority. The next planet takes care of the babies where they're fed and housed. All inhabitants look after the young. Again, the protection of the babies is paramount to these beings, hence their suspicion of others, as I said before.'

'So, what's the combined six planets for?' asked Louis. 'They kinda got everything covered.'

'The sixth planet is for the dead.'

'Whoa, hang on a minute,' said Charlie 'we can't be landing there!'

The next vision was not what you would expect. Large amounts of Abarist stood upright shrouded in a thick substance of sticky saliva, inside the bodies disintegrating. Other living Arbarist monitored the process. When all signs of the body were gone, the shroud was taken back to the food processing planets as fertilizer.

'So,' said Louis 'nothing is wasted, they will never be overpopulated.'

'That's a bit gross' said Charlie.

'But highly effective' said Louis impressed with these beings.

'What are the spaceships for?' asked Louis.

'They are only there for emergency, if they have to leave the planet.'

The screen showed a vision of the Arbarist standing tall to show a close up. The head of the alien was similar to a praying mantis, a strong mandible, and long thin arms with ten very active fingers. Long legs with long flat feet with toes to dig with. A dome structure shaped like a mushroom seemed to hover over their heads.

'What is that thing on their head?'

'That is their mode of travel Louis.'

It was most magnificent.

'It's incredible' said Esouli.

The dome started to pulsate. Energising, it had the same movement as a jelly fish, lighting up with the increased movement, slowly lifting off the surface. Smooth flowing flight, then hundreds of them lifted into the atmosphere. It was an extraordinary sight, different colours floating to their destiny.

'Oh Dude!'

'I know Charlie. There are no words! What are their defences?' asked Louis.

'It's very interesting,' said Esouli, 'remember how they embalm their dead in their own saliva?'

Both boys nodded in unison. Again, all eyes returned to the screen. The Arbarist appeared. It spat at an object and within seconds the object ignited into a blue flame. Nothing was left.

'Wow, how dangerous has spitting become? And we're gonna go walking with these dudes?'

CHAPTER 34

Jason and Tristan sat in an exclusive restaurant together, both looking like Hollywood movie stars. Women of all ages tried not to be obvious in looking.

Jason showed Tristan an image of Genevieve on his phone.

'Wow Dad. She is hot.'

'Now son, I want you to come and look at the development site. Money from investors is pouring into my accounts. Genevieve has invested a significant amount and groundworks have started. We can grow wealthy and powerful.'

Jason was throwing down bourbons, getting generous with his conversations. Tristan was watching closely. Planning. Learning. Tristan's little voice had become voices, each one competing to be heard.

The finest food was ordered off the menu, Tristan impressed Jason with the wine selection, which coincidentally, he had looked up on his phone, whilst on the toilet. Jason talked about the plans for his political career, Tristan was bored with Jason constantly talking about himself.

'Why don't you come with me tomorrow, have a look at the plans. I could pick you up around midday.'

'Sounds perfect Dad, I'll text you my address.'

'How about a game of golf?'

'Why not,' said Tristan, beaming a smile at Jason, 'I played at school.'

Tristan's silent voices were becoming angry. Whispering in the background.

'That's right Dad, ignore the school thing. Don't mention how you abandoned me.'

Tristan smiled, 'Can't wait.'

'How about,' said Jason starting to slur his words, 'we go to this private little club I'm a member of, and I tell you son, it offers whatever you desire, if you know what I mean?'

Tristan laughed accordingly, 'Sounds good,' whilst quietly thinking to himself what a pathetic fool Jason truly was.

Jason called for his car and driver. The men left together looking like lifelong buddies.

Tristan woke to the sound of his security alarm buzzing, someone needing to see him. Tristan checked the identification pad. It was his dealer due for a drop off and pick up.

The exchange was brief, no small talk and no pleasantries. Two hundred thousand dollars was handed over, fifty thousand given back in a package with more supplies. The dealer was dressed in a supermarket uniform, the delivery truck belonged to the supermarket. Home delivery of groceries was a perfect way to distribute to his customers. Tristan took the money to the kitchen, opened his top cupboards and pressed a hidden button. A false backing exposed a deep cavity full money, close to two million dollars.

Tristan didn't spend his time at his fancy boarding school studying mundane courses. It didn't matter what he did because good old Daddy donated large amounts of money to keep him hidden out of sight and out of mind. Tristan had spent hours studying the financial systems and how to manage large amounts of money without creating suspicion. He borrowed money to portray legitimacy, he purchased a travel agency to give him freedom to do anything he pleased. The ability to manipulate his own personality to fit in wherever he needed to. He used his money to look impressive with the high rollers. He invented a history that would make him acceptable to where he needed to fit in.

The travel agency was a thriving business, the staff were paid well above the average wage. All his employees had their own homes, as well as their own cars. For this generosity his staff handed out and accepted packages. It was an elusive process and it worked perfectly.

Many women in his circles pursued his affections, however Tristan was not interested in relationships. He didn't really know how to have personal friendships. The best friends he had lived in his head, they helped him, laughed with him, talked to him and advised him.

Jason arrived at the address texted to him. His son looked the part, expensive golf clubs, costly golf wear. Tristan paid the manager of the local sports store to open on a Sunday and have everything he needed to be delivered. He glided into Jason's updated car, a Mercedes Sports, top of the range.

One of his chattier voices was getting louder.

'Find out everything, get the dirt. Get the dirt.'

It kept going, becoming invasive. Tristan turned the music on to drown out the voice.

'It's a beautiful machine Dad.'

'It is that, kind of suits me I reckon.'

What a bloody wanker.

'It does, matches your debonair style. So is your development advancing, have you had any trouble from the tree huggers and black fellas?'

'Well, we have had a little issue with some ridiculous drawings, but it's amazing what greasing palms does, you know promises of large deposits, adjusting a few documents or omitting certain information.'

Jason lifted his head, laughing into the wind.

'That's probably a bit over your head son, but don't worry I've had a lot of practice.'

'And there it is.'

The little voice was happy.

'You're going to make a great politician Dad.'

They both laughed into the wind. The music went up, the top down, Jason knew he was being admired even while driving.

The Mercedes purred to a stop at the development site. Heavy earthmoving equipment stood like soldiers waiting for orders. They studied the site and plans together.

'I have to admit, this looks impressive.'

The secluded entrance was gone, bulldozed away. Structures were in progress to display the intended resort.

'So obviously there have been dwellings around here, how did you manage to get them out?'

'Yeah, just a shack over there, like I mentioned before, oh and some bullshit about Aboriginal art. I got around that by mentioning a few vandals here and there. Come on, let's go, I'll show you the model.'

'So how much has been invested so far? I might be interested.'

'Oh son, this is for the big players, you hang onto your savings.'

'Would you believe $100 million so far, and it's still coming.'

Tristan had his phone recording the conversation, Jason wouldn't notice anything. He was too absorbed in his own life.

'Before we go, how about we have a look down this track.'

The lake was still, water birds sat peacefully, whilst wildlife grazed at the water's edge. The beautiful cliff in the background caught the sun and reflected its many colours into the atmosphere. The abundant vegetation and majestic trees complimented the exquisite lake.

'Wow!' said Tristan, 'This is nature at its best.'

'But it does not make money son and besides all this animal life can just bugger off elsewhere or be shot.'

Jason laughed at his sense of humour, looking at Tristan waiting for him to laugh.

'Okay then.'

Tristan replied, forcing the best smile he could.

High on the mountain in an ancient pine tree sat the Tawny and the Wedge tail looking down at the humans below.

'How did you get around all the environmental issues, I mean this is very pristine and the Aboriginal art, how the hell? The recording was still active.

'You have to understand Tristan, in the world of big business, money can buy you anything. I suggest that if you suffer a conscience, let it go now. It will get you nowhere.'

'I guess you have connections in local government, you know, you're fairly high up now and you command a lot of respect.'

Jason laughed arrogantly, throwing his head back like some psycho kookaburra.

'Try Federal. Listen son, join me, become my right-hand man. This is just the beginning. I'm going to win my seat with your help.'

Jason poked him in the chest.

'The money and the power can be yours as well.'

Tristan put his hand on his father's shoulder.

'This all sounds very interesting Dad.'

Bridget sat in her car, she knew she shouldn't, it was gone, all of it gone not a trace of her life was left behind.

Isobel had explored every avenue to try and stop the development, it seemed she was being cut off from everywhere. The power of money was at work.

It was after five in the afternoon. Work had stopped and all was quiet. Bridget was nervous, her anxiety had been bad of late and Isobel was treating her with herbs. Bridget did some deep breathing. There was no one around. Getting out of her car, she made her way towards the machinery. They felt like alien monsters on a mission to destroy. Bridget had a backpack, clothes, towel and items to do a certain ritual. Standing at the edge of the lake, all the wildlife stayed quiet no fear within them. Bridget discarded her clothes, she walked into the lake until she disappeared, and the lake water was still. Time went by, a fin broke through the waters, a dolphin jumped out of the lake, over and over it went around the lake, and it was like it had been set free. The lake went still again. Momentarily, Bridget's head appeared and slowly she walked out of the lake and wrapping herself in the towel.

It had been a long time since the Vodoxium saved her life, she had never tested its long-term effects or if it had any, knowing at some level she was getting support from inside the mountain. Bridget's instincts seemed to be very strong, images and messages kept coming into her dreams. The entire vision of what she needed to do played like a movie in her head, she knew exactly what to do.

She pulled on the gown gracefully, with the sun slowly disappearing. Her lone figure gathered a stick and began drawing a large circle in the sand beside the lake. She then drew another within, continuing until there were seven. From her bag, she withdrew seven crystals, placing them on the right side of the circles, all aligned, similar to planets. Bridget then held in her hands a wand of crystal Blue Kyanite. Standing in the centre she faced the mountain.

Speaking in a clear voice.

'I call to the Ancient Keeper of the Universe, I summon the power of energies to my crystals aligned. Danger approaches our most blessed place. I call to you for your restored power.'

Bridget repeated this seven times, the blue kyanite in her hands started to feel warm. Looking to the mountain, a low cloud formed over the lake. A strange musical noise could be heard, time stood still, the cloud swirled coming alive. High on the mountain Arume stood magnificent in his appearance. Bridget held the blue crystal and it got warmer. Arume's words came to her.

'Remember the gift I give cannot be used against human beings.'

Bridget acknowledged, she got to her knees. High above, an orb appeared, it hovered over Bridget. The blue crystal started to pulsate, Bridget felt the power, it was like an injection of hot water into every vein, artery and capillary. Bridget's skin turned luminous blue, then back to normal, the power was overwhelming.

She woke slowly, the sun had set, the Tawny and the Eagle stood at the water's edge watching Bridget, as she spoke in a strange language with soft words, the two birds took flight.

Bridget gathered her items put them away safely. She was about to get her torch out. The torch wasn't necessary, tiny stars dropped like fairy lights to guide her way. Her happiness was intoxicating. The abilities wouldn't last long, hopefully just enough.

The bulldozers, excavators, backhoe loaders and many trucks, stood like threatening monstrous aliens, against the backdrop of day's end. Bridget pondered the best way to treat the aliens, making it simple for the initial intervention. She put her hand on each machine and imprinted it with her thoughts. Returning to her car, she looked to where her home once was. She would deal with that later.

Isobel was busy in the kitchen, the smell of herbs and fresh salad vegetables spread throughout the little beach house. Turning she met Bridget's gaze.

'You did it.'

'I had to!'

Something was happening in the kitchen, lettuce, tomatoes, capsicums, cucumbers, mushrooms, onions danced in the air above the kitchen bench. They landed perfectly into the salad bowl.

'Oh dear, I must be hungry.'

The wine was poured, the laughter was a long time coming.

'You two sound like you're on drugs,' Simone said looking from one to the other.

Isobel put some orange juice in a wine glass.

'We're celebrating happiness.'

The Tawny and the Eagle sat in the pine tree. All was good for the moment.

Seven in the morning, the work trucks arrived, the men stood around having a smoke and drinking their coffees.

'Well fellas,' said the foreman, 'let's get this knocked down, there's a lot of money invested in this, including mine! Let's go.'

David Levey climbed on board his hydraulic excavator supplied by the local council, all fuelled ready to go. Turning the key, music, loud music, classical music began to play. The workers all turned on their machines, again music, the same music. The men sat dumbfounded; confused. The foreman yelled, furious.

'What the bloody hell is going on?! This is sabotage, probably from those bloody tree huggers!'

He was on the phone, firstly to a mechanic, then Jason Blackwell.

Jason Blackwell was furious. He sent investigators to the worksite, demanding 'Who did this?!'

CHAPTER 35

Louis couldn't believe where he was, face to face with another lifeform on another planet. Charlie was visibly shaking as the deadly spitting beings that embalm, investigated the human bodies.

Esouli, and what was obviously a leader amongst these strange beings, communicated fluently.

'They smell kinda weird.'

Charlie whispered to Louis, looking into the face of another species.

Large eyes flickered pitch black, with red pupils that expand and contract, strong jaws with a snapping sound. The two boys couldn't move, their bodies now so close to these unbelievable, yet terrifying looking aliens.

A strange humming sound commenced, the domes above the beings began to pulsate energising its flight. All the beings began to take off together. It was an astonishing sight, illuminated domes like a thousand umbrella's lit up, green and violet in colour, dispersing to their selected planet.

Esouli, Louis and Charlie watched until they could no longer be seen.

'Who the hell would believe us?'

'No one Charlie, no one.'

'We need to get back to the ship before you two start gasping for air.'

'Oh good,' said Charlie, 'if I died then the big bugs could embalm me.'

Louis put his hand over Charlie's mouth, pointing him in the direction of safety, giggling quietly. As soon as they entered the craft, Fudgunkel stood waiting, tiny hands-on tiny hips.

'Come on, come on. Hurry up, smelly boys.'

Little bells tinkled, the tiny pixie creature huffed and mumbled, Charlie and Louis burst into fits of laughter.

'This is our new mother, if only Isobel and Bridget could see this.'

Charlie wrapped his arm around Louis's shoulder.

'Come on bro', Fundy Guts must be obeyed.'

The smell of planet Abarist was washed off, a healthy feed of hydroponic fruit and vegetables, and some luscious almond ice cream finished off the meal. Esouli was busy charting a course from the Milky Way to the Andromeda Galaxy roughly 2.5 million years away. Louis loved watching the magic.

On the huge screen before them, a vision of the Milky Way galaxy appeared.

'Since man walked planet Earth they have looked to the stars in wonder. Earth's galaxy itself is one of billions of galaxies. It is infinite and expanding. The human race has always had a fascination with the universe from the big bang theory, black holes and dark matter. Unfortunately, that passion does not extend to your own planet. Until the entire human race awakens, their evolution and comprehension of what is beyond will never be available to them.'

'You sound like you're not really impressed with the human beings.'

The big warrior looked curiously at Louis, his huge ears moving backwards and forwards.

'Well, it's not that so much, it's that money and power come before the health of your planet, and that makes us all extremely sad and frustrated. Many of your scientists have theorised this much. The universe is infinite, and matter is spread over 93 billion light years. The Milky Way is around 100,000 light years in diameter. The Andromeda Galaxy is roughly 3 million light years away.'

The screen before them was a mass of electronic light fusing together. Deep tunnelling images that just went on forever.

'This is fantastic!' stated Louis.

'What are we watching exactly?' asked Charlie.

'Galaxies in the universe, they range from dwarf galaxies with tens of millions of stars, then to great galaxies with trillions of stars.'

'So it just goes on forever, there is no end.'

'That's correct Louis.'

'What about different dimensions?' asked Louis, excitement stimulating every nerve in his body.

'Yes Louis, they exist, 'The Multiverse', called a Parallel Universe.'

'It's a theory,' said Louis, 'that two universes collided to cause the Big Bang.'

'That is true Louis, its effects had a dramatic change, especially to planet Earth.'

'Oh man, this is just way too much for my feeble brain to absorb.'

Esouli laughed and ruffled Charlie's hair.

'I know,' said Esouli 'but just remember with the power of Vodoxium we can travel forever.'

'How many species are out there Esouli?'

'More than we could count. Many are inhabited by very advanced races that have adapted to the environments and you have encountered some already. Many planets only have insignificant insect life some are just arid lands with toxic surfaces and air. Other planets are burning out slowly. Some are covered with water bubbling at high temperatures and poisonous fumes.'

'Are there other planets like Earth with Suns and Moons?'

'Indeed, there is Charlie.'

'What's going to be our next stopover?' asked Charlie.

'Yaramist.'

'What is it like?' asked Louis.

'Well, perhaps we will wait. It's a very complex environment and interesting inhabitants.'

'So Big Fella, how exactly are we going to stop the hideous munching Dradask?'

'At the moment I am sending information to all the 'friendlies' for the movement of the Dradask.'

'Can you watch their movements?'

'So far they have only landed on burnt out desolate planets, HOWEVER, they are moving with haste.'

Preparation had begun for departure.

'The next planet as I said, is Yaramist. We will not be able to land due to a strange phenomenon.'

'What is it?' said Louis.

'Let's wait and see. It's hard to explain.'

It was calm to start with, but it wasn't long before that changed. The craft was getting assaulted with a meteor shower. The ship started to change shape, becoming very long in shape like a pen. A large swirling mass was ahead.

'Oh God, tell me we're not going in that.'

Charlie was terrified.

The closer they got, the energy was pulling them in. Once inside many other objects could be seen, space debris, old satellites, disc shaped objects swirling out of control.

'Holy shit. This is like a PlayStation game.'

Charlie's knuckles turning white.

'This is a violent black hole; the energy is extraordinary and some of what you see here are spaceships that have to wait until they are spat out.'

'How long could they be in here?' asked Louis.

'Many years, as in human years.'

'That would mean the occupants would be dead inside.'

'I'm afraid that's right.'

Esouli assured the boys they were safe. There were explosions of gold and orange before their eyes, dazzling colours swirling so fast it was nauseating. Then darkness. The ship slowed down; green luminous slimy bell-shaped objects hovered in the distance. Hurtling towards them, each impact spewed slime all over the ship making it difficult to see. Black fur balls stuck to the craft.

'What the hell are they?' Charlie's voice screechy.

'They're waiting until we reach the ocean.'

'The ocean?'

'Yes Louis, there is an ocean in this vast black hole, when we reach submersion, they will morph into true creatures.'

The darkness slowly turned to light, bright light, the largest moon you could ever envisage greeted them.

'Are there any weird things living on it or in it?'

'No Charlie.'

Esouli handed them dark glasses.

'It's for protection, the brightness could harm your eyes.'

The ship started to move fast again, ahead was a worm hole heading straight into it. It was bumpy, turbulence rotated the ship, it went on relentlessly, then came the relief of serenity. Floating in water the little black fur balls started to move. Tiny hands started to form, forearms like human baby arms grew quickly. An abnormally larger head for its small reptile looking body two large eye and a large mouth. In completion, a lizard like being was adorned with bat wings. As soon as they fully emerged, they luxuriated in the water, frolicking like seals, finally to find a habitat they needed.

'They have waited a long time to reach the ocean, they can now survive and maintain the ecology of their environment.'

'Oh wow,' said Louis, 'this is amazing. Those poor little guys just wanted to get home.'

The ship came out of the water, back into space. In the distance appeared another large planet.

'How far have we come?' asked Louis.

'Two and a half million light years from planet Earth.'

They approached the planet in the distance. It looked extremely fertile, covered in vegetation, beautiful lakes, full of black water.

'The trees are moving!'

'Yes Louis, the entire planet moves.'

'Why is the water black?'

'Because Charlie, they are endless, we assume to the centre of the planet. Inside is a gel-like substance that holds anything forever that falls in.'

Esouli moved his hands across the screen, it showed the inhabitants. A grazing type animal could be seen feeding on the abundant vegetation.

'Now these fellas really enjoy their tucker.'

With faces like teddy bears, their bodies similar were to a hippopotamus.

'They look so peaceful.'

'They are Charlie, and there lies the problem and the solution.'

'I get the feeling we are about to hear the plan,' said Louis.

'The creatures you see are what we call Queffle, and the planet is Yaramist. The Dradask are heading for Yaramist. They are attracted to the Queffle to eat, plus the vegetation is lush and very appealing to the travellers. Having said that, the attraction the Dradask will have for this planet, hopefully could lead them to extinction. The problem we face, and this will be your part, is to get the Vodoxium sphere and rescue their captives before they end up locked into the centre of Yaramist. When the time comes our ship will invisibly align with theirs. Your new abilities will allow you to enter as smaller lifeforms, then revert to yourselves. Remember the sphere can be reduced to a small item. It will be at this point all your abilities can be used to try and rescue the beings on board, they can be reduced to very miniature status to collect with ease. The Queffle are proficient in avoiding the waterholes, they have lived in harmony for a very long time, we must also ensure that continues.'

The boys sat in silence; Charlie found his voice.

'We are going to confront the Dradask?'

'We can do this Charlie, but I think we need to keep practicing our skills intensely.'

The golden triangle moved serenely through space, changing shapes as it goes. Travelling craft are a familiar sight, billions of stars and planets, all different, millions of lifeforms however insignificant existing on and on forever.

CHAPTER 36

Genevieve was receiving the last treatment on her face. The surgery was extensive. Underneath the surface skin, delicate work was undertaken. Microsurgery and specially designed fillers helped to restore her face.

'Give me that mirror.'

She snatched it off the nurse carefully studying the surgeon's work.

'Are you sure my eyes are even?'

'Yes Miss St Day, we have measured every day for a month.'

'When is the surgeon coming?'

'After lunch Miss St Day.'

'Good, I want my goat's milk bath now. Send in those idiots that work for me!'

Rosa cautiously entered her bedroom.

'Well, here you are, I want a full massage after my milk bath, my surgeon is coming after lunch, and I want to look good. Hair, makeup and I will have the white Ralph Lauren gown, the Armani sandals.'

Genevieve's manager was aware of her incident, because it was an urgent situation, Rosa and Vivian had to accompany her. This was a precarious situation for Genevieve's privacy. Max insisted both ladies sign a non-disclosure agreement about her incident and personal life.

Rosa and Vivian had been stuck with their boss for three months solid and were going crazy. The only redeeming feature was Max insisted that they have significant bonuses. The plan they had could no longer come to fruition or they would spend a long time in prison. No pictures or evidence allowed. Vivian handed Genevieve the phone.

'It's Mr Blackwell.'

'Hello darling. Yes, I miss you terribly.'

Rosa and Vivian took a moment for a break.

'What the hell are we going to do Vivian, we can't get away from her, it sounds like she is going back to Australia. Our plans have gone, she does not even recognise that we have families.'

'Rosa, please listen to me. You have to be patient. I have something that will benefit us, but I can't discuss this now, trust me.'

'Rosa, where are you?! I need my massage.'

It was after lunch, Genevieve had pureed vegetables and vitamins. She sat waiting and looked radiant. There was a slight change in her appearance, but it could be put down to Botox.

The surgeon was stunned at her beauty, he examined her face, this was one of his best jobs.

'When can I leave?'

'Well Miss St Day, I am happy for you to go at your leisure.'

'Good. I'll have my secretary settle my account.'

'May I ask if you are happy with the results?'

'Yes, very much, I think I am even more beautiful, if that's possible,' Genevieve laughed, amused at her own words.

The doctor, somewhat shocked at her response, smiled and left.

'Rosa, let's go! start packing. Vivian, get the account paid and got the jet organised.'

Genevieve couldn't drag herself away from the mirror.

'And I will need my fur. I want my exit to be superb.'

Rosa was exhausted cleaning up after Genevieve and packing up all her clothes, shoes and make-up.

The jet plane left America at 5pm, again Rosa had to go through the massage and pampering, then going through the routine of giving her the vitamins and her sleeping pill. It was going to be a long flight with coordinated stops for refuelling, two stopovers, then Australia. Genevieve liked to sleep and when she did wake, she watched the latest soaps and read fashion magazines.

She was sound asleep induced by a sleeping tablet, Vivian and Rosa could finally relax. They enjoyed dinner together, Vivian set the computer up to show Rosa something.

'What am I looking at?'

'Accounts. You know how she has had her surgeries and everything she purchases? I pay with her credit card.'

'Yes,' said Rosa 'I understand.'

'Well, I have added to the cost and then transferred the excess to this account.'

Vivian enlarged the figures for her to see one million dollars had been skimmed from her account.

'Half each Rosa, when the time comes.'

'Shit Vivian, can we get caught?'

'No, I manage her tax returns. Her investments are returning a fortune and that's all Max is interested in. Don't worry, Max is helping himself to a bigger chunk than I am.'

Vivian poured Rosa a glass of wine.

'Relax Rosa, you deserve it. You wait on her hand and foot and get abused non-stop.'

'Yes, that's true.'

The two women had a quiet lunch, then settled down for some rest.

Rosa spoke softly as she relaxed.

'I miss my family and Paris.'

'I know my friend; I just want to find a little cottage with some chooks and flowers.'

'If we invest carefully Rosa, life will be better.'

The two women drifted off to sleep.

CHAPTER 37

Jason Blackwell was yelling down the phone.

'Are you people mad?! Are you on drugs? Machinery that plays music when you turn them on. Get more machinery in there now!'

Another loud crash up the wall, this time a whiskey glass.

The door to his office slammed open, Jill jumped in her chair, her nerves on edge.

'I'm going to the site.'

His face was red, burning with anger. The pressure was on Jason from his investors, they wanted results.

Isobel and Bridget sat on the verandah having morning tea. Fresh scones loaded with homemade strawberry jam. The soft sea breeze dancing with the wind chimes hanging high. On the front of the local paper the headline read 'MACHINES TURN MUSICAL. Police could find no evidence of interference it remains a mystery.'

'It will stall them for a short time, I know. No doubt they will employ a security company.'

'Any ideas?'

'I have a few,' said Bridget.

Jason Blackwell met the foreman at the site.

'Get on that machine and start it.'

Music, orchestral music, swirled in the atmosphere.

'Get off it! Try the truck.'

The same music continued.

Jason screamed at the foreman.

'Get more machinery in here now! And get this shit out of here!'

His phone rang.

'What?!'

'Oh Jason, you don't sound very happy.'

'Genevieve!'

'Yes, it is! I've not long landed in Sydney. At the moment I'm in my penthouse. How about dinner tonight?'

Jason's mood changed.

'How would you like to meet my son?'

'What?'

For a moment Genevieve thought he meant Louis.

'Tristan can't wait to meet you.'

She exhaled in relief.

'I'll organise the restaurant and the time. Rosa!'

'Oh God, here we go again.'

'Long black sequined dress, my white fur, black shoes, massage, make-up and hair up. Come on stupid, I want to look ravishing. Diamond drop earrings and the teardrop necklace for my superb breasts.'

Vivian spoke softly.

'See I told you you're worth more money.'

'What are you two whispering about? Now come on, massage.'

Genevieve clapped her hands in an act of demanding dominance.

It was organised that Genevieve would meet him at the restaurant of choice. She purposely arrived late and chose a restaurant that had an entrance allowing everyone to see her. She was exquisite, every head turned. This was what she loved.

'Oh my God Dad. Is that her?'

'It certainly is son.'

Once Genevieve had enough of being admired, Jason escorted her to the table. Introductions were done. Genevieve had an extraordinary story about where she had been. These idiots would never know the difference.

'Charity events, fashion shows, anyway I don't want to bore you with my escapades. Now Tristan, tell me about you.'

The entire evening Genevieve St Day spent looking at all the patrons, watching them, watching her, Tristan was aware she was not listening, she was a perfect match for his father. Obnoxious, self-centred and perfectly plastic.

Tristan closed his computer, he couldn't find anything more relating to Miss St Day's busy schedule, he couldn't find much on her past. This intrigued him. Between searching his father's business activity and Barbie's past, his little friends were excited, giggling in his head.

Jill looked up from her desk, the smell of Chanel overpowering the room.

'Mr Blackwell is expecting me.'

Sitting quietly watching her reflection in the window, Genevieve saw Jason approach, two flutes of Veuve Clicquot, Genevieve's favourite Champagne. After toasting their business venture, Jason handed Genevieve a tiny satin box. He flipped the lid, got on his knees and looked into her beautiful face.

'Will you marry me?'

Genevieve went into one of her past onscreen roles.

'Oh Jason, I don't know what to say. It's magnificent.'

She put it on her finger, forgetting he was supposed to. The size of the diamond sent her into a spin.

'What sort of wedding would you like?'

'Big Jason! Very big!'

'I was hoping you would say that.'

They laughed together and clinked their glasses.

'Rosa, Vivian, get in here now! I'm getting married. Get your pens and paper out and write down my wants.'

'Firstly, let the press know and I mean ALL the press, including international and if they want photos, last year's Paris photo shoot for Designer's Awards. Contact Chanel, Armani, Lauren and Dior. I want their latest wedding designs. And a list of the best venues. Next, find me the best wedding planners. Now move Vivian! Rosa, massage!'

The date was set, the pace was going to be hectic. The preparations had begun.

Tristan was fascinated with Genevieve St Day he still couldn't find too much information. He sat in his car watching the building hoping Genevieve would leave soon to have lunch with his father.

She drove off in a limousine, Tristan was amused at her antics continuously in the Hollywood star mode.

He rallied forth a special personality, vulnerable, bumbling young man, devoid of a family and innocent.

He buzzed the intercom.

'It's Tristan Blackwell, could I please come up?'

'Miss St Day is not here, she will be gone for a long time.' Rosa replied.

'Well I have gifts, could I give them to you?' asked Tristan.

Rosa looked at Vivian, she nodded. 'Very well.'

He walked in like a shy schoolboy. Flowers, champagne and chocolate truffles. Studying Vivian, she was tall and thin, undernourished, with her heavy framed glasses resting on a thin nose, sallow faced and stressed to the max. Nothing good in life going on here. Then Rosa, a bustling little woman, who must eat too much from stress. She had to be the one that cleaned up after Miss St Day, the one that gets bullied the most. Rosa's motherly instinct started to stir, she suggested coffee.

'Do you know what? I've never tasted champagne and I saved for this bottle. Cost a lot of money you know.'

The women looked at each other.

'Why not?'

Vivian got the glasses.

Sitting back relaxed feeling tipsy, the women listened to Tristan's story of abandonment and boarding schools. Tristan described what it was like on Family Days,

Sports Days, to have no one. The stories didn't have to be embellished, it was all true, from the age of five. Rosa had tears running down her cheeks.

'That is so awful. All I can say is Miss St Day will be a good match for your father.'

'Rosa!'

'It's alright Vivian, Rosa is right.'

The large bottle was empty.

'Tell me about your boss?'

'She does not have any interest in anyone but herself.'

Rosa's tongue was very loose, she wanted to unload and she did.

Tristan viewed all the paperwork on Genevieve. The explosive knowledge that Miss St Day was the previous tragic Lucy Blackwell. What was she up to?

Returning home and sitting in his own lounge room, he laughed, she hates him.

All the voices laughed. Then they stopped.

'I have a brother, I have family.'

Tristan rang his private detective. He decided to sit back and watch the stitched-up blonde and his father play out their roles and see how the show ends.

Genevieve had shown Jason her favourite locations in Paris for their wedding and reception, and perfect accommodation, the Shangri La Hotel Paris. It has a magical setting, oriental design influences and classic French décor. Her second choice Le Maurice located opposite the Jardin Des Tuileries, overlooking the rooftops of Paris.

'Look Genevieve. How about we honeymoon at these places? I'm going to win my seat, I need to be seen as humble, portraying to the working class that I am in touch with their lives and problems.' Jason laughed.

'Not that I give a shit, we can still have a big wedding, but here in Australia.'

She let him suffer and grovel a little longer, laughing on the inside.

'Alright Jason, I'll do this just for you.'

She didn't give a toss, as long as people admired her beauty, that's all she needed.

Tristan maintained his friendship with Rosa and Vivian. He took them out for tea and dinners. He heard all about the wedding plans, Tristan actually felt sorry for these women. It's not an emotion he fully understood.

CHAPTER 38

Esouli was tracking the odd spaceship manned by the Dradask. Only one more planet and Esouli would be able to see the stolen race.

The big warrior spent many hours taking the boys through their shapeshifting abilities. It was going to be imperative to have it fine-tuned. Special eye sensors had to be worn, tiny touch sensors on the sides allowing Esouli to see and hear everything the moment they leave the craft. Esouli especially wanted the boys to practice shifting into the smallest creatures, such as mice, insects and small birds. He explained that if fear could not be controlled, they could not shapeshift.

'This is so hard,' said Charlie.

'Visualise boys. Concentrate on the entire animal. It's important that we reduce the time. I need to get the time down to seconds for your change, we are going to do something radical.'

'Oh, that does not sound good.'

Charlie was looking very concerned.

'I'm sending you to a dark space in a section of this craft.'

'What do you mean dark?'

'I'm sorry Louis, but I have to do this to keep you both safe. You will be in the dark; you will be given scenarios of fear and I need you to shapeshift under intense fear.'

'Shit, the bloody dark!'

'It'll be right Charlie, we can do this, we have to do this.'

It was a system of tunnels, dark tunnels. The object was to make your way through the maze to the end. When you shift, a light came on to view your success.

The first practice was terrifying for the boys.

A couple of minutes into the dark tunnel, Charlie was grabbed by an unseen claw. Louis yelled at Charlie to shapeshift. Charlie was screaming. He couldn't do it. Louis floundered around in the dark, something grabbed his ankle, he wanted to scream, he visualized a cat, it started to happen, but he couldn't hold his concentration, he was half cat, half human. The light came on, he returned to human form.

Charlie moved on feeling his way, something was crawling on his head. The scream was coming, he continued thinking to himself.

'Mouse. I'm going to be a bloody mouse.'

Charlie had a mouse body, but still his own head. The light went on. Louis moved on into the tunnel his adrenalin was surging, all his senses heightened, something was crawling up his leg, squeezing it. It was starting to hurt. Louis started to breathe deeply. He visualised a spider, it squeezed harder, he visualised harder. Then it happened, a complete shift. Then the light went on.

'Well done,' said Esouli. 'Now keep going.'

Charlie on the other hand felt hopeless. He sat telling himself how useless he was. Louis could hear the tone of his voice in the distance.

'Charlie Crane! You can do this. I'm not doing this shit on my own!'

Charlie started to giggle.

'Okay dude. I'm gonna do a cockroach.'

Charlie moved on waiting for something to crawl, grab or choke him. There it was some slimy thing wrapping around his wrists and poking him in the back. Charlie took deep, very deep breaths, he could feel it happen. He felt okay, the light went on, there in the floor a complete cockroach.

It took a long time, nearly four weeks before Esouli was happy with the time frame it took the boys to shapeshift. They had an in-depth discussion on the training and why it was so important to Esouli.

'It is so crucial that you can shape shift quickly, the Dradask are brutal without any rational thoughts, feeding and destruction are their driving force. Again, I don't know who the beings are that they have captive. It's obvious these beings are flying the craft. Until you're aboard I will not have contact. It appears not all the Dradask are on board, the majority of the population have been left on a small planet to eat it out. No doubt the others were meant to return to pick them up in the craft they hijacked. Yaramist would sustain the entire population for a long time.'

Esouli moved his hand across the vision screen, he spoke more, and an image of the very unusual spacecraft appeared. It was three tiered discs joined by columns that moved and adjusted with the craft, the viewing windows were very visible. It was made of shiny blue metal, the discs spinning in different directions generating its power. It was a magnificent craft.

'This is what we're boarding?' asked Charlie.

'Yes Charlie it is.'

'Are we shapeshifting to get in?'

'That's the plan. We will be becoming invisible so you can board.'

'How small are we going?'

'There's a waste hatch on the bottom disc that services all three compartments. I will monitor the hatch for automatic openings, that will be the entry point.'

'Cockroaches. That's what we're gonna be, hey Louis.'

'Probably' said Louis. 'We are a bit creepy.'

'Oh man, that's lame.'

The boys feeling confident with their fine-tuned abilities.

They all studied the unusual spaceship. Esouli was puzzled, Louis was good at reading body language. He spent a long time reading his mother's moods.

'What's wrong Esouli? You look concerned.'

'This spacecraft is most unusual the energy system is baffling. It could be using Vodoxium and its own energy force. The sphere tells me it is there, the design is advanced. It is imperative we get the sphere, if we don't the entire mothercraft from the mountain cannot leave earth.

'What about the others around the planet, can they move?'

'No.'

'Oh God. This just got bigger,' Charlie sat heavily in his chair.

'Do you think the Lanorigal could still be alive? asked Louis.

'It is possible.'

'Well, we've got a big rescue ahead of us' said Charlie.

'It's looking that way' said Esouli. 'They now have an advanced spacecraft, and advanced beings forced to help them.'

Arume appeared on the screen, the boys had left to practice again in the dark zone finetuning their shapeshifting and visualising techniques. The Vodoxium was no longer in their systems. Arume felt weapons at this stage of their life was too early.

'My dear friend, do you feel the boys are ready?'

'I do Arume. They have worked hard. I do fear their entry into the mysterious craft. I think our plan will have to be changeable, depending on what is inside. I will guide them step by step. The implants will give us clear vision and hearing. The atmosphere is very heavy around the planet. Once the timed hatch is open, I will be guiding their every move.'

'It is going to be difficult Esouli for you not to rescue and intervene. These boys are our warriors for the future.'

Arume's vision started to fade. Esouli set the screen to their travel path. The craft was in his vision, he had problems seeing inside the craft, the structure of the metal was heavy and unknown to Esouli. The boys and Esouli would have to plan as they went. The preparation was to begin, he felt unsettled with the unknown.

That night the boys went into their pods to sleep, tomorrow was the day the missions commenced.

Esouli packed their suits with vials of Vodoxium, a backpack that fitted tight to their bodies. The next morning the boys had a quiet breakfast. All on board were in a state of unease, each boy lost in his own thoughts of what was to come, they looked at each other.

'You ready for this?'
'Nope, but we're doing it anyway, I guess a lot of people depend on us.'
Louis put his arm around Charlie's shoulders.
'We've got this.'
Together they examined the craft they would be entering, looking at it from all angles.
'Bloody hell, it looks massive Louis.'
'I guess where about to find out.'

CHAPTER 39

The tetrahedron triangle became invisible, slowly and carefully Esouli aligned the craft to the hatch.

The boys had special suits for when they were in human form. The moment had come. Esouli embraced them both and encouraged breathing exercises to keep them calm. He assured both that he would be watching at all times. The boys were quiet, keeping calm, concentrating on their purpose, but going into the unknown was a chilling prospect. Two cockroaches left the secure craft and entered the hatch, they were quick. The hatch closed. Esouli waited for contact.

Once inside the enormity of the ship was incredible. The boys turned back into themselves and turned on the contact receptors and moved forward to get a clear view. Scanning the bottom area of the craft, it contained roughly 500 metal suits, perfectly lined up.

'What are they Esouli?'

He was scanning the suits.

'They appear to be single control transporters. They're a strange shape, two little domes on the top and room for arms and legs.'

Charlie was fascinated.

'Whoever gets in these are only about a metre and a half tall.'

'Ish' said Louis.

'Maths was never my thing.'

'I need you to scan the entire space, move through carefully.'

The boys moved, scanning up and down.

'Wait!' whispered Esouli, 'Turn right.'

A luminous panel, small with a power source surging through was attached to the wall. Esouli's technology scanned the panel.

'This part of the ship can disengage, and it has its own flying power. It's a safety net for escape. There has to be something to release the transporters.'

Louis bent down looking under the suits, while Esouli scanned them.

'The release is under the suits; this is very clever. Wait there is another one inside, two escape plans.'

Charlie and Louis now moved towards the tunnel area heading to the next level. As they looked into the tunnel, air started to swirl around.

'Do either of you have anything in your pockets?'

'I have a chain I used to wear,' said Charlie.

'Throw the chain in tunnel.'

The air lifted it quickly to the next level.

'Will this lift us?'

'Yes Charlie. I have scanned and stored all information on this level. It's time to move up, you don't need to shift for this. When you get to the top shift immediately to something small or invisible.'

'Let's do invisibility.'

The boys did a high five and jumped in the tunnel, the forceful atmosphere grabbed them up like a tornado. Tumbling onto the next level they instantly became invisible. Esouli scanning quickly. There were two distinct areas to this second tier. In a half circular area, pods the same size as transporters looked curious. The boys moved forward slowly. Looking into a pod not knowing what to expect, they came face to face with a little being, blinking in fear. On further investigation only about forty of the pods had a life inside.

'They appear to be locked in as prisoners.'

Esouli continued scanning.

'This is all that is left of this race.'

'You mean the rest have been eaten?'

'Yes Louis.'

'Do we stay normal so they can see us?'

'Wait Charlie, something is coming. Quickly shift!'

Charlie was having trouble.

'Quickly!'

'Alright!'

'It's coming.'

A Dradask came from the tunnel floating towards the pods. Louis and Charlie were so close they could touch it. It's hovering tentacles settling. It touched an area on the floor and all the pods opened. The little beings started to squeal.

'It's their fear call,' Esouli's voice in their ears.

Slowly out of its ever-widening mouth, a long thick forked tongue sprung forth. The tongue swept over every pod, then touched each being. Their squeals got louder. Louis's emotions started to heighten he could feel his tears welling. His body was starting to become visible.

'Louis be calm.'

'It's going to eat them!'

'You can stop it, just breathe!'

'I've got it,' said Charlie, shifting into a big juicy Queffle and heading up the next tunnel, making a grunting noise.

Its tongue was wrapping around the little being closest to them. It started to lift the squealing body, slowly killing it. A big healthy grunting Queffle caught his attention slipping up into the tunnel, being far more appealing, he dropped the little being back in its pod. With its tentacles rotating, it floated with haste into the tunnel, the hideous tongue waving in the air, chasing the lone Queffle.

Charlie landed back as a sparrow, leaving the frenzied Dradask looking desperately for the tasty big Queffle.

'Nice move,' said Louis. 'That was quick thinking.'

'Thanks dude, my native instincts kicked in.'

Esouli had assessed the beings, he imparted his findings to the boys.

'The two oval domes on their head are a dual brain. If you place your hand gently on both of one, they can all communicate with you. You have to hurry, the Dradask will come back.'

Hands gently touched the oval shaped brains. The beings had an insect appearance, with eyes high on their round face, soft green with long lashes, two holes for a nose with a soft membrane half covering them, and a tiny mouth with a permanent slight smile. They were a dark yellow in colour. A long body, with refined fingers, all six long for intricate work. Insect like arms and legs, tiny feet with six toes.

'They look fragile' said Charlie, 'and there is not many left.'

Louis was relaying the message to Esouli.

'I would say they are hungry and on the decline. They are from several galaxies. Their home planet became volatile and was starting to burn out from the centre. Of the entire population, only five hundred boarded the ship and made their way to the third galaxy. They stopped on a planet compatible with their needs. What they didn't realise, the Dradask were busy feeding on the other side. When the Dradask sensed food the entire population put their massive tongues in the air to determine the direction of the food.'

Louis again placed his hands on the head of one being and communicated their escape, now all the pods were opening. The unusual beings just watched them, distress and fear on their faces. They communicated they could not leave the one flying the craft, as they were all deeply connected.

Esouli relayed the concerns. Louis asked what they are called.

'Jomonial.' Esouli replied, 'Their original planet had the same name.'

'How are we going to keep them from being eaten Esouli?'

Louis was feeling anxious.

'The ship has landed, now it won't be long before it topples and sinks, the ground will begin to shift to accommodate the arrival. You will have to move up to the next level and rescue the one flying the ship, they will not leave otherwise. You will need to shift now and move fast.'

The next tunnel will take you to the navigator. The boys repeated the jump, being gathered once more by the spiralling air, it landed them in the highest disc. Louis and Charlie's hands started to appear.

'Esouli our hands, we can see our hands.'

'How is you're breathing?'

'It's getting hard.'

'Quickly, hide behind those support pillars.'

There was a strange smell and sound in the air. Slowly they peeped out from their hiding position. The sight was repulsive. The Dradask, about twenty of them, with more lined up waiting, were grunting and shoving each other. They were in a feeding frenzy.

Remnants of what could only be described as a garden. Fruit and legume shaped objects lay shrivelled and dead. It looked like a very advanced food growing system, similar to Arume's people. More dead vines hung sad and desperate, everything was pulled apart.

'This is the Jomonial's food supply. They must be starving.' Louis whispered.

'Poor little guys,' said Charlie 'they're probably not feeling the best.'

The boys studied the scene further. A large pool of froth emerged, the Dradask excitably crowded around the edge. Large black blobs floated on the surface.

'Oh my God,' said Charlie 'we saw this in the crystal pool.'

Tongues and long claw like fingers pulling the black slime apart desperately trying to get out. The spawning Dradask made a guttural sound, the smell like black putrid garbage. The adults long forked tongues sipping into the spawning pond. Slowly they wrapped their tongues around the baby Dradask. The young starting to make louder noises understanding what was about to happen. Loud rotating teeth, pulled the babies into their mouths, flesh black in colour, and black slime flew into the air.

Louis and Charlie's minds went into a seizure. The noise and the smell assaulted the senses, the sight horrifying.

Esouli's voice came to them.

'Boys breathe deeply.'

Another noise distracted them. A high-pitched squeal. Taking another look on the roof of the craft, movement attracted the boys' attention. Coming out of what looked like paper wasp nests, delicate flying beings. Hovering over the slime pond feeding more spawning Dradask their own babies in small sacks were the Lanorigal.

'It's the Lanorigal.' Louis was excited. 'We have to save them!'

'Oh Christ, it's getting worse, this tongue shit is not cool.'

Suddenly the entire craft moved sideways toppling over. The top disc would sink first. The Dradask's tentacles started to rotate and hover, the big monsters crashing and scrambling to get to the top level.

'Quickly boys you have to move.'

'Esouli, we can't go completely invisible.'

'In your backpacks you have a vial of Vodoxium. Charlie, walk towards the Lanorigal and their nests.'

It was hard with the ship was still moving.

'Open it, hold the vial up to them, open your backpack and they will come to you.'

One little creature came towards Charlie, fear expressed on its face. It hovered in front of Charlie, blue wings beautiful in the light with a meerkat looking face and a bird-like body and big brown terrified eyes. The creature raised its arms up, then shifted into a little blue straw like figure. Charlie put his hand out and placed it in the backpack. With a great flurry all the little beings left the nest in great haste, one by one dropping into the back- pack with desperation and the hope of safety. The ship moved again throwing them off balance.

'Do it now boys, drink the Vodoxium.'

Charlie could hear the little straw people chattering it made him smile. The Vodoxium was surging throughout their bodies.

'In your packs you have a tiny pocket-knife. Remember in your training if you give yourselves a small cut, you can conjure a weapon. We didn't want to have to do this, but if you don't rescue the last Jomonial they will cease to exist, it's their leader.'

The boys moved into the tunnel gathered up once again in the turbulent wind and lifted to the control centre, they both chose tranquilizer guns with hundreds of cases.

Instantly they hid, the noise was deafening, the Dradask were terrified roaring and hovering, trying to stay upright, smashing into each other all their tongues pointing and quivering at the one being, expecting it to save them.

'Are you ready Charlie?'

'Yep. Let's do this!'

They started firing their tranquilizers. It took a while, but one by one they dropped. The Dradask were confused, they lay like big helpless logs. The rotating tentacles spinning like wheels, mouths still crunching, strange sounds hard to distinguish what emotion they were expressing.

The Jomonial creature clung onto the chair in front of the navigation panel. He was very afraid, eyes blinking fast.

'What do I do Esouli?' Louis cried frantically.

'Be calm Louis and repeat these words.'

He moved toward the Jomonial, speaking the words as instructed.

'Elian, Elfinian, Eldanlai.'

His brain started to light up and pulsate. The craft moved again, slipping further into the never-ending blackness, extinction of their lives was moments away. The Dradask piled high, unable to get upright, rolling and crushing into each other, guttural roaring masses of tongues, frantically thrashing in the air. The little being did an unexpected thing. He ran to Louis, jumped into his arms and hung on for dear life, wrapping his arms around Louis's neck.

'Run!' was the only word they heard from Esouli.

The boys headed for the air tunnel crawling was the best option to mobilise. Louis told Charlie to go first.

'What are we gonna do when we get to the bottom?'

Charlie was being strong but felt like jelly inside. Rolling into the tunnel first, the craft felt like it was falling again, Louis scrambled behind. The little alien hung on tighter. Louis and his guest floated down, unbeknownst to them, peering into the tunnel above, a Dradask, his ravenous tongue in pursuit. It started wrapping around his torso. Louis couldn't think, the little being started to make a crying sound. It was pulling them toward its deadly cavity closer and closer. The crunching noise getting louder. The ship was falling, and it was too late, fear paralysed Louis.

He smelt roses, time froze, nothing moved, the noises stopped. What the hell was happening? Louis opened his eyes, a hologram of his grandmother appeared before him, he couldn't speak.

'Louis my beautiful boy, listen to me, I want you to concentrate. You have time to get out of this. Visualise the lake NOW.'

He sat at the edge of the secret lake, his little being was beside him. Hundreds of animals also inhabited the lakeside. It was so peaceful.

'When my vision fades you will shift instantly and sever that tongue. You need to think now what you are going to do. I can't hold this much longer it takes a lot of power.'

Louis's mind was racing, his heart was pounding in his chest, blood racing through his veins. His right arm was free, he closed his eyes and concentrated he could see what he needed to be. The muscles in his arm started to change, it was shifting into a powerful shape, it was like a moth coming out of a cocoon. His right arm was now a powerful samurai sword massive in size and ready to remove the anaconda like tongue. The sword came down. The creature roared, stinking brown sticky substance poured out of the dying appendage, spinning around the tunnel, it unravelled and fell, flailing and convulsing to its death.

Louis's body was again his own and free. The Jomonial now safe still clung tight, they drifted on down the tunnel. Louis jumped into freefall to the last air tunnel. Charlie and the other Jomonial were all waiting.

The little guy jumped off Louis and ran to his family. Massive chatter and very vibrant brains lit up the craft. Charlie grabbed Louis in a massive hug. Louis hugged him back.

'Quickly Charlie, we're just about done.'

As soon as Louis spoke the word the craft shuddered. The Jomonial were busy at the control panel, it was activating.

'I've been handling a few brains,' said Charlie 'these fellas confirmed this part of the ship can separate, like dropping its arse end like a lizard.'

A strange rumbling sound echoed in the craft they were in complete darkness and falling further into oblivion. Louis and Charlie couldn't move, petrified with fear.

'Oh God Charlie, we've failed.'

Suddenly the craft stopped, the metal in the ship started to swirl around, the energy was incredible. It could be felt vibrating through their bodies. Their part of the ship was completing a separation, the craft was reversing, however it was getting pulled by gravity into the dark holes on the Queffle's planet. It wasn't powerful enough to get free.

From the viewing panel they looked back into the depth of the planet. The rest of the craft could be seen disappearing. The Dradasks' faces crowded against their own viewing panel, the mouths still open the teeth rotating, pushing and shoving each other. Were they aware of sinking into extinction? The craft was being devoured and the planet was closing in fast. It was a race against time, the ship slipped sideways, Louis and Charlie fell, they were sliding with uncontrollable force. Both boys shape-shifted before any impact. A large ball and a tyre slammed against the internal structure. Shifting back instantly, the Jomonial put themselves safely in the travel pods.

A shaft of light could be seen. The triangle ship hovered above. Esouli was terrified he was going to lose the boys. The craft wasn't going to make it, the planet closed around it wedging it sideways. At the last moment before total closure, a small miracle happened.

The large viewing window broke away before it was swallowed completely, escaping into the atmosphere, all the pods free and flying at an incredible speed, like bullets out of a gun. The boys looked at each other, there were only seconds left.

Louis yelled at Charlie.

'Shift!'

'Into what?!'

'Something that flies. NOW!'

The planet Yaramist had swallowed everything forever. The dark hole closed over, the Dradask and the ship digested into the remarkable planet. Esouli could not see properly. The Jomonial's craft blocked his vision. The top of the Tetrahedron opened up like a time lapse flower blooming, the Jomonial descending to safety.

Esouli was in shock, frustrated with anger, and fear. Arume's despair was deep as he watched helpless. This was devastating. The future was now very unsure. Many beings saved, but the two crucial lives lost. Esouli sat heavily, heartbroken they were gone, a guttural cry of sorrow echoed within. The warrior in a state of devastation went to greet the Jomonial, feeling empty. The huge triangle ship moved slowly, the Jomonial needed to be fed and the gardens on board had produced what they needed.

Arume had communicated with the Jomonial. It was agreed they would be homed on Helomedes until a planet that was suitable for their needs and sustainable could be found. A terrible sadness had taken over the ship, Esouli , wept.

The forlorn little Christmas creature searched the outside environment. He was distraught and would miss the boys terribly. Even though he acted grumpy, they made his life lots of fun. He jumped off the navigating chair in front of the panel to follow Esouli. A dazzling white light caught his attention from the corner of his eye.

Running back to look at the outside world, a star doing very unusual movements shooting around the sky with erratic gestures, it fascinated Fudgunkel. That was not all, an unexpected eagle was chasing the star. Fudgunkel ran to Esouli making weird noises, grabbing and swinging off Esouli's coat and pointing to the outside, so excited he couldn't talk. Esouli searched the outside darkness. His eyes darting frantically.

'They're out there!' screeched Fudgunkel.

Something dazzling attracted the inside viewers. The face of an eagle and a dancing star, that appeared to have wings, hovered for all to see from within.

'Oh my God! It's them!'

Elation, laughter and a massive sigh of relief left Esouli's lungs as the top of the triangle opened.

'I knew it! I knew it!'

Fudgunkel danced, his bells tinkling, hands clapping, and some tears were quickly wiped away.

It was like the universe exhaled. The two boys ran into Esouli's arms, a delicate tear ran down Arume's face. The boys picked up Fudgunkel showering him with kisses, he complained and laughed. He had saved their lives.

CHAPTER 40

Collin Stephens sat in his old Mercedes, another bag of screwed up Macca's hit the floor, adding to the pile slowly reaching the bottom of the window. The file was nearing completion on Lucy Blackwell, he had to use all his usual contacts to do so.

Her journey had been a long one, mysterious flights but Collin could fill in some of the gaps. It wouldn't be hard to put together, considering the change in her looks.

Collin was overweight, smoked and spent a lot of time in his car. He was shabby and smelly, that's why Tristan chose him, no one took any notice of him, or if they did, it was with revulsion. Tristan slid into the passenger seat, Collin coughed and farted at the same time, that was his greeting. He slipped the bearded man the envelope and took the file. Tristan tried to hold his breath for the transaction and avoided conversation.

The trail went cold when it came to finding Louis's whereabouts. Tristan read the hospital files on Louis, the abuse and neglect. He closed the file and sat back in deep reflection. Their lives so different, but somehow the same. Louis was rescued, but he was not.

He needed to find someone in the system to find his half-brother. Tristan had people working on his father's affairs. It was like trying to put a human jigsaw puzzle together, the piece he didn't need was his mother's.

'The picture is not going to be complete,' he said out loud, 'but then again, no one's picture is complete.'

Jason sat watching Genevieve, she was beautiful, but regrettably she was as boring as bat shit. He searched his mind trying to think who she reminded him of, he smiled, there had been so many.

'Jason?'

'Oh, um yes?'

'What music and flowers?'

Jason put his phone down.

'I tell you what, I trust you and your exquisite taste.'

Jason had texted his secretary to ring him with anything to get him out of here.

'I'm sorry my beautiful bride to be, I have to go. Don't forget to check the weather forecast for our special day.'

Newspapers and popular magazines had been put on notice for the pending wedding. Popular chat shows were buzzing with speculation. Vivian had contacted and sent all the invitations Genevieve had indicated.

The wedding dress was exquisite, it was a sleek body-hugging dress, low cut at the back, off the shoulder. It was white lace threaded with gold. It had a gold lace trail. A soft veil attached to a diamond headdress. Gold strappy sandals with tiny, embedded diamonds were simply exotic. Diamonds for her ears and throat. Genevieve daydreamed about her vision on the wedding day. She will sparkle. The more cameras, the better. Genevieve was by herself feeling relaxed, an hour's massage did her wonders especially for her skin and muscles.

Her entire plan was falling into place, she started to giggle. She was going to dump him after the honeymoon in Paris. She would then leave for Hollywood and commence work on a new series she demanded Max Dupre arrange.

She laughed out loud, 'I can't wait to dump you.'

This was going to hurt Jason tremendously and ruin his path to politics.

She laughed again out loud, talking to herself.

'He's so in love with me,' she kept chuckling.

'I better not set foot back on Australian soil and then I'll sack those two lazy assistants.' She had the letters ready.

Genevieve danced around her lounge area.

'I can't wait for the wedding. I'm going to be the most stunning beauty they have ever photographed.'

She was like a child with not a care in the world.

Vivian heard everything. She slipped away carefully.

CHAPTER 41

Tristan had gathered a lot of information pertaining to his father's business dealings. Money could buy you anything in this world. Council employees certainly open up when bulging envelopes are handed out.

His father had certainly been busy clearing the way for his development. Tristan had got his information using fraudulent ways, false identities as ASIC officials and Federal Police. But what the hell it worked. They will never know who and how they got the information from.

Dear old dad had wined and dined many wealthy and influential investors in the development. The money came pouring in. Jason got greedy and careless. He started skimming the investors' money into an account for his campaign and enhancing his lifestyle.

The curious damage to Aboriginal ancient rock art, it took some time to uncover. Jason demanded one of his council employees get rid of them. A Parks and Gardens employee had his car paid off to do the deed on the art. Tristan decided to take a drive to the site and visit the lake again. It was a beautiful day he pulled up at the site. Lots of bushland had been clear felled. The earthworks were underway to create an impressive entrance. Blasting and removal of waste was due to start around the lake in the next week.

Tristan got clearance from the site manager, he had to don a hard hat and high visibility vest. He looked at the dead vegetation stacked up ready to be removed. It made him feel forlorn, skeletons of a once vibrant life. He didn't understand the emotion or why he would even feel it. He moved on towards the lake, everything was quiet, and the lake was still. Small rock wallabies and bird life drank in peace.

Soft grasses and flowering shrubs swayed slowly in a stirring breeze. The sun reflected off the mountainside. Birds took flight the closer Tristan got, with the exception of two. He couldn't define what they were, as they were hidden in the shadows.

He felt drowsy, the sun was warm, and sweat trickled down his back, it felt like crawling insects. He removed his clothes down to his boxers, it was too tempting. The water felt like being wrapped in fine silk. He swam to the centre of the lake, floating on his back his body tingled, returning to the soft sand, he fell into a kind of twilight sleep, his eyes partially open. The two birds could be seen more clearly. A huge eagle and a tawny frog mouth sat side by side looking at Tristan.

He smiled and waved.

'Hey fellas. How you doin'?

The birds looked at each other. Tristan laughed out loud, he actually felt happy. Looking around closely at the lake and mountains it made him feel peaceful, another different emotion.

When he got to his car, all the workers had knocked off for the day. He walked towards what was once Bridget and Louis's house. Something caught Tristan's eye, a piece of paper flapping like it wanted to be noticed. Shadows passed over head, the two birds settled in a Bunya pine.

Tristan gently lifted the paper out of the soil, although faded and stained the writing was still legible. It read, 'Afternoon tea in the fridge for you and Charlie. I love you Louis, see you after work. Bridget.' Somewhere, stored in his mind, the name Louis was familiar.

He drove slowly, listening to his favourite Indi music, there was a traffic jam ahead, it looked like a caravan had decided to go its own way. Tristan sat waiting, looking around, a parkland was on his right. A rose garden was in full bloom. Different colours, randomly planted, he could actually smell them in the air. Roses. Rosa! That was it! The newspaper clipping, 'Louis', was the boy's name. He got straight on the phone.

'Collin, write this name down. 'Louis Blackwell' and 'Bridget'. I don't know the last name.'

He gave Collin the address of what used to be their home, he assumed. Next Tristan called Rosa, he organised to take his two favourite women out for dinner. Strange thing is he did actually like Rosa and Vivian, they were kind and treated him like he mattered. He wanted to have another look at the items Vivian found in the bottom of Ms St Day's briefcase.

Tristan waited in his car outside the penthouse. Jason and Genevieve were attending a cocktail party for socialites, the wealthy and TV personalities. He watched her exit the front entrance, a limousine pulled up to meet her. Her hair was piled high on her head. A body-hugging red dress, strapless, black pearls contrasted with the red. As always Genevieve was determined to outshine any female within her vicinity. She is like a fashion warrior, taking out all the competition.

Rosa and Vivian have become very fond of Tristan, he was kind and thoughtful.

'Can I ask a question?'

'Of course,' said Vivian.

'What are you ladies going to do when 'IT's' married off?' Rosa giggled.

'Go home,' said Vivian.

'And we can't wait!' said Rosa.

'I was wondering if I could take a look at those secret items in the bottom of 'IT's' briefcase?'

'Of course you can! In fact, you can keep them,' said Vivian.

'But don't you want to keep them for when your work is finished with her? You know, as an investment.'

'We don't need to,' said Vivian with a rather mischievous smile and a tilt of her head.

'Oh, I see,' said Tristan, returning the smile.

Tristan laid everything on the table. There it was, a tiny clipping, it was Lucy Blackwell's mother's obituary.

'Louis Blackwell, the dearly loved grandson.'

'I think I have found my half-brother...I hope.'

'My god Tristan that's wonderful.'

Rosa started crying. She couldn't help herself, she put her arms around Tristan's shoulders. He froze. No one had ever touched him with affection. Rosa kissed him on the head, he felt a warm rush, a feeling of security. He laughed, feeling embarrassed at his reactions.

'We are going to miss you, Tristan.'

'And I you.'

The phone rang while driving home.

'I can confirm your question.' Collin coughed up some phlegm.

'That was the home of Bridget Sherwood and Louis Sherwood, formerly Blackwell. Your father used forged documents to remove them. He paid them $180,000 and threatened them with further legal action if they didn't get out and they would get nothing. He used a paid off solicitor to do the dirty work with nasty letters. She had no money to defend, no one would touch it considering who Mr Blackwell was.'

'So where are we now?' Tristan's voice had a tinge of excitement.

'Still trying to follow the trail. I'm guessin' it won't be long.'

'Okay. Thanks Collin. Stay on it.'

He felt disappointed, but it was just a matter of time. He waited for the voices to have their say and laugh. Nothing. No Response. His head was quiet. Tristan smiled and drove off.

CHAPTER 42

The Jomonial and the Lanorigal were exhausted, some of the Jomonial were close to death. Esouli and his helpers were busy trying to feed and heal. Drops of Vodoxium were put in their mouths to try and regenerate their body systems. Food was prepared to entice them to eat. Everyone was deeply worried that their deterioration was beyond rescuing. The little Lanorigal beings recovered to good health however, they were nervous and stayed very close to Charlie, they had been through horrendous times having to feed their own to the Dradask. Esouli discovered they were taken off the same planet as the Jomonial.

Louis and Charlie came out of their pods.

'Oh my God, I am so hungry.'

Charlie's familiar voice put a smile on Louis's face. Fudgunkel was waiting for them.

'Come on, into the shower. You two stink. Come on!'

Charlie and Louis shuffled off. After eating, the boys met with Esouli for debriefing and to see how the boys were feeling.

'How are you boys coping?'

They both sat back, quiet and reserved.

'We didn't get the sphere,' said Louis feeling so desperate.

'Now the ship with all the living lifeforms can't leave the mountain, and it's all my fault.'

'Dude wait a minute, I failed as well, you can't wear this by yourself.'

'Boys, please. What you did was incredible. You saved remnants of two very important species. This is a backward step admittedly, but we can find a way around it.'

'How are they all doing?' said Louis. 'They didn't look good.'

'It's going to take time, they have lived a terrorised life with the Dradask.'

The craft moved quietly through space, Louis and Charlie fell into a state of melancholy because they didn't get the sphere.

The boys sat, literally staring into space. Esouli walked up behind them.

'I need you two to come with me.'

'Where to?'

'One of the Jomonial is in trouble.'

'What do you mean?' said Louis.

'We can't open his pod to treat him. He can't hear us due to the metal and its peculiar elements, or that's what I'm assuming.'

The boys went with Esouli to a different level. When the ETs set eyes on the boys, excitement, chatter and little brains flashed wildly in unison. They all gathered around the boys. The Lanorigal flying around their heads.

'Well! I guess you guys are very popular.'

Charlie and Louis smiled and gently touched the gathering beings. The Jomonial tugged at Louis's coat and pulled him towards the unopened pod.

Louis and Charlie looked in the pod, Louis frowned.

'What is it?'

'This is the one that navigated the ship.'

'How can you be certain of that?' asked Esouli.

'He has a tear in his suit, see.'

Louis stepped closer, then something happened. His brain started to glow slowly. Louis put his face closer to the pod, the opening slid back, it frightened Louis, he jumped back, nearly knocking Charlie over.

'Something's happening.' Esouli was confused.

The ship started to glow and vibrate, it seemed to speed up.

'What's happening?' said a panic-stricken Charlie moving towards Esouli.

'The sphere,' said Esouli, 'it's here.'

Louis hurried towards the pod. He was awake, Louis helped him out, supporting him to stand. The extra-terrestrial put his arm around his back, in his hand was the sphere. It too was traumatised, slowly coming to life knowing it was safe.

'Oh my God,' said Charlie, 'this little fella saved everything.'

'He only wanted Louis,' said Esouli.

The little Jomonial fell down.

'Quickly he needs help.'

Louis picked him up and placed him on a treating bed. Esouli got to work he put a tube in for feeding and a drop of Vodoxium in its mouth. The little ET was put in a deep sleep to heal and restore. Louis sat by the pod watching and talking to his very sick new friend, he dosed off into a dream state.

He had a huge tongue wrapped around him, another tongue pulling his body in half, blood gushing into his mouth. Louis woke sweating and fell off his chair, his heart tachycardic, panting, he strained trying to stand up. A light caught his eye, twin brains were activating, the eyes opened, tears rushed blurring Louis's vision he quickly wiped them away, relief at last, his new mate was going to live.

Arume appeared on the screen to talk to Esouli.

'Hello my old friend! I trust all our travellers are well?'

'Everything is on track and all is stable.'

'We have found a planet that may suit our homeless beings.'

The boys were trying to show the Jomonials how to kick a ball. It was hilarious, Charlie was breathless from laughing. They were clumsy but determined to try. They made a strange noise, that Louis assumed was laughter, the Lanorigal flew in the air, buzzing from one to another. Esouli's voice could be heard asking for their company. It was explained to all present regarding a future for their friends on board. Arume explained with translation that all assistance would be given to settle on a new viable planet, and all support from Helomedes would be given to reconstruct their homes and their lives.

The screen became alive. A view of the planet as they slowly approached. It was half the size of Earth. As it became clearer the landscape looked like geometrical formed stripes. A closer look defined the pattern. Lines of small hills, small streams of water meandered around the hills. Flat savannah grassland between the hills. Growing at a set distance umbrella style trees enhanced the interesting pattern. The surface vegetation included yellow moss. The entire planet was an organised display.

'This is incredible' said Louis, 'there are two small suns what's the air quality like?'

'It's not as highly concentrated as Earth but considering the size of the future inhabitants it may be suitable.'

The landing was quiet, Louis detected nervousness in the Jomonial, he put his hands gently on his friend's brain. They followed closely with Louis.

'I think you have some special friends,' said Charlie, giving Louis a flick in the head.

'I'm not the only one, look up! You too have company. I think we have some very nervous dudes.'

It was full daylight. It felt cool, the suns felt warm. Breathing was slightly laboured for the earthlings. The Jomonial and the Lanorigal were busy processing the elements, collecting data, their brains highly tuned.

Louis and Charlie decided to investigate further. They felt the moss, it was soft and pliable with no odour. Charlie felt the water, it was very cold, obviously coming from inside the planet. It was odourless. Charlie tasted it. Louis bent down to taste.

'It's good,' said Charlie.

'Can you believe we're standing here on another planet, another galaxy?!'

'I know,' said Louis.

'It's become normal.'

'Yeah it has.'

'What do you think of this place?' asked Charlie.

'I guess it's going to be hard for them to start again.'

'I think they will be okay, going from a terrible place to a good place.'

'You thinking about Bridget?'

'Yeah, I miss her.'

Louis changed the subject.

'I guess these guys have a lot of abilities we are not aware of.'

The little flying Lannies landed on the boys.

'I think these guys should go back to Esouli's planet. There's only a few of them and all perched on me.'

They all gazed at Charlie, gentle little faces, you couldn't help but love them.

'I could take them home.'

All the Jomonial stayed with Louis, together scanning the planet. Something felt uneasy in Louis, the Jomonials brains started to light up, the Lannies started to chatter. Louis's brain started to tingle something was happening deep in his brain.

'Louis, what's wrong? You look weird dude!'

'I think they're trying to talk to me, my head is scrambling with noise.'

'We better get back, you're looking really weird dude.'

The glowing brains stared pulsating. It was relentless. Louis held his head, Charlie was terrified.

Louis fell to the ground still holding his head, Charlie knelt down beside him holding Louis. Esouli bent down to hold Louis's head, Charlie screamed at Esouli.

'Do something!'

Then it all stopped. Louis slowly sat up.

'Shit dude, that scared the crap out of me.'

'I can hear them.'

'What?'

'What are you saying?'

'I can talk to them. They're terrified of new beginnings. They watched the Dradask eat nearly the entire race. They destroyed their home, ate their babies and captured them. They want to come with us to Helomedes.'

'Then, so be it,' said Esouli. 'Let's all get back to the ship, the air quality is changing.'

A strange odour was coming out of the moss.

'Oh Jesus,' said Charlie 'that's vile!'

'Quickly to the ship.'

The Jomonial started to fall to the ground.

'No!' was all Louis could say.

Esouli's arms shifted into huge hands. He gathered them all. Louis and Charlie visualised a bag. The Lanorigal flew into them.

'Run!'

That night all the beings sat together eating. It was decided the Jomonial and the Lanorigal could colonise Helomedes. Arume was happy for that outcome, pleased they were all safe. Their planet was already a multi-alien planet. Esouli had analysed the moss. Spores were released at a certain temperature, but not visible. They proved to be deadly to lungs.

'That explains,' said Louis, 'why nothing else lives on the planet.'

'Well, it looked pretty groovy,' said Charlie.

Louis chucked a bread roll at him. Peace settled once again.

CHAPTER 43

The boys lounged at the navigational panel, the Vodoxium swirled captured within the structure of the Tetrahedron. Its emotional elements allowed it to understand verbal communication. The boys were learning the intricacies of the craft.

'You know bro, it's like this craft is alive.'

'Well, I guess,' said Louis, 'considering its powers, that sounds about right.'

Esouli joined the boys at the panel. He showed the boys how to extend the visual screen to extreme distances.

It was a beautiful thing to watch. Luminous lines, swirling circles, strange noises, then commands and coordinates were fulfilled.

'While you are both here, I need to tell you that we are taking a detour on our way to Helomedes.'

'We goin' via Macca's drive-thru?'

Louis burst out laughing.

Esouli gave him a gentle shove.

'So where's this new digs we're going to?'

'It's the planet Silabistis.'

'All these weird names.'

'Do you boys remember, or have you ever heard of Area 51, the United States Air Force facility?'

'Oh yeah,' said Louis, 'it's somewhere near Nevada.'

The coordinates came up on the screen, 37 degrees, 14 minutes North latitude, 115 degrees, 48 minutes West longitude. All the information regarding the site came up.

'There is supposed to be a massive underground construction.'

'You're right Louis.'

'They were supposed to have found an alien in a crashed spacecraft.'

'That is also correct Louis.'

'Do you remember seeing or hearing about documentaries about people being taken and returned by aliens?'

'Yeah,' said Louis, 'people reckoned they were taken into ships and had all sorts of experiments and probes done on them.'

'They called them 'The Greys',' said Charlie.

'Wow,' said Louis, 'you do know your stuff.'

'Oh, don't tell me we're goin' to the Greys planet?'

Esouli laughed.

'Don't suppose they have Macca's?'

Charlie looked at Esouli.

'You're serious?'

'Why?' said Louis.

'They need help with food production, but I need to tell you guys something, and it is going to be hard to process.'

'Not again,' said Charlie. 'Do they have three heads and drink blood?'

Esouli put his hand on Charlie's shoulder.

'It's okay Charlie, they're not dangerous.'

'Are we really going there because of food? Do you trust them? What about the Vodoxium, will they be responsible?'

Esouli put his hand on Louis's shoulder.

'It's okay they are friendly.'

'How will you help the food production?'

'We will give them a device similar to your iPad, powered by Vodoxium. It contains all the knowledge to set up growing facilities, plus one small vial and a great variety of seeds specifically selected.

'Are they vegetarian?' asked Louis.

'Yes, but they do supplement with insects and worms.'

'Oh God! Worm burgers and cockroach frappes,' said Charlie.

'The good news is,' said Louis, 'they don't eat meat.'

The two boys giggled together, impressed by their own comments.

'Now, back to our original conversation, about the Greys visiting Earth. The reason for the visits and abductions? The Greys are an old race that have existed for thousands of years. They control their breeding to ensure a sustainable planet. They are advanced with technology in regard to building spaceships. This was how they went about their mission undetected. Until the craft crashed. They are an experimental race and that was the reason for the flight to earth. The Greys took humans to investigate the anatomy and physiology and study the immune system. The reason they did this was to save their race from becoming extinct.'

'What do you mean?' asked Louis.

'They became weak and sick and started to die. They became frantic and afraid for their very existence. They gathered stem cells, eggs and sperm, tissue and blood. From this they created a new and stronger being.'

'You mean they are human and Grey cross?!'

'Yes Louis.'

'Holy shit!'

Charlie and Louis looked at each other speechless.

Before the boys could descend into a mood of doom, Esouli spoke again.

'The area we are going to, requires us to enter a huge black hole.'

'Jeez, this is just getting better. I love black holes,' said Louis.

Esouli continued, 'This particular one has gathered many items.'

'A big second-hand shop.'

Esouli laughed at Charlie's sense of fun.

'The craft itself is going to shape shift to ease our travel. Our guests will have to enter their pods. The Lanorigal will have to be kept safe.'

'That's okay, I'll sort out my little buddies. Can we stay in our chairs if we get strapped in? I really want to see this.'

The Tetrahedron with its passengers changed direction. It was a magical sight accelerating into darkness, a brilliant glow of gold disappearing.

CHAPTER 44

Bridget studied the development site. Tiny shrubs, grasses, and ground covers pushed their determined way through the soft churned up soil. Fresh and full of life. The weed spraying sign fading in the afternoon sunlight. Holding her precious crystal tightly, the power pulsated in time to her own heartbeat. Inhaling deeply her mind focused on the sacred environment.

'Who the hell are you?'

Bridget remained unmoving her mind quiet.

'You!'

A hand went on her shoulder trying to spin her around. Bridget turned by her own free will, looking into the face of the very attractive Jason Blackwell.

'Oh, I'm sorry. Are you looking to invest?'

His voice slipped into the silky salesman tone.

'No, I'm not.'

'Then what are you doing here?'

'Just looking.'

'Then you need to leave, you're trespassing.'

'I'm just looking at the view.'

Bridget studied his face to find a resemblance of Louis.

'Don't you know who I am?'

Jason not used to people ignoring his commands.

'I know exactly who you are, and do you know who I am?'

'I couldn't give a rat's arse who you are!'

'Well Mr Blackwell, I'm the woman who used to live there.'

Bridget pointed to her old home site.

'Oh, the jam cooking, herb growing hippie.'

Bridget felt the anger pulsating its way to her mouth, a noise above interrupted the passage of anger, an eagle floating, soft and peaceful. She decided to walk away with her dignity intact. Jason Blackwell laughed into the wind at his own quick wit.

Bridget had fluctuating emotions about Jason Blackwell. Firstly anger, then frustration and then she burst out laughing. What an arrogant, vile person.

'Well Mr Blackwell, I obviously have the only decent part of you, your beautiful son. I have more than you will ever have.'

Bridget laughed again, mainly for the fact she was talking to herself. Bridget, Isobel and Simone watched the sunset on the verandah. It was a stunning evening, the sea rolled gently in its rhythmic way. Plovers and seagull calls carried into the slow darkening night.

A distraction fluttered into the Bunya pine, the big eagle and his tawny frogmouth buddy settled on a branch, low enough to be at eye level with the people on the verandah.

'Look Mum, Bridget, we haven't seen these fellas for a while.'

Simone pointed at the tree.

Everyone sat silent sipping homemade lemonade and eating Isobel's French fries.

'You're such and old hippie.'

Bridget burst out laughing, after relaying what Jason Blackwell had said.

'Now where's my joint?' said Isobel.

Over the distant mountain an orange glow spread into the sky, slowly a magnificent full moon greeted the night. The ocean glittered like diamonds in the sun, it felt akin to the dawning of a new world, fresh and untouched. Magpies started to settle into the Bunya. Galahs came screeching in for rough landings, and on it went, kookaburras, cockatoos, parrots. The Bunya was at capacity, the higher the moon went, and the birds became quiet.

'What's going on?' said Simone. 'This is weird, but somehow really awesome. Bridget, any idea what's happening?'

She was unable to take her eyes off the tree.

'They're excited I can feel it, the blue crystal's glowing on the table. They're safe. It's done.'

'Are you sure?' asked Isobel.

'The birds are the message.'

'Charlie and Louis are safe then?' asked Simone.

'It was said there would be a message, and this is it.'

Isobel wrapped her arms around her daughter.

'Will they be home soon Mum?'

'I'm guessing they could be.'

Slowly one by one, each bird took flight, single file. It was an extraordinary sight, the line of birds in a silhouette against the divine amber moon.

CHAPTER 45

Jason Blackwell was swinging backwards in his large office chair, smiling to himself. Jill rang through a call it was the site manager.

'Yes Rex, what can I do for you? I hope you have good news.'

'Well, I don't know how to say this, but, um...'

'Oh, come on.'

'...the development site, it's back to the way it was.'

'What the hell do you mean 'back to how it was'?!'

'The bushland, it's back and bigger than it was before.'

'I'm on my way, and by the way, you're sacked.'

Jill heard the raised voice, she waited, the window smashed, the door opened with a fury and Jason stormed through.

'Oh Mr Blackwell, don't forget your appointment at 4:30pm.'

'Shut up you stupid bitch.'

Jill sat stunned. She turned on her computer and started typing out her resignation.

Jason maintained his fury, desperate thoughts smashing his brain. One thought in particular was tormenting him, he had played the stock market with investors' money and lost heavily. He arrived at the apartment calm and precise in movement. Scrambling through his walk-in robe, behind his suit he extracted a gun case. He pulled out a semi-automatic rifle and three rounds of ammunition. Driving carefully not wanting to attract any attention, he was convinced someone was purposely sabotaging the development. He was sure it was a radical greenie group and convinced they were camping secretly around the lake. He remembered the Aboriginal art. Yeah, probably some sort of revenge. Wait until I get their arses in court.

Jason dialled a number on his phone. He demanded the person on the other end to go ahead with the explosives to demolish the huge rock walls that surround the lake.

Jason laughed.

'Think you can beat me?!'

He was gobsmacked. The bushland regrowth was inconceivable, even the growth from where the weird shack was had grown back. The anger was returning, he walked the path to the lake. Looking around the entire area, it was almost like the lake was protected. Walking on he reached the lake, birds of varied species, wallabies and grey kangaroos drank from the lake. Many birds rested in the massive trees. Jason looked around for signs of camps. He searched, but he found nothing. The anger started to surge again and again, he yelled his frustration into the wind, birds lifted into flight, fear on their wings. A large eagle stretched his wings, disturbed by the human.

Jason had his rifle loaded, his frustration and anger heightening. Face red with rage he fired one bullet off, it felt good, another one, then another, the adrenalin pumping.

Mooki prepared for flight, Jason caught his movement out of the corner of his eye, he started randomly firing. Jason laughed like a maniac excited over the kill, releasing his frustration felt so good. When the majestic animal fell to the earth he screamed with pleasure feeling total satisfaction.

The pain felt like a burning rod going into the eagle's chest, everything became darker and smaller.

He laughed, 'Huh! Take that, you ugly bastard!

The maniacal laugh continued as if he had somehow resolved everything. The magnificent body came to rest on the soft grasses. Silence fell all around, nothing stirred, Jason was unnerved, feeling spooked, he started to run, faster and faster. Sweat poured from his body, fear enveloped him as if something was in pursuit, reaching the car, he turned on the engine for the air conditioner, then locked the doors. He didn't know why he was full of terror. His heart slowing down, hands squeezing the steering wheel to stop them shaking, the urine hot against the skin in his groin. The journey home eventually relaxed him, he needed to plan for his next move, the euphoria waning from the kill, and reality crowding his thoughts.

Darkness crept slowly around the mountain, still nothing stirred, many eyes watching the mountain. The opening to the inner mountain stirred, it was a pitiful moment, Arume emerged, his eyes moved to the devastation on the ground. He lifted into the night air. The lake glowed a beautiful blue, laying on the ground, a being the same as Arume, a delicate exquisite creature. He gathered his own in his arms, holding it close, his tears fell to the ground turning into pearl like drops. They soared into the atmosphere transforming into magnificent green eyes blinking and looking down on the scene below, and gradually vanishing. Arume glowed in the evening light and still holding his own, they ascended into the mountain. It was a mournful sight, the Tawny frogmouth sat alone. Lost. A sadness could be felt by all.

Back on board, the spaceship burst through a wall of coloured water, it felt like being spat out of a huge mouth. The craft then drifted slow and peaceful. Above them a yellow sky scattered with stars; the brightness was spectacular.

'That was short and sweet.'

Charlie was in awe of the vision outside.

'Something's wrong,' said Louis, his voice high.

Esouli was alert, an unbearable feeling settling heavily.

Louis adjusted the huge screen, moving lines, organising coordinates. His face was frantic, trying to find Earth.

'What's wrong?' said Charlie, concerned not understanding was what was happening.

Slowly coming into form, the mountainside was revealed. Arume could be seen clearly drifting toward the mountain entrance, a glorious being like himself cradled in his arms. Esouli and the boys looked on in sadness, gutted at what they were witnessing.

'How did this happen?' Louis and Charlie, eyes filled with sorrow.

CHAPTER 46

Jason was deep in thought, he had to get access Genevieve's money so far the share market fiasco had been hidden.

The phone rang.

'Hello beautiful woman. How about dinner tonight at our usual place? I have something really important I need to ask you.'

'I would love to darling. Rosa, now! I'm going out!'

They sat together at their usual table, perfectly positioned so all the patrons could see her.

Jason had rehearsed the scene he was about to act out. He held her hand gently looking at the diamond he had to fork out to impress this self-absorbed woman. He looked into her eyes.

'Look I know we set the date for our marriage and everything is organised.'

Genevieve's heart nearly stopped, she thought he was backing out.

'Can we bring it forward?'

Genevieve exhaled and laughed.

'Of course, my darling.'

Relief flowed through over his brain.

'You know I can't wait to be your husband and the honeymoon in Paris with you, it's a dream come true.'

'Oh God, I'm good,' she thought. She absorbed the compliment, the adoration fed her ego, better than food.

'Not long to go now I'll have all the money I need.' He smiled vacantly at his soon to be bride as he thought. 'I won't have to spend too much time with boring Barbie. The Paris trip will be something irritating, but worth it.'

Jason's thoughts were interrupted by the waiter, Genevieve didn't notice a thing, she was busy watching the people watching her.

Genevieve stretched out in her bed, Jason had already left, something about stupid explosions. Vivian had spent the previous evening and the morning adjusting all the arrangements. She had been abused, yelled at, cursed and called names.

Genevieve burst into hysterical laughter each time Vivian informed her of the difficult tasks she had given her.

'That's what I'm paying you for idiot.'

In eight days, she would be Jason's wife again and he has no idea. Again, she laughed, her plan working perfectly. Thank God for confidentiality, those two cows can't say a word. Her impeccable handsewn wedding dress was on its way from Paris. The photographer was rebooked and that's all that mattered.

Genevieve thought about Tristan, she supposed that weirdo should know about the change.

'Vivian, contact that Tristan and tell him about the adjustment.'

Genevieve studied her face close up in a magnified mirror, it looks perfect. She had to be careful, it was stitched so intricately, remembering the warning.

'Oh well, Rosa, massage time and make it snappy.'

Genevieve was out for the evening with Jason. Tristan, Rosa and Vivian sat very relaxed on the lounge. Leftovers of a Chinese banquet scattered across an enormous coffee table. Two and a half bottles of wine had done their job.

'I am to inform you Mr Tristan that the wedding date has been brought forward, it seems your father can't wait to marry the demon from hell.'

The raucous laughter was contagious, Rosa fell off the end of the lounge only to create more laughter.

'So seriously ladies,' said Tristan, straightening himself up, 'have you got your plans in place?'

'Oh, indeed we do,' said Vivian. 'The moment she heads off for the wedding, a taxi will be picking us up and heading to the airport.'

'Do you have enough, you know, finances again?'

'We certainly do.'

'We can't wait,' said Rosa, 'to see our families, it's been so long.'

Little tears fell off her cheeks, generated by the expensive alcohol.

'Speaking of families,' Vivian felt herself becoming emotional, 'did you find your half-brother?'

'It's been a hard trail to follow, you know when kids get into care, a lot of secrecy to protect them.'

'I understand,' said Rosa.

'I do have a couple of leads.'

'I hope you find him Mr Tristan, you need a family.'

'You know what? I'm gonna miss you two.'

'Let's exchange contacts,' said Rosa, still teary and emotional.

CHAPTER 47

Marcos Manuel struggled with the vegetation, he made it to the lake, he was angry.

'How the hell am I supposed to do this, it's a bloody forest.'

Jason Blackwell was determined the demolition was going ahead.

'For shit's sake, I can't even get a vehicle down here.'

He dialled Jason.

'Why wasn't this cleared? I can't get my bloody truck into the site!'

'It was cleared. I was there a few days ago, it's not that bad!'

'Bullshit, it's a bloody jungle.'

'Just do what you've been paid to do.'

Marcos ended the call. Jason threw the pen holder up the wall, no one sat at the reception desk.

Marcos did many trips to the site and back, he loved working with explosives, watching structures falling to earth, it was like releasing his own internal frustrations. It had taken all day to position his weapons of destruction. Tomorrow he would return and blow the hell out of this place, he laughed at his own words. The clean-up was going to be massive.

'Hope that Blackwell's got plenty of money.'

Marcos was exhausted, angry and needed a drink. He arrived home, showered, grunted at his wife and commenced to drink copious amounts of beer. When he drank his fill and reached that place in his mind that caressed his ego, a dinner waited in the oven for him. No one went near Marcos in the evening, his teenage kids stayed mostly at friends' places. His wife waited for the usual. He opened her bedroom door, spewed abuse, staggered to his own room only to fall into an alcohol induced sleep.

A new moon greeted the night sky, peeping over the mountains, its big face reflecting in the lake. A colony of bats moved quietly across the sky, heading for their feeding grounds. Around the hour of two in the morning, sounds of the night ceased. High on the mountainside a small beam of light escaped the opening, the light expanded, the entire area glowed in a brilliance of mauve.

Arume's tall, elegant figure appeared, ripples stirred on the lake. The tawny frogmouth flew out of the opening alone this time, he perched in his usual tree.

Arume's sorrow for the loss of one of his own ran very deep. Tonight, for the first time, his powers were going to be used on planet Earth. It had always been forbidden, however the situation had become urgent. One human was determined to fulfil his greed.

His gown falling to the ground and his body glimmering in the light, the coloured scales were so vibrant. His vents opened and closed down his back. Lifting his arms, a thin membrane appeared like a glider possum's. Raising into the air the mystical form then plunged into the lake. His body could be seen under the surface, moving at a powerful speed, around and around. Exiting like a bullet and he landed delicately on the mountain ledge. Standing perfectly still and lifting his right arm, an intense beam of light scanned the areas where Marcos secreted his devastating wares.

Soil and rock drifted into the air, the beam detected every planted explosion, suspended in the atmosphere, moving them like a conductor. Looking like giant tangled spiders, Arume's magic moved them to the entrance of the lake site. The tangled mess was draped over the huge development sign, like hideous, mad Christmas lights. It was a freakish vision to behold. The tawny frogmouth and Arume disappeared back into the mountain.

Rumbling could be heard in the distance, dark clouds and flash lightening worked together moving towards the mountain. Light breezes grew into serious wind. The clouds bunched and dropped, only enveloping the mountain and the lake, then released the contents. The rain saturated everything. The mass of dynamite hanging over the enormous sign was rendered inactive.

Marcos stirred from his alcoholic slumber, dried up dribble stained the sides of his mouth. He sat at the kitchen table with his morning coffee, the house empty of people. Texting Jason, he reminded him to put the money in his account or otherwise the demolition would not go ahead. One quick check of his account balance before heading out and a big smile spread across his face, he turned on the engine.

Marcos's mood didn't last upon reaching the site. He walked around the massive sign mouth open. Comprehension was difficult, he couldn't find a swear word to mouth what he was seeing. He took photos of the curious arrangement, then forwarded them to Jason with a message.

'Don't know what you're playing at, don't contact me again.'

Jason studied the images. It took a few seconds to realise what he was looking at. The chair crashed up the wall. The crimson flush of anger travelling up his face like a blood elevator. His thoughts racing. Who the hell is doing this? It could ruin him.

He paced backwards and forwards. He stopped.

'Alright,' talking out loud, one thing at a time.

By the end of the day Brenda Long sat at the desk, all requests from her new boss had been attended to. Brenda was in love. Jason Blackwell he was the most handsome looking man she had ever seen.

Jason and Tristan relaxed having lunch overlooking Sydney Harbour.

'You ready for the big day?'

'What? Oh, yeah 'the wedding'. Apparently I'm organised.'

'And the honeymoon?'

'Yep, just turn up for that too.'

'Is there something wrong Dad?'

'You could say that.'

'Can I help?'

Jason unloaded his stories about the lake development.

'So, you think someone has been sabotaging the site?'

'Not anymore.'

Jason detailed his plan.

'So how are your finances running, will they hold up? The investors must be getting nervous.'

'As soon as I put a ring on a certain finger a financial boost comes my way.'

Jason laughed.

'You need to find yourself a wealthy, dumb, 'Barbie'. And of course, looking like me helps.'

Jason laughed again.

Tristan gave a false laugh.

'How much is she worth?'

'Last time my unauthorised man checked, a cool 35 million.'

Tristan looked at his father with a false smile, he wasn't about to disclose his visits to the lake. He did wonder who was willing to play around with explosives to protect the site.

CHAPTER 48

Bridget, Isobel and Simone boarded the Manly ferry back to the city. It had been a wonderful day. First the aquarium, followed shopping, then a long outdoor lunch in the Corso. A slow walk to Fairy Bower Beach and back, double cones of Dutch ice cream and hand- made chocolates topped off the visit.

Settling into the train, Simone yawned, got herself relaxed and fell into a well needed sleep, her head resting on Isobel's lap. Bridget found a newspaper on the seat across the aisle. Isobel watched the world pass from the window seat. Bridget let out some weird laugh.

'You alright? You sound like you're having some kind of choking fit?'

Bridget shoved the paper in her face.

'Look at this.'

'Wow.'

'Notice the surroundings?'

'It's all grown back, this is fantastic.'

'Read on.'

It went on to say that Mr Blackwell would be employing 24-hour security, then recommencing preparation for construction.

'Well,' said Bridget, 'we will have to wait and see what happens.'

'If only he knew what he was destroying,' sighed Isobel.

'He's not a man that would care, greed knows no boundaries.'

'You're dead right Bridget, my wise old friend.'

'Oi, that's enough of the old.'

They giggled like teenage girls.

Tristan Blackwell sat in his car at the end of the street. He observed the activity at Isobel's house. He hadn't yet sighted Louis or Isobel's son. He assumed they could be on some sort of school holiday camp.

CHAPTER 49

The ship moved closer to the black hole. The enormous energy sucking it in was of an inconceivable force. Inside the craft it felt safe.

'I wonder why they call them black holes? Mum says my stomach is a bottomless black hole.'

Louis laughed.

'I know a little bit. It's a place where gravity pulls so much that even light can't get out. So, we are not supposed to see black holes, but this incredible craft allows us to see something no other human will ever see. This one is called 'Supermassive'. The scientists say that black holes have masses, could be a million suns together. Every large galaxy has a supermassive black hole at the centre.'

'Okay teach, that's enough for one day, you're makin' me nervous. How long before we come across the big bugger?'

'About half an hour' broke in Esouli, 'we need to prepare, the craft is beginning to change shape. Our little friends are in their pods.'

'I better go and put my dudes away.'

Louis joined Charlie to settle their friends into safety pods. All the food production areas were sealed off, it all changed shape as the ship did masses of vegetable plants fresh and preserved, all produced by the energy of Vodoxium, protected and able to feed its inhabitants for months.

'It's incredible to walk through a craft and having it change and adapt around you.'

'It is that technology Louis, that could only be dreamt of on earth.'

Everyone was safely seated, the powerful force drawing the craft at phenomenal speed. It was mesmerizing.

Once deep inside, the display was spectacular. It was like a continuous bucket of every colour on the spectrum being thrown in your face. Chunks of meteorite flew past. Scraps of metal racing madly to nowhere.

'What is that small stuff?' asked Charlie.

'Satellites, space junk,' replied Esouli, 'anything that gets sucked in.'

Rivers of stars streaming like lightning going that fast, a piece of space junk with USA still visible toppling over and over, crashing into anything in its way. A saucer shaped craft tumbled over and over.

'I wonder if anyone was in that? It's probably been in here for years.'

Small planets crashing into each other, brilliant colours again flashing into the turbulence, gold, orange and silver particles exploding. It was magnificent to watch it fell like rain. Everything suddenly slowed in the hole, darkness came, then without warning extraordinary brightness, like millions of mirrors reflecting off each other. The Vodoxium shaded the craft to protect the inhabitants inside. Miniature suns sparkled a gorgeous yellow, just hanging motionless, the boys continuously bombarded with the radiance of space. A heavy mist then fell around.

'Is this cloud?' asked Louis.

'I'm not sure,' said Esouli, also intrigued.

Louis bent forward to investigate small objects clinging to the outside of the craft.

The mist was like lace or snowflakes all joined together, once noticed they disintegrated, it was soothing and angelic to watch.

'Wow that was awesome!' Charlie just nodded.

Esouli had been observing the boys for a long time, they had certainly come a long way. The fears now turned to curiosity with willingness to protect each other and the vulnerable. Arume and he had spent many hours discussing their adjustments, and their personalities. It was agreed that the training and experience would prepare them for a new world, if and when necessary.

The atmosphere outside started to move again, the craft adjusting itself, changing shape, up ahead a strange and curious sight was looming.

'What the hell is that?'

Charlie and Louis were straining to see more.

A tunnel was forming, the ship was being drawn in, deeper and deeper, they were inside a tangled rainbow, churning, wild coloured snake like objects wrapping themselves around the bullet shaped craft, then slipping free to continue the crazy journey. The boys had to close their eyes it was hypnotising to watch.

'Don't look Charlie, it will make you vomit!'

'Don't worry dude, I got this!'

As quickly as it arrived, it was over. Calm and blackness replaced the craziness again. The craft floating in the darkness, it was serene for a moment after the utter chaos. The ship again responded by lighting up again.

'I wonder if anything lived in this?' asked Charlie.

'Possibly,' said Louis. 'I remember seeing docos on creatures that live in dark waters of our own oceans. Freakish looking, but able to survive in what seems like nothing. You know, no one is going to ever believe a word we say about all of this.'

'Yeah, I reckon we would be medicated out of our minds.'

'Well, at least our mothers will believe exactly what we have experienced. I can't believe that I've come from my past to this.'

Silent moments passed.

'What was it like, you know, before us?'

'It was pretty bad.'

Louis took a deep breath, eyes cast down.

'The neglect was fairly extreme, like I said before, my mum drank a lot. She was scarred physically and mentally.'

'Did you get fed properly?'

Louis smiled at this.

'No. She wasn't bothered. She was always in trouble with the DOCS.'

'You had a Granma though?'

'Yeah, and I loved her so much, it all went bad when she died.'

'What was that?!'

Louis bent forward, all eyes alert.

Curiosity got the better of the creature lurking outside. All beings inquisitive of each other. Charlie gave his version of the creature.

'I reckon he looks like a giant stick insect. Yeah! But he's got a membrane joining six stick legs. I wonder what he eats?'

'Oh God Charlie, always the food.'

'He's got a big mouth, long compared to the size of his head.'

'Yeah,' said Louis studying the creature.

'He's got no teeth, he's got filters.'

The creature started to move, the membranes opening and closing. Two antennae positioned on his head lit up with his body movement. It was a fascinating sight. The boys waved at the prying little creature, feeling slightly silly. The creature studied the boys, moments passed, he lifted his right stick arm with his four stick fingers. He then did an amazing thing–he waved back. The boys looked at each other and burst out laughing. Charlie waved both hands, the creature did the same. Louis was so excited he jumped up and down, their friend did the same. It was an unimaginable moment.

Out of the dark waters, two larger creatures of the same appearance hovered each side of the smaller one. The bigger ones watched for a while positioning themselves in front of the smaller creature. Slowly all three drifted back into the dark waters.

'Do you realise what just happened Charlie?'

'Yep, Mum and Dad came to get the stick kid!'

'Besides that?'

Charlie gave a blank look.

'We communicated. We are in the guts of some black hole, billions of light years from Earth, we found a lifeform and made contact!'

'Well, when you put it like that.'

'Yeah, it sounds like a drug induced dream.'

Louis gazed into the dark waters, astonished at what just happened.

The craft started moving, the pure Vodoxium energy creating brilliant lighting to scan the depths below. The boys and Esouli watching with curiosity as the ship charted its own course. The waters swirled and sparkled, cloudy, then black.

Eventually the waters cleared, a strange but somehow familiar sight lay before them.

'I think,' said Esouli, 'we are looking at an ancient city.'

Large colonnades lay like slain beasts. Massive blocks of stone, fallen and smashed. Exotic carvings sculptured into decorative shapes and animals.

'How on earth is this in a black hole?'

'I don't know Louis, but this is astonishing,' said Esouli.

'What was that? Did you see it?'

Charlie's voice was squeaking with excitement.

Ghostlike creations, tall, opaque, but slightly visible human features. Gliding in the water, long wispy figures like streaming clouds.

'What are they?' asked Charlie.

'I can't really say if they're spirits or real,' said Esouli taking the controls.

The boys kept watching, hoping to get another glimpse of an ancient past lost forever.

'Could it have been a planet?' asked Louis. 'This hole must have consumed an entire planet.'

'It's not unusual,' said Esouli.

The craft moved closer, knowing the occupants were captivated, the lost souls came closer giving a more defined image. The faces looked haunted and sad, large dark eyes and mouths turned down. Drifting in and out of their fallen home, locked in a time of great loss.

'Oh shit, I really feel sorry for these poor buggers.'

'I know,' said Louis, unable to take his eyes of the strange wispy creatures. 'They know we are watching. Pity we can't help them.'

'I'm sorry Louis, but they have probably been in here for millions of years.'

'So, are they really dead, or what? I guess they could be spirits.'

The magical triangle moved off leaving the lost behind. Eventually natural light could be seen. The craft gathered speed, it went into freefall, then picked up in a turbulent slipstream. The surroundings were getting smaller and smaller, until it was nothing more than a tunnel. The triangle changed shape to fit. All beings were yet again well secured, ready for another visual feast.

The craft slowly morphed back to its normal shape, waiting for direction, floating peacefully in an amber sky with black puffy clouds moving up and down like bouncing balls.

'Jesus, everything changes so bloody quick, my eyes can't keep up with it.'

Charlie covered his eyes for a moment to give them a rest.

Esouli did his magic again, adjusting coordinates, the huge screen beeped and swirled, and it communicated with him. Visions of deep space appeared. Distant moons and suns flashed on the screens. Thousands of planets passed by, many fertile and many desolate and frozen. A meteor shower could be seen ahead, bright flashes, zooming across the sky.

'God, this is just unreal,' said Louis.

'You can say that again.'

'It's like the brain is trying to catch up, so much to see.

'Remember Charlie when we camped outside in summer and looked up at the night and wondered what was out there?'

'Yep and here we are slap bang in the middle, or somewhere in the Universe. You feeling homesick Louis?'

'Are you?'

' Yeah I am.'

'He-hum,' Esouli interrupted the boys. 'There's a group of aliens on the second level wanting a game of kickball. Anyone interested?'

The boys jumped up in readiness.

'Before you go, if the estimates are correct, we will be entering the Silabistis atmosphere in 48 hours and after our visit we are heading back to Earth.'

'Woohoo!' yelled Charlie. 'My skatie and surfboard here I come!'

CHAPTER 50

The smell of vegetable fritters and brewed coffee drifted and mixed with the smell of the rolling ocean.

Isobel, Bridget and Simone enjoyed their breakfast listening to plovers and seagulls in the background, their calls carrying on the wind. It was a beautiful morning on the east coast.

Simone came in with the daily paper and joined the ladies for breakfast.

'Oh yum! These fritters are divine.'

'You can thank the feathered girls out the back for that.'

'You mean your spoilt feather babies.'

Isobel laughed at the reference to her chooks.

Simone carefully slid the mobile phone in her direction while the ladies were distracted reading their papers.

'Mum, is that where Aunty Bridge used to live?'

Isobel raised her eyebrows at Simone's sneaky phone grab as studied the short article.

'Look at this Bridge, seems Mr Blackwell is having some trouble.'

It was brief, stating more interference with machinery at the development site.

'We have to go and see for ourselves.'

Bridget was on her feet undressing out of her pyjamas as she went.

Slowly they drove down Lavender Lane, coming to a stop opposite Bridget's old home site.

'Holy shit!'

Isobel opened the passenger door, Bridget followed, her mouth gaping open. Her garden had grown back to absolute perfection, with the exception of where the house used to be.

'Oh Bridge, it's like everything is waiting for your return.'

Bridget absently nodded.

'Look Mum. Look!'

Simone was pointing at a very strange sight indeed.

'Can I help you people?'

A security guard stood in front of the car. Isobel jumped in before Bridget had time to react.

'What the hell is going on here? I've invested a lot of money into this development.'

'Oh, it's just a small delay.'

'How on earth did that bulldozer, truck and grader get wrapped up in very unusual vines?'

'It's, um…well, we think it's just protestors. Nothing we can't sort out.'

Isobel did a final dramatic scene.

'This is just not good enough. Vines for god's sake. Mr Blackwell will hear about this.'

Bridget hurried to the car before she burst out laughing, Simone wasn't sure what to think. Once the car was turned around, Isobel burst out laughing.

'Unusual vines' so, what sort of vine is it Miss Bridget?'

'A species that will have them pondering for a long time. I wonder how long events like this will occur?'

'Well,' said Bridget, 'probably forever if necessary.'

An understanding look was shared between them.

A vehicle coming the other way heading toward the site, it was the local news.

Tristan parked his car in a laneway, waiting for the news people and their cameras to leave. He was so curious to see what the women were up to. So far nothing had turned up about the location of the two boys. Collin Stephens was in a quandary, there's nothing he couldn't find. Tristan's voices started chattering, but no clarity in their messages. The music went up in an attempt to drown them out, it seemed the more time he spent with his father, the more intense the voices became. As soon as this bloody wedding was over the better. He hated being near his father and that stupid thing he is marrying. The intrigue as to what she was up to had him weirdly curious. Whatever it was it was happening on the big day.

Tristan remembered how good he felt after the swim in that lake. He grabbed his gym towel, explained his presence to the security guard showed his ID and headed off. The curiosity about the machinery overwhelmed him, he had to take a closer look. The vines had penetrated into the machinery, thick and strangling, he googled invasive vines in all areas of Australia. Nothing matched.

The water was cold and invigorating. He laid on his back floating. Weightlessness felt good. Every muscle in his body rested, every nerve hushed. Tristan's mind went back in time, his first memory, being dropped off at boarding school in a taxi with his bags. The prevailing emotion that never left him, loneliness. In his mind's eye he could see his five-year-old self watching, hidden, all the other boys with their families, the kisses and cuddling. Tristan saw his younger self being made fun of, even by the teachers. He had no one, he still has no one.

His emotions started to swell inside him, he left the water and sat in the cool shade. His throat constricting with pain, he tried to hold back the tears. It was hard, too hard. They fell like hard rain against a window. The pain escaped at last. Reluctant at first, deep sobbing ragged noises kept coming, wave after wave of liberated pain until he was spent and exhausted. Sleep finally took charge, the best he was to ever have.

All the pain that little boy felt was gone, something warm and content had taken its place.

The sun had well and truly set when Tristan awoke. The moon was in the dark side of its phase. He sat quietly, feeling no fear as night animals stirred and the wind whispered its presence. He was quite happy just sitting in silence beside the lake.

Thoughts of the day presented themselves, wanting to be dealt with. Two women, the little girl, the vine clad monsters, the untraceable boys, this place. It was like a fascinating feelgood drug.

Deciding to trace his steps in the dark proved difficult. Something ran over his foot, he laughed, thinking how silly he must look. He could hear a kind of clicking sound close by, he followed, so far so good, he hadn't fallen over. It continued and Tristan followed. A ray of light could be seen up ahead from the street. The Tawny frogmouth sat low on the branch of a tree he made another call.

'So, it was you, thanks buddy, couldn't have done it without you.'

He saluted to the night bird.

'This place has a certain magic my feathered friend. Oh, and I love the vines.'

Tristan giggled like a little boy, the little boy who was now free.

CHAPTER 51

Genevieve sat opposite Max Dupre and her accountant.

'Well my dear, you enjoyed getting back on the catwalk?'

'I did Max, when Paris is willing to pay two million for my face and body, why not? I must say it was exhilarating.'

Greg Yadley was gobsmacked by Genevieve's beauty.

'Now, Mr Yadley, how have my investments been performing?'

'You will be pleased to know that to date you are now worth 35 million dollars. I have your portfolio for you to look over. Your popularity with the magazines has been lucrative.'

'By the way,' Max jumped in, 'we have a very substantial offer for exclusive coverage of your wedding.'

'I was actually wanting as many photographers as possible for my wedding.'

'But it's a huge amount!'

'It's not about the money Max, it's about camera's worldwide coverage.'

'Of course, Genevieve. It's your choice.'

'Now moving on gentlemen, I wish to discuss something of the utmost importance to me. Please listen carefully. My husband to be is expecting me to invest more in his silly little development, some resort thing. I have told him after we marry, I will transfer twenty million into his investment account. I would like you to personally send a guarantee to him that this will happen. My secretary has all information.'

'I can certainly do that Miss St Day.'

'I haven't finished yet Greg. The moment we are married, and Max will keep you informed of that, do not transfer a cent. Do I make myself clear?'

'Did you say, 'not to'?'

'Yes. I shall be leaving Australia for good directly after the wedding.'

'I'm sorry Miss St Day, I'm confused.'

'Just do as I ask you stupid man. Stop asking questions!'

She uncrossed her elegant legs to stand, turned on her beautifully designed stilettos Tut Tar Max, her perfume lingering in the air after she left.

'My God she is so rude.'

'Oh, that's mild to what I usually endure, now how much is she really worth?'

'Closer to 40 million dollars with my careful investing.'

'Good, I think we deserve our retainer.'

'I really can't argue that!'

Max Dupre sat in silence with the accountant.

'What the hell is she up to Max?'

'With that woman, it's not worth asking.'

Genevieve's plane was fuelled and ready for take-off. All the wedding garments and staff aboard. She went ahead and booked her honeymoon for one person in Paris, and that's where she would stay.

'Rosa! Get in here and hurry up, stupid waddling duck.'

Genevieve laughed and mimicked Rosa's walk.

'Yes Miss St Day.'

'When the jet reaches its height of safety, I want the usual massages, sleeping tonic, and my clothes ready. I assume the other idiot has my magazines ready, and I would like to watch some of my TV series and the fashion show I just starred in.'

Rosa was exhausted, she had to massage Genevieve's body for two hours with her special oils. She watched herself and read about herself the entire time. Rosa gave her the sleeping tonic, then she was dismissed.

Vivian had chicken salads and crusty bread ready for her and Rosa. They waited half an hour to ensure she was asleep.

When they finished dinner, Vivian produced some documents from her briefcase and handed it to Rosa.

'What's this?'

'Well as you know, in four days the wedding will take place. I have booked a taxi for us to exit in, when she is delivered to the wedding. Our luggage is organised to be delivered to the airport where we will pick it up.'

Vivian handed Rosa the computer to access a private bank account in the Cayman Islands. All the information was given to Rosa, everything was verified.

'Oh my God. Vivian, this is for one million dollars.'

'You have deserved every cent for the bullying and humiliation. Let's not speak of this anymore, all details are in your satchel. This is our last trip with her. In just a few days it'll be over.'

'I can't believe this. I can have a holiday and my mother-in-law can move out into her own place.'

'Now listen to me Rosa, people will take advantage of you, you must be wise and careful.'

'I know what you mean Vivian, don't worry, I realise my family are not exactly angels. I'm thinking as far as they know, there is only enough for a bigger house and a holiday.'

'That's good my friend, always have an escape plan with something hidden.'

The two women opened a half bottle of champagne.

'Are you going to be okay Vivian?'

'Yes Rosa. I'm going to be perfectly fine, let's keep in contact.'

'Yes,' said Rosa, 'let's make a regular get together.

They both put an agreed date in their phones.

Jason Blackwell swam the length of his pool back and forth, it helped to settle his surging rage. He was informed of the incident with the vines. He sacked the current security service and employed a more aggressive agency.

His nerves were starting to affect his lifestyle. The investors' money hadn't returned what he needed. The email from Max Dupre had bolstered his confidence.

Jason knew Genevieve was worth more, but first he had to marry her, there were no prenuptials.

'You're not drowning are you Dad?'

'Tristan, I was just thinking about you.'

'So, you ready for the big day?'

'Like I said, I just turn up and our suits are on their way from Paris. And you my boy will just have to do as you're told like me.'

Tristan nodded as the snide voice in his head began to whisper. ''My Boy' since when have I been that you smirking idiot?!' The voice, that bloody voice. Tristan tried to block it out. Why won't it stop. It's only when I'm around this dickhead.

Jason pulled himself out of the pool, tall, tanned conceited. They relaxed sipping cool drinks. Jason smiled constantly. Thinking, calculating and planning his moves, all to ensure the comfort for his future.

'What are you thinking Dad?'

'Everything alright with the development?'

'It will be, I've employed a new security firm.'

'Do you ever think about your past wife and child?'

Jason put his drink down and looked at Tristan.

'I didn't know you knew about that.'

'Well Dad, every astute businessman knows it's in his best interest to gather as much information as he can.'

'True, but I don't think it's that interesting. Anyway, to answer your question, I haven't seen the kid. I left long before it was born. As for her, I would never want to set eyes on that ugly monster for as long as I live. Now that's all in the past, rather think of my future. Come on, join me in the gym.'

Jason lifted weights in front of the mirror, he knew Tristan was watching.

'You could look as good as me son, with more hard work, tighten up that flab. Get some sun.'

Tristan could feel the vomit rising with revulsion and resentment. Outwardly he smiled at his father. Jason was busy studying himself from all angles, he punched his abdomen.

'Yeah, I'm not too bad.'

Tristan's phone alarm went off, it was his safeguard to get away from his father or any situation.

'I have to go I'm meeting with an associate.'

'Well then, I'll see you at my wedding.'

He woke that night, cold but sweating, as he did regularly. Tristan laid back on his bed, he allowed his mind to travel down the long tunnel to the past, the little boy standing at the steps of his boarding school. Every day was the same. Long and lonely, he was bullied, intimidated, he was entertainment for others.

Tristan could clearly see in his mind's eye the first night alone in his bed in the four-bed dormitory.

The room was in total darkness, something was under his bed, hissing noises surrounded him. His mattress was moving, the five-year-old Tristan was terrified, as his tears fell, maniacal laughter echoed with blatant torment. He curled up in his bed shaking, not knowing what was next to come.

His blankets came off, the contents of garbage bins emptied on top of him, snotty tissues, vegetable scraps, paper and other sloppy substances. He didn't move, like a half dead animal waiting for the final attack. His entire body shaking, hot urine trickled, the dampness spread.

More laughter.

'She's pissed her pants!'

'Sissy Trissy!'

They kept chanting.

'Sissy Trissy!'

He was then known as 'Sissy Trissy'.

'Jesus Christ that stinks!'

The blanket landed back on top of him. Tristan cried himself to sleep, without making a sound. There was not one person on planet Earth to turn to for help. He was alone and that's the way it remained.

The voices in his head kept him company.

Tristan focussed his thoughts on learning and spent hours in the library, it was quiet and safe. He excelled in most areas. Sport was a different story, at every opportunity he was pushed, tripped up, and laughed at. The favourite torment was to take his clothes whilst he was showering. Tristan was always found by the cleaner, sitting in his towel staring out the window.

When holidays came, Tristan was relieved, he was the only one left at the boarding school. He slept well, ate in peace, and enjoyed his own company. At Christmas time he overheard the staff making comments about him not being wanted. Gifts of guilt arrived with tags 'Love your Father.'

Tristan became an observer of life, of people and their habits. He became invisible and that suited him. He watched cruel bullying imposed on new inmates. Tristan had become a boring victim, the difference with other students they had parents to protect them.

By fourteen years of age, he had acquired a substantial amount of guilt money, asking for more always worked. He was tall and had sprouted a lot of facial hair. Getting into the local pubs was easy and a false ID helped. Always the observer, he watched the secret drug trade in the pub when the lights went down and the music went up. As anticipated Tristan was approached to purchase a deal, cocaine was the favourite. This was the moment he planned for. A kilo of cocaine was organised.

By the time he was 17 he already had a car and a licence. Amongst the wealthy students Tristan became a god. Business was booming, the invitations rolled in, parties, sports events, however he declined. Personal involvement was foreign to him, his best friend was his new sports car. He didn't need people.

Tristan's mind was disturbed having awoken from his horrendous night's sleep. It always happened after spending time with his father. The thought of the lake and the peace he felt, pushing away the aroused voices. It always began with whispers, then louder, insulting him, repeating his father's words of ridicule over and over.

Tristan understood why he was so messed up. His empty life, devoid of human contact, the abandonment, he read enough books on psychology to understand, he just didn't know how to break into humanity. Tristan's only ability was to put on a positive, confident, well-educated businessman persona. He could mould his personality to blend and fit in anywhere, he was accepted and trusted.

What confused him most of all was his curiosity with his half-brother, the two women and the mountain lake. The need to know them was inexplicable. Every day now he felt constantly drawn to the lake and he felt cleansed and refreshed each time he swam in it.

On this particular day, high in a mountain blue gum the scruffy grey bird shook his head and observed the human floating on the lake. He waved at the bird, feeling silly.

'Hello old mate!' Tristan laughed freely.

The waters felt like an elixir, massaging every layer of his body, trying to fix the broken parts. The voices had become quiet, a cool breeze danced across the lake bringing the soft grasses to life. Birds checked in with each other, their calls echoing around the mountains. Tristan was in a twilight sleep, he was sinking into the lake, and he couldn't move to save himself. He was going to drown. Panic overwhelmed him, lower and lower. The struggling stopped he was still breathing. What the hell was happening?

It was dark and peaceful. His body became upright, and the fear was gone. In the distance a pinhead of light could be seen. It became bigger. It was a brilliant white light, almost blinding. He could see a figure of something in the light, it was tall but hard to define, and it didn't come any closer. A voice came to Tristan's ears.

'You must be patient in what you seek Tristan, maintain the secret. In time you will understand your purpose.'

Tristan sat up abruptly, taking a deep breath, he was on his towel at the side of the lake. Did he just dream that?

'I was in the water. How the hell did I get here?'

Although he was confused, he felt calm. He laid down again closing his eyes. The words came to him, 'patience', 'the secret', and 'his purpose'. Something warm and wet was touching his face.

'Shit, what now?!'

Sitting next to Tristan, looking very pleased with himself was a small, scruffy dog with a multitude of colours and hair hanging over his face covering a most happy pair of brown eyes.

'Well! Hello there and who might you be?'

The little dog wiggled with excitement, his tail slapping the ground. His fur was soft, he had never touched an animal, the dog snuggled into his armpit. The rush of an unfamiliar feeling spread throughout his body, a deluge of emotion that brought a flood of tears, they waited a long time to be set free. They laid together absorbing each other's security. Tristan now understood the words that he heard.

'Well then little mate,' looking into its furry face, 'probably time we went. I could do with a feed and I reckon you could too.'

The little dog sat on the front seat and had the belt around him.

'I think your new name is going to be 'Mate', after all you're the first mate I've had.'

Tristan dialled Collin Stephens in his car.

'Hey Stephens. I want you to drop the investigation for now, and could you contact my lawyer, ask him to commence a name change for me. I'll keep Blackwell, hang on a minute. Okay Mate, pick one, Tristan's out, so here goes, 'George', 'David', 'Elton', 'Angus'.'

The little dog tilted his head in a confused look.

'Okay, what about 'Maurice', 'Freddie'?'

Tristan burst out laughing.

''James', 'Sam'?'

Mate barked.

'Okay Sam it is. 'Sam Blackwell'.'

'You alright Mr Blackwell?' asked Collin suspiciously.
'Yep, never better. If you could get onto that I would be grateful.'
He hung up.
'Well Mate, that's the end of 'Sissy Trissy''.

CHAPTER 52

It was 5:30am, the big day had finally arrived. At around 12 midday or thereabouts she would be on her way home. It felt so good, only a few more hours and this dreadful woman would be out of her life forever.

Vivian was already on the phone, making sure everything was in place.

'Please for god's sake make sure the limousine arrives exactly on time. Leave very early in case of traffic.'

Rosa had a coffee and a bowls of oat ready.

'Oh my god Rosa, this is going to be hell.'

'Come, sit Vivian. Have your coffee and make sure you eat your oats.'

'Did you see the gold veil that arrived late last night? I have to attach it to the hair somehow. It's amazing to touch and it's worth a fortune. I have never seen diamonds on shoes.'

Rosa giggled.

'Lucky person who gets them in the charity shop.'

Vivian laughed into her coffee.

'Oh, have you made preparations to leave?'

'I've hidden my bag for a quick getaway.'

'I must admit, I too have packed light,' said Vivian. 'I can't wait to go home.'

'Thanks to you,' Rosa took Vivian's hand, 'I can have some peace in life.'

'Well, you know it works both ways, I couldn't have tolerated this without you. Our taxi is ordered for the moment she gets out of that limousine and down the aisle.'

'Oh dear, she's going to be angry when she yells for her servant. I'm gonna be called every nasty word she can think of.'

'Rosa, where the hell are you? Don't you know what day it is?'

'And here we go.'

Both women moved with a sense of urgency as usual.

The intercom was running hot. The hairdresser, makeup artist, nail technician, beautician, all arrived carrying their tools of the trade to create a masterpiece. The photographer was last, waiting to take pictures of the final product. It was six o'clock in the morning.

Vivian suggested providing breakfast, however Genevieve declined.

'I'm paying them to work, not eat.'

'I was thinking I need to do some exercise this morning. Get my personal trainer.'

'Um, Miss St Day, you don't have one.'

'Well get me one you smart bitch.'

Rosa ran from the room. Vivian heard the conversation.

'I've got it Rosa, now deep breath.'

Genevieve did her muscle toning regime followed by a one-hour massage from Rosa. She had Genevieve's bath ready, aromatic oils drifted in the air. After her bath, Rosa had to apply a light spray tan, just a light gold, massaging her body again with purified oils from Paris to enhance her tan. Her body was luminous, she turned in front of the mirror, pleased with the result. Next the hairdresser piled the hair, using artistic patterns. Her hair was platinum blonde like white ice. To complete the look, the makeup artist showed Genevieve the portfolio of diverse alluring faces to choose from. She chose an Egyptian goddess look to highlight her gown and veil.

Rosa had all the clothes, jewellery and shoes ready. Before Rosa assisted her into her gown, she sprayed her body with expensive perfume. The jewellery and veil were the last to apply. Rosa's back and her feet ached, she felt weak from hunger.

'What the hell are you doing fumbling around in my hair, just clip the damn thing to the diamond pins.'

It was 11:30am, the white limousine waited patiently.

'Remember you two are not travelling in my limousine. You have a taxi I believe.'

Genevieve burst out laughing.

'Imagine, the likes of you two in a limo – the hired help.'

The magnificent cruiser waited at Darling Harbour. It was luxury at its finest, enough to cater for nine hundred guests. The dining room elegant and tasteful, massive chandeliers, subdued lighting and neutral colours added to the exquisite ambience. Tables draped with gold and white tablecloths were adorned with gold wine goblets, ice white crockery and gold cutlery. Each table featured centrepieces of golden ivy. Large white leather lounges were strategically placed for comfortable relaxing. Waiters dressed in black pants, white shirts and gold bow ties. All busied themselves with final touches. The food was sourced from boutique farms across Europe and Australia, the menu was mouth-watering.

Genevieve chose the beautiful cruiser, so other vessels could surround it and cameramen would have access to her for hours. Everything Genevieve's mind could conjure, was then Vivian's job to bring to reality.

The golden carpet to the cruiser was ready. All the guests arrived at 10AM. This was a purposeful act so no one would miss Genevieve's entrance. Music and the best French champagne served in pure crystal flutes kept the guests entertained.

The marriage was to take place under the magnificent chandelier and the altar at the front of the cruiser. The area was opened up to allow photographers access. For those who could not get a perfect view of Genevieve St Day, relay screens were positioned to view the proceedings, every moment was being filmed.

Jason and the newly named Sam Blackwell arrived together in a black limousine. Their suits matching black, black vests, pure white shirts, a gold tie, black satin lapels. A gold pin sat on the lapel with six diamonds catching the sunlight. The men looked divine and extremely handsome. Women of all ages gathered, guests and onlookers alike, to look at the splendid men. The cameras flashed like a lightning storm.

Ocean vessels of all sizes bobbed up and down in the water, surrounding the big cruiser, waiting for the woman of the hour to arrive.

The guests, dressed in the most glorious clothes, from the world's best designers. All were occupied mingling and chatting. Stories of Hollywood, relationship breakups, investments, surgeries and their latest real estate acquisitions were only a few of the topics.

Waiters kept topping up glasses and tongues began to loosen.

Genevieve St Day was elegantly assisted out of the limousine by the chauffeur, and then it began, the mass of flashing lights began, relentless and repetitive calling her name. Just the way she expected it to be.

Sam put his head down to hide his amused smile, she was magnificent in one way, but so terribly hideous in another. Rosa and Vivian took their last glimpse of Genevieve St Day surrounded by guests, photographers and the public. The taxi disappeared, headed towards the international airport. Jason was astonished at the vision before him, she was perfection.

Genevieve felt engorged with pure exhilaration, this was her favourite environment. She was like an Egyptian goddess from head to toe, she carried herself to perfection, like an opening scene to an American blockbuster movie. Genevieve lingered, turning so every angle could be captured.

Jason was feeling bored, for some reason he started to feel unusual. Sam watched her approach, soon this circus will be over, and he could exit his father's life, he couldn't stomach much more.

'You alright Dad?'

'Yeah, just getting sick of waiting.'

'Take some deep breaths, she's nearly here.'

The heat from the cameras and lighting started to create tiny beads of sweat. Trickles began to run down Genevieve's neck.

She demanded that the ceremony and vows be done in the shortest time possible. She was only interested in the ring and its worth.

She began becoming uncomfortable, her face felt hot. She could hear people's comments on how beautiful was. She composed herself long enough to say, 'I do'.

The magnificent ring glided on her perfect hand, the diamond was impressive, she held up her hand for the camera's.

'Goodness, this heat and sweat is unbecoming.'

She signalled for a serviette, laughing saying it was the excitement from having so many people watching. They giggled accordingly. It was not sweat. Warm bloodied fluid dripped onto her hands. She slowly touched her face, mounds of sloppy wet skin folded over her fingers. The front of her wedding dress slowly stained. Genevieve could feel something touching her cheek, her eye had dislodged. Her face was sliding off the bones again. She couldn't think, her brain was in a frozen with shock.

Jason felt dizzy. Feeling unsteady, he took a deep breath trying to fill his lungs. He reached out and lifted the veil, he saw the stains, but nothing was registering. He was to kiss his bride, his beautiful bride

Sam watched confused. What was all that shit over her wedding dress? Why was she holding her face under the veil?

Jason lifted the veil, folding it back over her hair. She screamed as her hands pushed at the flaccid pulpy mess. First, a moment of silence, time stood still, each brain trying to register what was happening. Then chatter began, the cameras went wild.

One word could be heard above all the noise.

'Rosa!'

No one came.

Jason couldn't take his eyes off the familiar grotesque mess. Darkness was surrounding him, all the noise started to fade.

'Lucy, how the hell?'

The handsome figure slowly folded onto the floor.

Sam dialled for two ambulances to be in attendance. The cameras were blinding, the crowd hysterical, some were even laughing. His brain endeavoured to absorb the very disturbing event unfolding before him.

Genevieve clawed at Sam for help. Bits of skin clung to the elegant lapels of his jacket, the cameras capturing every bazaar moment. Grabbing her wrist, he could feel her shaking with rage. Her blood began running through his fingers.

'Get me Rosa,' a guttural coarse voice demanded.

'Listen to me Lucy, calm down and listen. Rosa and Vivian have left the country and your husband appears to have had a stroke. Whatever this is you have created is over.'

Still holding her wrist, he watched her face transform from absolute beauty to a deformed mess.

Lucy became a wild animal trying to lash out at Sam. Kicking, spitting, her once refined speaking voice, now filled with poison and ugly language. Sam looked toward the celebrant who had just married this pair of psychos.

'A little help would be good.'

Reluctantly he put his arm around Lucy's shoulders, pulling the veil over her face, and guided her to a seat. Sam stepped back demanding a wet towel from one of the waiters who looked totally dumbfounded by the events unfolding. He wiped his hands clean of her clinging body waste.

Jason remained still on the floor. No-one rushed to his aid and Sam realised why. The smell was disgusting. The sea breeze shared the repulsive aroma with all the well-dressed guests.

'Oh Jesus! He's shit and pissed himself.'

Sam's mind was in overload. The sound of sirens penetrated his brain freeze.

'Thank Christ for that.'

A waiter walked up and dropped a tablecloth over the unconscious body.

Sam watched the ambulance officers load the broken disaster of humanity into the back, the doors closed. Mr and Mrs Blackwell disappeared into the traffic.

Turning slowly, Sam looked at the crowd gathered. Everything that just happened had now become breaking news around the globe.

'You may as well enjoy the food and wine.'

The limousine and chauffer waited in the distance.

Sam was aware hundreds of cameras pointed at him, waiting for something. They received no more than a quiet dignified exit.

The back of the limo felt like a comforting escape cavity. Security, away from thousands of eyes penetrating into the very core of his humanity. Were they secretly waiting for more unhinged drama? He looked back at what he left behind.

'How the hell did I just manage that?'

The driver enquired to the destiny.

Rather reluctantly he responded.

'To the hospital. Follow those sirens.'

Sam felt exhausted, alone in the waiting room, he was the only next of kin for both of them.

All information about the very odd couple admitted together was scarce. No Rosa or Vivian or a caring secretary to fill in the blanks. The head of the Emergency department sat down next to a very tired Sam. He introduced himself as Doctor Byron.

'Your father has had a stroke. It is a blood clot or bleed in the brain. He could have neurological damage and other significant complications, but at this stage it is not known. We consider his condition critical, and he will remain in intensive care. Mrs Blackwell in the past, appears to have had major surgeries to her face. I have performed some repair work, and I'm not sure any surgeon can restore her face. In my opinion the damage is irreversible'

The doctor was very matter of fact. Sam didn't really mind, after all he felt no emotion for Mr and Mrs Blackwell. As the doctor left Sam sat pondering what he should do. He didn't want to be responsible for either of them. He phoned his lawyer. He gave his lawyer all the information he had regarding both the Blackwell's finances and their contacts. It was arranged that a home care service would attend to their needs while in hospital. He felt sorry for anyone having to deal with either of them. He just wanted to get away.

CHAPTER 53

Esouli and the boys worked together on the gigantic screen. It was misty, lines were jagged, and the beeping was intense.

The ship was trying hard to get a visual on Silabistis. Meteors and dust storms raged outside. Silabistis has its own satellite - some technology borrowed from Earth.

Just when frustration levels were reaching their peak, visibility found its way through.

'I do believe folks we have found the Greys' planet.'

'Woo-hoo,' said Charlie.

Esouli spun the planet on the screen, it started to zoom in, and images came into focus. The first vision was a very unusual landscape. Massive plateaus could be seen followed by enormous, jagged mountain ranges.

'God, it looks like some big giant has stomped all over the planet!'

'Yeah, I see what you mean,' said Louis, 'big footprints oozing the mountains up the side, let's hope he does not exist.'

Tall manmade towers like upside down wine glasses stood erect and dominating. Sleek spacecraft rested, ready for take-off at any time.

'Seems to be activity inside the towers and look at those weird building.'

Louis was curious and slightly puzzled. Against the skyline suspended in the air stood constructions similar to giant windmills.

'Could be where they live.'

'According to analysis, it looks like they have an underground area. It's most likely manufacturing and it is expansive!'

Esouli was also intrigued.

'The black mountains contain many different minerals and rare earth minerals. They mine these elements to construct living areas, the factories and build the spacecrafts.'

'What are those big rectangle buildings?'

Louis pointed at the screen.

'I believe,' said Esouli, 'that houses the food production, plant foods and insects for protein.'

'What's that on the mountains between the next footprint?'
'The native forest.'
Louis zoomed in for a closer look.
'Wow, it's so dense and fertile. I recognise some of them from earth.'
Esouli spoke again.
'Deep springs run all over the planet. Freshwater rivers slowly bring the powerful minerals to the top. The Greys appear to have a very structured and orderly planet and society.'
'What do you mean?' asked Louis.
Both boys looked to Esouli, needing to understand where they were going.
'Everyone has a purpose and a job, from what I know there is a hierarchy of leaders. Everyone has to follow rules and regulations. Each individual has a job to do, population is controlled, so sustainability is maintained.'
'Wow, it sounds like school.'
Esouli smiled at Charlie.
'That's the Greys way. It's what they call a productive secure life.'
'So what goes on behind the mountains?' asked Louis.
'There doesn't seem to be any data on that.'
'What else do they make in the factories?'
'Spacecrafts and probably weapons Charlie.'
'They produce clothing, their own technology, equipment, I would say all gathered from Earth, human stuff.'
'Did you just say 'stuff'?'
Charlie and Louis smiled at Esouli's description.
'Is there any way we can look at the Greys?' asked Louis.
'Yeah, that would be great,' agreed Charlie.
'I have to admit,' continued Louis, 'there's something weird about the whole crossbreeding thing.'
A vision of an unusual city became clear. A group of Greys, young looking, walking around what looked like a shopping centre. Simplistic in design, no fancy lights or advertising, the basic needs covered in the basic way.
They weren't unpleasant to look at, they seemed to be the same height, the same physique, and perfectly proportioned. A close-up showed a beige coloured skin, the eyes were large and all the same colour - black pupils, dark grey eyes. The nostrils were large with a defined ridge running down the middle. The cheek bones were very high, the ears smaller with larger ear canals. The young Greys arms and legs were longer and the fingers and toes, long and tapered.
'They look pretty cool.'
Louis leant forward having a close look.
'They don't have hair and how do you tell male from female?'

'Their organs are internal. The females have lighter eyes and studs in the ears.'

'When you say 'internal', how do they reproduce?'

'That Louis, I do not know. They are an advanced race. If they have other abilities, we are unaware, they remain very secretive. It seems they look after the planet environmentally, that's always a good sign.'

'If you expand the vision, you will see some do look slightly different, minor human attributes, like hair and different coloured eyes.'

'Dude! Your right.'

Charlie pointed to some in the background.

'Do they know we are watching?'

'Most likely Louis.'

'Well,' said Charlie, 'I do remember our big bone crunching buddies, so hopefully these dudes have got their shit together.'

'Do they speak English?'

'Yes Louis, plus their own language. I think they do some signing as well.'

'Wait', said Charlie, 'zoom back more to the left. What are those ones? They look different, really ugly.'

'I think it's got something to do with ranking and leaders.'

'Well, I do kinda like the Star Trek suits.'

'As I said Charlie, a very structured society.'

Esouli turned his attention to the outside.

'We are now in their solar system.'

The craft continued to change shape as needed, the boys particularly liked the 'flying saucer look'. Louis's favourite was the shark shape, minus the fins. Burnt out planets drifted to nowhere, toxic cloud formations heavy with dust were common. A satellite changed direction to observe the craft.

'We are being watched boys.'

'Can they actually see us?'

'No, it's okay Charlie, the Vodoxium shield protects us.'

That night all the craft's travellers ate together. Louis looked at each individual watching the easy way everyone got on, he turned his gaze to Esouli. He was magnificent, frightening, and as gentle as the black Labrador he found that day at the markets. Everyone was so gracious, innocent and a threat to no-one.

'You look troubled Louis.'

Esouli's voice broke into his inner thoughts.

'I was wondering how much Vodoxium you are giving the Greys?'

'You have concerns about that?'

Louis took some time to answer.

'What bothers me is the human part of the Greys, you know, considering our history and the rigid structure of their society.'

'You feel it could be used in a negative way?'

'Well, yeah, that is my thinking. It's not sitting easy.'

'I understand your concerns. To be honest Arume and myself had the same thoughts.'

'Really?'

Louis searched the big warrior's face, trying to guess the level of concern.

'We have decided after much conversation that we are only giving a vial of Vodoxium and not a sphere.'

'How much power will that generate?'

'Very minimal, just enough to power the greenhouses!'

'It can't be used for anything else?'

'What is your thinking, Louis?'

'I guess maybe the Dradask are fresh in my mind. Maybe this lot have ideas of invasion considering the advancement in the technology.'

'Our visit to Silabistis has changed somewhat, and I will need yours and Charlie's help. We need to observe as much as we can in the way of weapons manufacturing. Another area we must try and observe is the population density.'

Esouli continued.

'I'm anticipating guided tours of the facilities. You two will probably be introduced to Greys your own age. How do you both feel about this?'

'Well, I just love getting to know aliens, because it went so well last time.'

Charlie was looking at Esouli with his cheeky grin.

'I think our little friends should stay on the ship.'

'That's a definite,' said Charlie, 'and I think we need to be really observant.'

The boys looked at each other remembering another time on board the ship of death. The powerful craft accelerated making its way to planet Silabistis.

CHAPTER 54

Number 106 woke to the usual brain piercing alarm. Every day the same thing, over and over. They didn't get to just rest, like robots off they went to the daily routine.

106 always stayed in the steaming cylinder longer. The daily ritual cleaning of the skin, then into a cylinder of gel-like substance to stop the skin from cracking and bleeding. A slight defect in the cross breeding.

When 106 was created a mistake was made, she was pure human sperm and a test tube designed grey ovary. The sperm was meant to be spliced with a grey. When she was born it was in perfect form. It was decided early on not to flush her away as many others were. She could be of use in future studies. The girl watched her reflection on the metallic wall, she was fourteen and showing definite signs of being more human than Grey, thicker than normal hair on her head and body.

106 couldn't understand why she wanted to know so much, the only information she was allowed to access was what she was made for. Live and work, then die or be killed when your usefulness has come to an end. Fitting in was hard, she looked different. There were many times she felt like running away but no-one knew what was beyond the mountain ridge, only dark frightening rumours.

The receivers on her wrist activated, she was called to her superior. Her heart started to race. She had never been summoned before. She always tried to act invisible. She stood, very nervous before two of her superiors, her bladder was filling.

'We are having a visit from representatives from planet Helomedes. They will be delivering to us a most powerful energy that will help with food production. On board are two human males similar to your age. You have been assigned to be their guide.'

'They're full human?'

'Yes 106, as you are half. Leave us now, you will be activated when required.'

CHAPTER 55

The craft changed shape to land on top of the unusual platforms. 106 was waiting, hovering in a transporter, a powered pad extremely sleek and advanced.

'Wow,' said Charlie, 'that looks like a Frisbee in a dome.'

The boys were fascinated, the two ships side by side. The hatches opened in unison, all the occupants staring at each other. 106 was in shock, she couldn't take her eyes off Louis and Charlie.

'Do you think she speaks?' asked Charlie in a whisper.

Esouli moved the boys forward, hands on their shoulders.

'Greetings,' said Esouli, introducing the boys.

106 finally spoke putting her hand out, copying the Earthlings to hold and shake. They boarded the Frisbee like craft, Esouli had to duck to enter. It adjusted as necessary to accommodate him, the metal seemed to shimmer. The craft moved off, gliding slowly giving everyone a good view of the planet.

The strange, jagged mountain range and the pale suns seemed very close. Beyond these, mountains and plateaus. This landscape repeated itself for as far as the eye could see. The vegetation was compact and massive.

They passed the suspended structures, also built out of the shimmering metal.

'They look like metal windmills,' said Louis.

'That's where we live,' said 106 looking very nervous. 'They rotate to let us out of the tower. The big rectangular buildings are for manufacturing everything we need.'

She pointed to other buildings.

'They are for our food production. The minerals and metals are mined from the mountains. I um, believe our power source is copied from your planet, solar power. The minerals are reconstructed to give us enough energy for our needs.'

'So, dude, what's behind the mountain ranges?'

'My name is 106 Female.'

'Oh,' said Charlie, 'why are you a number?'

'I was experiment 106, but something went wrong. I have too much human DNA.'

'Oh, I see,' said Charlie, elbowing Louis to stop staring.

They were shown to their living areas.

'It's kinda Spartan,' said Louis.

'Their entire lives seem Spartan.'

Charlie tried looking for anything interesting.

Food was delivered by young Greys, emotionless and non-communicating. The boys opened containers of food that looked like breakfast cereal and green and yellow drinks. Reluctantly, the boys tasted the food. Esouli was amused.

'It tastes like a mixture of nuts and seeds or something like that.'

Louis looked at Esouli.

'What exactly are we eating?'

'I believe it's a mixture of insects, worms and berries. Very high in protein, all dehydrated and the drinks you will find familiar fruits and vegetables from Earth.'

Charlie laughed.

'Mum would love this stuff tastes like food she eats.'

'Well,' said Louis, 'saves eating animals.'

Esouli left, escorted by a standard Grey, who looked more military. They were to negotiate the Vodoxium and its use. The boys went off with 106 to look at the shopping areas and the food production. They boarded the transporter, but this time it wasn't closed in.

'Wow, we're going in a convertible.'

Louis giggled at Charlie's joke, 106 looked at them confused. Smiling and laughter were a foreign expression.

'She thinks we're mad.'

More giggles.

The food production was massive, hundreds of young Greys worked on the production lines, hectares of vegetables and fruits and berries. Hydroponics were set up under mesh domes.

'What's in those huge cylinders?'

Louis pointed.

'That's where they dry the insects and certain high protein berries.'

Tubes ran across the top of the vegetable and fruit production. Jumping onto the transporter, they moved on to another dome. Yet again, more of hybrid people working the production line. Thousands of breeding boxes alive with insects, all visible to watch the growing process. Various breeds of worms in all stages, growing and feeding.

The packaging and storage areas were gigantic.

'Are you guys planning on a disaster? There's enough food stuff here to last years.'

'They must have known you were coming dude.'

106 looked at the boys without answering. It was an extraordinary sight watching the process. No talking, just automatic people like robots.

'Oh God, this is so weird, they're like ants in suits.'

'Big suits Charlie.'

'Hey 106, why do those dudes look different?'

'You must not look at them.'

The alien girl turned them around to stop them looking.

'They are the 'Standards'.'

'What are the 'Standards'?'

'Supervisors with bigger brains.'

'Where did they come from?'

'The laboratories.'

'They do have bigger brains.'

Louis spoke quietly.

Their head WAS bigger! Extending out at the back, with large veins pulsating with extra blood. They had a straight nose, wrinkles on the forehead, larger drooping eyes and a larger mouth, with a much bigger body.

'They supervise us.'

106 tried to sound important in her new role. They watched the Standards poking and yelling at the young Greys to work more efficiently.

'Yep, they've got too much human. Can we go now?'

Louis headed to the transporter.

They transported to the area of food outlets, something like supermarkets but not much choice. Everyone was given a ticket to receive their food and drinks.

'Everything is so regulated, do they have any fun time?' asked Charlie, watching the automated blank way they operated.

'We are told we play sport like you on planet Earth. We have swimming pools it helps with our skin.'

'Well, I'm gonna ask,' said Charlie, 'do you have any electronic games or music?'

'I know what you mean, we have seen visions of your Earth and the things that happen with your young people. We are forbidden. It will make us less intelligent. Our Prime Leaders look after us. They give us the magic water every day to make us strong.'

'What's a Prime Leader?' asked Louis.

106 discreetly pointed out a Prime standing up on the tower lookout. Louis and Charlie strained to look.

'Damn they are ugly.'

Charlie nudged Louis. The head was larger again, no nose, just holes, heavily wrinkled brow and long slits for eyes. A bigger body and a big star on the chest area. The mouth looked like a slash across the face as an afterthought.

'So those guys are all Grey?'

106 just nodded. Her wristband beeped again.

'I have to go. You need to go back to your quarters.'

'You seem frightened.'

'The forests are frightening at night, lots of noises and movement. No one goes there, we don't know what's in there, but our leaders tell us we could be killed and eaten. We must hurry, you have to be in your living area.'

'Okay Onesie, whatever you say.'

'Hey that's a better name,' said Charlie grinning, putting his earphones in.

Onesie was intrigued watching Charlie. Louis nudged Charlie, looking at Onesie.

'Let her listen.'

The strange little alien's face lit up, a huge smile, she felt her mouth.

'What is this?'

'It's music.'

She repeated the word. The transporter moved off as nightfall came in more suddenly than expected.

'Do we really have to stay here Esouli? Can't we go back to the ship?'

'It's okay Charlie, we have to show goodwill for our mission.'

All were settled in for the night, locked away until sunrise.

Outside in the unusual forest surrounded by the jagged mountain range, lifeforms began to stir. Tiny primate like animals, long ears, and large eyes to see at night, tiny sets of wings along its spine gave it flight to move across the treetops. In other trees another species also a ground dweller, big in form but very agile with long limbs covered in black fur, long fingers and toes, a gentle face similar to a sloth, but the most peculiar attribute, three pouches on the underbelly with teats, only breeding when the population begins to decline. Strange animals of flight with long tentacles like an octopus used for finding food and a long body with fan-like wings, using huge eyes to find food. Many creatures, tree dwellers and ground living, moved through the lush bountiful forest.

There is another species living in the forest. However, they are not native to the environment. When the Greys began experimenting with human and Grey crossbreeding using sperms and ovaries trying to perfect a stronger race many babies born in incubators developed hideously or deemed deformed and inferior. They were flushed away and ended up in the forest waterways, eventually floating well into the outside world. Most of them died of exposure. Those that survived were scooped out of the water and placed in warm pouches and nurtured by the forest animals giving them milk to live.

Once the experiments became stable in their health, the milk, the nutritious fruits that grew from the giant succulent trees and long black beans, that when squeezed produced a thick yellow substance, all sustained the throw away lives. Slowly they grew, hideous in their different forms, vulnerable in the struggle to survive.

Louis was looking puzzled at Esouli.

'Did you find anything unusual in the tour of the weird regime?'

'I sat with the Prime Greys and the Standards. They would like to colonise another plateau and they need Vodoxium for the power source.'

Louis looked at him intently.

'Did you see any weapons?'

'Nothing sighted yet.'

'So, um, what are their future intentions?'

'Yeah?' added Charlie, 'Do they intend to get all weaponed up and go back to Earth to take over?'

'Well, they say there is no reason to return. They felt earthlings are aggressive and too comprehensive to understand.'

'So is that why they have such a boring lifestyle and are so regimented. They're kind of like robots.'

'I have observed that too Louis.'

'I gave Onesie my iPod to listen to. You should have seen her face. It was priceless,' said Charlie, with a huge smile on his own.

'I feel sorry for them,' said Louis, 'especially Onesie because she is more human than Grey.'

'It's difficult to understand for you boys, but it is their way. Now, if you boys will excuse me, I'm feeling a little tired.'

'That's odd,' said Louis.

'What?'

'Esouli, tired.'

'Well dude, we have eaten our bugs and worms, drank the fruit juice, no games, or computers, nothin' to do but sleep.'

'Remember Onesie, as you call her, will be here for you two in the morning to do more looking around.'

'I love that flying skateboard. So, what are you doin' Big Bro?'

'Big Bro will be discussing the energy factors of Vodoxium.'

'How did the Prime and Standards come to be?' asked Louis.

'Well, I'm assuming they are the original crew, the Standards are the lesser version, before they harvested human beings.'

'Oh God, all that mixing up of people's stuff. It's disgusting.'

Louis then threw a flat pillow at Charlie hitting him square in the head, the pillow fight and anything else, was on.

Breakfast was served the following morning.

'You know this stuff isn't too bad,' said Louis, scraping his bowl.

'Well dude, give me Weet-Bix and Nutri-Grain any day! Having said that, the juice is good.'

'It's real fruit Charlie.'

A knock at the door interrupted the breakfast talk.

'That must be Onesie because the Big Dude has left.'

'I'm now 'Onesie'?'

'Yeah, see, 'One-oh-six', get it?'

Onesie smiled at the boys but could not figure out their strange actions.

The dome closed over the platform.

'This is so smooth, it's an incredible machine.'

Louis was busy scanning the environment, the sterile architecture, the lack of colour and vegetation, designed to suit the blandness of the grey's lives. The craft moved higher and higher heading towards the jagged mountain tops, almost black in colour. Veins of shiny mineral ran through the mountain like a huge vascular system. The craft started to wobble slightly, they scrambled to remain upright. It was becoming unsteady. Onesie was frantically trying to rectify the stability.

'What's happening?'

Louis's voice was calm.

'I don't know, I have no control.'

'Oh shit,' said Charlie, 'the skateboard is going to crash.'

Both boys thought in unison of shapeshifting, however Onesie's reaction and emotions became hugely distracting. The screaming was ear piercing. Jumping up and down with nothing to hang onto, Louis lurched forward, grabbed Onesie and the three of them began to freefall. Desperate noises came from all three. The boys couldn't come up with a saving intervention. Charlie fell first. It was surprisingly soft. Louis and Onesie followed in a tangled mess. Onesie continued to make guttural noises and jumping.

'What the hell is wrong with her?'

Louis looked at Charlie quizzically.

'I think she is experiencing emotions unknown to her. She doesn't know what to do.'

'Can you feel that?'

'We're sinking Charlie!'

'My skin is tingling and hot.'

'What have we landed on?'

'We are being digested, come on quick!' said Louis, 'We have to move.'

Louis's mind was trying to absorb the amazing vegetation.

'It's so huge, it must be the soil. The flowers are massive.'

'I feel so small,' said Charlie, 'like an insect.'

'I want to go home. This is not nice.'

Onesie continued to whimper like a wounded puppy.

Louis turned and grabbed Onesie by the shoulders and made her listen.

'Look at me and listen. You have been bred to feel nothing, to experience nothing. You are having a real human being experience. Please be quiet, listen and do as I say.'

'Wow! Dude, that was some speech, and um, if you look up into the monster ferns, there are some strange fellas watching us and I'm not sure if we look like food.'

In that instant a sudden downpour of rain seemed to come from nowhere, the three ran towards a huge bell-shaped flower, drooping down big enough to house a dozen adults.

'It does not do this on the plateau,' said Onesie.

'Because you have no vegetation.'

Louis's face was beaming with delight.

A yellow substance covered them like confetti, the huge flower was disturbed, dropping its pollen.

'Oh my God, this is incredible,' Louis gently touched the petals, studying the structure.

Onesie however was holding her head, panting, once again overcome by emotions.

'I need some of our water.'

'There's plenty of water,' said Louis, filling his and Charlie's canteens from the most pure and pristine water hole he had ever seen.

'I don't think it's the same.' Louis again held her shoulders.

'Breathe with me.'

He handed her the drinking vessel she took a long drink.

'That tastes so different, and so good.'

Onesie looked delighted at the taste experience.

'Pure rainwater, hey Louis.'

'What's wrong with me Louis?'

'I guess your emotions are flooding your brain. You were not designed to feel anything, but you have been stimulated. Your life is so dull and regimented that's why you are feeling fear, anguish, confusion, and I guess, lots more to come.'

Movement! Something was coming in under the huge flower. A long tentacle with a flap opening and closing. It was the size of a Python it came further in seeking out the occupants.

'Looks like we have a nosey visitor.'

Louis put his hand down so it could smell.

'Well so far no teeth,' said Charlie.

No sooner had the words got out, when a huge lobster like claw started to slice open the huge bell- shaped flower. With care, the huge petal was pulled back like a stage production curtain. Louis, Charlie and Onesie were looking at the most grotesque, deformed creatures the human imagination could conjure.

''The Underneathers'.'

'What? Who are they?'

'You mean, WHAT are they?' said Charlie.

'It is a rumour we are forbidden to talk about.'

'But what are they?' asked Louis again, intently looking at Onesie.

'Experiments flushed away.'

All the beings stood in silence absorbing each other, the shapes, the abstract jigsaw of their bodies.

Small to medium size blobs, small arms and legs with large hands and feet. A large mouth and tongue with tiny teeth and eyes hidden in jelly like skin. Small holes as ears, experiments created, born, let to live, observed then flushed away and survived. They survived, nurtured by another lifeform, fed by the forest, the minerals in the water strengthening their immune system. The mysterious mountains and forest giving life to the lifeless. Other lifeforms started to appear tall and thin, weak bodies with large square shaped heads, antennae on the head, this enabled them a level of intelligence so they could survive. The skin tone was similar to human beings, the internals similar to human but devoid of a reproductive system. Small crablike beings scurried along the ground, human eyes blinking. Human like feet with multiple toes, gave them the ability to run fast. Tiny front arms fed a human, little human ears moved to catch all sounds. Another in the line up to view the imposters and seemed to be more dominant. It was the size of a fourteen-year-old boy, the body in proportion, however the head was a triangle shape. Two small black piercing eyes, a small mouth, pointy little nose with flappy transparent ears.

The last one visible looked slightly human, but that was where it ended, there was no head. The abdominal cavity opened and closed with every slow breath that showed a hideous version of a human face. Pale washy blue fleshy eyes, a flat nose spread across the centre of the face. An ugly large flaccid mouth, blue veins tracking like moving worms. Randomly spread teeth, pointy and appear when the mouth moved. Tight pink skin stretched over the pathetic figure angry noises emanated from the discarded mistake. A brain that went beyond just survival instincts, the cries of pain and frustration seemed to be in the communication. Communication between these beings was a series of grunts, eye movements and signals of their extremities and pitched squeals.

'Oh God. These poor creatures. I'm thinking,' said Charlie, 'they have experimented with more than humans!'

'I think you're right Charlie. This is extraordinary on so many levels.'

A tentacle moved behind the stunned three, ushering them onto a path.

'Looks like they want to keep us as pets,' Charlie mumbled, coming out of his shock.

'Well,' said Louis, 'they don't appear to be meat-eaters.'

Onesie moved like a robot, all her emotions on overload.

The strange gathering moved toward one of the dark mountains, a cacophony of noises only creatures could understand. The vegetation fascinated Louis.

'The structures of the leaves and stems are incredible. The smell of the fruit is pungent. Look at the shapes of the fruit and the abundance, I bet it's edible. The soil must be incredible.'

'Dude, I hate to interrupt your gardening hour, but aren't you a little concerned about our living status? Let's try shapeshifting.'

'I don't think we are in any danger at the moment.'

'It's the 'at the moment' that worries me.'

The strange mob stopped suddenly, noises ceased, a rumbling in the distance could be heard. The canopy of the forest started to shake the sound came closer.

'What is that? This is going from bad to worse. Shouldn't we run?!'

'Too late Charlie.'

A large head appeared from the dense undergrowth.

'Holy shit! It's a worm.'

'A massive earthworm', replied Louis, a smile of amazement on his face.

A huge translucent body the size of a semi-trailer, displaying its organs, shuffled across the path. The tiny eyes and toothless mouth gave it a gentle look.

'My Nan would love this, the forest, flowers and fruits.'

Charlie put his hand on Louis's shoulder.

'Dude, do we have to do the Louis Attenborough thing?'

Louis laughed.

'It's a worm Charlie!'

The oddball group moved on, strange gaits and groans. Ahead an entrance to the mountain could be seen, the creatures seemed to be excited. The tentacled being gathered the three up and directed them to another entrance.

At first darkness enveloped them, they huddled together to maintain touch and security. Onesie was panting with fear.

'Should we try shifting? This is getting weird I can't even see my hand!'

'Just give it time Charlie!'

They waited, each hearing their heartbeat. Shards of light started to appear. It increased exposing the inside. Scene by scene it lit up. It was as stunning as a cathedral. Everyone was speechless. Before them was a designed internal mountain, carved stairways, leading to chambers via more stairways. Platforms on each level, luminous colours in the rock itself played with light, casting a multitude of colours throughout the entire environment. A pulley system was in place to deliver to the platforms. High up on the further platform someone appeared, they all strained to see. It started to move down the staircase, jumping on the elevator and floating to meet the strangers.

'He looks human.'

Charlie's voice was high-pitched in disbelief echoed around the carved- out mountain.

'You're human,' Charlie blurted out the words in utter shock.

He watched the intruders, studying their faces. He was older than the boys, it was hard to define his age. Large dark grey eyes, with a very slight ridge running down his nose, a strong body, his other facial features human, his hair thick and matted. Louis studied his clothes. They were loose fitting and made of a fabric that looked like woven plant material and matching soft shoes.

'Um, I'm Louis, this is Charlie, and this is Onesie.'

'Silence. What number are you?'

He looked at Onesie.

Her little voice mumbled, '106'.

'So, you were not flushed for being too human? Interesting. I call myself 'Day'. Follow me.'

They followed Day to the first landing. They entered the chambers one after the other. A large cushion like seat made from the skeleton of a very big plant covered with a soft plant material, same as Day's clothes looked very inviting. A table sat between them similar to a dried upside-down huge lotus plant. Each one studying the environment didn't notice the small primate like animals entering with cups of water.

Everyone settled into the plant lounge. Day watched the trio with curiosity.

'Um, this water is very refreshing, kinda like an energy drink,' blurted out Charlie in nervous chatter.

'You are human beings from planet Earth. I must say they haven't copied you very well.'

'You speak very good English,' Louis venturing into an uneasy conversation.

'Yes, I do.'

'How are you able to speak English?'

Charlie kicked Louis under the table, worried Louis was being too pushy.

'Come with me.'

Day jumped to his feet, his manner very stern.

Louis found it difficult to read his mood. They followed, bothered, but strangely excited. Up the carved-out stairs, Day put his hand out for everyone to stop. A loud rumbling noise could be heard coming closer. Between each floor, large tunnels had been created and went on endless.

'Oh God,' said Charlie, straining to look into the tunnel, 'it's our big wormy mate.'

Louis noticed a slight upward tilt to Day's lips. Day communicated with some squawks and a high and low whistle. All his organs pulsated to his heart-beat, Onesie couldn't move, amazed at the vision. The big worm moved on slowly, once into the dark the big worm's body became a brilliant ice blue light, showing the way ahead.

'Follow me.'

All obeyed without hesitation.

'We are following a worm down a hole.'

'It's okay Charlie, I don't sense danger. I think he wants to show us something.'

Day finally started to talk.

'I want to show you how I am able to speak English, why I am aware of your arrival, and why you are here.'

They came to a plateau, the worm moved on then stopped. Day stood in front of a rock face, smooth with unusual colours. He put his hands on the wall, veins started to appear in the rock. The entire thing started to swirl, the same blue light as the worm lit up the wall, followed by an opaque appearance which gradually cleared. Louis and Charlie moved forward in anticipation of what they were about to see.

Row upon row of the Grey populated a large factory, packaging food and making uniforms. Charlie spoke without thinking.

'So you have watched and listened to their existence?'

Louis was fascinated.

'How are you able to do this with what looks like solid rock?'

Day spoke with confidence.

'Areas of these mountains have a dense gathering of a certain element. As you have witnessed the worm lights up to a vivid blue. I call this mineral 'The Seeing Mineral'.'

'And let me guess,' said Charlie, 'his favourite food is Seeing Mineral?'

'This is awesome!'

Louis's face so excited.

'What is awesome?' asked Day.

'Just look at his face dude! This is their life, their entire life. Just a process line. Forever?'

'Yes. What was your name?'

'Charlie.'

'Yes, Charlie.'

'What happens when you get old? I don't see any older Greys!'

'No one gets old, I will explain later.'

Day had his eyes downcast.

'We must move on,' Day mumbled, 'it is very important you see what else is being manufactured.'

'The big worm has made these tunnels?'

'Yes, and there is more than one.'

They moved further downwards, the huge worm body lighting the way.

'Don't know about you Louis, but I'm starting to feel a little nervous.'

Onesie on the other hand looked surprisingly confident, walking side by side with Day, her head held high.

'My instincts are telling me it's okay Charlie.'

'I hope you're right because we are currently in a galaxy billions of light years away from Earth, walking into the bowels of a planet following a giant earthworm. Who the hell would ever believe this?'

Charlie giggled at his own humour.

'Everything we have experienced would make us look totally insane.'

They came to another landing and stopped abruptly. Day did his magic with the rock face, the others watched spellbound by the life force he conjured with his hands. No one could speak, eyes wide, flickering, absorbing, hundreds of Greys each in uniform. All stood in lines, not moving, as far as the eye could see.

'Soldiers.'

'Holy shit,' Charlie's voice was just a whisper.

Louis opened his mouth, nothing came out.

'That's not all, come.'

They moved emotionless, trying to process the confronting image. Following on, the atmosphere changed, all nerves on edge, everything seemed to be getting worse, the next sight confirmed their instincts.

Day spoke.

'This is what they are preparing for.'

Massive spaceships, troop carriers, most of them finished with hundreds of Greys working on process lines.

Charlie spoke first to no one in particular.

'What do they need all this for? Are they under threat? They remind me of metal turtle shells.'

His voice faded out.

'These ships are about to be powered by the energy source YOU are giving them.'

His voice was angry.

'They intend to colonise any viable planets they can find.'

The next question was obvious for Louis.

'What about all the beings that may already live on these planets?'

Day's eyes went cold, looking at Louis.

'You saw the weapons and those ships are also loaded – ready to kill!'

'These Greys, they act differently. They look automatic.'

'You're right Louis, they look braindead.'

Louis and Charlie looked at each other, Louis felt the panic rising through his body, it got to his mouth.

'We have to get to Esouli, he was told it's to help with food production.'

Day put his hand on Louis's shoulder.

'We only have a few days.'

'Oh my God, you mean there's more?'

Charlie's voice became hysterical.

'You asked me what happens when they get too old to work.'

Their journey continued in silence.

'This is the end now,' announced Day, 'the tunnel goes no further.'

Day manipulated the viewing wall, Louis and Charlie almost not wanting to see.

'This is the latest weapon. This will help you understand why I had to escape. Being too human was dangerous for me and a threat to them. I think you call it 'Freewill'.'

It was like a massive warehouse on one side. The Greys were busy stacking strange looking handheld instruments.

'What are they?'

Louis held Day's look.

'I am not sure if Onesie is ready to see this, or for that matter you two as well.'

Louis took a deep breath.

'I think at this stage,' said Louis, 'we need to know everything and if it's okay, we need to know how you know so much about planet Earth. How can you speak English?'

Day watched Louis's face.

'Of course. I was wondering when you were going to ask that. Are you ready?'

'Go ahead.'

Day expanded the viewing field.

Older looking Greys, each worn out, were standing in line behind each other with their heads down. It was a miserable sight. Younger Grey soldiers stood in front holding the strange instruments they viewed previously.

'Is that a weapon?'

Charlie looked to Day, waiting for an answer.

Other Grey soldiers stood still just watching. The weapon was a long sword shaped weapon with round orbs ranging in size from small to large. The soldiers pressed something to activate, the orbs filled quickly with a brown mist, aiming it at an old Grey. It was shrouded in the mist instantly. The body started to disintegrate and melt. In a matter of seconds, it was a pile of granules. The once living being gone, now just a mess on the floor to be dealt with. A vacuum machine sucked up the remains. And it continued. Another old Grey stepping forward and becoming a product for the vacuum. There was pain on their faces, the only emotion ever witnessed in the short life given to them.

'Why don't they react? They can't do this.'

Louis was distraught, Onesie fell to her knees in shock and Charlie was speechless. Day gently lifted her. She was crying. Onesie put her fingers to her eyes, feeling the tears not understanding the sensation.

Louis was angry.

'And we thought they were passive and innovative.'

Louis looked at Day.

'What do they do with their brown stuff?'

Day's eyes studied Louis.

'Feed it to the insects, that they eat!'

'What the hell is wrong with them?'

Charlie put his hand on Louis's shoulder.

'This gives a whole new meaning to recycling.'

Charlie looked at Louis.

'Sorry I'm now feeling very nervous.'

Day stepped forward.

'We will go back to our living area and talk. I need to show you other things.'

'Oh no,' said Louis, 'not more shit like this?!'

'No,' Day responded gently, 'I think you will find this intriguing.'

'By the way,' said Day looking at Charlie, 'why are you a different colour.'

'Well,' said Charlie, 'my ancestors were the first human inhabitants on what is now called Australia, it was later colonized by white people.'

'Interesting' was the only reply.

Once settled back into the living quarters, Louis studied the environment he sat in, his eyes absorbed everything. The furniture, the drinking and eating vessels, utensils, the bedding and the clothes.

'It's all made from plants.'

'What?' said Charlie, stuffing food into his mouth. 'Everything?'

'Yep, and the food's not bad.'

'The water,' said Day, 'is spring water from under the mountains, its packed with beneficial minerals.'

All the creatures and Day dwelled within the mountain, each having their own place to live. Each being working together to survive and live. Onesie ate and drank in silence. Her once dormant brain, now tingling and working at a higher level.

'Are you alright Onesie?'

She looked at Louis.

'I can't go back there; I want to stay here.'

Panic began creeping into her voice.

'I think it's way too late anyway for her to go back,' Charlie added between mouthfuls, 'they will know by now she's missing, and they will punish her and probably use the compost weapon. I think it's best Onesie stays here for the moment.'

Day sat down and gathered his thoughts.

'I think it's time I explain to you how I became aware of your language, and your way of life on planet Earth.'

Day began, relaxing back into his comfortable plant chair.

'As you are aware, the Greys visited Earth decades ago. They went unnoticed taking on the form of humans until one of their ships crashed. It was the last one to leave earth and the Grey was weak and sick. Besides collecting humans to harvest ovaries, sperm and large amounts of blood, they stored hundreds of hours observing life on your planet. This showed how humans interact plus the history of the human race, especially conflict. The Greys focused heavily on the human wars, the aggression, and the disregard for human suffering. That's what they decided to copy. They were so excited. They infiltrated laboratories performing some very immoral and inhumane experiments along with using powerful drugs. They chose strong human men for the sperm. They wanted to maintain their specific look, ugly and aggressive. When I was made, as with all the others, the process was much the same as you breed animals artificially on Earth to eat. We are not born to parents, the sole purpose of our life was to produce food, clothes, weapons, and everything to support the armies you viewed. For some reason, they age early.'

'I think it may be because their brains have no stimulation. It's just a thought.' Charlie went on, 'Are they still making you know, your kinda people?'

'Only when stocks get low.'

'But do you have, you know, genitals?

Day looked uneasy.

'I'm human in that respect. They harvested female human reproductive systems, it took a long time, they perfected ovaries and artificial wombs they don't want the complex human brain, just a working body.'

'What about the other severe looking Greys?' asked Louis.

'The Primes and Standards, they actually have organs, but not very active sperm so they crossed it with human sperm to maintain the 'Superior' ones, and that's how they control the others. What I'm about to tell you and show you is repulsive.'

'Oh shit, this is starting to sound like a horror movie.'

'Follow me.'

They all looked at each other, they followed the trail again, however this time they took a detour. No one spoke, the air was tense. Day stopped he hung his head, took a deep breath, put his hands on the wall, it lit up and seemed to pulsate, and then cleared. Every inquisitive eye, hungry to see what lay beyond.

'What the hell?' Louis couldn't speak, he felt sick.

'Oh shit I'm gonna spew, this can't be real?!'

True to his word, Charlie splattered the ground with vomit.

In what looked like huge cryo vac bags hanging from large hooks, were bodies of the Primes in various stages of growth. Machines filtered blood and many other fluids into the mass of flesh and bone quivering and growing. Onesie fell to the ground crying in fear, making a strange statement about needing her water. One bag showed a head and torso with arms slowly growing, blood, and flesh mixing together. Large slits for eyes moving around captured in time and waiting. Another huge bag suspended near completion of the body within, hands and feet yet to grow, the eyes alert darting from left to right. In all, six huge transparent bags in different stages of repulsive growth, looked more like a slaughterhouse production line. The silence continued words hard to find to express the horror before them.

'I'm sorry but you needed to see this.'

'I have to record this as well for Esouli, they must not have the Vodoxium.'

'Christ, just when we thought we had seen it all, these weird fuckers growing big meaty Primes in bags.'

'What else do we need to see, this is appalling, and Helomedes must be made aware.'

'Every Prime and Standard are made like this.'

'What about us?' Onesie finally spoke.

'I'm sorry Onesie, this is where we are all made.'

They followed Day further. Housed in artificial wombs hundreds of living foetuses, still growing, suspended in artificially made amniotic fluid.

'I was one of these?'

'Yes, as was I.'

'What is the entire process for these ones?'

'Well Louis, when the ones like Onesie become older, some will become soldiers, the rest will have all the various jobs you have witnessed, until they become too old. The Prime and Standards take longer to grow, and they only need minimal numbers to instil enough fear.'

'Who does the experiments?' Louis's voice had a slight shake.

'The Primes, and only the Primes. The energy source you intend to give them will empower the Primes and Standards making them stronger with the ability to produce with quicker growth. It will enable them to take over planets and travel in their ships through solar systems, black holes and survive as far as they want. I can't explain it fully, I don't have the knowledge.'

'It's okay Day,' said Louis, 'we understand. Do they intend to go to Earth?'

'I'm not sure Louis, but I do know that they do not like human beings.'

'How did you know you were different and what made you want to escape?'

Louis was fascinated with Day's life, and his incredible strength of character.

'When I first went to the process lines, I started to have thoughts, I wanted to know how things worked and I started to look more human. I loved looking at the forest and I would sneak around seeking anything to stimulate my brain. I have a brain and I wanted to use it. I saw the Primes watching me, the stuff they make you drink wasn't working well enough to their liking. I knew they were going to kill me. One night I found my way to the laboratories, and I saw all the embryos growing in the bags with tubes inserted into them, all at different stages of growth. It was at that moment, full of fear, I decided I couldn't go back. I made the decision, I jumped down the flush chute.'

'Holy shit.' Charlie couldn't help himself. 'What happened?'

Day smiled remembering the moment.

'At first, I was numb with fear until I hit the water, it was running fast and I started to sink. I couldn't understand what was happening, then everything went black. When I woke, I felt fur against my skin, I put my hand out to touch it, I remember how good it felt, so warm and soft. When I became completely awake, I had a group of creatures looking at me. These beings are the ones you have seen around us, native to the forest. They fed me, sheltered me and I survived. I learnt about the forest, the plants, the animals and the water. As time passed, we learnt how to communicate, my brain seems to absorb and understand, it had come alive. The forest and mountains have become my home, the plants you see are more than just plants.'

Louis stood up in excitement beaming in his eyes.

'What do you mean 'more than plants'?'

'Here we go.'

'What do you mean?'

'Tomorrow I will take you to the forest and show you something you don't have on Earth.'

Day smiled watching the two boys interact. Louis sat back down, an expressive thought on his face.

'I made many discoveries in this forest and the entire environment, the waters alone are magical.'

'Remember the areas for the viewing, I watch everything and listened to everything that came from Earth.'

'Did they film all the planet? But how?'

'They copied your technology. All those satellites have been used by the Primes and Standards to gather information. They intend to find the planet that has the source of the energy you are giving them.'

Louis and Charlie moved at once.

'We have to get back to Esouli.'

Louis and Charlie readied themselves to leave.

'So that is his name, that strange enormous being.' '

Yep that's our dude and we have to get back to him,' Charlie was sounding very nervous.

'Please Louis, Charlie, don't get alarmed, I will help you get back. I estimate you have two more days before they expect your gift, they're being very cautious.'

The boys followed Day.

'Wait,' said Louis, 'if Onesie does not come with us there will be questions and suspicions.'

All eyes turned to Onesie.

'He's right,' said Day.

Onesie looked forlorn, but knowing she needed to control her emotions and act as herself.

'I know what I have to do.'

Onesie felt strong inside, she gave a tentative smile her eyes downcast.

The hover board was located, still in functioning mode, quietly they headed back.

'I didn't get to see the forest,' said Louis watching it disappear.

'Well,' said Charlie, 'I have a feeling we are going to.'

That night Onesie was punished by being locked into a small dark room with only water. She had been away too long and scratched the hover board. She didn't drink the water.

The boys were relieved to see Esouli. There was much chatter about their adventure. Esouli used the stored memory screen. Both of Louis's eyes were scanned, all they had seen and done was portrayed on the screen. Esouli watched in utter despair and at the same time awe as he viewed the rejected deformed lifeforms, the magnificent forest and the entire environment, magical in its beauty. The hidden weapons and the manufacturing of them, the fleet of spaceships and armies left Esouli in shock. And the most horrifying of all, the bodies being made, and the monstrous image imprinted on everyone's brain.

What do you think?'

'I think you boys have stumbled across something that could have been disastrous for many planets and their inhabitants.'

'They want your planet Esouli and the one in preparation.'

Louis couldn't read Esouli's face.

'I need to discuss this with Arume.'

Esouli left their living quarters, making his way towards the Prime Grey's headquarters. The big warrior's arrival was announced. He was greeted warmly and offered a seat.

'You look concerned,' the rather large Grey commander said, walking toward Esouli.

'We have a problem,' said Esouli.

'And what would that be my new friend?'

'Your plan has been uncovered.'

'We will have to rethink our approach.'

'What do you mean?'

Esouli was handed a drink, he drank with the Commander in an effort to be diplomatic.

'My travelling friends have discovered a species of intelligence living in that massive forest between the plateaus.'

'Why would that concern us?'

'They are aware of your plan.'

'What plan is that? How would it stop our intentions?'

Esouli didn't feel right, it was difficult to think.

'They um, they live in the forests.'

The commander laughed, others automatically did the same on cue, too afraid not to.

'I'm just reporting,' said Esouli.

'Well my friend after the next two suns rotations, we will destroy the forests and whatever is living in there will be burnt alive. It will be good practice for our soldiers.'

Esouli had to be told to leave.

'We will be entering and taking your ship, those creatures on board will be eaten and you will all be disposed of.'

'Yes, of course.'

Esouli left. He felt weak, it was difficult to understand or hear what they were saying. He felt totally numb as he staggered feeling weaker.

Day closed the viewing wall, his heart was racing, his feelings totally mixed up, fear, anger, and confusion. What was going on? What was he going to do? He paced up and down. The little primate creatures sensed his distress and jumped onto his shoulders. They snuggled into Day's neck, he patted them gently, wondering why the boys weren't with Esouli. He ran to the next platform to look for the boys. They were resting, but not asleep, leftovers of the food and water they took with them could be seen on the floor. They seemed relaxed; surely, he could not have misjudged them. Louis finally said something, rolling over to look at Charlie.

'Did Esouli seem just a bit strange to you?'

'Dude, this entire show is strange.'

'No, seriously Charlie, he just kinda got up and walked out. We usually talk about everything, and we contact Arume together.'

'Maybe he's worried.'

'He just looked vague and slow, just not himself.

'That's it!' yelled Day, looking at the boys, slapping the viewing wall.

They have given him the control drug in the water, like all the other Greys. They must come back tomorrow. Day was frightened the boys would be drugged. They must not drink the water. He just had to hope they only drink the forest water. How was he going to get to them? He paced again, but nothing was coming to his mind. He had to save the forest, his home and his friends. Day ran into the forest, he kept running until exhaustion forced him to sit on a moss covered fallen tree trunk. Tears of frustration ran down his face, he held his head in his hands, cursing the Greys. A shadow passed overhead, blocking the stream of light touching the forest floor at Day's feet, something hit him on the head, then landed in his lap. He picked it up slowly, it was a flat pebble showing a carving of a tree. Day looked up following a bird call, and a large black bird demanded he make eye contact. The bird practically yelled at him. Day studied the pebble, looking up at the bird.

'What?! What is this?'

He remembered he was going to show the boys the massive plants and their defences, but now he needed more from the forest, he needed an army. Day sat with the tiny creatures, pondering the stone, turning it over in his hand, frustration rising, not knowing what to do. Little bags began to fall on his head and into his lap. Day opened each one. The first contained seven small stones. The second, seven black flower petals, the third, a bag of golden sand, the next had seven oval shaped pods with a liquid secured inside and diagrams of what to do. The next bag contained a folded piece of soft bark. A drawing of a tree, with information about all the items. An arrow pointed east down a path. Day had to drink from one of the pods delivered to him, it felt like warm honey on his tongue his body felt strange, tingling, his eyes turned inward. In his mind he saw the tree, he saw himself laying out the items from the bags, and he knew what he had to do. He began his journey with fresh eyes. The name Delimderay was to be the one he sought.

Day headed off with his pack. The tree he looked for wouldn't be hard to miss. He moved quietly in the undergrowth, large fronds and leaves above his head. There were pungent smells of flowers and decomposing undergrowth. At one stage Day had to stop for a giant snail crossing his path, large tentacles poking around his head.

Flying bats, the size of dogs swooped overhead. Enormous snakes, their tongues smelling the air, watching him as they hung relaxing in the trees. Huge butterflies displayed their magnificent colours. A humming noise played from thousands of wings in flight. Day felt so small amongst this breathtaking world. An enormous spider fell clumsily to the ground, six big eyes, and long flowing hair. Its big pulsating abdomen was gurgling getting ready to dissolve Day. Fangs like elephant tusks adorned a gaping hairy mouth, he couldn't think or move. It came closer, he could smell it, putrid, rotting leftover creatures dangled from its mouth.

Crashing noises distracted both of them, six eyes moved to the right, Day was waiting to see what else was ready to eat him. A loud snapping sound pushed through the undergrowth. A big rambling skeleton, jaws crashing together headed towards the spider. Day froze. The skeleton resembled an extinct dinosaur from planet Earth, its tail swaying from side to side. Day pondered briefly how a skeleton could portray life. The spider started to move off, but the impact was explosive. Its abdomen burst on impact with the massive skeleton, bones and black stinking sludge splattered heavily into the air. Day ran for cover under a large floppy leaf just in time as bits of undigested animals and dripping black liquid covered the area. The big spider moaned in agony as the skeletal creature lumbered away minus a few bones.

Once he was convinced it was safe, Day stepped through the mess and went on his way. The pouches holding the items began to vibrate, he could feel it through his body.

'I must be getting close.'

Day was talking out loud, it helped with his nerves. It wasn't hard to miss the towering tree ahead. Pushing through the low vegetation, getting closer, it was like opening the final curtain to something magnificent. Before him stood a colossal, ancient beauty.

The trunk was gnarled, and weather beaten, the size of a sprawling mansion with deep openings, like manmade doorways. Standing in awe, his body was alive with anticipating nerves. He could feel many eyes watching, vivid colours reflected from the last rays of evening from one of the suns.

The branches went on forever and were sturdy enough to walk through. Masses of leaves differing in shape adorned the tree, all different shades of green and gold.

He bent down and began the ritual, the small white stones placed in a horizontal line, seven in total. Seven black petals placed between each stone he made a closed oval shape with the gold sand. Last was the six remaining pods, three on each side of the white stones.

Standing in the oval, he began to speak the summoning words, carved on the tree, 'O A SI EXAR, O A LE MAOL, O A KI KOLI'.

Day repeated this seven times, not a sound could be heard. Above, dark clouds formed, a slow rumbling and crashing could be heard above the trees. Forked lightning savage in its force hit the ground. Just when Day was feeling vulnerable it started to happen. The entire tree lit up and brilliant white light moved down the trunk, something was coming from within the tree. Time seemed to pass slowly, what appeared to be a door started to move. He had never felt so alive, the energy was incredible.

The light was blinding, he put a hand up to cover his brow. A turbulent mass was forming inside, a head could be seen, like a monstrous seahorse. Slowly emerging with a long spine covered in feathers and two sets of wings, its soft membrane quivered, large clawed feet, followed by strong forearms. The entire being was breathtaking. Its long tongue licked the air, moving it towards Day, it was getting closer. The two made eye contact, huge yellow eyes with pupils shaped like a daisy, intrigued Day. A long pointy orange tongue investigated him intently. The strange creature sat back on his strong back legs and studied Day, he didn't know what to do under heavy scrutiny, so he just started to talk nervously.

'The forest is in trouble, um, er, the plateau race is going to destroy all lifeforms within the forest and then burn it to the ground. We face an army of weapons. I need your help Forest Lord.'

He looked pleadingly into the captivating eyes. Nothing seemed to happen. Time was standing still, he went on, not knowing what else to do with the silence.

'They have a poison that's being used against our friends, I need to reverse the effects and save one particular being. We have Earthlings that want to help us.'

The silence continued, the creature swayed to and fro, his beautiful eyes closed, a soft musical sound floated on the air. The tree started to light up with the brilliant white fire, it started to spread fast across the top of the forest. A circle of gold flame travelled around Day. The forest was growing, butterflies became as big seabirds, with normal size ferns reaching the size of small trees. Vines as thick as human legs, flowers appearing the size of open umbrellas. Day was feeling lightheaded and very tired, his body slumped to the ground in the golden oval.

He awoke slowly, the tree was gone, it was dark, something was moving towards him. He held his breath, whatever was coming it was bright. The big earthworm slid his way to the opening, Day smiled with relief. His old friend had found him. He could now see the pods had grown to the size of a human head full of fluid.

'This will stop the poisoning,' Day laughed. 'Come on my big friend, we need to get back.'

Day strung the pods together and used a vine to get on board the worm. He couldn't take his eyes off this new forest. Enormous trapping mushroom plants fleshy underneath, opening and closing, moving independently. Anything caught would suffocate and be absorbed. Vines with long barbs, moved like snakes. Pitcher plants with long tongues, swirled salivating sticky pollen spraying into the air. He wasn't sure what it did. Day started to laugh.

'Now THIS is an army.'

He laughed more thinking about what Charlie would say. A blast of wind nearly knocked Day off the worm. Wasps the size of large birds darted across the brilliant sky circling like fighter bombers. Monstrous bell-shaped flowers were in drop and capture defence. Higher up Day noticed masses of canopy covered trees with pouches hanging, containing an unknown substance ready to spew out its contents. It seemed they were placed strategically for the first line of defence.

The ground ahead was swirling and spinning into an unknown vortex. The big worm punched his head into a tunnel. Day bounced into the air heading into the gaping hole, his body went stiff, he had never felt so much fear. He closed his eyes waiting, feeling very weak, something was wrapping around his waist, he was being flung into the air, he was wrapped up like a cocoon. Next minute he was rolling on the ground and landed in front of his mountain home, his head was spinning, all the pods intact.

CHAPTER 56

'Okay,' said Onesie, 'I need you two to remain calm and listen to me very carefully!'

The boys stopped what they were doing to look at Onesie, her transformation was incredible. It was like a rebirth.

'I have put in place some distractions so we can get out of here. The young Greys have not had their drugs that make them mindless, I figured that out when I missed the water drinks they give us and I drank the water from the forest. It flushed the mind-numbing poison out of my body. My mind is alive, and by the way, we DO have abilities. I've given them real water.'

They could be heard everywhere, and they were loud.

'Hey, that's my music!'

Onesie smiled.

'It is Charlie, and they love it. I have rewired the security doors and they will not close. I have been to see your friend and he is very unwell. They have been secretly giving him the poisoned water since you arrived. It's been given to subdue his powers. Day will have the cure, to flush out his system and save his life.'

'How do you know that?'

'I think I tapped into an ability I didn't know I had. Now, this is what we are going to do. You are going to shapeshift into young Greys, we need to get back to the forest...'

'And get that stuff for Esouli,' interrupted Louis.

'The army are going to commence warfare on the forest soon, you both need to do this and do it now!'

'Okay then,' said Charlie looking at Louis, 'we better do as we're told.'

They commenced to put themselves into a trance-like state, doing everything they were taught. Onesie watched captivated, wondering if the Greys had a similar ability, then realised they must have for them to have lived on earth. Slowly all characteristics of the boys started to fade. The process was complete, the boys looked at each other touching their faces.

'Oh jeez, my skin feels like a sand suit.'

'Good description,' said Louis, feeling his arms.

They quickly left the living pod. Music played and the young Greys no longer appeared to be like zombies. No walking in straight lines or empty actions, they were now communicating, looking at each other and observing their surrounds.

The three made a run for it while the distractions were all around them. They were nearly there. The massive forest towered over the plateau, they slowed down, not believing what was in front of them, they were petrified.

'Move and we will shoot to kill.'

There was no way out, guns pointed at their heads.

'You are prisoners, let your deaths will be a lesson to all.'

Behind them, out of sight of the soldiers, a large vine crept slowly, positioning itself, then it moved at extraordinary speed, striking like a snake, wrapping them up like parcels, flicking them into the dense forest. More soldiers could be heard running, angry voices and shots being fired. The three parcels rolled onto the ground at Day's feet. Charlie and Louis started to transform back while still on the ground. Day watched excited by their abilities.

'This HAS been a strange morning.'

Before a word could be spoken, painful roars could be heard from above, brilliant red wasps, like helicopters, spitting acid like substance exploding on contact, burning holes in the soldiers' suits, reaching their delicate skin. All were confused, never expecting to be challenged.

It was aggressive and proficient. The forest was going to fight back. More soldiers came, all ordered into the forest. They were brainwashed not to feel fear, only to please their masters. The forest floor greeted its prey, sucking them into the unknown. Massive pitcher plants licked and entwined their victims, dropping them into the melting pot of gut juice and slowly turning them to liquid only to spew them out again. Giant mushrooms enveloped their victims, suffocating and draining them of all body fluid. With the leftovers discarded, they looked like paper floating away on the breeze. Large balls of pollen smashed into the soldiers' faces, instantly shutting down their lungs. Their bodies lifeless on the ground as black shiny claws emerged from the ground capturing limp bodies, pulling them into their world to store as food for the unknown lifeform.

While the chaos continued and escalated, Day led the others into an enormous waiting flower. They held on tightly to the filament as it lifted and carefully made its way, weaving through the jungle. Soldiers could be heard, bullets kept firing. Day saw all his creature friends huddling together and terrified. The flower landed near them and they ran to him crying and trembling. He directed them to a secret chamber that was deep in the mountain where they had food and water. He assured them he would be back. They clung to him as he felt his heart breaking for them. His eyes filled with tears. He landed back on the portable flower, and they continued on their way to the tower where Esouli remained held prisoner. The soldiers were in panic mode with groups assembling everywhere, the battle had begun. Onesie led them to the secret tunnels under the garrison.

'He'll be heavily guarded.'

She was breathing heavily as she continued running hard in panic.

'They will have troops waiting for us at the other end.'

'Oh great,' said Charlie, stopping to catch his breath, 'we should have stayed as Greys.'

'Don't think it will make much difference, they're going to shoot to kill anyway.'

'Keep running,' said Onesie, 'I have a plan.'

The sound of what seemed like hundreds of footsteps was getting closer. Something very unusual could be heard.

'Can you hear that, Charlie?'

'It's my music.'

Bruno Mars music was playing loud.

Onesie opened the heavy steel door, no security system, no one was alerted. The music was louder, the scene was riotous. They were met by hundreds of young Greys dancing and singing. The soldiers were confused and unsure what to do.

'And this is the diversion? Very impressive,' said Charlie, 'especially the music.'

'Quickly we have to move into the tower, the Primes will order the killings.'

'What?! They will kill their own?' asked Charlie, looking from Day to Louis.

'They will wipe them out just to make a point, remember they studied human wars.'

The tower was in darkness with a staircase leading to the top. Quickly they all moved as the music played. Bullets and screaming created a chilling feeling of fear around the planet.

Upon reaching their destination the sight was devastating. Esouli was unconscious and chained up like an animal.

'Quickly,' said Day, rummaging through his backpack to find the pods with the liquid to save his life.

Louis and Charlie held Esouli's head, frantically trying to get the fluid into his mouth, he still had a swallowing reflex. Nothing was happening. Distraught, they slapped his cheeks with tears streaming down their faces.

'This can't be happening. He can't die.'

Suddenly, his eyes started to flicker as Esouli took a deep breath.

'Can you please stop slapping my face.'

'Woo-hoo! Thank God.'

The boys hugged Esouli, laughing, but still crying. Onesie and Day looked on absorbed by the intense emotions. Day looked at Onesie. Tiny smiles formed around each of their mouths. Esouli got up slowly staggering as he reached his full height. Day and Onesie were gobsmacked by his size and looks.

Louis's voice broke the moment.

'Where is the Vodoxium?'

Esouli's wings stretched out of their hidden place, the vial of Vodoxium rolled onto the floor from the wings on his lower leg.

'Oh, thank God!'

The chains snapped off.

'They know there is a sphere in the ship.'

A strange smell floated on the air loud explosions could be heard.

'We have to get out of here.'

Esouli took the lead. Outside, a vision of disaster met them. Day was horrified as fireballs exploded in the forest with butterflies, birds and insects trying to escape. Panicked and frightened calls faded onto the wind.

'We have to stop this I can't let this happen.'

Day was shaken and horror struck.

The Prime leaders watching the destruction were excited and clapping their hands.

'We need to get to the ship'.

'They will send their ships to bring you down', said Day trying to run and talk.

'I've de-activated them,' said Onesie.

Laser guns fired close to them. The ship could be seen, high on the landing pad. It was pulsating, aware danger was imminent and ready to leave, but not without its passengers. Suddenly, the group were surrounded.

'Did they just appear from nowhere?'

Louis looking at Onesie.

'Must be a developed ability.'

Esouli started to feel weak again, they had hit him with a dart of poison.

'Shit no!' Louis's face in shock.

The group huddled together around Esouli, as the Primes moved in.

'Get on your knees!'

They did as commanded, the Prime leader stood over them, his reptilian looking face laughing.

'I will kill you one by one until you give me the Vodoxium sphere, including the one you have hidden, and you can watch each other die. We are going to take your craft, it's over for all of you. We will dominate, and Helomedes will be ours followed by Earth.'

Day saw the flames rising in his forest. The Prime produced a huge sword, as Onesie was pulled out of the group by her head, and she was first. With his sword raised, the other Primes cheered, waiting for the kill. Louis could feel his heart thumping in his ears. He could feel Charlie's as they held each other and Esouli held all of them.

'Surely Nan it can't end now, help us!'

Roses! He could smell roses. Louis exhaled heavily, tears flowing with Charlie uncapable to move or respond. Day was shaking. Surely the ritual would save them and the forest, he was bewildered and terrified. Esouli struggled to focus, his mind confused and dull.

The suns paled as something was blocked the rays. Something was wrapping around them, scraping them up. They were thrown into the air as darkness encased them with something sticky and smelly underfoot.

'Oh God, what now? I hate this planet.'

Charlie clung tightly to Louis.

'I don't know Charlie; we still have our heads.'

They were inside a massive pitcher plant, each of them clinging to the edge watching.

A spectacular sight was unfolding below. A Venus fly trap, the size of a two-story house, its immense red mouth open, was approaching. It crept up behind the Primes and Standards who were exhilarated with the smell of death and pain all around them. Clapping hands and making high grunting sounds they jumped up and down. The Primes and standards had been distracted by the impending killing of the others taken by the monstrous plant, not realising they had been rescued. Before they registered what was happening the hungry colossal plant opened its enormous mouth and grabbed up all the Primes and Standards swallowing them in like a starving dog. The big head lifted into the air, its teeth locking them in forever. Slipping into the guts of the plant, burning and melting into the deadly acid, the roars of pain echoed around the forest. Able to be seen from the outside, their revolting faces imprinted into the fleshy plant for all to see. Each victim's hands seen trying to rip apart the tough structure. Time stood still, all those watching fascinated by the gigantic plant consuming the contents. The huge head of the plant swayed from side-to-side digesting. Moments later, boots and uniforms were flung into the air. The once proud star worn by the Primes now falling blood soaked to the ground.

The escapees suspended high above the forest, captured in their own plant carrier witnessed the demise of the cruel laboratory mistakes. The deadly but gentle plant rested its head on the forest floor. Slowly crawling out they all made their way to the safety of the mountain. Heavy plump rain began to fall.

'Shit that rain hurts.'

Esouli drank more from the pods to flush the poison.

'Follow me' yelled Day, protecting Onesie with his arm.

'Seriously dude, I'm over running from shit.'

Louis giggled at his friend, relief washing over him.

Once all were safe inside, Day rushed to the lookout to watch his forest, they all followed, it was still burning with fury. High above the incredible landscape tall, unusual trees with a single canopy, swirled around like sprinklers and that's exactly what they were. Spinning and showering the entire forest below each drawing water from the underground rivers acting like nature's windmills.

'That is extraordinary, imagine if we had that on earth.'

Louis couldn't take his eyes off nature at its best.

Onesie's voice broke into everyone's eye feasting,

'I have to go back and help my friends. The brain altering poison should be wearing off the soldiers.'

'What will happen if they're not under control?'

'They will be in total confusion Louis, not knowing what to do. They have been indoctrinated since around my age.'

'But the young are now like you, able to think and process.'

'That is true, but I am not sure how the soldiers will react. They have been watching all the footage from Earth, a lot of cruel psychological education.'

Day led everyone to the viewing areas. The soldiers were like wound up toys, coming to the end of their coils, walking into each other, falling over, empty eyes, blank faces, feeling nothing. The young Greys on the other hand were organised, directing the mindless soldiers to their barracks to lay down, like insects at the end of their lifecycle, their poison replaced with water.

'I would not trust them Onesie, they should be locked up and observed closely.'

'I totally agree,' said Day.

'I think,' said Esouli, 'I shall return to our ship. Our little friends will be frantic, and I need to speak to Arume about the future of this planet.'

'What do you mean?' Day looked shocked.

'I mean the weapons, and the amount of fighter craft.'

'Oh, I see.'

'I think my friend its time you come out of hiding and have much more input into how the future of your home should look. And you Onesie are an extremely brave girl.'

With that Esouli's wings appeared, strengthening exercises throwing off the last of the poison from his system. The magnificent warrior lifted into the air gracefully and made his way towards a very anxious spaceship. Onesie and Day in awe of his magnificence.

'He's pretty cool hey Bro? nudging Day.

'Yes, Charlie he is 'cool' as you say.'

'I really think I should go and see what is happening.'

Onesie was getting anxious.

'We can come with you.'

Louis was keen to see how the others were coping.

'Oh shit, all I want to do is go home. Seriously I'm so over weird shit happening.'

'It's over Charlie, I think we are safe now.'

'Well, I hope there's no more of that bloody poison.'

Louis put his arm around Charlie.

'Come on big fella we can do this. Let's hitch a ride in a big plant.'

The four friends boarded a friendly plant that tossed them onto the plateau. Something was happening in the forest, the massive vegetation was moving and re-shaping, unravelling and returning to normal size. The environment had a different feel, music still played quietly, the young Greys had ceased work on this particular day, they relaxed and ate in peace. Louis and Charlie went to look at the soldiers, they were a pathetic sight, forlorn and non-responsive.

'It's going to take a long time for them to come back to any state of normality. What do you think will happen now with this planet?'

'I reckon,' said Louis thoughtfully, 'they need to feed that weird shit growing in those bags to those plants in the forest.'

'What about the baby bags, God knows, that's their future population.'

'They really need to find another way, but that's for them to decide. Come on Charlie lets go and see our lovable aliens.'

Day returned to his poor deformed beings, they were so pleased to see him, they hurried toward him excited and making funny little noises. He communicated the events and how their lives were now safe and free.

Even though peace had come to the planet, the little creatures did not want to leave their mountain home or the forest. The fear of the other world was too hard to overcome.

Day enjoyed a drink with his friends all the while thinking about Onesie. He had grown very fond of her. Strange feelings he didn't quite understand. Tonight, was the first time in the history of the young Greys, they would all eat together in the food hall, they could talk, laugh, and be the race of Greys they were meant to be. He could hear the strange music, he liked the two human boys, they make him smile and it made him feel good.

Louis looked around at all the activity, listening to the chatter and watching the Greys interact with each other.

'Alright, what are you thinking?'

'I still can't believe this is real.'

'Well dude, if it's a dream it's a bloody long one.'

An in-depth discussion took place between Esouli, the Greys and Day. They decided they would manage the planet together and continue self-sufficiency. Onesie interrupted.

'I think you all need to come and see this.'

They all headed towards the soldier's barracks. It was cold and dark more like prison cells than soldiers' barracks. Onesie pointed inside the barracks. Every soldier had disintegrated within their uniforms, they were dust.

'What happened to them?'

Onesie looked at Day.

'The drug. This is what occurs after long-term use. All of them were given or rather forced to take it by the Primes.'

Esouli looked at Louis.

'You looked worried.'

'You do realise that when this generation of Greys die, that's the end of them?'

'Yes, that's correct, and they are aware of that.'

'What will they do? They were made in a laboratory.'

'I will leave them the Vodoxium. Hopefully it will strengthen their immune systems and maintain their blood cells. The waters from under the mountain should help restore their cells.'

'But what about all the spacecraft and weapons?'

'They accept their fate, but we will be watching and will intervene if they wish to continue their existence. They will need to use the weapons and crafts, only if invaded by hostiles. Their nature is passive, they know how to seek knowledge. Day will take them into the forest to explore and learn.'

'Can we please go home? Seriously guys, I'm so over this planet!'

Louis and Esouli couldn't help laughing, the look on Charlie's face was priceless.

Onesie and Day, with all the young Greys, waited to see them off. Everyone shook hands, Charlie and Louis gave Onesie a hug.

'If it wasn't for you Onesie, we wouldn't be leaving.'

'Thank you, and I'm glad you have a real home now.'

'Yep, he's right, now can we go?!'

The craft was fully energised, all life on board so happy to see the trio.

'Thank God!'

Charlie sat heavily in one of the pilot chairs. The craft was secured, pulsating, almost singing. The crowd below looked up in awe as it took off. From the great viewing area all on board watched the population become smaller. The gigantic forest had gone back to its normal size, moving and reshaping like a giant landscape still being painted.

'I was thinking,' said Esouli, 'we could make one more stop.'

'No!' said Charlie.

'You've got to be joking?!'

Louis jumped out of his chair.

Esouli burst out laughing at his own joke.

They heard tinkling, quick footsteps coming closer and decisive.

'Come on, off to the showers. You all smell.'

Tiny hands clapped.

'Come on!'

'Oh great, back with the bossy midget weirdo!'

All the little creatures followed, flying around the boys heads much excitement and strange little noises of contentment.

CHAPTER 57

Sam and Mate had finished a long run on the beach and were relaxing eating fish and chips together whilst watching a beautiful, mottled sunset. The phone interrupted the moment.

'Collin. What's up?'

'You home?'

'I will be in about half an hour.'

'Good, see you then.'

Sam smiled, looked at Mate.

'Well Dude, our warm and fuzzy friend is coming to visit.'

Collin shuffled his way in, Sam got a whiff of mixed odours, cigarette smoke, hamburger and a touch of whiskey.

'You got any scotch?'

Sam handed him a glass and a bottle of single malt. He slammed a file down on the table, Sam studied the paperwork.

'Your lawyer has sorted those two weirdos out, it's all in there.'

Collin drank down his scotch and just looked at Sam.

'Oh, right.'

Sam pulled out a wad of cash and handed it to Collin.

Collin got up grunting, 'Nice dog' and left, taking the bottle of scotch with him.

He read the file with Mate's help. Genevieve St Day, the former Lucy Blackwell, was living in public housing on a disability pension and managed by the NSW Trustee and Guardian. She was allocated drop-in support as she was diagnosed with mental health problems. Her bank account was used to pay off her husband's debt. Compensation was paid to Bridget Sherwood for illegally removing her and her son from her home. Jason Blackwell dodged a jail sentence due to his health status. He was now a resident in an aged care facility requiring 24-hour care. He was receiving speech pathology and had made some improvement. Mr Blackwell unable to mobilise, was awarded a disability pension for his diagnosis and declared bankrupt. Jason was also financially managed by the NSW Trustee and Guardian as no relative had come forth to advocate for the care of Mr and Mrs Blackwell.

Sam sat back exhaling as he thought about the entire situation, including the boys and the mysterious lake that he now visited regularly. He knew that Bridget, her friend and daughter frequented the lake often too. What was it about that place? The boys were still away, another strange situation.

'So, Mate,' the little dog sat up listening intently to Sam, his head moving side to side, 'I was thinking we might 'out of curiosity', take a visit to see Mr and Mrs Blackwell and close this chapter permanently.'

The following day Sam put in the address to Jason's aged care facility in his GPS system. He made sure Mate had his seatbelt on and off they went, music playing.

He was required to be let in at the front door of Gardenia Lodge. Mate was left in the car under a tree, windows quarter way down with some water. Sam looked at a line of old people in various stages of sleep-in lounge chairs. It was confronting. They looked like empty vessels; souls already departed. It was pathetically sad. A smell of urine mixed with the smell of gardenias filled the air.

Jason was curled up in his bed, Sam sat in a lounge chair facing him. After a few moments his eyes started to flicker, both his eyes ectropion, dry and sticky. He recognised Sam his speech slurred.

'How are you feeling Dad?'

'I want to go home.'

He mumbled in a saliva filled mouth, his eyes pleading.

Sam made a decision to tell him the truth.

'Dad you don't have a home, in fact you have nothing left.'

His eyebrows raised in recognition.

'Your wife's money paid out what you owed, combined with the sale of all your possessions. You certainly got yourself in a financial mess and you dodged a jail sentence due to your health status.'

Jason formed a 'Nooo', coughing on his saliva.

'And there's more, the women Genevieve St Day, was your former ex-wife Lucy Blackwell. All she did with you was for simple spite or revenge, I'm not sure why. She planned to leave before the honeymoon and cut you off financially.'

Sam knew he was understanding by his facial movements and tears trying to escape.

'So, nothing you both conspired went to plan. You're now on a disability pension and it is managed by the NSW Trustee and Guardian. Oh, and the house you took off that woman and her son illegally was compensated out of the settlement of your assets and the title returned. Another interesting thing about that woman is, she is also the foster mother of your other son. The one you had with Lucy Blackwell and abandoned.'

Jason's noises got louder, his eyes flickering from side to side, his legs moving under the sheets.

'Take me home.'

It was clear, it took all his concentration and physical effort to get it out.

'What? Take you home with me?'

Jason was moving his head up and down.

'Well Dad, I don't think I will be doing that, kinda like when you wouldn't ever take me home from boarding school! Do you remember Dad, dropping me off at boarding school when I was five and never coming back?'

Jason was shaking his head from side to side, anger expressed on his face. Sam looked at his father, he felt nothing, nothing at all.

'I'm leaving now, and I won't be back.'

Jason Blackwell let out angry low moans, his face grimacing, his legs flailing around. Sam kept walking.

Mate did his excitable greeting routine, as if he had been away for years.

'Now YOU buddy, I DO love. Well, my little hairy arsed friend, that went as expected, now off to see the other one.'

Resetting the GPS they headed for Fernhill Road, Fairfield. Sam eventually found the street. It was a poor area, community housing for low-income people. Sam found her flat number; he could hear the TV daytime soap operas. He knocked quietly, the door opened slightly, he couldn't believe he was looking at the same person. He found it difficult speak and he knew his mouth hung open.

'What do you want?'

'It's Tristan.'

Being Sam didn't matter at this particular moment, he felt very uncomfortable, she opened the door wider for him to enter. The flat was small and stale. It looked like she lived on the lounge surrounding her were empty wine casks, a bulging ashtray and frozen food containers. The carpet was old, thread bare and stained. Lucy's look matched the room. Stained track pants, t-shirt with holes and dried food clinging to both. To finish the look, a pair of old Ugg boots with an unpleasant smell. Worst of all was her face. The red pulpy skin hanging in folds down one side of her face, the weeping fluid running down the folds, her mouth sagging. The eye that hung halfway down her face stared at him, milky and dead. Her hair was now a dull sandy colour mottled with grey. She was incredibly thin and hunched over.

'Have a good look you cocky little bastard. It's not forever, I will be back.'

She was snarling like a beaten mongrel dog.

'I'm the world's most famous model.'

Magazines scattered all over the floor, pictures of her, glamourous and beautiful.

'When I get all my money Genevieve St Day will back.'

Sam decided to play it cool after observing the many medications packed in a Webster pack. He also noted she had missed many.

'Look, I'm not staying, I'm just delivering information because I happen to be the only person nominated in both your lives.'

'That's a damn lie, bloody smartarse. I have a manager.'

'Okay, yes of course you do. Jason is in a nursing home, he is bedridden.'

'Ha-ha! That's the best news I could hear.'

Sam was nervous, here goes.

'All your money paid off everything he owed. The moment you spoke the words 'I do' your money transferred to his account.'

'But that was not my instructions, her mouth was opening and closing. That stupid accountant got it wrong.'

Her pulpy face was getting flushed, and the eye seemed to be enlarging.

'Jason was in a lot of financial trouble. He was facing bankruptcy and jail. You are now on a disability pension and financially managed by the NSW Trustee and Guardian.'

'That can't be right, I had millions.'

Her voice was getting louder, clenching her fists.

'I need my face fixed, I need my servants, all my clothes and jewellery.'

'It was all sold to pay for your wedding.'

She came at Sam with closed fists, spit flying everywhere.

'You've got it, you miserable weirdo. You've got it.'

Sam left closing the door behind him. She opened it and hurled the ashtray at him, just missing his head.

'You'll pay for this!'

She was screaming hysterically. Curtains from adjoining flats moved, curious heads trying not to be seen.

Finally, Sam and Mate were on the road again, relieved he would never have to see her again.

Sam looked over at Mate.

'You know dude, I think I prefer dogs to people.'

On the way home Sam decided to swing by Isobel's place to see if he could spot Louis and his Aboriginal mate. He parked the car in a laneway that allowed him to see the front of the house. He listened to music, stroking Mate's head, they were both dozing off until a loud dirt bike screamed past. Sam sat upright and rubbed his face. This was becoming so strange. It was as if the boys didn't exist.

'I wonder where the hell they are? You know Mate. That lake, the boys, this family— they're all connected.'

He made a call.

'Yep.'

'You got a lot on?'

'Nope.'

'I'm going to text you an address can you watch it for a week?'

'Yep, and I'll text you my bank account details.'

'No worries.'

Sam laughed at Collin's bluntness he knew Collin was happy to live in his car. He drove off, deciding on another stopover.

'I think you might appreciate a walk to the lake old Mate.'

As Sam drove away, Karen Landy pulled up.

Sam put his car in the usual place, out of sight. Mate was excited, running ahead. The growth around the entire place was incredible, Sam walked to where Bridget's house once was. Bridget's garden had grown back.

'It's like it's waiting for the house to come back. Alright dude, now you've finished pissing on everything, let's go.'

They walked towards the overgrown path. Sam suddenly felt confused. He picked up Mate, his body felt weird. Something was sucking them into God knows where. He was in a long black tunnel travelling at a phenomenal speed, it felt like all his insides were going to be sucked out.

He woke up in his car, Mate was sitting in the passenger seat looking at Sam with his head on the side.

'What the hell was that? How did we get back here?'

Sam's mind was racing, trying to make sense of what just happened.

'Have we been here the entire time, did I imagine that? I must have gone to sleep, but I remember walking the path.'

Sam's thoughts got distracted by a car pulling up, Mate was watching intently, excitedly wagging his tail.

'You like the look of that car dude or what? I don't believe it.'

Bridget, Simone and Isobel got out of the car and headed towards the lake.

'God this mystery is getting intriguing. Come on, we're gonna try again.'

He put Mate under his arm and headed to the lake, trying to be quiet. Just as before he awoke back in the car. Sam laughed.

'Hey dude, we're having a ground hog day.'

He started the engine.

'We're doing this again tomorrow my fluffy little buddy.'

Bridget needed to send an alert to the boys. She followed the ritual for Arume to acknowledge their presence, the Tawny Frog Mouth sat alone high in the trees camouflaged watching. The message for them to return soon was paramount.

'Do you think they understand?' asked Simone.

'They do my darling girl. How about a treat on the way home? I think we all need a treat.'

Bridget winked at Simone.

'When did Miss Landy say she would be back?'

'It was open-ended ten days, but I have a feeling it could be random. That impromptu story of yours was a lifesaver. Do you really have an uncle in Arnhem land?'

'Well as a matter of fact I do, and he does live by the traditions.'

'Has Charlie ever visited before?'

'When he was around five, we took a trip to Arnhem Land, but he was too young to learn his traditional ways, it's something he wants to do.'

'I think Louis would insist on going.'

'Yes, I am sure he would.'

'Well, that's our story Bridge my friend, I just hope they get back soon.'

'I don't think she is very impressed, and I could be in trouble. My God if I lost him it would destroy me.'

'That's not going to happen.'

'I hope not. You know that saying, 'Bad things happen to Good People'.'

'Not you, my friend. Not you.'

'I really miss Charlie and Louis.'

'We all do Sweetheart.'

'Why did you lie to that woman Mum?'

'Sometimes the truth has to be adjusted to protect people.'

'Does that mean animals as well?'

'Okay, what have you done?'

'Those bloody people in that greenhouse neglected their guinea pig. She was running around in the yard, no food or water, chased by cats, so I 'took' her.'

'How?'

'She came for food under the fence.'

Isobel was smiling, as was Bridget.

'So, where is this little piggy?'

'In the garden shed.'

Both women burst out laughing.

'No wonder I'm always short of carrots and lettuce. I guess we have a guinea pig.'

When they got home, the escapee was presented, introduced, and 'Dolly' moved from the garden shed to her own house inside. Simone, all excited about the boys coming home and Dolly, skipped to the mailbox, one of her favourite jobs. Returning, she handed Bridget an envelope.

Bridget nervously and frowning opened a letter from a law firm.

'Oh God, I wonder what this is about?'

Bridget went quiet, resting the letter in her lap.

'What's wrong Bridget?'

Isobel read the lengthy letter.

'This is wonderful.'

'It was fraud. Everything they did was fraud. My home destroyed for nothing by that Jason Blackwell for a development.'

'Well girlfriend, karma came along and kicked his arse big time. He's in a nursing home now and owes millions. You going to take it? Three hundred thousand is a lot of money Bridge! The land is yours again, you could build.'

'I think I need a drink.'

'Yep, good idea.'

They sat on the veranda sipping chilled wine.

'I keep thinking about the name 'Blackwell', Louis's former name. Do you think it's a coincidence?'

'Hard to say, but I do know you have some decisions to make.'

'What would you do?'

'Take it and build a cute little cottage. The garden is waiting for you. Besides that, the lake needs a keeper since the discovery of those drawings.'

'Okay, that's what I will do. Louis needs his home back and so do I.'

Bridget had a restless night in bed. Her mind wouldn't shut down. Karen Landy and Louis, scenarios of what could happen kept running on a loop. For some reason the footage of Jason Blackwell's disastrous wedding kept playing in her dream state mind too. The woman under the veil, the blood and fluid flooding down her dress, all over the floor, people getting swept along in the mess.

Bridget woke panting in panic.

'Why the hell am I dreaming about that stupid wedding?'

Laying back down throwing off the blanket, reaching for a dark chocolate, the soothing sweet taste good for nerves. Something was moving outside, the full moon changing from night to near daylight between drifting clouds. The tawny frogmouth sat relaxed his feathers slightly ruffled by the night breeze. The sound of plovers calling going about their night activities.

'Your friend is missing,' spoke Bridget quietly, making eye contact.

A dark shadow moved past the window, Bridget flinched, it went backwards and forwards three times, she was intrigued, reaching for her lamp, it stood still. The clouds cleared at the same time. It was the body of Arume, but the face was a skeleton of an eagle. They watched each other until Bridget spoke. It was the message they needed. The boys were on their way home, clouds blocked the moon as darkness fell like a veil of black lace over the night. Just as quickly as he appeared, the window frame was once again empty.

Collin Stephens stood back looking at his trade, an old- style camper van, more comfortable to live in for days on end. The camera was set up to run non-stop for twenty-four hours. The van had a good view of the house and looked a natural part of the coastal environment. Collin decided to take a walk on the beach, it was getting boring. After six days it was time to shower, and it only cost two dollars at the amenities block. A trip to the supermarket, the bottle shop, finished off with fish and chips for dinner.

He laughed.

'Wow, getting paid for having a holiday.'

His bottle of rum and packet of cigarettes to kept him company.

Crawling into his van, ready to enjoy his feed, he replayed his video camera. Someone else was watching the house. He used his zoom lens. Scrambling through the rubbish to get into the front seat he rummaged to find his glasses. Karen Landy had her binoculars on the house scanning the windows and garden. He took down the number plate.

'Looks like she only stayed an hour.'

The laptop was pulled out from under the seat, he got to work searching the number plate.

'Well, that's interesting, so you're from Child Protection Services.'

The car was registered to Family and Community Services. Collin forwarded his information onto Sam.

Karen Landy sat in her car finishing off her coffee and sandwich. It had been over a week with still no sign of the boys. It was now a case of two boys missing.

'How could I have got this so wrong? I trusted Bridget I know they're both lying. Who the hell is that strange man living in the camper van?'

Speaking aloud eased her frustration.

'Jesus. Don't they realise it can become a police matter?'

Knocking on the front door, it was Isobel that answered the door inviting her inside. Taking a seat Karen began prodding. Both women seemed relaxed.

'Have you heard from the boys?'

'Yes,' said Bridget a little too eager, 'they will be home at the end of the week.'

'But they're supposed to be home now Bridget, surely you must both be concerned?'

'No not really,' Isobel maintaining eye contact.

'Look,' said Karen, sitting forward in her chair. 'I'm getting a lot of heat from this and the police could become involved any time now.'

'The police?'

Isobel was getting unsettled.

'Tell me Miss Landy, this wouldn't have anything to do with the colour of my skin?'

'Of course not. I also don't know if you're aware, but there is some strange man living in a campervan watching your house. Look, your children haven't been sighted and I have a job to do remember!'

Bridget spoke up.

'It's some old man living in his van. He walks the beach, uses the amenities block, and he's not interfering with us.'

Karen was aware she had upset Isobel and she had to be careful there was another child in the house.

'Look, I'm leaving now and I apologise if I upset you, but remember I have a job to do.'

Bridget walked her to the door, feeling nervous. Karen gave her a stern look and left.

'Oh shit, shit and more shit.'

Bridget was close to tears. Her heart pumping hard and fear was raging in her brain.

The two women sat in silence trying to process what had just happened and the consequences.

'They have to come by the end of the week.'

Isobel grabbed Bridget's hand.

'Time for a protection spell.'

Sitting face to face holding hands, they began to breathe deeply, slowly clearing their minds and centring themselves.

'Elements of the sun, elements of the day, please come this way. Powers of the night and powers of the day, I summon thee to protect me. So, mote it be.'

They repeated this three times.

'Should we go to the lake?'

'Yes, one more time and we will repeat our spell with our altar.'

Collin Stephens moved on in his van, that Child Services woman kept watching him. He updated Sam on the visit and the women visiting the lake again.

CHAPTER 58

The boys slept for long hours into the journey, completely exhausted from their experiences and the many moments of heightened fear. Both their pods opened simultaneously. A tinkling sound could be heard getting closer.

'Oh God, that's not who I think it is?'

'Yep, it is,' said Louis with a yawn.

The little face was nose to nose as his little hand smacked Louis across the head.

'Come on, get up! You stink.'

Fudgunkel moved on to Charlie, sniffing his body, another smack across the head.

'Poo, poo. You stink too!'

The boys crawled out of their pods and staggered to the shower cylinders, yawning and scratching their tired, dirty bodies.

A large banquet was being prepared. All creatures on board taking direction from Dorfund with the Jomonial and the Lanorigal having their strange conversations and face pulling arguments, Fudgunkel got little pieces of food thrown at him when he wasn't looking. The little human faced dragonflies cleaned up and reorganised the tasty foods.

The banquet finally came together. All creatures busied themselves delivering and serving food and drinks. There was happiness in the air, everyone so happy the boys and Esouli were back safe. The Jomonial and the Lanorigal relieved to be finally going to their new home Helomedes. It was a great scene. Esouli watched the boys, and all the others on board, he had to talk about one more stopover. He knew they would react, but it is something they needed to see. Charlie stuffed food as fast as he could, not interested in talking. Louis couldn't stop giggling at Charlie. Louis also couldn't help throwing a fruit fritter which landed right in the middle of Charlie's forehead. Charlie stopped chewing, pulled it off his face and shoved it in his mouth. Esouli got splattered with a very ripe tomato, it dripped and fell in his lap, the food fight began, even Fudgunkel joined in. Esouli flicked bits of sticky pancakes off his pointy big ears.

Once finished the boys joined Esouli in the chairs at the cockpit. The control panel was alive and navigating their course.

'I need to have a talk to you boys about our travels.'

'Oh no, something's coming. Where are we going now?'

'I knew it!'

'I promise Charlie, no more aliens.'

'I have a message from Arume. We need to be back on Earth by the end of Earth's week calendar. Apparently, people are looking for you?'

'Who?'

'Some woman called Karen Landy.'

'Oh shit. Mum must be getting pretty stressed out. Are we going home?'

Louis concerned for Bridget.

'This could get serious. Remember my situation.'

'In about an hour's time we will be entering the Milky Way.'

'Woo-hoo. Finally coming to our own solar system.'

Louis and Charlie smiled at each other.

'But first...'

'No, no, you don't.'

Charlie let out a howl.

Esouli put his hands up in defence.

'So you don't want to see Earth Two?'

'Are you kidding? Earth Two!'

'Yes please!'

'So where exactly is this planet?'

'Once we enter the Milky Way galaxy, we will be diverting off our navigated path. Earth Two is in a kind of parallel universe to Earth, minus a populated planet.'

'What do you mean?'

The boys looking confused.

'The planet kind of hides behind Mars, billions of galaxies make it impossible to be found from Earth's scientists.'

'So, what about the colony on Earth Two?'

'Patience Louis, its better you wait and see, rather than I try and explain.'

'Now this planet Mars, what's the story?'

'What do you mean Charlie?'

'Well, why is it dead?'

'It wasn't always dead.'

This sparked Louis's interest instantly.

'What happened?'

'Mars is much older than Earth. Life on Earth is about 3.8 billion years old, but Mars is older. Your scientists declared it 4.5 billion. It's actually seven billion.'

'What happened?'

'Mars as it is known to Earth, once sustained life. It had vegetation and an unusual landscape compared to Earth.'

'Did it have life?'

'It did Louis, for about one billion years, and a small colony of inhabitants.'

Esouli stood up waving his hand as if holding an invisible wand. A hologram of the red planet was in front of them.

'Let me show you, rather than explain. This is Mars today. A desolate planet, sad in its landscape with broken rocks scattered everywhere, red mounds of strange hills, covered in large empty craters and rock formations stacked on top of each other. Sand geysers spew forth the skeletal remains of past vegetation.'

'It just stood up and died.'

'It did Charlie.'

'Oh wow, look at this!'

Louis was excited, his mouth open looking at the hologram.

It was Mars one billion years ago and the difference was astounding. Giant succulent trees stood strong, their thick green stems with thin branches and plump leaves and vibrant flowers adorned the trees. Thick red moss covered the ground, spongy and damp. Tiny pools of water the size of dinner plates constantly fed the aquifers. Tall, lush tufts of green and red grass dominated the environment. Large mountain ranges in the background eclipsed the sky. Holes could be seen in the mountains in no particular order. The landscape was repetitive in its design. Movement in the sky caught the boys' attention. An animal resembling a large green frog glided across the hologram sky, yet it had webbed wings and legs like a pterodactyl. More of them followed coming out of the holes in the mountains. They landed with precision around water holes feeding on the on the moss. They watched each other to ensure that all had enough to eat and drink.

'Holy shit! Do you realise we are looking at creatures from a billion years ago? This is sensational.'

Louis's face was beaming in awe.

The large tufts of grass moved radically as small creatures rummaged around.

'Cockroaches.'

Charlie pointed at them.

Hard-shelled animals the size of a land turtle were very busy feeding. Two distinct areas on the shell opened to show large bright green eyes blinking slowly. Tiny claw-like feet with multiple toes carried the strange creatures to their next destination which happened to be downwards into the earth.

'How are they eating?'

Everyone watched intently.

Long serrated tongues came out from under the shell, it cut and scooped the grass and moss, folding it up in its tongue and disappearing under the shell.

'This is incredible,' Louis breathed out 'watching creatures going about their billion-year-old business was extraordinary. You said some creatures colonised the planet.'

'That's right Louis, but they were not native to Mars.'

They zoomed in on a temple construction. Large slabs of rock stacked on top of each other. Water cascaded down the temple making it shine like a beacon. A deep moat surrounded it. The hologram zoomed in again so close, Louis and Charlie automatically raised their hands to touch the strange construction. Long white fingers could be seen between the rock layers, cooling them in the water.

Multiple sets of hands appeared all doing the same. Then their bodies emerged, like tiny white ghosts, they slid down the temple wall like dripping honey, seeking the water for comfort.

'Oh my God, they're translucent. Those sad black eyes and so frail.'

'Oh man, they look kind of like a sea dragon with little human legs. Look at the tiny arms.'

Charlie kept talking until Louis interrupted.

'The face has a human look about it, their eyes three membranes when they blink, so beautiful and delicate. What are they doing in the water?'

'Feeding on minute plankton.'

'You know, they don't really look like they belong on Mars.'

'They didn't Louis.'

'What happened to cause all this to end?'

'Are you familiar with asteroids or minor planets?'

Both boys turned their curious attention to Esouli.

'We have in science.'

'Well, as you would have learnt, there are millions of asteroids of many different sizes. They're basically left over from your solar system about five billion years ago. The asteroids are irregular shapes with giant craters and hundreds of miles across. Double asteroids also exist, some are a solid mass, but others are honeycomb. Mars had what we call Trojan asteroids. Many asteroids orbit Mars.'

'It was an asteroid?'

'Yes, Louis it was. Some asteroids crashing into other planets can be beneficial to create a water supply, however in this case it was a disaster. It is rare, but this time it was a massive metal asteroid, the huge crater cannot be seen by NASA or other telescopes. The planet projected closer to the Sun and the impact was devastating.'

The hologram came to life.

'We can watch it?'

'Yes Charlie.'

Mars appeared again, serene in its simplistic landscape, the green tinged sky accentuating the vegetation. Louis felt sorrow, knowing what was coming. The asteroid was massive and solid, almost demonic, lurking towards its victim. The speed started to build, getting sucked into the planet's gravity. Louis felt his heart racing. Charlie couldn't move as they both stood frozen unable to look away. As if in slow motion the massive bully pushed his victim into a spin. The wind velocity was tremendous as the sand and soil was picked up forming into a gigantic tornado. Everything in its path was levelled destroying the entire planet. Like dominos, they all fell. Mountain ridges exploded sending lumps of rock running and bouncing to their final resting place. All the vegetation was torn from its roots and disappeared into the churning, volatile red monster. It was evident, as it moved across the planet swallowing and spewing out, nothing would survive.

Esouli fast-forwarded to present day.

'Holy shit that was a wipe out.'

Louis looked at Charlie.

'Those poor creatures, nowhere to run or escape. So there still could be water in the planet?'

'That's right Louis, unfortunately the atmosphere of Mars is now too thin, and mainly made up of carbon dioxide and nitrogen. I can see this has disturbed you boys.'

'Could this ever happen to Earth?'

Louis's face was still pale from shock.

'Over billions of years ancient craters on Earth's surface indicate large objects have come into contact with Earth. It would depend on the size of the asteroid or comet. The Earth was hit sixty-five million ago. That created the Ice Age and the extinction of dinosaurs.'

'Where do you think the out of place creatures came from?'

'We think perhaps they originated in another galaxy, way beyond your solar system.'

'But that would mean somewhere cold!'

'Yes, it would Louis. We think their home planet may have been destroyed by the volatile environments as many were.'

'But how did they get to Mars?'

'Probably somewhere on Mars is the remnants of a spaceship.'

'A spaceship? Do you have anything on the hologram?'

'We did capture an extraordinary craft leaving Neptune a very long time ago.'

The hologram was flashing again, nothing was coming. Everyone sat down waiting and watching. Finally, after half an hour the screen activated, static at first and cloudy. Lights could be seen, brilliant white and rotating. The spaceship was breathtaking in its construction.

'Wow, it's shaped like a huge daisy.'

'Oh yeah,' said Charlie with his mouth open.

They all studied it in silence.

'It certainly is different in design. The power source is intriguing.'

Esouli studied the craft from all angles.

The main cockpit was a huge round structure, but underneath incorporated long additions, six in all, made from black metal with blinding yellow lights adorning the six wings. Slow rotations moved the craft.

'It's spectacular,' said Louis, unable to take his eyes off the unusual craft.

'That could mean the entire race lived on the ship?'

'It appears that way, although the centre of the craft is expansive enough to accommodate the entire race.'

Charlie's voice broke into the moment.

'How did it end up on Mars?'

'From what we can gather it entered a black hole, maybe unintentionally. To go through a black hole, as you well know, is extremely dangerous unless you have an adaptable craft and the right power source.'

'So somewhere on Mars, that beautiful craft is buried forever?'

'Yes Louis, along with that extraordinary race from an unknown planet.'

'You know,' said Charlie, sitting back in contemplation, 'who would ever believe we had a conversation about how we saw life on Mars a billion years ago? I'm thinking when we get home, everything we have seen and experienced has to remain our secret.'

Louis started to giggle.

'Imagine telling the kids at school everything?'

'Oh mate, imagine the fun they would have on social media. While we are on this subject...'

Louis looked at Esouli, unsure how to say what had been bothering him for some time.

'What is it, Louis?'

'How, I mean, what do we do and say when we get back home?'

Esouli looked from Louis to Charlie. The silence grew as the boys each drew a deep breath.

'Remember I said we would make one more stop before Earth?'

The boys kept looking at Esouli.

Louis made a slight grunt, Charlie swallowed.

'When we arrive at our next destination everything will be clear and you will see how you fit into the future.'

'Is there a timeline, I mean do we finish school?'

Esouli put his hand up.

'Yes Louis.'

Charlie looked from one to the other.

'I am talking in the future, beyond your school life. Look boys, I know this sounds all mysterious, when we arrive at our next destination the explanation will be obvious to you. I know you are anxious to be home, only a little bit longer.'

'Well big fella, I'm up for some serious skateboarding and surfing.'

Esouli smiled at Charlie.

'One more a week.'

'Good, now I'm hungry, let's eat.'

CHAPTER 59

Simone was the only one who heard the knock on the front door. Karen Landy had had enough, this would be the last visit.

'Hello Simone. Is Mum home?'

Simone yelled to her mother and hearing Karen Landy's voice, they looked at each other. The moment of serene ocean watching had been broken, replaced with stark reality.

'Please, sit down Karen,' Isobel pointed to a single lounge chair.

'I'll stand, this isn't going to take long. I've tried to help both of you and have been more than fair and patient. I have had to report the boys as missing persons to the police.'

'You did what?'

Isobel's voice was loud and angry.

'I told you where they are! How dare you disbelieve me!'

Isobel moved toward Karen Landy, shaking with rage and on the verge of tears. Bridget moved in front of Isobel, avoiding making the situation worse.

'I didn't have an option you both know that.'

'You're going to have us put in jail because the boys are on holiday.'

'The police will be here with a search warrant.'

Karen's insides were shaking, her exterior showing no emotion.

'Get out of my house. Now!'

Although Bridget's legs felt weak, her heart rate elevated. She found her voice.

'You had better go Karen. This was totally unnecessary.'

Karen let out her breath as soon as she locked the car door.

'I hate this bloody job.'

The car moved off slowly.

'What the hell did she do that for?'

Isobel was in tears, in Bridget's arms.

'Bloody hell Bridge, they have to come home or we are going to jail.'

Simone heard everything. She was in tears and hysterical. Isobel gathered her up in her arms, kissing her face. The scene was pathetically sad. Someone else had just watched the arrival of Karen Landy and her dramatic exit.

Collin Stephens had planted a camera in the tree in the front yard.

The two women had to be strong for Simone, they had to make sure she was secure. Isobel sent Simone to get ready for bowling.

'Listen Bridge, we need to talk and figure out how we are going to approach this.'

Bridget made her vegetable fritters and baked potatoes for dinner. She needed to keep her mind occupied.

'Am I going to be sent away Mum?'

Simone's little face was crumbling into tears.

'Oh God, no my baby girl. That will never happen.'

'Will Charlie be home soon? Will we ever see him again?'

'My darling, everything will be okay and the boys will be home soon. Now please don't worry, nothing is going to change.'

Simone had finally fallen asleep after her outing. She didn't want to leave Isobel's lap. They ate in silence, minds racing.

'How are we going to put this Bridge? As it is the police will come and search for anything unusual.'

'We remain calm. No negative reactions or outbursts.'

'Yeah, yeah I know I lost my shit.'

Bridget giggled, and accidentally snorted.

'You fired up girlfriend.'

'She just made me so wild.'

'I know. She makes you feel like you're a really bad person. I wonder when they will come.'

Bridget got up to wash up.

'I think very soon. Let's get this place cleaned up, keep ourselves focused and strengthen our minds.'

'You're right Bridge, they will be judging everything.'

As sure as the sun comes up, the knock on the door came later in the evening. Two detectives and two uniformed. Fresh coffee and fruitcake were offered, as the shared room by the boys was searched. The large, bearded detective stretched himself while sitting on the lounge in readiness, his pad resting in his lap. He pushed his glasses up that had begun slipping down his nose. Then the questions began.

Simone sat between the two women, all relaxed and enjoying the coffee and cake. The big detective wrote down Bridget and Isobel's responses, the other one just watched them. The story was told of traditional lands, the location and the remoteness. Explanations were given about learning how to find bush tucker, animal tracking and the healing properties of plants. Isobel then started to talk about the

Dreamtime. Bridget watched them closely. Their body language indicated they were not interested. The next question was directed at Bridget.

'Why did you send Louis? He does not identify as Aboriginal.'

'They're very good friends and he desperately wanted to go for the cultural experience.'

The two uniformed exited with a bag containing the boys' belongings. Isobel stood up, as did the detectives.

'Why have you got their stuff?'

'Your questions will be answered when your statements are taken, we expect you both at nine o'clock.'

They left their cards on the table.

Walking to the car, a conversation began between the two detectives.

'They're hiding something.'

'I think you're right, but we have to tread carefully, it's the black fella influence.'

The bearded detective sighed after his words.

'I hate these bloody cases.'

It was a long night for both women, thinking of every scenario possible for how their day may turn out.

Breakfast was had together, keeping the mood light for Simone's sake. They dropped Simone off at school then headed to the police station. Reciting a protective spell together they pulled up in the station carpark.

'Deep breathing time Isobel.'

They held hands and closed their eyes. The moment was interrupted by a thud on the bonnet. The large tawny frogmouth sat staring. He blinked twice, shook his feathers then lifted into the air.

Bridget was in the interview room. The large, bearded detective slammed the door to unnerve them. She didn't know his name as she hadn't looked at their cards or taken notice. He sat down grunted and stared at Isobel. She could smell stale alcohol, Bridget focused on what looked like egg stuck to a hair near his mouth.

'Can you tell me why you would send Louis away to strangers, so far away? You fostered him to adopt, is that right? Don't you think that is rather irresponsible? You still want the kid? From where I'm sitting it does not look like it. Did you want to get rid of him, are you sick of him?'

'What? I love Louis, he's my world.'

'Is that so? I don't believe you!'

Bridget's heart was racing as she thought, 'Oh my God, they think I've killed him.'

'He's been missing for some time now, hasn't he Isobel?'

'He's not missing.'

Her throat was starting to ache, trying to hold back tears, her bladder was filling and it was hard to swallow. He kept staring at her. He leant forward, the ugly hairy gash looming close, his eyes bloodshot, like a demon hungry for a victim.

The door opened Bridget physically jumped. A voice broke through her fear.

'This interview is over.'

Standing at the end of the desk dressed in the most exquisite suit Isobel had ever seen was the most perfectly groomed man. He didn't look real.

'Miss Bridget Sherwood?' she nodded.

'I'm your legal representative, Jerome Clayburg.'

She was handed a beautifully designed card. He turned to the detective.

'I will be representing both Miss Sherwood and Ms Crane.'

He sat himself down and placed his black leather briefcase on the table.

'Now detective, what were you saying? Detective Silver is it not?'

Still staring at Bridget, he pushed the chair back, scraping it on the floor slowly. He gathered his paperwork, not making eye contact with the intruder and left without a further word.

'How do you do? I'm Jerome Clayburg from Clayburg and Newel.'

Bridget looked at the card.

'You're a barrister.'

'That's correct.'

'We, um, I mean Isobel and myself can't afford a barrister.'

'Well young lady, it's your lucky day. You're not paying. Now if we could get out of this offensive dungeon, I would be most grateful.'

They sat drinking very expensive coffee and gourmet sandwiches.

'Ladies at this stage I will be delaying any further procedure with this little charade, long enough for the return of your children. Please, eat up. Now, where was I? Oh, yes. The person paying your account wishes to remain anonymous at this stage. If you would be so kind to write down your contact details, emails, phone numbers and address, I shall keep you updated. In addition, don't be surprised if the establishment watches your movements. They are convinced the boys have met some devastating end. Your benefactor assures me the children are safe and well. For now, it has been a pleasure meeting you, enjoy your meal. I shall be in touch.'

Isobel couldn't take her eyes off him.

'I feel like I've just been in a nineteen forties movie with a refined English actor.'

'Oh goodness.'

'What is it Bridge?'

She was googling the wonderful Jerome Clayburg.

'He's extremely well-educated, from a wealthy English family with titles. He rates as the top law firm in Sydney and London. Do you think we are safe Izzy?'

'Sounds like it, for now.'

'Who on Earth is this benefactor?'
'I wish we knew Bridge so we could thank them.'
Sam finished his coffee from the window seat. He watched the ladies leave as he completed his phone call with Jerome Clayburg.

CHAPTER 60

It was no longer a story, no longer a dream, they were witnessing something extraordinary.

'It looks huge,' said Charlie, unable to stop watching the miracle getting closer.

Esouli smiled.

'It's twice the size of planet Earth.'

The opaque screen came to life giving a more refined vision.

'Earth Two has the same landscapes as Earth One, but as you can see is much bigger. There is only minimal desert area due to the constant wet weather patterns. There are billions of hectares of untouched forest.'

As the tetrahedron got closer and they could rotate to see the entire planet, a variation of forests, temperate deciduous broad leaf forests, all semi evergreen and moist. Louis was excited beyond belief.

'I can see sparse trees and parklands, and what looks like swamp forest and mangroves. This is just awesome. Fertile savannahs, they go on forever, green and lush.'

Lakes and rivers fed the landscapes. The mountains were covered in tall timbers all lush, ancient and perfect. Low cloud tried to hide the gigantic beauties. Smaller exquisite vegetation was in bloom. It was a picture-perfect landscape, designed by an inspired artist.

'What animals are there here?' asked Louis.

'Pollinators, bees, insects and birds. This is nearly a blank canvas. The transition of life will be done with great care, keeping in mind man will only play a small role.'

'How will you manage overpopulation and inbreeding?'

'Our scientists have the technology to manage this without pain and trauma for all animal life.'

The oceans were vast surrounding the enormous continents. Aqua in colour, pristine they were already the perfect marine habitat. Louis and Charlie's eyes and minds feasted on the wondrous sight.

The approach was slow as they waited for an opening. The boys were brimming with excitement.

'So where are we supposed to park this baby?'

No sooner had the words come out of Charlie's mouth than something could be seen emerging out of the treetops. A triangle shaped object came into full view. The peak of the triangle opened like a flower. Their ship descended inside, fitting perfectly. Louis couldn't wait to see the dual planet.

'I wonder if they've got skateboards.'

Charlie put his arm around Louis's shoulder and together they walked onto the new world. Louis breathed in the air; it was the best thing he had ever smelt. His nostrils tingled.

'God Charlie, smell that.'

'Did you fart bro?'

Louis giggled as they all followed Esouli.

Bending down Louis touched the soil. The forest was so lush with mixed shades of green, delicate ferns, ground succulents and blossoming shrubs all protected from a filtered soft canopy.

Ahead was an incredible construction towering into the sky. Colossal trunks of bamboo were constructed into living apartments. Crystal panels became energised by the sun. Inside compact living apartments and laboratories it was clean and fresh. Reticulating water from the deep springs serviced the entire building. A large dining area looked very inviting. Made from natural products, mudbricks, timbers, clear sheets of crystal and products made from their hemp plantation.

'Well, I have to ask, what sort of food do they eat? Is there a kitchen? Seriously guys, I need to know.'

They moved onto a huge landing. Spread before them were acres of vegetables, fruit and nut trees and hot houses for raising seedlings.

'Does this answer your question wormy guts?!'

'Oh yeah!'

Everyone else headed for the forest exploring and flying in complete safety. The flowers, the smells and native fruits enticed them further into the beautiful planet.

'What are those other buildings tucked away in the forest?'

Louis stretched to see.

'That is where we turn our hemp, bamboo and timber into products.'

'This is amazing, it's just so beautiful. Imagine, Earth once looked like this. The Sun seems paler Esouli.'

'It is Louis that is why we have refined the solar system into building materials.'

'You mean all the materials have solar?'

'That's right. We transport our crystal sheets from Helomedes.'

'How many people live here, and will we live here?'

'That's a good question Charlie. What you see here will be replicated across the planet. We haven't put a figure on population, but we need many good people to sustain a lifestyle and manage our sanctuaries to preserve what we take from Earth. We want a peaceful planet but we have to be prepared at all times.'

'Is the Vodoxium is being used here?'

'That's right Louis.'

'So again, my question about food and any fun stuff?'

'I could live here.' Louis was totally captivated, 'My God this is a feast for the eyes!'

'Well dude I'm thinking food feast.'

Plates of fruit, vegetables, honey and rice bread with luscious fruit drinks, were placed in front of the guests. Plates of roasted nuts with incredible flavours finished off the meal. Charlie rubbed his belly with satisfaction. Louis was keen to meet the people already living on this beautiful place. The enormous bamboo structure was extraordinary. It was layered in a square design supported by some of the native timbers crafted into beauty. Charlie and Louis were introduced to some young people. Everyone seemed happy and relaxed, loving all the different jobs, working in laboratories and experimenting with new varieties of fruit and vegetables creating new tastes and shapes.

Esouli sensed Charlie didn't feel quite as excited as Louis. Travelling upwards to another level, Charlie found something more appealing.

'Holy crap. A games room, thank God. I thought it was going to be work and vegetables. Four other kids were busy playing. As soon as they noticed the boys their excitement couldn't be contained. They introduced themselves.

'How the hell did you get this technology and these games?'

Charlie grabbed a controller.

'We transferred them from the ship to keep it interesting for the younger ones.'

Charlie's little group of friends settled down to watch him play. Louis looked over at the gardens and greenhouses. He made his way down to talk with people going about their jobs. It was all so interesting and welcoming.

'I can hear birds.'

'Yes Louis. You're not going mad. There are lorikeets, galahs and many others. We had to introduce the birds for a balanced ecology, plus the bees for that delicious honey. We have actually introduced much birdlife to Helomedes. They adapted well.'

'Can you really take everything from Earth?'

'We are doing our best. There are many people on Earth as we speak gathering as much as possible.'

'Are they coming here?'

'Yes. As you can see there's plenty of room. How about we take a flight over the forest and have a bird's eye view? We have a transport system that our people use to check the environment.'

'You just said 'our people'.'

'I did Louis. This is the planet we created. It's taken thousands of years to get it to this stage.'

'How old are you?'

'Way too old!'

'Why don't you use the Vodoxium for the energy?'

'We use enough but the history of humans on planet Earth, the love of weapons, we don't want to tempt fate.'

Charlie joined them looking over the forest. Louis caught Charlie up on the conversation and a look at the planet.

'What are we going in?'

'There's a special craft we use powered by Vodoxium that's supplied by Helomedes one small crystal at a time.'

'What is Helomedes really like?'

'Well, I guess you would call us advanced in comparison.'

'To whom?'

'Well Earth to begin with. Our food production is as this planet. The constructions and landscape are different.'

'Do they all look like Arume and you?'

'Well Charlie we have many beings living on Helomedes, rescued from dying planets and invasions. There's a colony of Arume's people, male and female, only small, as is mine.'

'You all get on?'

'We do Charlie. Peace is our main concern and survival of small vulnerable species. Hey, I have an idea!'

Esouli looked from Louis to Charlie.

'Oh no.'

'It's okay Charlie, this is simple. Without landing we can take a look at Helomedes. You will be able to see the geography, environments and constructions.'

'Sounds great,' said Louis 'we do have to get home.'

'What's for dinner tonight?'

'Oh my God Charlie, you're always hungry.'

'Probably got a big tapeworm curled up inside.'

'Thought you didn't want to talk about worms?'

'I'm still hungry!'

They moved to the top floor. From the extreme height, the birdlife could be seen and heard. High misty clouds painted themselves into the landscape. The colours were unusual, an amber glow bounced off the tree line. A strange sound could be heard coming closer.

'Oh shit, it's a fair dinkum flying saucer.'

A shiny gold dish was heading towards them as a landing pad extracted itself from the building. It looked like some kind of sea animal and the colour was incredible. Louis was stunned.

'Are we gettin' in that?'

It was a beautifully designed craft with a long tail made especially for passengers. It got closer and finally landed. Blindingly stunning and sleek and made of an unusual metal with windows, similar to a plane. It looked like a metallic stingray.

'How do you get in? I don't see any joins.'

At that moment the hatch opened. Esouli directed them to the front. It was similar to the tetrahedron craft within. The control panel was invisible but lit up to voice command. The front of the ship opened up to give a perfect view of the world outside. Charlie leaned forward to touch the unusual metal. It was cold as ice. Louis and Charlie's little friends went into the passenger area.

'Hey Louis, look at our little dudes, all human-like boarding a plane.'

The boys smiled with total affection. The craft moved off over the forest. It went higher and higher, silent and smooth. Large areas had been cleared to grow hemp. All species of timbers were used in constructions. Stands of massive bamboo, different varieties, strong and durable. Shade houses were scattered everywhere.

'Look! They've got quad-runners or lookalikes.'

'I know. Solar-powered and built on Helomedes.'

Esouli laughed at Charlie.

Two half-built towers were underway. The craft got faster and headed towards the lush mountains.

'Hang on, look Charlie!'

Pointing downwards to the right of the craft, Esouli started to laugh. Secluded in parkland, a natural swimming pool, positioned under a waterfall, people could be seen swimming and relaxing. Further on was a tennis court designed out of the natural landscape, a baseball and mini-golf course and to top it off a skate park using the huge bamboo designs for the best skaters. The craft landed with ease so all on board could have a good look at some of the food production and the fun things to do.

'Do you eat the chooks?' asked Charlie.

'We could, but no-one wants to kill them!'

A small woman with greying hair and a smiling face, put out a soil covered hand.

'Hello. I'm Janice and I just love growing things and by the way our eggs are the best.'

Introductions were done.

'What were those sausages made from?'

'Oh those. Corn bread and herbs, combined with our beautiful eggs.'

'The storage houses are massive. It all looks so colourful and fresh. It's just total food art.'

Janice laughed.

'You are right Louis. It is a beautiful creation. Let me show you something we found growing.'

A large purple-brown coloured fruit that looked like a massive pear sat waiting on the cutting table. Janice opened the fruit from the top, she plunged her hand inside and pulled out a clear membrane bag full of seeds. The boys were intrigued, picking it up and feeling it. Janice squeezed out pearl like seeds. She handed them to the boys to feel and taste.

'They taste like pears and grapes,' said Louis, 'and the membrane feels like Glad Wrap. This is unbelievably brilliant.'

Louis was in his element.

'We try and find a use for everything.'

Janice was in her element.

'Thank-you Janice, this is just awesome.'

Charlie was gobsmacked with everything especially the skate park.

That night a magnificent banquet was enjoyed by all on the planet. Board games were presented, and everyone joined in. Charlie was laughing with a girl his own age. Louis sat back for a moment absorbing the incredible place, the hidden worlds, the incredible journey.

'Are you okay Louis?'

Esouli's voice interrupted his thoughts.

'You boys do remember we will have to leave here. We need to get back on track to Earth, it should take two Earth days. Do you still want to see Helomedes?'

'Hell yes!'

'But we don't land, that's the plan remember?'

Louis agreed.

'That sounds better' added Charlie.

'Okay Sooky, I get it.'

The boys settled in for the night. It had been a big day of discovery with both dropping off to sleep in minutes. Esouli sat watching them for a while, he had grown very fond of both boys. They will grow into great men. Louis had been chosen a long time ago and Charlie just happened to be in the right place at the right time. That was the best thing ever. He got up and went for a walk through the forest. The night was still and clear and the waterfall ahead could be heard, serene in its music.

A voice greeted his arrival.

'They are sleeping like tired babies.'

Maeve Beaumont sat elegantly at the side of the pool, the mystery that surrounded her on Earth still remained.

'Are you sure you don't want to see him?'

'Well, my old friend I've seen him, heard him and he is beautiful. I don't want him distracted at this stage. I would love to hold him in my arms, but that will come, and I do like Charlie.'

'What are you going to tell him when that day comes? He saw your dead body.'

'The truth.'

Maeve Beaumont spent years travelling the world. She loved remote places and exploring the vast corners of the world. Maeve liked to mix with the locals and native people in touch with the environment. History fascinated her. She wrote many papers about her findings and the impact of over-population and plundering of resources in pristine areas. Maeve wrote about the destruction of fresh water and forests. She was not popular with oil and gas companies and developers. It never bothered Maeve. She was fascinated by the unusual, the mysteries on the planet, fed into her imagination and added suspense to her writings. Maeve's story began with an organised trip to one of her favourite places to explore.

The weather reports for San Juan, Puerto Rico was nothing unusual. Maeve's plan was to venture by boat to the far point of the Bermuda Triangle, sailing into the centre. She had equipment that could detect anything unfamiliar or paranormal. The crew were organised, although not keen, but the money was good. The wind started to pick up halfway to their destination. The sea was beautiful, midnight blue and the air pristine. More time passed as the winds became stronger. Clouds started to form unusually fast, dark and ominous. The oceans became turbulent, and the boat started to rock. The waves intensified, washing over the craft. The environment became as dark as night, it was like being in a giant washing machine. Panic was setting in and the crew wanted to turn back but Maeve wanted to ride it out. Maeve was on the deck about to plead with the men to keep going. At that moment a huge wave smashed into the boat, like a monster tongue ready to flip its victims over. Maeve lost her grip and her balance as the monster wave tossed her overboard like a ragdoll. The crew couldn't see her. They quickly tossed a life buoy plus an inflatable raft overboard and headed back to land. It disappeared quickly hidden between the waves.

Maeve found the raft and clung on, her mind trying to have an assembled thought. It was hard to catch her breath as fear and adrenalin began racing through her veins. Closing her eyes and she gathered all her strength to get into the raft. No sooner had she exhaled in relief and exhaustion, than the raging winds ceased, and the sea settled to calm. It was silent. Abnormally so. Millions of stars decorated the black sky. Maeve's body began to relax, she just sat back looking around. A fraction of the black sky appeared to be opening up. At first Maeve thought it was lightning, but it was burning orange and getting bigger. A tunnel was forming, the raft was getting pulled into the unknown. Maeve just hung on as she laid on her stomach, her face hidden and that was the last memory of that night.

The pod opened slowly. She felt like she'd died and come back to life. Her eyes scanned the surroundings and instinctively knew she was not on Earth. The moment Maeve sat up, a door opened and a strange little creature like a dragonfly with a tiny delicate human face entered. She watched it fly towards her with a tiny container of fluid. It handed the offering to Maeve. She couldn't help smiling and knew at that moment that she was safe.

Never in her wildest dreams or her vibrant imagination, could Maeve engage in a more invigorating conversation than with the Elodites. She was bewitched by Arume's beauty. The females had more delicate smaller faces, like little dolls. The army of warriors, impressive in their original form, she found fascinating in their ability to shape shift.

Maeve was shown everything on Helomedes and Earth Two. In return she imparted all her knowledge of plant life, animal life, Earth's ecology systems and natural resources. In everything they were on the same level, and she fell absolutely in love with the magical Elodites. Maeve admired and applauded their pure intentions, their wisdom and compassion. She heard their plans for the dual planet and witnessed the wonders of the Vodoxium.

Before Maeve was due to return to Earth, there was a gathering of people, all returning at the same time. It was at this event, that Isobel, Bridget and Maeve met. Arume foretold of their connections, the arrival of Louis and the lake. It wasn't in specific details. They were asked to be aware of signs and told they would instinctively know them. Maeve was prepared for her passing on Earth and that it would be her Avatar created by the Vodoxium. That's what Louis had witnessed. The people would return to Earth Two at a time in the future. It was then suggested that Louis was not to know until his final ascension to the dual planet. Arume informed each person that they may be called upon to undertake a task on Earth. Maeve stayed on the magnificent new world. She had much work to do with the anticipated reunion with her grandson.

The following day people entered the tetrahedron to return to Earth. The arrival happened at night settling itself into the mountain, inside the mothership. A car was waiting to disperse the arrivals to their destinations.

CHAPTER 61

It rained all day and they were nearly home. Isobel slowed the car down, as they approached the corner just before home. Simone strained her neck to see clearly the unusual colours in the sky and reflecting in the trees.

'Oh my God. What now?'

Three police cars were parked in front of the house. Karen Landy was standing in front of the police cars.

'What's happening Mum?'

Simone began to cry, fear fuelling her tears. Bridget and Isobel exchanged looks they took some deep breaths. A suited detective with uniformed police waited. Karen Landy spoke first.

'This is an official visit, the police have new information regarding the boys, you are required to go with the police for further questioning. I'm here to keep Simone secure.'

'What the hell are you talking about?!'

Bridget put her hand on Isobel's arm.

'It's okay we can do this we have nothing to hide.'

Isobel explained to Simone she would be safe, and everything would be okay. She was sobbing. Karen Landy forced Simone into the police car.

'If anything happens to my child, the entire country will know about it.'

The women held hands in the police car, feeling the hot terror of each other, Bridget practiced deep breathing and Isobel felt the rhythm.

The women fronted two new detectives from the Missing Children's Unit.

'I'm Detective Lester and this is Detective Jenna. You have stated previously that the boys had gone to the top end to be with a relative of Charlie's to learn about the culture and explore the traditional lands. You stated Louis went along for the experience.'

'That's correct,' was Isobel's reply.

Detective Jenna focused on Bridget.

'Don't you feel as a foster parent you are negligent sending Louis off to unknown places and people?'

Sam's phone rang, Collin Stephens was breathless informing him the women and girl had been taken away.

'Why are you breathless?'

'I think I'm about to be arrested.'

The phone went dead. Two uniformed officers caught Stephens in the laneway near Isobel's house. They took the phone and handcuffed him. He was being held under the suspicion of child abduction. Sam made a phone call to Jerome Clayburg. Sam didn't know what to think. Breaking news interrupted his thoughts. It stated two females and one male had been apprehended for questioning relating to the disappearance of Louis Blackwell and Charlie Crane.

'Oh shit, shit. They've got Stephens.'

Sam's mind was trying to absorb and figure out what to do next. They probably have his phone.

'Oh Christ, now the media is involved.'

'Miss Crane, we have spent weeks investigating the travel plans of your son Charlie, we can't find a trail of transport purchases and no-one has sighted your son Charles...'

'Charlie. His name is Charlie!' Isobel interrupted.

'Can you explain why there has been no sighting of an Aboriginal boy and a Caucasian boy travelling together?'

'I can't explain why people are unobservant, but I know they're safe and will be home soon.'

'Do you know how pathetic that sounds? You can't explain. How do you think that will sound in court? In case you're unaware the boys have been posted as missing. It's on social media and mainstream media. This is becoming very serious, and you could find yourselves serving a very long jail sentence. Would you like to take a guess on what people think of you? Is your son dead?'

Isobel could only see an angry face, squinting his pig-like eyes through thick glasses. She felt disconnected, his voice seemed miles away as the fluorescent light flickered. Saliva was rushing into her mouth. She was going to vomit. Isobel was given a vomit bag and a can of lemonade, then left alone. Detective Jenna pulled his chair up close to the table.

'Well Bridget, what I can't understand is why you bothered to foster a child only to get rid of him somehow. Don't you think he's been through enough? Did you kill him?'

He kept glaring at Bridget.

'He's not dead!'

She didn't mean to yell.

'Where the hell is Louis Blackwell?'

'He's safe. He'll be home soon.'

'Then where is he, considering we can't find a living trail of him, no evidence, no sightings, no travel reference? Have you killed him?'

Bridget could feel the blood surging through her body, her ears were ringing, her heart wobbling in her chest.

'Who are Collin Stephens and Sam Blackwell?'

'What?'

'How are they connected to you?'

He slammed his fist into the desk yelling at her, spit landed on her check, his eyes getting closer, leaning into her. She said nothing. She had difficulty breathing due to fear.

'You're cold Bridget, but mark my words, we will get you behind bars.'

The door opened startling Bridget. Jerome Clayburg walked in.

'How are you?'

He directed his conversation to Bridget. Sitting down slowly he extracted his leather covered notepad out of his briefcase and a beautiful gold pen.

'Now, shall we proceed? What evidence do you have?'

Detective Jenna got up, walking out, before angrily pushing the chair into the table.

'Well my dear, we seem to be in a bit of a pickle.'

'Where's Isobel? Is she alright?'

'She is after a rather tough interview.'

'That detective asked me about people I have never heard of. What's going to happen now? Can we go home? And poor little Simone.'

Jerome Clayburg put his hand up to silence Bridget.

'Now I want you to listen to me carefully. In view of the fact that the children are still missing and shrouded in some mystery to their whereabouts. Another consideration is that this story has now become viral as they say. I am recommending that you and Isobel stay here on remand for a few days until I can sort something out as a defence for you both.'

'But we haven't done anything wrong.'

'Bridget, you know how the public react to missing children. Your lives could be in danger. Please heed my words. This is in your best interest. The public feel the children have been murdered.'

Jerome Clayburg was calm and poised. Bridget on the other hand was a swirling mess of emotions. She couldn't speak. So many thoughts scrambling through her mind, the boys, the mountain, the future of Earth.

'I have asked that you be kept together, checked by a doctor, there is money for toiletries and clothes. You haven't been charged with murder as yet, but now the media have taken a huge interest, your lives are at risk from radicals. Simone is in care.'

'She will fret. What about her guinea pig?'

'Her what?'

'Guinea pig.'

'Oh, well uh, leave that with me. I can assure you I will not be babysitting a guinea pig.'

Bridget smiled at Jerome's facial expression. The sides of his mouth had a slight tilt upwards.

'Well, my dear, are we clear on everything?'

'Yes and thank you.'

Isobel was frantic for Simone. She couldn't stop crying, thinking about her baby girl with strangers. The female doctor came to assess both women, they were prescribed a sedative to reduce their anxiety. The doctor was brief and not exactly friendly.

They both sat on the one bunk, having changed clothes, had something to eat, and used the bathroom. They waited until all was quiet before having their conversation in whispered voices.

'Did you get asked about someone called Collin and Blackwell?'

'Yes,' whispered Isobel, 'do you think Blackwell is related to Louis?'

'I don't know. There's something very odd going on here.'

'I agree. They should be on their way home.'

'It will happen Izzy, they can't charge us with anything.'

Bridget held Isobel's hand.

'Our lives could get very uncomfortable. We need to keep a look out for a sign.'

Isobel paused.

'You know after this we will need to take the final ascension. Do you think Simone will cope?'

'So much is unknown. Did you take your Valium?'

'No Bridge, we need to be on our toes.'

'Exactly.'

The women drifted off to sleep on the same bunk.

It was about three in the morning, there was an enormous moon. A stream of moonlight rested on the floor in their cell. Leaves on the tree outside made dancing shadows, Isobel stirred to waking, as did Bridget, they both watched the floor. Time went by, they kept watching, then a shape appeared in the moonlight. A definite shape of a tawny frogmouth.

'Thank God!'

They embraced in relief. Isobel stood in the beam to give recognition and knowing, the bird flew off.

'Well Mr Stephens?'

'Yes Detective. What can I do for you?'

'Why are you living in a campervan and watching the home of Isobel Crane and Bridget Sherwood?'

'It was just a job.'

'A job to do what?'

'To look for Louis Blackwell.'

'What's your relationship to Sam Blackwell?'

'Well Detective, you probably already know that. He's Louis Blackwell's half–brother and he wanted to get to know him. He hired me to find him.'

'So!'

'Detective, am I going to be charged?'

'Did you ever see the boys?'

'Yep.'

'How long ago?'

'Oh, weeks ago. I can't remember precisely.'

'Why are you still watching?'

'Well, that's obvious Detective, waiting for them to come back.'

'You know where they are?'

'Nope. No idea.'

Detective Jenna slammed his diary.

'You can go.'

Collin sniffed back a nose full of phlegm, scratched his head and walked out, giving the detective a crooked smile.

Sergeant Darley phoned in to Detective Jenna.

'There's nothing here.'

'Okay, that will do for tonight.'

Sam watched the unmarked car move off, watching from the rooftop. Collin Stephens had filled him in on his interview. Sam couldn't fathom anything with the exception of the lake, somehow it connected them all. The energy and the lake attracted him as well. Sam's mental health had now improved. No more voices, no more anger. He really wanted and needed family. Sam wanted a new life, but he was not exactly sure how to go about it.

The women were told their lawyer had arrived. Jerome Clayburg looked very solemn. He sat and met each woman's gaze. He opened his iPad and turned it on for them to see. The women were horrified, they were on trial by social media.

Isobel's house had murderer painted on the front, the public wanted blood.

'I need to know where your children are.'

Isobel spoke up.

'Like I said, a remote area with my relatives in Arnhem Land and they're five regions and five hundred kilometres from Darwin.'

'That story with all due respect, is becoming very stale and now unbelieved. The prosecutor wants you both charged with murder, as does most of Australia. Unless you start telling the truth you will both be sentenced. You have one week.'

Jerome Clayburg got up and left, clearly frustrated with both women.

They didn't say a word until back in the cell.

'You okay Bridge?'

'Yep, you?'

'We've had our sign. We are never going back home.'

Bridget looked intensely at Isobel.

'Not on this planet.'

That thought now working its way into acceptance.

'You know what we forgot?'

'What?'

'The chooks.'

Bridget couldn't help laughing.

'Oh my God Isobel. Here we are locked up accused of murder and you think of chooks.'

Bridget was still giggling.

'I reckon,' said Bridget, 'our chooks have entered that mountain.'

CHAPTER 62

They moved on further over tall timbers, another trip of discovery over an unusual mountain range. Before the boys could get over the excitement of what they had already seen, their eyes absorbed a breathtaking pristine coastline. The waves rolled onto a pinkish coloured sand, combined with the greenish colour of the sky and sea, it was like an ancient, faded seascape painting. Sunlight was starting to fade, they hovered for a while watching the magnificent sunset. The colours were incredible, but it was time to go, they all took one last look.

'I think I understand now why you have to be careful. An equal society where everyone is working for the same thing.'

'That's right Louis. People who are happy with what they have, to enjoy the world as it is and not change it for profit, greed or because they can. Minds working together not being led. Our young and older people, and people living with disabilities are all together in harmony. Everyone working, experimenting and most of all enjoying. All of our productions, science and laboratories is for all.

'No bosses and everyone just work's together for the one cause!'

'Why Charles, I think you have it. Now you understand our careful selection of who comes to live on this planet. We have observed and followed people's lives since they were born. People from all walks of life, all countries, no religion, no political parties. We are still watching and selecting.'

'When you say, 'all walks of life', who exactly?'

'Some are professionals Louis, hands-on people, homeless and older people. Many people you will meet later. People who are deep thinkers, kind, empathetic and balanced. Many qualities that we want in this world. Some of our most enthusiastic people have disabilities, both physical and mental, but their heart and mind are superb. Planet Earth is failing, societies are becoming estranged and human qualities are becoming negative and destructive. The planet is dying. The weather patterns are violent, it will be more difficult to produce food. Fresh water will become less available. The human being has become detached from environments. I guess we are going backwards in our evolution.'

'My Nan used to say that. She used to say losing our connection and our way.'

'She is right Louis.'

'You mean she was right.'

'Yes, of course.'

Esouli changed the subject.

'Tonight, you will meet and talk to many people living here and ask as many questions as you wish.'

'Oh food. Yeah, when?'

'Oh my God Charlie!'

Esouli left the boys in the dining room to eat with the others. Everyone greeted the boys with enthusiasm. Fresh food and drinks were prepared by those rostered for the kitchen.

'It's just like Macca's on a Saturday afternoon, minus the meat,' added Charlie laughing and a little bit nervous.

People sat around and openly answered questions about their past and present life. Louis was totally captivated how it all came to be. A very lively sixteen-year-old girl sat next to Louis, wild curly hair dancing around her freckled face with smiling deep blue eyes introduced herself as Louise.

'How long have you been here Louise?'

'Well Louis,' she giggled at their names being familiar, 'since I was seven.'

'Seven. Wow! What about your family? Don't they miss you?'

'Slow down Louis, I'll start from the beginning. I was born in the country and lived on a farm, that part of my life I didn't mind. The problem being I was kind of invisible to everyone. I spent a lot of time with animals and hence they became my preference. I didn't really fit in anywhere and always felt different. I didn't feel any connection to family or so-called friends. One night I was lying in bed watching the night sky as I did every night. For some reason I felt a strong connection to space. I used to dream and imagine another world to live in. I was tuned into the world around me. I hated seeing land and forest cleared, animals being bred for meat. I hated hearing about wars and devastation to people and planet. I instinctively knew it wouldn't get better. I felt so much and worried so much, I had no one to talk to and it started to make me sick. All I had in the world was a big black dog, I talked to him, and I talked to the sky every night. I wondered and imagined incredible things. One night after another disconnected day at school, with no real friends, being targeted by teachers for daydreaming and speaking too softly. Tears rolled down my cheeks, my funny big dog licked them off and started to whimper. I sat up in bed just to see a bright beam of light on the ground in the paddock next to the house. The big dog was tugging at my clothes. I can remember being frightened but excited. I knew I was leaving.'

'Didn't you miss your family?'

Louis was spellbound by her story.

'No. No-one would miss me, and it was mutual. I couldn't see the craft, just heavy low cloud with bursts of blue lights. My dog walked ahead, and I followed into the fog. I can still remember the feeling. I felt so happy and calm. I woke up in a pod after having the best sleep ever. When I woke my big dog was waiting patiently. Then the most incredible thing happened.'

'I know the next part. He turned into our massive warrior known as Esouli.'

They both started to laugh. Charlie was busy at another table listening to many stories behind the arrival to this new earth.

Louis was bumped on the shoulder as another teenage girl sat down beside him.

'Hello, I'm Cassidy.'

Louis was captivated by her beautiful skin and her glistening hair. Cassidy has an interesting pre-arrival, they shook hands.

'Go ahead Cassidy.'

'Well, obviously I'm African, from Kenya. From a very early age I was aware of poaching, and I used to sneak around alerting animals to poachers. I used to look at the night sky asking for help from somewhere to save my animals. It was heading towards sunset on this particular day, and I was fairly tired. I had a good day spooking animals to save their lives. I was unaware that they were onto me, shots were fired, and I was on the run. I could hear a vehicle getting closer. Every now and then I still feel that fear. My heart was pounding, and my legs felt like jelly as a bullet went past the side of my head. I was waiting for one in my back. I could almost feel it. Then the strangest thing happened. I was running on air upwards, higher and higher. The next thing I know I'm waking in a pod after an amazing sleep.'

'I know! Our big warrior dude was waiting patiently!'

Cassidy put her arm around Louis.

'You are a funny one my new friend.'

Louise stood up.

'How about people introduce themselves.'

The first voice from the back was that of a tall thin Asian man.

'Hey! I'm Jimmy a mad Horticulturist.'

'Shirley. Florist from Canada.'

'Susan, Teacher, Ireland.'

'Chen, China, Mathematician.'

And on it went. The introductions, various jobs and careers, people from all over Earth. Louis noticed a guy in a wheelchair.

'Did you get here the same way?'

'Hey, I'm Rashida from Egypt, Scientist. I guess you're wondering about my chair?'

'I'm sorry,' said Louis, 'I didn't mean to be rude.'

'It's okay.'

'I knew the ship was coming, my computer kept getting this message, a date, and a time, so I just waited. There was activity in the Earth's solar system, but I couldn't identify it. Every instinct, every cell in my body told me it was real. When the time and date came around, a vision of a location came on my computer. I got in my modified car, taking nothing and followed the GPS. It was two in the morning. I sat waiting, hoping I wasn't wrong. The anxiety was overwhelming because I wanted it so much. I must have fallen asleep, I don't remember, but when I woke up, I couldn't see a thing. There was a heavy blue mist, then I woke up in a pod, and the rest is history. My parents died in the car accident, and I survived, so I'm very happy to be here.'

The life events for these people were all similar, people knowing that something was coming. The characteristics of all these people was similar. They all possessed an underlying deep instinct, a knowing that crept into their soul and psyche from a very early age.

Charlie and Louis rested in their beds, both pondering the day's events, the people and the planet.

'Hey dude, you think we could live here in the future?'

'I think I could very easily,' said Louis. 'What about you?'

'I think I could. What do you think will happen?'

'What do you mean Charlie?'

'Well how will it all happen? What about Mum, Simone and Bridget? I wonder when this will happen, do we get a warning?'

'That's a lot of questions Charlie, I guess we will be home soon and just go back to our old lives.'

'And do what? I know it's going to be hard, knowing that one day this will be home, like living a temporary existence.'

'I suppose we will look at Earth differently now.'

'Yeah, I think we will Charlie.'

'I don't know Louis, will we fit in again?'

Louis aimed a pillow at Charlie's head.

'I will. Not sure about you, being weird an' all. Now let's get some sleep.'

Both giggled into their pillows.

'Esouli is going to show us something tomorrow, apparently an outstanding addition to the planet.'

'Well as long as it doesn't try and eat us,' Charlie sighed 'I wonder how Fudgunkel is going, bossing our buddies around?'

'Do they really take any notice?'

'Probably not. You know I'm really going to miss out little friends. They have become a big part of our lives now. It all has.'

Louis and Charlie went quiet, so many thoughts from their journey, so many into their future.

The morning sunlight on Earth Two was beautiful to see. Looking over a new planet from high up, was truly magnificent, so fresh and perfect. Thoughts of his grandmother and Bridget crowded into his mind, with a strange sense that his grandmother was somehow watching. Bridget would adore this planet. His throat started to hurt, tears started to swell, ultimately spilling over.

'Don't jump.' Louis quickly wiped away his sadness.

'It's alright,' an arm came around his shoulder, 'I had mine this morning.'

Breakfast was served for those going to work early. Mounds of fresh berries, plums, apricots and yellow fleshy bananas. Pancakes made from nutmeal, drizzled with wild honey. Plump jams and planet grown tea and coffee tasted so good enhanced by almond milk. A tray of vegetable sausages was slid under Charlie's nose. He laughed at the sight and smell.

'Everything tastes so good.'

'Have you seen all our hothouses?'

An older man sat opposite the boys. His skin was weather worn and his hands indicated a life in, as well as a love for the soil and his work.

'We have seen many,' said Louis.

'My name is Jarne. I work with the herbs and spices. You will love the aroma. How about I meet you for afternoon tea?'

'Charlie, you okay with that?'

'Suits me. I can tell Mum what I saw. You know she loves herbs.'

The unique craft felt like it was just floating through the sky. A strange cluster of cloud could be seen ahead. As they got closer, it could be seen as a spiral of clouds travelling up and down continuously.

'What the hell is that?'

Neither boy was prepared for the frightening adventure.

Esouli spoke up.

'We are going into that, I want to show you something that is breathtaking, another reason this planet is sacred.'

'Okay.'

Charlie couldn't help himself.

'Is there anything that wants a feed. Secondly, how do we get out? Third, can we breathe down there?'

Esouli smiled.

'That will be 'No' to question one. Question two, the spiral works both ways if you watch closely. And number three, the air is pure and beneficial.'

The sleek machine slowed down as the was power cut. With one sudden jolt they floated down. From inside the craft, nothing was visible, it took about five minutes before they settled onto something firm.

'Are you ready?'

Esouli led the way.

The outside environment was blinding until their eyes adjusted. When that happened, the boys sat down in astonishment, their eyes gorging on the spectacular display around them.

'What is this Esouli?'

'This, boys, is a world within a planet.'

There were colourful smooth walls impregnated with crystals of every structure and colour.

'Wow, this is amazing. They're crystal walls.'

'Yes Louis.'

'I can see other gems.'

Louis touched the wall, running his fingers down the veins of spectacular colours.

'Amethyst, Amber, Ametrine and Arghanite.'

'How do you know this?'

'I used to study one of my grandmother's gemstone books. It was the colours that got me in. They say crystals are pure substances, they have molecules arranged in regular geometric type patterns. All these colours have a name. This one is Amazonite, probably because it is green. This is Bloodstone, see the blotches of red. See the Citrine, it's orange. Look this is Garnet, this is Fluorite. They're all here. Peridot, looks like Pyrite, this is incredible.'

'What's this one? It looks like an all-day sucker.'

'That's Rhodchrosite.'

'Yeah? It looks like strawberry and cream. Is that gold running like veins between the rough?'

'That's what they call Sphalerite. It looks like the spaceship.'

Louis looked at Esouli.

'Yes, we used it as an experiment. Our scientists found it durable and strong it will only be known to us. The mountains are full of gems and minerals. We think the power in the spiral energy is produced from the purity of this environment. It was like being inside a moving psychedelic chaotic mandala, the colours bouncing and reflecting shards of brilliant mixed colours, filling the entire internal world.'

'It's so warm and bright I feel like I could run forever, my body is tingling, what's going on?'

'Mine too Louis, it's the crystal energy.'

Esouli drew their attention behind them. A quiet river flowed. The boys ran towards it watching the water for signs of life, and there they were. Tiny fish skimmed the surface, disappearing in and out of fresh-water plants. Soft flowing lime-coloured ferns sprouted out of the rocks. Shrubs with lemon-coloured leaves pointed upwards for the light as tiny flowers of multiple colours crept along the rich soil like a vividly embroidered carpet. Butterflies with multiple wings, like a daisy rotated around, flittering around the delicate vegetation. Louis bent down to taste the water and smell the plants. Charlie joined him watching the coloured fish. Tiny feet appeared from under their body, then retracted. The boys stood in wonderment of the world they descended to.

'This is unbelievable. God, how many times have I said that?'

'Yeah, you're right Charlie. Imagine explaining this in geography. How far does all this go Esouli?'

'There's another point on this planet that meets up, so it runs through just like this. That's why the preservation of this natural phenomenon must always be a priority.'

'Does everyone know this is here?'

Louis was still investigating the wall of captive precious and semi-precious stones.

'People often come here for quiet reflection and to absorb the energy. Kind of like a natural health spa.'

'Could you imagine what they would do with this on earth?'

'Yep, they would mine the shit out of it.'

It was one of those places for sitting and watching the magnificence of natural creation, and that just what they did.

Jarne was waiting for the boys when they returned to go on their organised walk. They followed the meandering pathways still in amazement at the untouched beauty. Dragonflies, bees and assorted insects focused on their role. Birdlife talked amongst themselves, forever busy with their life's quest. The food production houses could be easily spotted, their massive rooves were opened to let in the sunlight, the bees and natures pollinators.

'This house is for vegetable and herb production, including many exotic spices.'

The aromas were powerful, mixing together it was an extraordinary sensation.

'Oh my God Louis, my snotty nose is all clear.'

Jarne laughed.

'They have many properties. Row upon row of every vegetable you could imagine.'

'These vegetables seem bigger.'

'We use virgin soil. The nutrient factor is incredible, and the water is free of contaminates with no need for additives.'

The herbs and spices lush in growth and masses of flowers cascading, creeping and standing tall, all happy in each other's company.

'What do you do with the excess produce?'

'Much of the excess food goes to Helomedes, we try not to waste. Our chooks eat very well.'

Jarne was excited to show off the beauty of his labour. The next house was full of drying herbs and spices ready to go into hemp pouches. Long tubes of crystal filled with water and oils, preserving many fruits and vegetables. Loads of chutneys and pickles. Discarded waste turned into enriched compost. Acres of orchards planted randomly between native trees and shrubs, tropical fruits, stone fruits and citrus trees.

CHAPTER 63

Jack and Madison Hillard sat under a tree having a cold drink of water, they had a good day collecting seed pods and dry flower heads for samples. This was the fifth year of living off the grid in the Blue Mountains, working for the CSIRO. They were also collecting secretly for the new planet. They loved being in remote places and exploring the terrain all over Australia. Their home was specially designed by Jack to erect with ease. They also had an attached greenhouse, all generated by solar panels. A rough bush track was used by their second-hand four-wheel drive to pick up supplies. A big shaggy dog of multiple breeds kept them company and busied himself with everything they did.

Jack and Madi met at university and rescued Monty from death row at a council pound. They both achieved a Bachelor of Environmental Science and landed this as their first job because they were willing to live in remote areas around Australia and its islands.

At the age of twelve years, both Jack and Madi were visited by Arume. They had a glimpse into a future life on another planet and their task on Earth. Like many others were told on Earth, it was the secret to be kept. Jack and Madi's thoughts, feelings and every fibre of their being, in regard to the preservation of Earth, aligned with all the other selected people.

Arume was getting very concerned for his people and the protection of the lake site. He had no choice but to call on others to help. Sam Blackwell had made himself part of the situation and he was now needed to help and get everyone involved to the safety of the mountain.

Arume spent long hours with others discussing Sam. They had been watching him for many months now to understand his personal growth as a worthy person to transition to the dual planet. They all agreed to accept him.

The Super Blood Wolf Moon crept slowly over the lake, Arume appeared on the ledge, emerging through the rock face. He lifted his arms and drifted to a strong upright Eucalyptus tree, he settled elegantly on a high branch, a silhouette against a glorious background of his comforting old friend. Nocturnal life stirred around the lake, those of the night ever alert for the mysterious. He uttered some ancient chants that carried into the tranquil night. The lake area became luminous and mystifying.

The statuesque being transformed into a magnificent white breasted sea eagle. He gracefully launched into the night, heading toward the Great Dividing Range seeking the Blue Mountains, parallel with the coast. This sea eagle was not ordinary, his power of flight far exceeded that of a normal bird. One stroke of his wings could glide him effortlessly over many kilometres. Soaring through the altostratus clouds, the lights below resembled an upside-down landscape, and he was looking at stars. It was cool and invigorating. Arume absorbed the beauty of the forests below, the rivers looked like silver trails. Shapeshifting intermittently, dipping up and down, he enjoyed the freedom under the cover of nightfall. A small light could be seen in the wilderness, his destination secreted away in lush tall timbers.

Jack and Madi sat listening to music on the small verandah, attached to the cabin. The big dog was looking into the sky made little warning barks, nothing too serious. The beautiful sea eagle manoeuvred into the nearest tree to the cabin. The couple waited. Not a word was said, they had been visited many times. Excitement surged through their bodies at the sight of him floating and shifting as he walked towards them. He greeted them both with a hand on their cheeks looking searchingly into their eyes. The sensation was like an intensive shiver down their spines and a total injection of magic.

Arume sat between them drinking cold water. He was thirsty and his body needed hydration.

The beautiful alien's voice had them captivated as he told them of the situation with Louis and Charlie and the distrust and suspicion of Karen Landy, including Bridget and Isobel's situation. Arume put his hand up making a large square. Instantly a hologram appeared. Jack and Madi could see his concerns, the people, the places and they could see Bridget and Isobel in the exercise yard. Next came the introduction and history of Sam Blackwell followed by the tetrahedron in the shape of a missile with wings making its way to Helomedes. Arume explained what needed to happen. It meant they would have to leave their hideaway and perhaps Earth. Jack and Madi were clear on the people and places they needed to deal with, including the escape plan that was imperative for everyone's safety.

With the moon was high in the sky now, it was time to leave. Arume stood in the small clearing. Silently, the sea eagle spread his wings and gracefully lifted into the path of the high moon. It was a spectacular sight, watching the vision becoming small as if heading to the moon.

There was much planning to do for Jack and Madi, needing to head back to civilisation and begin to put things in motion. They would check into a motel, so they didn't have to involve family and friends. Big Monty would have to go into a boarding kennel, they must have no distractions. If they got caught or attracted any attention, the end result would be disastrous.

The first thing Jack needed was a haircut and beard removed. They went to charity shops in upmarket suburbs, purchasing a well-tailored suit, shirt, black tie, and shoes. They found a leather briefcase for five dollars. Madi selected some tailored dresses and some stylish shoes and a handbag. She too had her hair and nails done. They purchased prepaid phones. Madi organised to pick up a different rental daily for a week. Jack rented the newest A-Class Mercedes, black with gold trim. That night they went through their plans, memorising each other's phone numbers. Jack had to sit in the Mercedes and practice the instrument panel. They laughed together looking at the comparison to their old Land rover. They drove the Mercedes to a local restaurant, enjoyed a magnificent cuisine and the best Australian wine.

Sam was watching the police parked in an unmarked car. It was becoming frustrating, wondering exactly what they expected him to do. He hadn't been to the lake, just the travel agency. He was organised, having groceries delivered and had his own gymnasium.

The buzzer activated indicating a visitor. He answered and could see on the video screen.

'What can I do for you?'

'I need to speak to you Mr Blackwell.'

'I'm not interested in buying anything and I donate online. Thanks, but no thanks.'

'I'm not a salesperson.'

'Okay what do you want?'

'It's in relation to the two women and the two boys.'

'You realise there are police watching you.'

'That's why I'm dressed like a lawyer and driving this expensive car.'

The door opened.

From the parked car, 'Well, well. I'm guessing lawyer.'

'Yep, maybe a barrister, that's a very expensive car. He knows we're watching.'

'What's the story here? Do they think this Sam Blackwell knows something about those boys' disappearance?'

'That's the theory. Oh well, I'm going to get more coffee, I hate these shitty jobs.'

Jack looked around Sam's apartment, it was pure luxury.

'My name is Jack Hillard.'

They shook hands. Sam made coffee then cut up some cheese with olives to go with some crusty bread. Jack was invited to sit. They settled down for morning tea.

'You mentioned the women.'

'What I am about to tell you Sam will sound like a story of someone under the influence of mind-altering drugs. Trust me Sam, it is all true. You have spent time at the lake I believe. Can you tell me about your experience?'

Sam felt reluctant to expose who he was to this total stranger. Mate came racing into the lounge area straight to Jack, sniffing and wagging his tail madly.

'That's unusual, he never goes to anyone.'

Sam felt it was a good sign. Mate and Jack became instant friends.

'Well back to your question. I had a very detached childhood, and I grew up into a very messed up youth. I used to do a lot of illegal shit.'

'Do you know Louis Blackwell is your half-brother?'

'That's why I started watching, I really don't know how to approach the situation. I know his foster mum is Bridget Sherwood. All I can say is that kid must have gone through hell, I'm very familiar with his real mother. I hired a private detective to follow their movements. That's when I found the lake. Look Jack, this is going to sound incredibly stupid. I started swimming in the lake, and it began to heal my mental health problems and I can tell you they were bad. I just wanted a family, but I didn't know how to do it, you know, approach them. I can tell you this, there is something unusual about the lake area, something or someone didn't want it developed. There's a strange sensation when you arrive, like you're being watched, but I felt safe as well. I love floating on the water and watching the birds.'

Sam stopped, looking at Jack so calm and poised.

'I can't believe I said so much.'

'Look Sam, I'm just going to put it out there because this is too hard and too big to summarise.'

Sam sat forward.

'The two boys are on their way back in an advanced spacecraft, with a really advanced race that have developed a dual planet. We have taken many samples of animal and plant life, including oceans to reproduce on this other 'Earth'. There are humans living on this planet, each specially selected and who are the best of humanity.'

Sam couldn't respond, so Jack continued.

'Inside the mountain on that rock face at the lake, is the mothercraft. You were being watched and helped to become well. We need you to help us get Isobel and Bridget out. My wife is looking for Simone.'

Sam still wasn't speaking. He was having so many different thoughts. Was Jack totally mad? Could it be the truth? Who the hell was he? Why did I tell him so much? Is he for real?

'Look Sam, I'm sorry I can't take this more slowly. I know you think I'm mad, let me show you something.'

Jack took off his jacket and he took a small vial of Vodoxium from his briefcase, he held it up to show Sam.

'This is a powerful energy source that has emotions, and it can do extraordinary things.'

Sam was feeling fear, convinced Jack had huge mental health issues. How was he going to get him out?

'I'm going to take a small sip and shapeshift.'

'Okay,' said Sam, now fully convinced Jack was very ill.

Feeling nervous but remaining calm, Sam decided to go along with him to avoid upsetting him.

'Okay Jack, how about a tiger? Show me how you change into a tiger.'

Jack took a small sip and concentrated. Sam was just about to run for the front door as Jack's head started to enlarge, his human eyes changing as a large cat appeared, complete with large teeth.

'No way.'

Sam jumped on the lounge, holding his head.

'No this is not happening.'

Jack's entire body had transformed to a huge Bengal Tiger sitting on his hindquarters panting. Sam couldn't take his eyes off the large animal and before his eyes Jack emerged out of the tiger.

'Okay Jack, just give me a moment, everything you have said is for real?'

Sam sat dumbfounded, he went to pat Mate for comfort still staring at Jack, Sam literally screamed. Sitting next to him was a goanna.

'Oh yeah, your dog's an alien.'

He then morphed back, licking Sam's face.

Madi rang Child Services where Karen Landy worked. Madi introduced herself as an advocate for Isobel Crane and Bridget Sherwood and wanted information on how Simone Crane was dealing with the separation. Karen Landy had an opening at 11am.

'Okay thank you, I'll take that. My name is Jade Maron.'

Madi arrived for her appointment and looked very professional. She held a folder full of paperwork. Karen Landy opened the conversation, slightly aggressive in tone.

'Look, I don't know why you're here, those women are going to be charged with murder.'

'It's not done as yet, and they are entitled to an advocate. Can you tell me how Simone is?'

'She's fine, going to school and she has her guinea pig and.'

'Is she seeing a child psychologist?'

'Yes, she is.'

'And do you have reports?'

'That's not for me to say. Now if you will excuse me Jade, I have to be going.'

Jade stood up to go, the file in her hand dropped scattering papers on the floor Jade got down on her hands and knees to gather them, Karen Landy was annoyed and unwillingly to help. Jade dropped a tracking and listening device into Karen's handbag, technically advanced from Helomedes.

'Could you please leave Miss Maron, I'm in a hurry.'

'Certainly.'

Madi pulled up in the shade of trees on the side of a road. Her earpiece and tracking pin in the charger socket of her mobile phone, she could actively see and hear Karen Landy.

Karen made a call to the local court to confirm Bridget and Isobel were entitled to an advocate. Her attitude was dismissive and angry. The next call was to make a doctor's appointment. Nearly two hours later there was a third. Madi had dozed off, the call woke her.

'Hello, Carol. This is Karen Landy. How's Simone?'

'I think she's okay, she doesn't say much. Look, she's going to school, eats, but spends most of her time outside with that stinking animal. She's just odd.'

'Alright, I'll be there tomorrow after school, I need to check in on her.'

She hung up.

'Damn! Stupid woman!'

Karen Landy was angry.

Jack rented a Catholic priest's outfit. The roman collar, white clerical shirt, black over shirt and black pants, completed with a heavy cross. He found a Bible in a charity shop. Jack had two crosses designed with empty chambers, perfect to store Vodoxium. He rang the police station, passing himself off as Father Constance, offering religious solace. Father Constance was informed they go into the yard between 2pm and 3pm.

'Thank you, officer, am I required to make an appointment?'

'No Father, you can just turn up.'

'Thank you. You have been very helpful.'

Detective Jenna put the directions into the GPS system.

'Who's this person we are looking for?'

''People' Detective Lester. Let's get coffee.'

'What's our first stop? Some sick dude in a nursing home.'

'What the hell could he tell us?'

'Who knows?'

Jason Blackwell sat slumped in his recliner, his hair now white and very underweight. He dribbled from the corner of his slack mouth onto the adult bib laying across his chest. The nurse woke him. He lifted his head to try and talk, but nothing came out, just a grunting noise. The detective introduced himself and Detective Lester. They put their notepads away and walked out, the smell was overpowering.

'Christ, that was a disgusting waste of time. So that's how we could end up?'

'That dude was very wealthy, influential and a real chick magnet.' 'Well, the only thing that he's attracting now are bloody flies! What's next?'

'This woman, Lucy Blackwell, a former international model, Genevieve St Day. Here, this was her.'

Detective Jenna handed over the phone.

'Wow she is a good-looking woman. Let's go and meet this stunner.'

It was an old block of flats, mainly housing individuals on welfare. Detective Jenna knocked on Genevieve St Day's door. It was quiet. He knocked again, slowly the door opened slightly to peep through.

'Lucy Blackwell?'

'My name's Genevieve St Day.'

'Okay, Miss St Day can we come in?'

She opened the door. Neither detective could find any words. She came out from behind the door, the sight of Lucy Blackwell was pathetic. Her hair hung in greasy strands. She had tried to apply her makeup to her fallen blotchy red face. The makeup was smudged, colours running into each other. Her watery eye did a slow blink sitting down on her cheek. Lucy had on a sequin dress that accentuated all the weight she had put on. Stains of all colours decorates the front of the dress. The lounge room was filthy. The walls were covered with her photos when she was the exotic Genevieve St Day. All her fashionable evening gowns and shoes lay scattered over the floor. Empty wine casks, take-away cartons, rotting food, an overflowing ashtray mingled with an underlying odour of urine. Lucy was drunk, tottering around in high heels. She picked up a sort of washed jam jar, offering the detectives a drink.

'Miss St Day, we would like to ask you questions about your son Louis.'

That statement triggered an instant change in her mood.

'What about that little bastard?'

'He's missing Miss St Day.

She started laughing like a maniac.

'I hope he's dead.'

She started yelling and stumbling over all the stuff on the floor.

'It's all his fault you know and that other bastard.'

She started throwing shoes and screaming, dribble flying in the putrid air. Both detectives left without a word.

'Jesus Christ, what the hell was that?! Clearly she hates her kid.'

'You think?! That kid would never go to her.'

The two detectives had lunch together putting notes in their pads.

'Where do you think those kids are?'

Detective Jenna looked out the window.

'Honestly, I don't know. But that thing we just left is going to be found dead one day. My God she's a pathetic sight.'

Detective Jenna slid his phone over.

'Read that, it's the family history.'

'That poor bloody kid.'

'Yeah, I think we can safely dismiss the parents as suspects.'

Sam, Jack and Madi were all together in the apartment enjoying a variety of takeaways. Mate was having the time of his life with lots of company. They had spent hours going over plans. Madi found where Simone was and the plan to take her had been formed.

'What happens if we get caught?'

'If that happens Sam, we will not be left behind. An extraction will be launched, and they will use any means necessary.'

'What if everything is exposed?'

'Then so be it, there will be no trace and no explanations.'

'How can you be so sure? If we all become a liability, why would they bother with us?'

'We have all been family for a long time and you don't leave family behind.'

'Well, you've got me there, I still haven't had a lot of family experience.'

'Oh shit!'

'What is it Sam?'

'Your dog, what about your dog? And Mate's coming surely?'

'Esouli will rescue him, if need be, but the plan is they both come.'

'That's the big warrior fella you told me about?'

'Yep and he's an expert shapeshifter.'

'What if I don't fit in or I don't like it?'

'You will be returned, but all memories of this will be erased.'

'I feel nervous. Do you guys feel the same?'

Madi gave Sam a hug.

'We are going to be fine. This is family.'

CHAPTER 64

The sight of the black hole looked terrifying. The craft was in the process of adjusting into a long bullet shape. All on board were getting secure for the incredible journey ahead. It looked like a gaping bloodied mouth waiting to devour a passer-by. All the energies were shut down, the force of the black hole was pulling them in at a furious speed. The boys and Esouli strapped in, all others were secured in their pods.

'You boys sure you don't want the pods?'

'No way, I'm not missing this.'

'Nope I'm right, I can handle this.'

Charlie winked at Louis.

It was like entering a monstrous burning tornado. It seemed to close in, then open like a gigantic valve pushing the craft in extreme turbulence.

'I can't watch this, it too hard and fast on the eyeballs.'

'Yeah, I know what you mean Bro, think I'm gonna spew.'

'Look away until it slows down.'

'I hope it's soon Esouli, my guts are not happy.'

As Esouli predicted, it was over in minutes. They both looked up as large molten rocks hurtled towards the craft, deadly fireballs crashing into each other causing extreme heat. What looked like shattered glass, bombarded everything in its path.

'This is very violent.'

'It is Louis, something unusual is happening.'

'It's like being inside a giant artery. The red is so vivid and it's getting hotter.'

Louis was taking off his jacket.

'You're right Louis.'

The craft started to hum.

'What's happening?'

Charlie was getting nervous.

'The ship is in stress it could be melting.'

'Oh shit! We're going to burn in an inferno. How long until we are out of this? Will anyone know we're in trouble?'

'A distress call went out before it shut down. Hopefully someone is waiting on the other side of this.'

Darkness fell like a blanket, the craft felt like it was still, or it could be travelling at incredibly fast speed. The heat was getting more intense.

'Will they be okay in their pods?'

'They're cooled inside Louis.'

Their fear became stronger in the dark. Another twenty minutes went by, Esouli kept the boys calm by taking them through what was going to happen. He had a small vial of Vodoxium to give some light.

'I've estimated by the time we get to the end the craft will be near disintegration.' Esouli continued, 'There will be another ship waiting for us, we are going to take a spacewalk.'

The boys looked at each other, sensing each other's fear, not knowing what to say.

'So close to getting home,' Charlie mumbled.

'We're not going home so to speak,' said Louis.

Charlie cleared his throat, trying to stop tears.

'What about the pods?'

'They can move independently towards the new craft.'

'What are you going to do Esouli?'

'I will be guiding you two. You will need oxygen, so suits will be worn.'

Louis was alarmed.

'How are you going to survive?'

'It's okay Louis, I'll wear oxygen, and have you both tucked under each arm.'

The panic could be felt even though Esouli was trying to be calm for the boys' sake.

'The atmosphere will be hot initially then it will get cold, I will be initiating my flying abilities to the extreme to get away quick.'

Beams of light gave them enough illumination to get into the suits and attach breathing equipment.

'They feel okay. Not too bulky.'

Louis helped Charlie strap on the oxygen packs and attach the head equipment. Then Charlie helped Louis with his gear. Esouli just had the head attachment and a backpack of oxygen.

'We're getting closer. The pods will be released first.'

The craft was just responding to Esouli's commands and touch. It was starting to open up, the humming was getting louder.

'Okay my friends, this is it. We are at the end.'

The suits kept the boys cool. Esouli was getting heat stress. He stood tall, his wings started to form. An enormous span, black, row upon row of thick feathers appeared on his lower legs to balance the flight.

'We have to go now.'

The boys moved like little robots, frightened beyond belief. Esouli's large arms wrapped them up and tucked them into his body. The pods were clear of the black hole and could be just seen in the distance getting smaller. The craft was in great distress. It was trying to survive and save itself. Its emotions high, it could not save the internals and the outer layer started to shed like a snake's skin. The Vodoxium gathering like a cocoon.

The second tetrahedron had only just received the message. The time spans were not going to coordinate to retrieve everyone before the oxygen ran out and no one was aware. The boys were ready, petrified with fear, but feeling secure in Esouli's arms. His wings started to move slowly, gracefully all in unison. The atmosphere was in turmoil. It took all Esouli's strength to negotiate the path out and remain stable. Louis couldn't believe how exhilarating it felt. It was getting cooler. It was so smooth and quiet, but very dark, with just the light of some rather large stars in the distant velvet night.

A large roar behind them broke the momentum of concentrated flight. Esouli turned just in time, to see a gigantic inferno, angry, blood red flames reaching out, twisting, explosions booming into the dark. The black hole had come to life for its end, spewing out toxic flames in multiple colours, reaching out to destroy any remnants of life. The black hole was burning itself out and expelling furious energy, an energy that hurtled all three in different directions at an extraordinary speed.

Louis finally steadied his heart racing, knowing he was using too much oxygen, his eyes searching madly for anyone. He watched the black hole burn into an angry dying blaze. Charlie was watching the same thing he was alone floating in the dark. Thoughts of home, his mother and Simone, the tears started to flow he was panicking. His rapid breathing activated the oxygen alarm. Was this his end? How could it happen like this? They were meant to go home. He was getting tired, finding it hard to keep his eyes open.

Esouli was frantically trying to fly looking for the boys, his oxygen was quickly diminishing, the ship was supposed to be here.

'I've failed and those boys will die.'

He could see the pods in the distance floating with no direction.

'Can I shapeshift?'

He tried but didn't have enough energy. The Vodoxium was wearing off, he had run out frantically looking for the boys. Thoughts started to fade, his huge body weakening.

Louis felt tired.

'My oxygen is low...'

He began to close his eyes permanently. He was aroused by something in his line of vision, blinking to stay awake. He saw his grandmother, she hadn't changed, the loving face, she smiled, she was waiting for him, darkness fell like a light turned out.

The dying spaceship was distorting and shrinking, the humming was now less, it was actually in pain. A stream of brilliant blue fluid moved upwards, a reverse fountain, it was pooling at the end, gorging itself into a luminous blue bulb shape, it kept getting bigger, then changing, escaping its burning shell. It was now an oval shape, splashing out like a star, then a rectangle. It twisted and swirled, then the stream finished feeding. A pure Vodoxium triangle shape revealed itself, saving power and discarding the remains of the ship. It was building up speed, brilliant blue against the black sky, it was searching for its occupants. All three were unconscious, drifting into the abyss. The pods couldn't find the new craft, hearts slowing, the strings of life melting away.

The Vodoxium was spreading itself, tentacles searching and shooting across the sky desperate to find all its lost cargo. With forked lightning speed it finally reached the drifting body of Charlie. Louis took longer he had gone further. Then multiple tentacles scoured the dark foreboding sky for Esouli. The luminous mass absorbed Charlie. The blood surged in his body, he was in a long black tunnel, and he was running, running towards the heartbeat. Charlie's eyes opened a luminous blue.

Louis's grandmother woke him up.

'It's time to go.'

It was bright. The ocean could be heard. No, it was his own breath taking in oxygen, he was being pulled somewhere. It felt secure where was he. Something held him, he couldn't move. The pods were guided into the Vodoxium strong tentacles, placing them tenderly in the blue saviour. All the eyes opened, then all went back to induced sleep to avoid anxiety and fear. Esouli's body floated, his wings stretched out, heading towards a supernova. It looked magical, his magnificent outline against the dazzling explosive colours. It was like and everlasting lightning flash.

The Vodoxium wrapped Esouli in a cocoon, the astounding energy needed to regenerate his life was immense. The tetrahedron moved with incredible speed toward the Vodoxium and its cargo. It was like a meeting of long, lost friends. The emotional attachment was beautiful and not fully understood.

The craft came to a stop, waiting, the Vodoxium formed above in precise dimension to its host below, everyone secure within. Ever so steadily the Vodoxium injected itself into the spaceship. It started to spin gently, lighting up, changing from a platinum colour to gold and then luminous blue. They became one. The craft was now more powerful, updated and ready to try out its superpower.

The boys remained in their pods. Arume and all who lived on Helomedes watched the monitoring screen incorporated into the pods. Deep concern could be felt, the boys were not responding well. Heart, lung and brain activity had not returned to normal. Esouli was highly stressed, he recovered with a strong dose of Vodoxium watching on. It had been five days, he paced up and down near the healing pods. Charlie and Louis's little friends had recovered well, they remained quiet, waiting for the boys to respond.

The atmosphere was sombre, nothing would be the same for everyone if the boys don't make it.

Everything was reaching crisis point on Earth, and now in the craft. Esouli was in talks with Arume. The boys were deteriorating and Arume was in deep distress.

'The only intervention at this point that will save their lives will be a rather significant injection of Vodoxium.'

A smaller female named Elus spoke in a beautiful, serene voice, 'You know what this will mean Arume.'

'Yes Elus, we cannot let these human boys die. They have come so far and proved they are pure.'

Elus spoke again, 'We all agree, we must take the acceptable path.'

They bowed their heads indicating confirmation.

Two crystal vials were handed to Elus. They were inserted into the top of the pods. The Vodoxium was going to circulate in their body systems. The outcome would change Louis and Charlie forever, it was a complete transfusion. They would no longer be human beings.

Many cells in their bodies would not have the same DNA. It was a long nervous wait for signs of improved life, everything seemed to be frozen in time. The monitors stirred; vital signs started to improve. Another twenty- four-hours went by, hydration was maintained, and deep sleep induced. All the signs looked positive. Their brain activity was slowly reaching full capacity with all the organs active and functioning.

All the creatures waited. Fudgunkel's tinkling was intense, he paced around mumbling continuously. Then it happened, a voice.

'That'd be right. The first thing I hear is the weird Santa's tinkling bells.'

Charlie's eyes were open. He sat up.

'Oh My God, I am so hungry.'

'For the first time I'm with you Bro, starving.'

The quiet atmosphere exploded, with an audible sound of relief.

The laughter, the cuddles and tears were followed by a thorough health check. The atmosphere was full of calm life again. The question left hanging, how different or who were the boys now?

Everybody ate together, Louis and Charlie only remembering small events, but busy shovelling food. Arume's people watched the boys closely for any changes, they were fitted with monitors to observe any abnormal behaviours and abilities.

'Do you get the feeling that everyone is watching us?'

'Dude I can't even go to the toilet without company.'

'What do you remember Charlie?'

The boys stretched out in their beds, getting alone time for once.

'Oh, shit man, I was so frightened. I remember thinking, I'm never going to see Mum and Simone again. I couldn't believe it was going to end floating in the stars.'

'I saw my grandmother, my thoughts much the same. I couldn't believe it was all over. Not seeing Bridget, everything I guess.'

Louis felt hot, sweat started to trickle down his head and face. He was pale.

'You don't look so good.'

Louis got up to leave for the bathroom. Charlie blinked his eyes. One Louis was leaving and the other one was still sitting on his bed. The one on the bed watched Charlie.

'Louis!'

The other one walked back into the room and resumed his place inside the Louis on the bed.

'Charlie you're see through!'

'Dude you just walked out the door and stayed on the bed at the same time.'

'I think we need to see someone.'

They sat around a beautiful carved crystal table with Esouli, four Elodites – two males and two females, including Elus. The boys sat together.

'It's like being in the Principal's Office.'

Charlie giggled nervously and watched his hands become see through.

Elus asked how they were feeling in her soothing voice. Each of them described the strange body experiences. Elus nodded to Esouli. A hologram came up of the boys floating in dark space. They saw themselves laid out with multiple tubes, leads and monitors attached.

'When you were rescued, your vital signs were nearly non-existent,' Esouli looked from one to the other, 'we tried everything in the human rule book. Neither of you responded, you were both dying.'

There was tension in the air, Louis and Charlie looked at Esouli confused.

'We made the decision to stimulate your entire body systems with Vodoxium, we couldn't let you die.'

There was a brief silence, Esouli went on.

'You both now understand the power of Vodoxium?'

They both nodded.

'The Vodoxium will never leave your systems.'

Louis cleared his throat.

'How different are we?'

Esouli paused.

'Neither of you are totally human.'

'So that's why weird stuff is happening.'

Louis spoke with an intense voice, 'How weird will it get?'

'Dude, we are aliens!'

They both looked at Esouli.

'You are going to have certain abilities and we intend to show you how to use and control them.'

'Like before?'

'Yes Louis, but then you only had a small oral dose.'

Elus spoke in her beautiful voice.

'We are sorry, and we apologise deeply to you both. We could not let you die.'

'Well,' said Charlie with his famous smile, 'I think it's totally wicked!'

They all looked at each other, not understanding. Louis put their minds at ease.

'He means we are both happy and thankful you saved us.'

Again, the silence and pensive glances, Louis looked at Esouli. The Elodites got up in their graceful manner and seemed to float out bowing as they left.

'Righto Big Fella, out with it.'

Charlie tapping Esouli on the shoulder.

'There's been some trouble on Earth.'

'Are our Mums, okay?'

Louis and Charlie both looking frantic.

'They're okay, however they are in jail.'

'What!'

'Please, just listen. A woman called Karen Landy assumed you two were dead.'

Esouli put his hand up.

'How could she think that?'

Charlie was close to tears.

'Because they can't find a trace of you on Earth.'

'But Mum had a plan about us going to the top end for a holiday with family to learn traditional ways.'

'That was a good plan, but I'm afraid a suspicion crept in and the authorities spent a lot of time trying to track you boys down and it came to nothing.'

The stress on the boys and the Vodoxium was having unusual effects, both now partially visible, then back again, turning into each other, then their mothers.

'Boys you need to concentrate.'

They both reappeared.

'Okay, let's do some deep breathing. Listen to my words. Everything is under control.'

Esouli put his hand on their shoulders, they all sat down, still taking in deep breaths.

'Although we have concerns, the situation on Earth is under control. We have our people ready to extract Simone, Isobel and Bridget and it's going to work.'

Esouli studied Louis's face.

'What now?'

'Well Louis, someone unexpected has surfaced. You have a half-brother. His name is Sam Blackwell. He has known about you for some time. He hired a private detective to find and watch you, unsure how to introduce himself. You have the same father. He could not find a trace of you or Charlie.'

'Go on,' said Louis.

'Because your disappearance and the media have exposed so much about your lives and now you are not totally human, it will be dangerous to go back to Earth. Your mothers, Simone and Sam will be leaving as well. The time has arrived earlier than we anticipated. Getting our people out is risky trying not to expose our existence.'

'The Elodites will be leaving us as we get closer to Helomedes and that will be in twelve hours. You will be able to see all of Helomedes from our passing location, then we will make haste to Earth. Our mothership will be ready to take us on board.'

'You mean this craft will fit into the big girl?'

'Yes Charlie.'

Louis jumped in quickly when Esouli finished.

'How do the crafts come and go without being detected by Pine Gap. They track everything that moves.'

'Oh great! Now we could be hit by a missile.'

Charlie started to disappear again. Louis grabbed him, his fingers falling through Charlie's arm.

'It's okay, I'm becoming whole again.'

'You know what, when we get back to the other Earth you and me Charlie are going to skate, swim, surf, eat, drink and sleep. We're gonna do nothing. We need a holiday.'

Esouli continued, 'I think that is a great idea, and you guys deserve it, I might even join you.'

'Oh yeah dude I can just see you on a surfboard.'

Louis and Charlie exchanged smiles.

'So how do we re-enter Earth again?'

'The craft can shift into the shape of satellites, then we can black out transmissions if they get too curious.'

'We won't be leaving the ship?'

'No, we will stay as we are, and our ship will integrate with the mothercraft.'

'Oh God, I hope it all goes to plan.'

Louis looked concerned.

'The Elodites will be watching, we will all be watching Louis. They are not on their own.'

While the journey to Helomedes was hastily underway, the boys had to begin intense lessons. Learning how to manage their altered states was exhausting. Initially it was painful to transform so many times to achieve perfection. Shapeshifting eventually came easily due to the amount of Vodoxium now a huge part of their anatomy. The second ability which was to become invisible, took great concentration. The boys studied and practiced meditation to help them take greater control. Next was changing body shape. Firstly, becoming super tall, they overdid the first attempt and hit their heads. The laughter was contagious for all watching. Becoming tiny was intimidating but had its advantages when Fudgunkel was on the warpath about their housework. The boys could change into each other, animals and other people. It greatly amused them and the audience on board. Their bodies could look like water or fire, enabling them to flood or burn. Learning to fly was extraordinary, the freedom was exhilarating, but not without a few hiccups. After a few crashes and mastering the art of turning in flight, they were left with a few bruises.

'Jeeze, the bloody birds make it look easy,' cried Charlie as he slid to the floor.

The ability to have strength took robust mind control, engaging and convincing the brain it could achieve the ridiculous, and eventually they did. The boys dedicated as much time as they could on the way to Helomedes. Reaching the planet was certainly a distraction.

'So according to our monitor we should see Helomedes.'

Charlie and Louis scanned the sky outside. The environment outside started to move, the boys couldn't believe the bizarre situation.

'Are you sure we are in the right place?'

Louis looked at Esouli confused.

'We have shields around Helomedes to protect the Vodoxium.'

When the shields parted exposing the planet, it was a sight of revolutionary advanced technology.

The first structure looked like a massive cartwheel with spokes. In its centre a huge triangle shape. The entire structure was so bright, pulsating with luminous Vodoxium. Brilliant blue and shades of purple. It was structured in six layers, joined by massive pillars. Smaller complexes surrounded the bigger structure. The tetrahedron slowed to hovering so the boys could absorb it all.

'The smaller ones are for food production. The two lower levels are where technology production and structures are made. Remember I said lots of our food comes from Earth Two?'

Just then, a ship that looked like a brilliant gold bowl, with a massive viewing window sped past, more were coming out of the big space station.

'They're checking us out and greeting us. They know we are not stopping.'

'How many dudes live here?'

'Five hundred of Arume's people and two hundred of us.'

'Is there a Mrs Warrior?'

Esouli smiled, 'Of course there is. We only expand our population when they can be supported by our systems.'

'Oh, good to know.'

Charlie received a quick flick across the back of his head. Both boys laughed.

After studying the space station, Louis's eyes were drawn to the surrounding landscape.

'What on earth are those towers? They look like giant pencils.'

'Whoa, look at those weird pom-pom tree things. They look like something Mum would knit and sew onto a hat and make us wear them to look cute.'

Esouli laughed at the boys.

They moved closer to the landscape. Strange animals that looked like flying Manta rays floated in the sky then secreted themselves in oval shaped openings in the strange pencil towers. Grasses of all colours adorned with fluffy tops swayed between the trees. Fountains of water squirted intermittently from the ground. Tiny pools of water plentiful in numbers housed many species of crustaceans and frogs taken from Earth to complement the ecosystems. Esouli pointed to the towers.

'They are formed from very dense crystal and covered with many varieties of vegetation. They are very cool and full of liquid crystal.'

The craft moved further on.

'If you look into the distance, you can see another space station like the first. There are ten stations around the planet.'

'The vegetation is lush; the soil must be very fertile.'

'It is Louis, lots of underground springs, it helps keep it cool for Arume's people.'

'So where exactly does the Vodoxium come from?'

'How about I tell you that when you're older.'

'Looks like there's plenty of liquid crystal!'

'It's never-ending Charlie.'

The craft hovered over the massive station below.

'I want to show you guys something. Keep watching.'

The entire station began to move, the foundation supports retracting. Each layer began to spin slowly then consolidated into one craft. It was miraculous to watch, like a new sun rising. Luminous, beautiful and powerful. A formidable sight.

'Are they all spaceships?'

'Yes Louis.'

It moved across the sky, moving up, further and further until it was a tiny light in the distance, just a dot. Within what seemed moments, the craft was back preparing to land.

'Holy shit, that's faster than the speed of light.'

They watched the ship unfold and extend to its former self.

'That's just totally awesome.'

'Yep. Awesome.'

The boys' mouths still open in disbelief.

Louis eventually spoke.

'You said once that other lifeforms live here.'

'That's right.'

'How do they all get on and what do they do here?'

'You have to keep in mind that these lifeforms have experienced extreme devastation, either by their planet self-destructing because of climatic conditions or meteors. Others have been taken over and have come close to being wiped out. We search for planets that can be reconstructed using our own technologies, trying to make them conducive to their needs.'

'Do you make weapons on Helomedes?'

'Only stunning weapons Charlie. We rely on our abilities and technology, only using them in extreme situations.'

'You guys could go on that renovation show, instead of houses, its planets.'

Charlie giggled at Louis.

The craft moved on showing the rest of the planet and other stations. The pencil pillars dominated the landscape, oddly shaped birdlife flittered through the towers. They looked more like flying ants and beetles with feathers.

'What other animals live here?' asked Charlie.

'Mainly insects, birds, lots of crustaceans in ponds. There is a native mammal and it's extremely secretive, living in underground caves.'

'What does it look like?' A very excited tone in Louis's voice, his curiosity with animals never fading.

'I guess the closest resemblance would be a wombat. It has a long beak-like nose so it can feed on the food in the ponds and insects.'

Esouli used the hologram to show the boys.

'Wow. What an amazing creature.'

They watched him poke at the food in the pool, skewered it on a little hook-like appendage, then it folded up into its mouth.

'They don't breed a lot, about two cubs every three to four years. Small colonies live together in tunnel type caves, but they never interbreed.'

A storm was brewing in the distance, black clouds, literally black.

'Look at that.'

Charlie was pointing to the sky.

'You need to watch this the storms are something different.'

The black clouds gathered in clumps, they moved as though life inside them was trying to get out. Multiple spouts appeared out of each, like lots of legs. Then water ran down the spouts and watered the ground below. The noise it made sounded like an incredibly low sigh of relief. Charlie and Louis laughed at such an unusual storm delivering its water.

Esouli took command of the ship. Arume appeared after the boys had gone to practice their new abilities. Fudgunkel was tapping his impatient tinkling toes.

'Greetings my dear friend,' Arume's voice was warm. 'The situation is getting dangerous on Earth. Our people are in fear of being exposed. The extraction plan is about to commence, I am afraid I may need to intervene to save our exposure. Can you come to Earth with haste?'

Esouli could always tell when Arume was concerned, his voice was strained.

'I'll see you soon my friend. We are on our way.'

The tetrahedron changed its shape immediately to stream-lined for its quickest journey to Earth.

CHAPTER 65

Jack arrived at the police station in complete Catholic priest dress and holding his Bible. It was the day before Isobel and Bridget were to be charged with the murder of Charlie and Louis. It was to happen at 3:30pm. Isobel and Bridget were in the yard from 2pm to 3pm. The timeline was slim. Once charged, they would be separated.

Jack spoke in a soft voice and maintained a humble manner. He was ushered into the interview room. Isobel and Bridget were already sitting. Jack sat down and hung his head.

'I have been sent by Arume. Take my hands as if we are praying. They can see us but can't hear us. In my hands is a cross for each of you. Within them is Vodoxium. Tonight, you need to practice shape shifting to a bird. Only use a portion. You need the rest for tomorrow.'

Isobel whispered, 'What's happening tomorrow Father?'

'Between 2pm and 3pm you will take the Vodoxium, shifting into the chosen bird. I suggest Magpies. At the end of the road will be a blue van parked waiting for you, the side door will be open, once in, we head to the mountain. You are both going to be charged with murder at 3:30pm by the police prosecutor.'

'Where's Simone?'

'She will be extracted tomorrow at the same time you will be escaping.'

'You are aware after tomorrow Earth is no longer home?'

They both nodded as if in prayer.

'There will most likely be protestors and media. When you're in flight go directly to the vehicle.'

'We understand Father.'

Isobel spoke quietly for them both.

'Look at those two pretending to be Christians, makes me sick. Sooner they're out of here and locked up for life the better.'

Detective Jenna was angry he couldn't find the bodies.

'This bloody media and those protestors are a pain in the arse. I reckon they're enjoying every minute of the attention.'

Detectives Jenna and Darley despised both women and judged them to be totally guilty. Opening the door with force, all three people inside flinched with the loud noise. Jack left without a further word. He wasn't sure how a Catholic priest ended a spiritual visit.

Madi drove to the vicinity of Simone's carer's home. She took a casual walk up the street carrying shopping bags. She wore sunglasses and a cap the weather was hot. A dry creek bed ran beside the house with a tiny gully from the house yard fence joining the dry creek bed. Madi fanned herself and drank water, giving the impression of having a rest, just in case she was being watched. The area under the fence was deep enough for Simone to crawl under. The difficult part would be convincing her.

Isobel and Bridget went back to their cell, hiding the crosses. After the lights went out, they took tiny sips and commenced trying to shape shift. It was hard not to giggle. Bridget's bottom half was Magpie, Isobel had a beak and human face, wings instead of arms.

'Oh, shit we are not very good at this.'

'Come on old girl, we need to clear the fear and concentrate.'

Another three attempts and finally two magpies perched in the jail cell. It was 3am and finally they were able to complete the shapeshifting within seconds.

Just after 3am under the cover of an ocean storm and very low cloud, the tetrahedron nestled into the mountain inside the mothership, undetected by satellites or human eyes.

Arume sat at the massive viewing screen with Esouli.

'It is so good to see you my dear friend.'

'And you. It's certainly been a journey. Our dual planet is ready for everyone.'

'You sound like it's coming to an end.'

Arume put his hand on Esouli's shoulder.

'I have an instinctive feeling, whatever happens we have to complete this for something far bigger than any of us. The human race has had long enough to awaken, but that hasn't happened. It's devastating, they have no idea what's coming.'

'Elus is strong and capable, whatever happens, something of me will still be here.'

They embraced, then sat quietly together.

Jack, Sam and Madi finalised their plans before going to bed for the last time on Earth. Sam cuddled Mate and talked softly to him, wondering what the hell he was doing and where he was going. He left the travel agency to his employees. His money he gave to animal welfare charities. His beautiful penthouse to the homeless for a sanctuary, his car transferred he to the travel agency. Sam kept a bundle of notes in his jacket, just in case.

'And you my little friend I'll keep in my jacket, even though you're a little alien.'

Sam tossed and turned for a few more hours, then dozed off about 3am.

Jack and Madi went through her plan. She would have the old land rover and hoped Simone would trust her and not hold up the timeframe they had set. Jack pulled Madi close.

'You could talk anyone into anything with that sweet face and voice. This is our last night on Earth, I feel like we should be celebrating or something, not really quite sure.'

'I'm glad we've got Monty with us.'

His big tail thumped on the floor at the mention of his name.

'We all go together. Sam's organised all his stuff.'

Madi laughed.

'Not worth leaving our old stuff to anyone.'

Jack grinned.

'They would be pissed off, having to get rid of it.'

They both tossed and turned also dozing off around 3am.

The next morning Sam ordered a huge breakfast to be delivered and treats for the dogs.

'Well,' said Sam, 'today's the day then.'

Jack and Madi laughed at the awkward moment.

'Just remember one bag each, just in case we have to run.'

'Great! I feel so much better.'

Sam laughed at his own words.

'Every detail is organised. The vans in place, clothes for the women and blankets and the cab is booked for us. Madi you should have plenty of time to talk her into leaving if you arrive at the time organised.'

They cleaned up the penthouse, took the dogs for a run, each person having many thoughts and absorbing the world around them for the last time.

The time had arrived. They all headed off in silence. Sam took one last look around. Madi set off, flicking tears from her cheeks at intervals. It was both sad and exciting. Madi had her shopping bags, hat and sunnies looking like a person walking home. Simone should be home from the day care centre, according to her formed patterns. Madi moved off the path and down the side of the fence where the ditch made a gap. It was a Colourbond fence and sturdy. Madi found a rock she could stand on to see over the fence. A forlorn sight met her eyes. A little girl sat with her legs crossed, cuddling her guinea pig rocking backwards and forwards. Madi watched and listened.

'Mummy will come back soon. Charlie and Mummy will come back and get me. We can go home then. Bridget and Louis will be our friends just like before. Its okay Mummy will come.'

She kept repeating this. Madi's heart broke listening to this poor little soul. She took a deep breath, clearing her throat.

'Simone.'

She stopped rocking.

'Simone.'

She stood up, still holding her guinea pig close.

'Simone, can you come to the fence.'

Madi waved.

'Can I talk to you please?'

Simone walked over, glancing back at the house. She looked up.

'Hello, my name is Madi. I'm a friend of your mum and Bridget.'

Simone's eyes widened with a flicker of excitement.

'What's your guinea pig's name?'

'Lottie.'

'Hello Lottie. How are you feeling Simone?'

'I just want to go home to Mummy. Do you know where she is?'

Tears fell on Lottie.

'Listen to me Simone, I need you to be really brave. I'm here to take you to Mummy. Is that okay?'

'The lady doesn't like me and hates Lottie. She calls her Stinky.'

'Do you think you could crawl under the fence?'

'Can Lottie come?'

'She certainly can.'

Lottie came through first and placed carefully in Madi's backpack. Simone crawled on her belly, Madi helped her up and hugged her. Simone felt safe and hugged her tight.

Karen Landy had to practically stand on the brakes to avoid smashing into the car in front. She screamed, angry and irritated.

'You bloody stupid old man!'

Her handbag went flying, emptying the contents on the floor. She pulled over, still cursing, gathering up her stuff. A small silver disc slipped through her fingers, she frowned in wonder, a little blue light was flashing.

'What the hell is this?'

She sat thinking.

'That woman in my office, crawling on the floor. Shit, shit!!'

Karen fumbled for her phone, calling Simone's carer.

'Where's Simone?'

'Oh, in the bloody backyard as usual.'

'Have a look!'

Karen was yelling.

'She's no not here.'

'Quickly have a look outside, down the road. Hurry!'

Panting could be heard from the other end.

'An old Land rover pulled out from the side of the road.'

Karen Landy called the police, she picked up the disc, it disappeared while holding it.

The two women were in the exercise yard. They drew little attention from inside the police station, the fences were very high. There was no chance of an escape. Voices could be heard from around the front of the building.

'This is it Izzy.'

They held hands and drank the rest of the Vodoxium.

'Let's do this.'

Starting to shrink, their bodies changed, beaks, head and feathers. Last the feet transformed, for a moment in time magpies with human legs and feet did look hilarious. They took flight, somewhat unbalanced, they followed the footpath, over the low shrubs. A large crowd was gathering, chanting, and lifting placards in the air for the media cameras to see. More cars were arriving, horns blowing, it was very disturbing, and the crowd wanted them dead. The fear and adrenalin made their hearts race, it used up the Vodoxium quicker than expected. The human feet hit the footpath, now totally naked, just a few steps to the van. A blanket was thrown over them, the van door slammed, and took off. The dogs greeted the women, as if they had known them for years.

A woman at the end of the pack was trying to attract the latest news car that arrived.

She was screaming.

'They're in the van.'

The women's clothes were found in the exercise yard. Police were running to the patrol cars with the woman still screaming, telling police the colour of the van. Quick introductions were done while the women got dressed.

'I think someone saw us.'

'That explains the sirens.'

Jack looked frantically in the rear vision mirror.

'We're going to have to ditch this van.'

Sam pointed, 'Turn right, next intersection, I have an idea.'

The women hung on to avoid being thrown around.

'Head toward the beach.'

'Does anyone know where Simone is?'

Isobel was frantic.

'My wife has her, they're on the way to the mountain.'

'Thank God.'

'Pull up over there next to that white service van.'

Sam jumped out, the owner had just finished surfing, Sam gave him five thousand dollars for the van.

'Dude, it's not worth a grand. It's a deal.'

He handed Sam the keys. They quickly put all the gear in the van. Monty and Mate jumped in all excited. They headed off again to the mountain. No one was speaking, too anxious and full of fear.

Jack's phone rang, it was Madi, hysterical.

'Shit Jack, we've been sighted, can you hear the sirens?'

'I know they're after us as well, where are you?'

'The last shopping centre before the mountain.'

'There's a McDonalds on the right.' Sam cut in, 'Madi, go into the underground carpark at the shopping centre, we're only minutes away.'

'Simone!'

'Mummy!'

Sam handed the phone to Isobel, they were both crying, unable to speak.

They looked frantically for the old Land rover.

'I see it.'

Jack pulled up behind. Simone and Madi got in, Isobel pulling her daughter into her arms. Monty licked Madi's face until she couldn't breathe properly.

'I believe you're Madi?'

Isobel's teared up eyes.

'Thank you. Thank you from my entire heart for rescuing my baby.'

Madi reached into her backpack and pulled out the guinea pig.

'Meet Lottie.'

They all giggled, and Monty thought he had a snack.

They were getting close to the mountain and the tension could be felt.

'Oh shit! No!'

'What? What is it?'

'Police helicopter.'

'Okay.'

Jack was trying to manage the situation.

'Everyone just stay calm, get all your stuff ready. Bloody sirens again. How the hell did they find us?'

'Of course,' Sam banged the dashboard, 'cameras on the tollway.'

'Alright they're getting closer and we're nearly at the mountain. Sam shoved Mate in his backpack, Madi had Monty's lead on him.

'We're going to have to run and run fast.'

The van came to a screaming holt, skidding to a stop, police cars behind them. The helicopter hovering above as more police were arrived.

Simone and Isobel were in front followed by Madi and Bridget, Monty was pulling Madi along. Jack and Sam ran behind them. A loudspeaker rang out telling them to stop. They kept running. Bullets started to fire above and around them. Bridget was hit in the arm, the pain excruciating, she fell to the ground, blood seeping into the ground. Isobel and Madi stopped to help, she yelled at them to keep going. Sam was hit in the leg. Jack stopped for Sam.

'No Jack! Take Mate and run.'

Many police had caught up to them. The menacing helicopter was loud and frightening. Monty and Mate barked hysterically, as Simone cried seeing all the blood.

It was over. Guns drawn, yelling at them to lay on the ground. Monty was about to get a bullet in his head.

Louis and Charlie were watching feeling helpless and agitated, Esouli tried to assure them it would be okay. No words could console them. Unbeknownst to all, Arume had appeared on the ledge holding a long sphere. He held it high and spoke some ancient words. The helicopter pilot nearly lost control watching Arume, and then the intervention happened. From the sphere, visible air waves shimmered, spreading as far as the eye could see. Across the entire country everything and everyone was frozen in time. Arume held the sphere. It was vibrating the energy was enormous, Arume was visibly getting weak, his beautiful body starting to fade in and out.

The mountain opened, seven pods drifted towards the people and dogs on the ground. Each body lifted into the atmosphere then gently settled into the pods. Sam and Mate remained together. All the healing modules drifted into the opening followed by Arume who was notably in decline. When the mountain sealed around the precious lives the healing both physically and mentally began. Police wandered around confused, having no clue what they were doing. The helicopter pilot took off not knowing what he was doing. The country resumed, just a glitch in life that no-one really stopped to think about. All those within the mountain, their identity on Earth now extinguished.

The boys raced to the pods, looking for their mothers.

'They'll be okay Charlie. Remember we've been there and done this. So, this guy is my half-brother.'

'Don't worry dude, you're better looking!'

'Oh shit!'

'What?'

'He's got an awesome little dog. There's another one here. Woo-hoo Charlie! We've got dogs!'

The injured were removed to another chamber to get the attention they needed. The boys were invited to watch. Bridget and Sam were placed in strange looking gowns. Esouli spoke as the process began.

'The gowns are impregnated with seaweed and Vodoxium.'

The bullet entries were exposed, and the entry sites opened.

'Whoa, it looks like a shell opening.'

The nose of the bullet appeared, then popped right out. The wound closed up and tiny crystals circled around the wound sites as if in some ritual dance then just disappeared.

'That's incredible. When are you going to wake everyone?'

'I really need to hug my Mum and Simone.'

'Me as well, and we need dogs.'

The boys were getting impatient waiting for all the pods to open. Fudgunkel clapped his little hands, the time had come. All the creatures on board had prepared a celebration feast. They too would be making the dual Earth home. It was a moment of high emotions, the pod people had finally recovered, they exited the place of healing. Many long embraces, tears, and continuous laughter. Jack, Madi and Sam watched and laughed, flicking a tear here and there. The dogs did the sniffing thing and decided they would share the territory. Louis and Sam were introduced. They hugged and for the first time in his life, Sam felt complete.

After everyone had eaten, talked out the adventures and the future, Esouli interrupted the crowd.

'My friends, I hate to do this, but I have some unfortunate news. Arume will be passing soon.'

'What?'

Louis and Charlie jumped to their feet.

'What are you talking about?'

'Arume requests you all come at once.'

His body was in a crystal cylinder.

'Let me explain what is happening. As you know the Elodites like to be cool and live near water. Their bodies are mostly liquid. What you are seeing is the outer shell of Arume. The liquid in the cylinder is Arume.'

'I don't understand.'

Jack's voice was distressed.

'Arume's powers, his essence, his spirit and his abilities are in the liquid in this cylinder.'

'In a way he still lives?'

'Yes Louis. The cylinder is very powerful.'

'What do you do with it?'

'In the future, Earth, may be required to enhance humans to actually keep the planet alive. At this stage the future of Earth is unknown. We have those humans who want to preserve Earth and those who wish to exploit it. All deceased Elodites have been preserved the same way and stored on Helomedes.'

It was a devastating moment for all, everyone processing the sorrow within them.

The following day, each person on board had a tour of the mothership, and all the stored life on hold. It was an amazing sight. Embryos, fertilised eggs, sperms, ovaries, everything that held potential life. Mountains of crystal compartments housing the precious lives suspended in the mysterious Vodoxium.

Next, they were shown the product samples of Earth's vegetation, all secure in their crystal essence.

The food production centre, lush and brimming with fresh food, vegetables, fruit, herbs and small nut trees with its magnificent aroma was phenomenal. Sam was astonished that so much life and the future was contained and hidden in one planet to be reborn on another planet.

'Well Brother, what do you think of this modern-day ark?'

'To be honest, I can't find a word. All I know is I'm so glad I made this decision and now I have a real family.'

Louis smiled at Sam.

'We can have lots of conversations about our childhood and find out who's was the most shit.'

'Yeah.'

They went to find the others, Sam putting his arm around Louis's shoulder.

'Let's go brother'

It was unanimously decided to spend the day looking at Earth and in particular their favourite places on Earth. Louis looked at his grandmother's favourite place, it still looked the same. He had mixed feelings, sad and excited. The past and future colliding.

'Oh no!'

Everyone looked at Isobel.

'What's wrong Mum?'

'The chooks. We left the chooks.'

'Have a look in the neighbour's yard.'

Madi was smiling at Isobel.

'Thank God for that.'

Simone and Charlie hugged their mother as they had a last look at home.

'The chooks and your house were given to your neighbour. I know they were good friends.'

Isobel hugged Madi and thanked her.

'Well, I for one,' said Sam, 'couldn't really care about my home. This is my favourite place now and that lake changed my life. I hope it exists forever and I'm so bloody grateful to be here.'

Bridget and Louis looked at her garden. It was beautiful and that was the way it was to stay.

Jack and Madi looked at the beautiful landscapes across the entire continent, their workplace. It had been their home for so long. That night many conversations flowed. Louis watched the people around he and Esouli.

'Something is troubling you, Louis. I was just thinking of Arume's ability that he used to save us. No one will remember what happened. Why do we have to leave?'

'We don't know how long memories have been interrupted for, the complexity of the human brain is puzzling. Arume insisted on this action, he didn't want to take any chances.'

'He actually died for us.'

Esouli put his arm around the boy.

'Not all of him. He would do anything to save the mission, these planets and all of you. As would I.'

Sam found Louis and Bridget together. She put her arm around Sam, he handed Louis his phone.

'I thought you might be interested. This is who your mother was.'

Bridget looked at the images of Jason Blackwell and Genevieve St Day. She remembered them standing and laughing together at her home.

'This is our father now, and this is your mother.'

Louis studied the before and after.

'It's weird, they are total strangers to me. The upside, I now have an awesome brother.'

Bridget hugged them both, now a family of three.

Back in her office, Karen Landy felt unsettled, something was disturbing her mind, but nothing surfaced.

Many people directly involved in the lives of those on board the ship also felt they were meant to do something, but the answers were not coming.

The following night all those aboard the mysterious spaceship ate together before departure, everyone having their private internal thoughts. Contemplation of what the future would be and what was being left behind. Outside low dark clouds formed together with winds gathering. Nature was under command to deliver a cover so the ship could leave undetected.

The mothership would be staying, her precious cargo and more gathering was still to be done. Any incidents that happen to any mothercrafts on the planet, would be transmitted to Helomedes. It was imperative that the ships be protected.

The time was approaching, the cover was a fully active storm. Everyone gathered to view the departure. Once above the storm, the ship would be undetectable from any technology on earth.

Sitting on the usual branch of his favourite tree, high on the mountain, the tawny frogmouth was a lonely sight. He too was waiting. All the nocturnal animals gathered near the lake's edge. A beam of light appeared from the mountain top, the point of the tetrahedron appeared. A warm shaft of light landed on the Tawny frog mouth, then it transformed into the figure of an Elodite, smaller than Arume, but just as magnificent.

A graceful Sea eagle settling beside him, the next generation of protectors of the lake and mountain.

The ship was ready. It hovered in the storm for a moment, farewelling the mothership and Earth, and all those watching. All on board observed everything. Once above the cloud and storms, the blue planet could be seen in its entire form, the most exquisite planet known to humans. It became smaller, then eventually it was gone.

Shawline Publishing Group Pty Ltd
www.Shawlinepublishing.com.au

9 781922 444837